PRESIDENT HAMILTON

A NOVEL OF ALTERNATIVE HISTORY

To Judi –
Thanks and
enjoy !

LEWIS BEN SMITH

ELECTIO PUBLISHING, LLC

President Hamilton: A Novel of Alternative History
By Lewis Ben Smith

Copyright 2021 by Lewis Ben Smith
Cover Design by Electio Publishing, LLC.
Original Cover Artwork provided by Annee Helmreich

ISBN-13: 978-1-63213-710-4
Published by eLectio Publishing, LLC
Little Elm, Texas
http://www.eLectioPublishing.com

Printed in the United States of America

5 4 3 2 1 eLP 26 25 24 23 22 21

The eLectio Publishing editing team is comprised of: Christine LePorte, Lori Draft, Sheldon James, Court Dudek, and Jim Eccles.

Publisher's Note
The publisher does not have any control over and does not assume any responsibility for author or third-party websites or their content.

President Hamilton *is a well-written and thoughtful answer to the 200 year-old question, "What if Alexander Hamilton had survived the duel?" Prior to the duel, Hamilton wrote that he wanted "the ability to be in future useful, whether in resisting mischief or effecting good, in those crises of our public affairs . . ." In Lewis Smith's work of historical fiction, Hamilton gets his chance but has to overcome political adversaries who fight to the end to stop him."*

–Douglas Hamilton
5X-Great Grandson of Alexander Hamilton

Lewis Smith tells the story of the founding of our republic, but following the road not taken. What could the country have been had the original sin of slavery been atoned for at a vital, early crossroads? Unlike much historical fiction, the engaging dialog of the cast is plausible and true to what we know of the founding generation. President Hamilton *is an alternative history of the nation as it could have been.*

Jerry W. Jones
Professor of History
Texas A&M University – Central Texas

"*Lewis B Smith's* President Hamilton *pays tribute to one of our most indispensable Founders — America's first Secretary of the Treasury Alexander Hamilton. In this immersive and vibrant tale, Smith captures the very essence of Hamilton's personality: a relentless man who was unyielding in his moral and political convictions. The story is well-researched, full of historical details that bring the period to life, even as it explores this great "What if" of the Hamilton narrative. You will find yourself cheering Hamilton on, in his mission to create "a more perfect Union" by liberating those held in the cruel bondage of slavery while simultaneously seeking to prevent the outbreak of Civil War. Would the United States have been a better, stronger nation with President Hamilton at the helm? Now you can answer that burning question.*"

– Elizabeth Matic, Administrator
ALEXANDER HAMILTON: LIFE AND LEGACY
Facebook Page

The alternative history novel President Hamilton *is that rare gem of a book that is both enjoyably engrossing, and thought-provokingly relevant to where we are now as a nation. Lewis B. Smith, author of historical thrillers* Theophilus, The Redemption of Pontius Pilate, *and* The Gnostic Library, *transports readers to an era in US history that should have been but sadly never got to be, and takes them along through a re-imaged timeline as they visit our struggling country in the early 1800s, and meet familiar figures from our heritage, not only as they were but as they may have been had the most tragic duel ever fought had a different ending. This is "what-if" at its highest stakes, and storytelling at its most intellectually pleasing.*

—Dai-Keag-Ity
Amazon Reviewer

THIS BOOK IS DEDICATED TO:

My wife of 36 years, Patricia Smith, who has loved me, inspired me, and endured me since we met on the playground in second grade.

My dear friend and beta reader par excellence, Ellie, who provided a great deal of thoughtful criticism and feedback to this manuscript.

And to Lin-Manuel Miranda, author of *HAMILTON: An American Musical*, who has done more to interest the millennial generation in our Founding Fathers than all of us history teachers combined!

And a special thanks to my friend and co-worker Annee Helmreich, for creating the magnificent portrait of Hamilton that adorns the cover of this book.

PROLOGUE
THE INTERVIEW AT WEEHAWKEN

ALEXANDER HAMILTON grasped the gunwales of the barge as the murky waters of the Hudson rolled beneath them. The sun was just clearing the horizon, and the bluffs at Weehawken loomed ahead, illuminated by early morning rays. Atop the island was a flat area, lush with summer greenery, about a hundred yards in length by forty in breadth. It was out of sight of the nearby docks and walkways, a secluded field where duelists had met off and on for over a century. There Hamilton would face a man he had despised for years, a man he believed had every intention of killing him—the Vice President of the United States, Aaron Burr of New York.

Hamilton was deep in thought. He did not want to fight this duel, and despite his contempt for Burr, he had no particular desire to kill the man. Alex had made out his will the night before, and in it he had announced his intention of throwing away his shot. As a Christian, Hamilton had come to detest dueling— especially since his beloved son Philip had lost his life in a duel three years before. Alex had no wish to die—indeed, he felt he had much to live for. He had not abandoned all hope of becoming President someday, despite the scandal of his well-known affair with Maria Reynolds. Someone would have to undo the damage

Thomas Jefferson was busily inflicting on the country, why not Alexander Hamilton? There was no other leader in the Federalist Party who had his credentials, or his political ingenuity. He was not yet fifty years old, and in excellent health. His prospects were still bright.

Alex knew he could have avoided this duel had he wanted to—but the cost would have been his personal honor. He meant everything he had said about Burr—the man was an unscrupulous snake who coveted power at all costs. Hamilton could not apologize to Burr without retracting what he had said, and he knew he had spoken the truth. President Jefferson, Hamilton's former cabinet colleague and current rival, had often denounced Hamilton as an ambitious, unscrupulous monarchist—a charge Hamilton resented. True, Hamilton lacked Jefferson's blind faith in the wisdom of the masses, but it was a far cry between believing the country should be led by wise, educated men of substance and property, and actually craving a scepter! Hamilton found it ironic that a man who accused him of royalist ambition should take as his Vice President someone who truly lusted for that kind of power. But even Jefferson had come to realize what Burr was, finally, and had already let it be known that he would seek reelection that fall with a different running mate.

Burr had seen the handwriting on the wall, and had switched parties yet again, trying to win the Federalist nomination for Governor of New York. Although he had not held political office in a nearly a decade, Hamilton was still the unofficial leader of New York's Federalist Party, and he had let it be known to all and sundry that he was adamantly opposed to Burr's nomination. Burr had lost both the nomination and the election, in which he had wound up running as an independent. Seeing his political career in ruins, he blamed Hamilton for his failure—and he was right. Hamilton took a certain grim pride in destroying Burr's prospects. He knew, however, he had not done so out of malice, but out of genuine concern for his country's future.

Now, months later, he was paying the price. In a newspaper interview, one of Hamilton's friends, Charles Cooper, had mentioned some of the things Hamilton had said about Burr at a dinner party, and the Vice President, incensed by the statement that Hamilton had a "yet more despicable" opinion he had left unuttered, had issued a challenge that Hamilton could not refuse.

The former Treasury Secretary looked at the portmanteau containing the dueling pistols. One of them, he knew, was the same gun that had killed his son Philip three years before. Philip—Hamilton still had to stifle sobs of grief when he thought of his beautiful son, a bright and shining light snuffed out before his time, killed defending his father's honor on this same bloody ground. He vividly recalled the raw grief on his sweet Eliza's face as their son had breathed his last, and closed his eyes, trying not to imagine her expression if he, too, died in the same place and manner.

"Are you well, my friend?" Nathaniel Pendleton asked him. One of Hamilton's close friends, he had volunteered to act as second in this "affair of honor."

Hamilton forced a smile he did not feel.

"Well enough, Nathaniel," he said. "My bosom and I have been debating each other."

The keel of the barge grated on the sand and gravel of the shoreline, and Hamilton rose and sprang lightly to the beach. A clear-cut path led up the bluff, and Pendleton and Dr. David Hosack followed after Hamilton as he briskly climbed up. Hamilton turned at the sound of their steps and frowned.

"Doctor, you should wait with the barge and the rowers. You will be called if your services are needed," he said.

Hosack nodded. Dueling was illegal in New Jersey, although it was not prosecuted as vigorously there as it was in New York. As the attending physician, he could be called on to testify in court if he witnessed the duel in progress. Granting the non-participants a level of deniability was customary in such affairs; the doctor always remained out of the line of sight, and the seconds turned their backs to the duelists at the moment of truth.

When they reached the top, Hamilton found that Colonel Burr and his seconds, William van Ness and Matthew Davis, as well as another man Hamilton did not know, had already arrived. They had already cleared away the brush that grew over the area during the spring. Pendleton and van Ness conferred for a moment, then Hamilton and Burr drew straws to determine their positions. Hamilton won the draw and chose the high ground, facing across the river to the city. The sun was now well above the horizon, so that its glare would not blind him.

"Gentlemen, now is the moment. Should either of you wish to end this affair, you may do so now," said William van Ness. "General Hamilton, will you apologize for your egregious insults to the honor of Colonel Burr?" During duels, it was customary to refer to one's opponent by his military rank, if he had one.

"Had the Colonel confined his demands to a single remark, I might have been prevailed upon to consider an apology," Hamilton said. "But what he has required is that I recant every opinion I have ever publicly expressed about him. That I cannot do and retain my honor. Will the Colonel modify his demand?"

Burr shook his head silently but refused to meet his opponent's eyes.

"Then we shall proceed," said van Ness. "Do you have the weapons, Judge Pendleton?"

"I do," replied Hamilton's second, opening the portmanteau and presenting the well-oiled dueling pistols. Burr chose first, and Hamilton followed. The two men walked ten paces and turned to face each other.

"You may each have a moment to confer with your men," said Davis.

Pendleton leaned in close to Hamilton.

"Do you wish to activate the hair trigger?" he whispered.

Hamilton thought for a moment and shook his head. He knew that each pistol contained a gear that made the trigger much more responsive, but he was more accustomed to giving the heavier pull flintlocks required. Besides, he fully intended to throw away his shot, so his aim would not matter.

But should he throw it away? This was the question that had raged through his thoughts ever since he had accepted Burr's challenge. The Vice President was a dangerous man, a man whose ambitions boded ill for the country. If he killed Hamilton, it was quite possible the consequences of that deed would destroy Burr's political prospects forever. But what if they did not? There was not another Federalist leader who possessed Hamilton's stature or connections. The party might well founder without Alex there to lead it. Jefferson detested Burr, to be sure—but Jefferson would not be President forever. Who would be left to check Burr's path the presidency if Hamilton died? James Madison? The diminutive Secretary of State was a brilliant man, but a poor politician. Burr was effortlessly ingratiating, a man who could easily persuade gullible people of his sincerity. His path to the Executive Mansion would be easier with Hamilton out of the way.

Still in an agony of indecision, Hamilton reached into his pocket and retrieved his spectacles. If he did decide to shoot, he thought, he wanted his aim to be true. He surveyed the ground one last time and nodded.

"Back to back, gentlemen," van Ness said. The Vice President and the former Treasury Secretary took their positions. Pendleton, van Ness, and the others stepped away from them and turned their backs.

"I will count to ten, and then you may turn, face each other, and fire at will," said Burr's second. "One, two . . ."

As he marked off his paces, Hamilton's mind was still racing. Finally, as van Ness got to the count of seven, he decided. He would let Burr shoot first, and then respond accordingly. Let God decide the outcome—if he died, then Burr was meant to go on to greater things. But if Burr missed—

"Ten!" Burr's second said, and the two men turned. Burr's face was twisted with wrath; he had been practicing with a pistol all week, and now he took deadly aim at his hated rival.

A shrill shriek broke the silence of the morning. It was only an osprey, stooping to catch a fish, but for that split second, to Alexander Hamilton, it sounded like the anguished scream Eliza had uttered the moment she saw Philip's pale, stricken face after his fatal duel. Hamilton swiveled his head to track the sound, and as he did so, his body rotated slightly.

The osprey saved his life. Burr's bullet struck his side, penetrated his clothes and skin, and then glanced off his ribs, leaving a long gash but going no deeper. The pain of the impact caused Hamilton to wince. He looked at his side, where blood was already staining his jacket, and then looked down the field at Burr.

The man's sneer slowly faded to shock as he realized that his shot had failed to finish his opponent. In that moment, Hamilton saw the fury in Burr's eyes suddenly giving way to fear. The former Treasury Secretary slowly clenched his jaw. Burr had indeed tried to kill him—and failed! In that moment, Hamilton saw all that he had nearly been robbed of—the love of Eliza, the best of wives and best of women, who had stood by him, forgiven him when he strayed, and comforted him in his grief when their son died. He saw Philip's face, his beloved son, killed by one of Burr's scurrilous minions. His beloved mentor, the father figure who had raised him from obscurity and seated him at the right hand of power, George Washington, stood tall in his mind as well, unbowed by age or sickness. Hamilton thought of himself as the guardian of Washington's legacy, but in his pride, he had nearly let Burr destroy that and all else he held dear. With that realization, he made up his mind.

He took careful aim at Aaron Burr's heart and pulled the trigger. Burr's eyes widened as the bullet struck home, and the

Vice President slowly sank to the ground, blood pouring down the front of his shirt. At the sound of the second shot, the seconds slowly turned around.

Van Ness quickly strode to Burr's side and spoke his name. Burr looked up at him and tried to speak. The Vice President's body spasmed. His eyes widened for a moment, and then closed for the last time.

"General, are you all right?" Pendleton asked, his voice full of concern.

"His bullet grazed me, nothing more," said Hamilton. "Let us go."

CHAPTER ONE

"A DUEL? Alex, how could you!?"

The smack of Eliza's hand across his cheek echoed through the house like a thunderclap. They had been married for nearly twenty-five years, and Hamilton had seen his wife hurt, angry, mournful, happy, and excited, but the emotion that now blazed from her eyes was one he had never seen before. It was pure rage; a towering fury that made him shrink back from her, combat veteran though he was. His cheek reddened from the resounding slap she'd given him, but her words hurt far worse than the blow he had taken.

"Our son died in one of those stupid, stupid 'affairs of honor,' and now you dare to go and engage in one yourself?" she shouted, her normally pale-tinted face flush with anger. "What would I have done if you had died? How could you even think about such a thing? To rob me of my husband, after fate has already stolen our sweet Philip from me? Do you think that I could possibly live without you?"

She burst into tears, but her gaze remained fixed on him and her anger did not relent.

"My dear Betsey," he said, calling her by the pet name she loved. "Please forgive me. Honor required —"

"Bugger your honor!!" she shouted, and he flinched. He had never once, in all their years together, heard her use that phrase. She grabbed the sides of his head and tilted it downward so that their eyes were locked.

"I am sorry," he began, but she placed her hand over his lips.

"I love you beyond all reason," she said fervently. "I have borne your children; I have stood by your side even when you betrayed your vows to me. I have counted myself blessed to be wed to the most brilliant man on earth. I did not complain when you paid more attention to my sister Angelica than you did to me. I have endured, I have forgiven, and I have always been proud to be your wife. But I want you to swear a vow to me, here and now, Alex, that you will never fight in another duel. No matter what the provocation, no matter how deep the insult cuts, you will NEVER do this to me again. Because if you do, I will leave you, and I will take our children with me. It will break my heart, and it will probably kill me—but I will do it. I cannot bear the thought of losing you. Am I clear? Will you promise me?"

"My dear heart, I could never refuse you," he said. "This was the end. Enough is enough, as they say. I will toss these pistols into the Hudson tomorrow, and never own another set."

She stared into his eyes for a long moment, trying to measure his words and the spirit behind them. Finally, she sighed deeply, and the anger in her eyes began to fade.

"Then we shall speak of this no more," she said, "but I meant what I said. Do not forget that, my sweet, irreplaceable Hamilton!"

With that she threw her arms around him, and he winced even as he returned her embrace.

"Oh, Alex, you are hurt!" she said.

"Burr's bullet grazed my ribs," he said. "It is but a flesh wound."

Doctor Hosack had bound the wound tightly before they left Weehawken, but the blood had soaked through the bandage and stained the clean shirt Alex had donned after the duel. He had spent an uneasy night in an inn afterward, uncertain how to tell Eliza about what had transpired, and the hard, lumpy bed had not helped. The gash in his side was not deep, but it was painful and throbbing now.

"We'll see about that," Eliza said. "Up to the bedroom with you! Junior, fetch me hot water and some clean washcloths, please!"

Alex's second son and namesake was eighteen years old and bore a distinct resemblance to his father, although he was not as much of a prodigy as his father and older brother had been. He had been listening to his parents' quarrel from the door to the drawing room, and now he ran to the kitchen to follow his mother's command.

Hamilton let himself be led upstairs. He was still shaken enough by the events of the previous morning, compounded by the unexpected fury his bride had directed at him, that he dared not resist. Eliza set him down on the edge of the bed and used a sharp penknife to cut through the white linen bound around his chest, exposing the wound to the noonday light streaming in from the window.

The bullet wound was a bit worse than he'd realized—an ugly gash about four inches long, still seeping blood around its edges. The skin had been peeled back by the ball's passage, and as he studied the wound, Hamilton realized that the white bone of one of his ribs was exposed. The flesh around it looked angry and red.

"I'm sorry," he managed to say before turning his head and throwing up the glass of brandy he'd drunk in place of breakfast. He had seen men killed, and done his share of killing, as a young man during the Revolution, but seeing one's own bones shining in the light of day was a bit too much for him. As young Alex cleaned up the mess, Eliza busied herself wiping the wound down with hot water and bandaging it with clean linens. Tears streamed down her cheeks as she worked.

"My Hamilton," she said after a moment, her voice catching. "A matter of an inch or so and you might have been lost to me forever! What were you thinking? Was Mister Burr so vile to you that you were left with no choice?"

Alex sat up, his head still swimming but the nausea gone for the moment. He leaned forward and kissed his dear bride on her forehead, his own tears falling onto her upturned face and mingling with hers.

"Oh, Eliza, my honor is dear to me, but not so much as you!" he said. "I will say this much, and then speak of this matter no more. Aaron Burr was a great threat to our Republic; he was the American Catiline, and I had to act the part of Cicero without the powers of a consul. I baited him, and he challenged me. But, as God is my witness, I let him take the first shot! I gave him every chance to repent of his bloody intention, but instead he did his best to kill me. I was not going to return fire, but then I thought of all that I had nearly lost—I could not help myself. I took my shot, and I killed a man. I killed the Vice President of the United States. Now I must ponder what to do next. Burr is not without friends, you know. I am afraid this matter is not settled yet."

"Do what you must, dear husband," Eliza said as she wound clean strips of cloth around his midsection. "But remember my words! No more duels, ever, or you will lose me and the children, whether you survive or not."

"Then my dueling pistols will be retired permanently," he said. "I have risked losing all that I love; I will not do so again. From now on, words will be my only weapons."

Hamilton stood so that his wife could finish applying the bandage, and then reached into his wardrobe for a clean shirt and waistcoat. He looked down at his trousers and saw that his blood had stained them, too, so he returned to the wardrobe and retrieved a complete change of clothes and began to get dressed.

"You need to lie down!" Eliza said. "You've lost a good deal of blood, and that wound will reopen if you strain yourself."

"I must speak to someone," Alex said. "It is a short walk, and when I am done, I promise to return and spend the remainder of the day resting."

"You should let it wait," she gently scolded him.

"Eliza—I must do this," he said firmly. "My conscience will not let me rest until I do."

"Your conscience?" his wife asked.

Hamilton bowed his head, and then opened his heart to his wife.

"I killed a man, Betsey," he said. "Not in the heat of battle, or under the moral cloak of a just war for one's country. I stared down the barrel of a pistol and pulled the trigger and watched his spirit leave his body. I need to know . . ." He hesitated and swallowed hard. "I need to know if my soul will be damned for all eternity as a murderer," he finished. She embraced him gently but made no reply, and after a moment he pulled away.

He retrieved his walking stick from the corner and gingerly made his way downstairs and thence out onto the street. He could hear the hue and cry of the great city of New York as it sprawled out around him, the fastest-growing city in America, and his adoptive home for thirty years now. It was a short walk from his house to Trinity Church, and the rectory where Bishop Benjamin Moore lived was right next door.

The news of the duel had spread rapidly, and a news crier was standing on the corner selling a special edition of *The National Gazette*, the Republican newspaper once edited by Philip Freneau.

"Vice President Burr Murdered by the Monarchist Alexander Hamilton!" the crier proclaimed. "Read all about it! General Hamilton guns down Burr in cold blood!"

On the next corner, a rival news crier for Hamilton's *New York Daily Post* was touting the alternative version of the story.

"Aaron Burr nearly kills Secretary Hamilton! Vice President killed in self-defense after shooting the Federalist leader!" the newsboy screamed out.

Hamilton took little note of either of them; the fact that Burr had shot first and wounded him rendered Alex legally untouchable. Duelists were occasionally prosecuted in New York, but when they were, it was invariably the person who shot first and killed his foe who drew the ire of prosecutors. As for New Jersey, where the fatal encounter had taken place, dueling was also illegal there, but prosecutions were quite rare. Hamilton was more concerned about the judgment of a much higher authority, and that was what drove him to the rectory despite the aching wound in his side.

Trinity Church was the tallest structure in New York City, its central spire rising two hundred feet into the air. There was a large burial ground in the back; Hamilton's son Philip was interred there. As Alex surveyed the modest marker that he and Eliza had placed over their son's grave, he swallowed hard and touched the throbbing bullet gash in his side. A matter of inches, and his own grave would have been dug right there, next to Philip's. He imagined how different life in New York—indeed in America— might be if Burr's bullet had found its mark. Would anyone remember Alexander Hamilton if he died now? Perhaps his tenure as treasury secretary might earn him a footnote in the history books, but Alex had little doubt that had he perished that morning, as Burr intended, his legacy would have been small and soon forgotten. No more, he swore to himself! America had not heard the last of Alexander Hamilton. His life's work was not yet finished.

Benjamin Moore was a tall, long-nosed Episcopal bishop of the traditional sort; his sermons were longwinded and pedantic, but he had a solid grasp of doctrine and was a sound scholar of the Christian faith. The Hamiltons rented a pew in Trinity Church and attended services occasionally, even though Alexander was not an Episcopalian. It was, however, the closest church to their former Wall Street home, and was not much further from the Grange, their current residence. Beyond that, Alex liked the man, pure and simple, and had ever since the first time he met him.

"General Hamilton?" Moore said when he came to the door. "Good afternoon, sir, what may I do for you?"

"I take it you have not heard the news, then?" Hamilton asked him.

"I have been in my study, preparing my Sunday sermon," Moore replied. "I have heard no news of anything today."

Hamilton sighed and summoned up his most engaging smile.

"I need to speak with you at length, sir," he said. "May I come in?"

"Of course, General," the bishop said. He was a courtly gentleman, only six years older than Hamilton, but he carried himself with the dignity of a venerable graybeard. "It was inconsiderate of me to leave you standing on my doorstep."

Hamilton entered and sat down on a comfortable, padded chair near the fireplace. Since it was high summer, there was no fire, but the drawing room was comfortable, well-lit, and inviting. Bishop Moore called for tea, and the maid brought in a steaming pot and two cups a few moments later. Hamilton gratefully took a sip and then leaned back in his chair, closing his eyes for a moment. All the adrenaline that had fueled him for the last two days was spent, and he felt sore and exhausted.

"So, what brings such a noteworthy person to my door on this fine Wednesday afternoon?" the bishop finally asked.

"I killed a man yesterday," Hamilton said, too weary for pretense. "I shot Vice President Burr. He had challenged me to a duel, and I would not retract my assessment of his character, so I met him at Weehawken just after dawn. I had fully intended to throw away my shot, but when he fired first, his bullet grazed me. But for sheerest chance, he would have killed me. In the heat of that moment, I returned fire and struck him in the heart. Sir, I am a military man, as you know. I personally killed men during the Revolution, and I felt that the righteousness of our cause removed the stain of that sin from me. But this was different. I looked at Colonel Burr down the barrel of my pistol and pulled the trigger and sent him to his grave. My conscience is deeply troubled."

"It should be," said Moore. "Murder is a mortal sin, my friend, and dueling is nothing short of legalized murder. It is a holdover from an age of barbarism and savagery and has no place in a civilized society."

Hamilton nodded sadly. He knew that Moore had publicly condemned dueling from the pulpit on more than one occasion.

"I have not always been a good man, Bishop Moore," he said. "But I have tried hard, in my latter years, to atone for the sins of my youth and to be a good Christian. I have tried to become a better man than I once was. I raised my children in the nurture and admonition of the Lord and read the Bible to them every day. I pray with them every morning, and I spend my own time in prayer each day. You are a man of God, sir, deeply read in the Holy Scriptures. In your learned opinion, have I damned my soul by doing this?"

"You have sinned, there is no doubt, General," he said. "You have killed another man in a violent affair that we dubiously call a matter of honor. I cannot think that God is pleased with what you have done. But I also believe that even the worst of sinners are not beyond redemption. While the Holy Writ teaches us that grace is given, not earned by our own works, I do believe that there is something to be said for making restitution for our sins. God accepts the sacrifices of a broken and contrite heart, General Hamilton. Is your heart grieved that you have done this?"

"It is." Hamilton nodded as he spoke. "I had no desire to kill Colonel Burr when we rowed out to Weehawken. But it was obvious that he had every intention of killing me. If I had thrown away my shot, I am sure he would have demanded another round of fire, and another. I could see my death in his eyes, and I killed him to save my own life. I was thinking of my wife and children at that moment, more than anything. I wanted to live for their sakes, and the only way to do that was for me to pull the trigger."

The Bishop sighed and rose from his seat, staring out the window into the busy New York streets. He remained silent for a long moment, and then spoke again.

"I cannot absolve you from this, General Hamilton," he said. "But you can atone for what you have done, I think. You say that the Vice President fired first, and that he intended to kill you. Were you struck?"

"Yes," Hamilton said. "The bullet grazed my side. An inch or two more, and it would have gone through my vitals."

"Then God spared you for a reason," Moore said. "His purpose for your life is not yet accomplished. Redemption remains possible. I would say to you, though—do not squander the second chance you have been given! Humble yourself before the Lord and seek His purpose for the life that remains to you. God does not hide His will from us, Alexander. If he has some object you are intended to achieve, He will lay it before you. Be attentive and listen for His voice. I do not think the gates of heaven are shut before you because of this one act."

Hamilton nodded and rose with a groan. The wound was positively throbbing now, as if someone was jabbing him in the side with a red-hot iron poker.

"Are you well, General?" the bishop asked. "Do you need me to call you a carriage?"

"I will be fine," Hamilton said. "The wound is painful, but not serious. My home is not far distant; I prithee come and visit me soon. Help me seek the will of Christ for the rest of my life."

"I will gladly do that," said Moore. "The Son of Man came to seek and to save that which was lost; how can I do any less? And you, neglect not the Lord's house on Sundays!"

"I'll be here as often as I can," said Hamilton. "That I promise."

With that he rose and made his way to the door, grateful he had brought his walking stick. The late afternoon skies were bright and clear; the day had gone from pleasantly warm to uncomfortably hot, and Hamilton's vision was swimming. As he made his way up the street, he saw people pointing and whispering. The word of Burr's death had spread like wildfire through the city, thanks to the intense competition between political newspapers. He was not afraid; he had braved angry mobs all over New York when he squared off against the powerful Clinton faction during the battle to ratify the new U.S. Constitution in the summer of 1788. Besides, Alex knew that Burr was not as popular with New Yorkers as he had been a few years previously—the man's constantly shifting political allegiances had disillusioned many of his supporters.

"Hamilton!" a familiar voice called. It was Nathaniel Pendleton, his second from the duel. "Egad, Alex, are you all right? You look as white as a sheet!"

"I am well enough, Nathaniel," he said, "but I am very weary, and this wound is paining me. Will you walk with me to my door?"

"Gladly," his friend said. "The city is all abuzz regarding yesterday's duel. Burr's faction is trying to paint you as a murderer, but most people don't seem to be giving credit to that idea. The fact that he shot first, and struck you, shows that you acted in self-defense. I think you will have no legal worries."

"That is comforting," Hamilton said. "I wish my own conscience would let me off as easily. I tell you, Nathaniel, as dangerous as Burr was, I still would undo this entire confrontation if I could. The Vice President's death is on my hands, morally speaking, even if I am not legally culpable."

"You said nothing of Burr that was not true," Pendleton told him.

"I know," Hamilton said. "The man was dangerously ambitious. But I wish there had been another way to end our dispute. Here, help me up the steps, please."

They had arrived at Hamilton's house as they spoke, but Alex found he simply did not have the energy to mount the few steps up to the front door. Pendleton took him by the arm and let Alex lean on him. Eliza was already opening the door by the time they got to the top step.

"Alex!" she said, and he could tell she had been weeping while he was gone. "Heart of mine, are you well?"

He summoned up the strength to smile, even though the room was spinning all around him. Her eyes anchored him, and his love for her was like a lifeline in a storm.

"I am absolutely fine, my love," he said, and then his legs buckled and he fell headfirst into the front corridor. He was saved from smashing his face on the floor only by Eliza catching him and breaking his fall.

"Mister Pendleton, please fetch us a doctor!" she exclaimed. "Junior! James! Help me get your father into bed!"

Hamilton protested feebly as his wife and sons half carried him up the stairs, but he no longer had the strength to stand alone. Alex Junior held him upright as Eliza stripped off his waistcoat and shirt. Both were stained with blood, and his bandage was soaked.

"Whatever it was, it could have waited!" Eliza snapped. "You have reopened your wound. Now lie back and be still. James, get me hot water and more clean kerchiefs."

"I will be fine, I am sure," Hamilton said, and then darkness closed in around him.

CHAPTER TWO

ARTICLE FROM *The New York Daily Post*, July 13, 1804:

GEN. HAMILTON GRAVELY ILL FROM WOUND INFLICTED IN DUEL

Alexander Hamilton, late Sec'y of State, is reported to be in grave danger due to an infected wound sustained from the pistol of Vice President Aaron Burr, who was killed by the General's return fire. Hamilton's wife and children are gathered by the General's side, and doctors report that he has been unconscious for the last few days, with a high fever. Medicines administered have thus far been ineffective and attempts to bleed him have been rebuffed by his family, who say that he lost too much blood from his injury for such treatment to be efficacious. Citizens of New York are gathering at local churches to pray for the General's speedy recovery; to which the author of this article adds his own fervent good wishes and prayers. The Post will update its readers as developments warrant.

Eliza Hamilton gently wiped her husband's brow with a cool, wet cloth. The fever had begun while he was out on his foolish errand, trying to atone for the guilt he felt because of the duel. When he collapsed in the foyer of their Wall Street home, his brow was already hot to the touch. The wound was inflamed and red; doctors had recommended cauterizing it, but she felt that such a drastic treatment so close to his heart might endanger his health even further. As for bleeding—she failed to understand how you could improve the condition of someone who had already lost a good deal of blood by taking even more. Not to mention Alex had a horror of being bled; he was convinced George Washington's doctors had hastened the President's end by draining far too much of his vital fluid after he fell ill.

Instead, she had poured the strongest whiskey she could find over the wound, and then focused on keeping it cleaned. She had found several small bits of cloth from Hamilton's coat which the bullet had carried into his flesh and had plucked those out with a pair of tweezers. The redness around the wound was beginning to fade, but the fever continued.

She knelt by the bed and prayed earnestly, begging the Lord to restore her husband to her. For all his faults, Alexander was the most perfect man she had ever met, and she knew that there was much good that he could still do for his country if God spared him from this ordeal. Her tears dampened the sheets as she begged for her husband's life, but Alex continued to toss and turn in his fevered dreams, sometimes aware of his surroundings, sometimes not. The children came and went, but she only left her husband's bed when the two youngest needed her attention.

As for Hamilton, he felt as if he were drifting; one moment burning hot, the next freezing cold. At times he was vaguely aware of Eliza or one of the children beside him; at other times he remained adrift inside his own mind. He was unaware of the passage of time, but on the third day he reached the crisis of his illness: his body's resistance was low, the infection had not yet begun to recede, and the thread of his life was stretched and frayed to the limit. He was unaware of all this; in his mind he was simply floating on a pillow of warm, comfortable darkness.

Suddenly he opened his eyes and found himself in a familiar place. He was standing under the shaded porch at Mount Vernon, overlooking the green lawn that sloped down to the Potomac as it lazily wound east and south to the Chesapeake. But all was silent; no birds sang in the shrubs, no slaves worked in the fields. He yearned to hear the familiar voice of George Washington, the man who had found Hamilton as a poor immigrant captain of militia and raised him to be his chief staff officer, but even in his fever dream he remembered that Washington was dead, gone nearly five years now. He did not anticipate the voice that suddenly sounded from behind him, but he recognized it instantly.

"Hullo there, Alex!" John Laurens said cheerfully. "I've been waiting a long time for the chance to talk with you."

In all his life, Hamilton had never had a closer friend than John Laurens. The tall, young son of a South Carolina planter had served on Washington's staff with Alex for several years, and the two of them had spent countless hours talking, drinking, chasing women, and planning their futures together. While Hamilton had never been sexually drawn to men—in fact, the concept repulsed him—the love he had borne for Laurens was in some ways greater than the love he felt for his dear Eliza. Uncluttered by carnality, it was simply pure affection for a kindred spirit, a young man who embodied everything the fatherless immigrant Hamilton had yearned to become. Laurens was already elegant, cultured, and wealthy when they met; Hamilton was poor, awkward, and desperate to prove himself greater than the squalid background he had risen from. They had bonded from the moment they met—and losing John in a meaningless skirmish at the end of the war had crushed Alex like no other loss in his life, save that of his son years later.

Laurens had died almost a year after the Battle of Yorktown, a few months before the Treaty of Paris had ended the war. Alex still recalled the stunned disbelief he had felt as he read the letter informing him of John's death; he had stared at the words on the page for the better part of an hour, his mind frantically trying to reorganize the sentences so that they said anything other than the grim message that assaulted his eyes. Since that day, he had never allowed himself to feel that level of brotherly affection toward any other human being. He could not tolerate the thought of feeling such deep pain a second time.

"You're dead, John," he said finally.

Laurens laughed, a sweet laugh of pure amusement that seemed to make the very sun in the sky shine brighter.

"Of course I am dead, my dear friend!" he said. "I'm as dead as British bullets and bayonets could make me. But surely you have not fallen into the trap of believing that death is the end of all existence, have you?"

Alex stared in disbelief a moment longer, and then lunged forward and caught Laurens up in his arms, embracing his old friend and laughing as he did so. He knew not if he was dead or alive, and at this moment he did not care. Laurens, the brother he had chosen rather than the one who had been born from his mother, was with him again at last, and that was all that mattered.

After a moment, he let John go and looked at him again. Those cool blue eyes stared back at him with that same amused affection that Hamilton had seen a hundred times in Washington's headquarters as they slaved away, helping the General run a mutinous, barefoot army and fight an impossible war against the most powerful nation on earth.

"Does this mean I am dead, too?" Hamilton finally asked.

"Not yet," Laurens said. "And maybe not at all. You are very ill, and right now you have one foot in each world. That's why you can see and hear me. I have a message for you; that's why I summoned you here, to this place we both loved."

"A message?" Hamilton said. "What message is that?"

"A storm is coming, Alex," said Laurens. "Look, even now it approaches!"

Hamilton turned his gaze to the river and saw a line of black clouds sweeping across the sky from south to north, obliterating the spring sunshine. Red lightning arced through it, leaving trails of sparks across the clouds. Booming peals echoed from it, but they sounded more like cannon fire than thunder. As the lightning grew brighter, Hamilton fancied he could see silhouettes in the clouds, the forms of soldiers locked in grisly combat in the sky. A tornado of fire swept across Mount Vernon, blasting the barn and outbuildings to splinters. It roared toward them, and the great manor house itself began to disintegrate. Trees were uprooted and the ground scorched and turned black where the firestorm touched. Alex cried out in fear and shock, and the vision winked out in a second. The sun was shining again; spring had returned, the grass was green, and the buildings stood as pristine as before.

"War," said Laurens. "A horrible, brutal war that will kill hundreds of thousands of Americans, leaving great cities in flames and dividing the country for decades even after it is over and done. It will not come in your lifetime, but your children will live to see it, and some of your grandsons may die in it."

"A civil war?" Alex said. "What am I to do about it?"

"You have to prevent the war by removing its cause," said Laurens. "The wicked institution of slavery will be the fundamental cause of this dreadful conflict. You must eliminate slavery in America before it takes root any further. There isn't much time, Alex! If this is not accomplished within the next decade, it will be too late. I don't like dropping this burden on you, old chum, but you are the only one who can do it."

Hamilton stared at his old friend, aghast at the implications of what Laurens had told him. He thought hard for a few moments, and then spoke.

"Why me?" he finally said. "I'm from New York; the Southerners detest me already, and certainly don't trust me."

"Better you than a New Englander," said Laurens with a wry grin. "Actually, Alex, it has to be you because there is no one else. No other national leader who commands the political resources you do is untouched by the scourge. Jefferson and Madison—both are hopelessly sold out to the slave labor system, especially Jefferson. John Adams is an old man, and a spent force politically. You are the only remaining Federalist of sufficient stature, and it will have to be a Federalist who does this—the Republicans' chief strength is in the South, with the slavers. You will have to become President, of course. Only from that office can you wield the power that will be required to make the Southern states see reason. I would start with Virginia, if I were you. South Carolina is far too dependent on slavery, but if Virginia leads, much of the South will be inclined to follow."

Alex sat down in one of the wooden chairs that lined the porch and buried his face in his hands.

"I don't know that I can do it," he said. "The Federalist Party is dying; right now, I am the only thing holding it together. Jefferson has adopted so many of our former positions we are reduced to a petulant voice, crying in the wilderness, often condemning the very positions we once supported, for no other reason than the fact that the President espouses them!"

Laurens shrugged playfully.

"I can't help you there, dear brother," he said. "I am no politician. I never rose higher in elective office than the South Carolina state house. But there is someone here who can."

Hamilton saw a shadow fall across his line of vision and turned around to see who was approaching. There stood George Washington, not the white-haired old man whose ill-fitting dentures had made his last years as President an exercise in misery, but the General in his prime, a regal figure who had drawn Alex into his orbit from the moment the young immigrant first laid eyes on him.

"Hello again, Mister Hamilton," said the President. "It is good to see you, my lad."

"Your Excellency, I—there is so much I wanted to tell you, sir," he began. Washington had always awed Hamilton, and seeing him now, restored to youth and vigor, made him even more intimidating. His relationship with the General was complicated; in some ways Washington had been like a father to him, but they were both were proud and stubborn, and had quarreled on several occasions, exchanging bitter words that Alex now regretted.

"You'll have to save it, Alex, for your time among us is nearly over," Washington told him. "Listen to me closely now. The window of opportunity for you to act is already closing. As you said, the Federalist Party—did I ever tell you, Hamilton, how much I hate the spirit of factions? And yet it seems no country can function without them! But you are right; the Federalist Party is dying. It is dying because it is divided. Many of those divisions are attributed to you. You have encouraged factions within Federalism; now it is time for you to preach unity. You are going to have to find a way to convince all those of the Federalist persuasion to rally behind you! Then you will need to appeal to as many Republicans as you can; for one faction alone cannot address this crisis. Make friends of your enemies, and allies of your adversaries. Mend your fences first, Alex, and then begin building bridges. It will take great patience, and great courage. There are more decent men in this country than you realize, and you will need the help of them all. But above all, you must become President. Only when you wield the power of the Chief Magistracy of the nation can you hope to avert the dreadful conflict that John spoke of."

As he spoke, Washington's form began to fade from view. Behind him, the walls of Mount Vernon began to shimmer and become translucent. Laurens laid his hand on Hamilton's shoulder, but that touch became lighter and lighter as he, too, faded.

"Your Excellency, wait!" Hamilton cried. "There's so much I have to ask you. I don't even know where to begin the task you've set me to!"

Washington was almost gone, but his voice, now thin and tinny, still reached Hamilton's ears.

"Find your allies where you can, from Virginia to Massachusetts!" he said. Then Washington, Laurens, and the beautiful Virginia plantation all faded from Hamilton's vision. Alex called out after them.

"Laurens! Your Excellency! Please wait!" he said, but even his voice sounded faint and weak in his ears. He found himself weeping as his world faded back into blackness.

"WHO IS Papa calling for, Mother?" asked little Eliza. She was four years old; an intelligent and curious girl with her father's wide eyes and her mother's long dark hair. Her family called her "Lizzie" to avoid confusion with her mother.

"John Laurens was his closest friend, back during the war, sweetheart," Eliza told her. "He was killed by the British many years ago. Your father is very sick; he is dreaming while he is half awake."

"Was Laurens an Excellency?" the little girl asked.

"No, your father simply called him by his name," her mother replied. "I think he may also be dreaming of President

Washington. 'Your Excellency' was what your father always called him."

"Is Papa going to wake up?" Eliza asked plaintively.

"Oh, my sweet Lizzie, of course he is," her mother replied, blinking back tears. "Your father is the strongest man I have ever known; he has survived so much in his life. The fact that he's alive is a miracle! It is a wonder he even lived long enough to come to this country, from what he told me of the island where he was born. A simple bullet scratch is not going to take him from us!"

Eliza believed that with all her heart, but she was still worried about her husband. He was ghastly pale, and there were dark circles under his eyes. Beads of sweat had popped out on his brow, and parts of his shirt were starting to soak through again.

Suddenly, the import of that struck her, and Eliza leaned forward to kiss her husband's brow. It was cool! The fever had broken at last. She smiled and hugged her little girl.

"Father's fever has come down!" she told Lizzie. "I think the crisis is passing."

"Good!" Lizzie said. "I want Papa to be better!"

"I want your papa to be better, too," a faint voice came from the bed.

"Alex!" Eliza gave a small shriek of joy. Her husband's wide, violet-blue eyes were open and looking at her with deep affection; for the first time in days, he seemed to be really seeing her.

"It seems that I'm not quite ready to enter the gates of Paradise yet," he said. He struggled to sit up, then gave a groan and lay back down.

"Papa! I'm glad you are awake!" said Lizzie.

Hamilton reached out with one hand and gently stroked his daughter's hair. She giggled with joy and climbed onto the bed, kissing his face repeatedly. Alex laughed at the purity of her love and concern for him. How marvelous it felt to be alive!

"Lizzie, go to the kitchen and tell cook to prepare some chicken soup," Eliza said, lifting the little girl off the bed. "Your father needs to eat and get his strength back. He's been through a grave ordeal."

The four-year-old scampered off, and Eliza took her husband by the hand, grateful to see him awake and aware.

"My dearest Hamilton," she said, "I feared I had lost you forever!"

"Apparently my wound was more serious than I realized," he said. "How long have I been abed?"

"Four days now," she replied. "I've been sick with worry!"

"You are the best and dearest of women, my love!" he said. "But I need to talk to you. I've been given a task, Eliza, something that I must work towards with all my might and main for whatever days I have left on this earth."

"A task?" she said. "My dearest husband, the only task you have before you at the moment is to rest, get your strength back, and fully recover!"

Alexander Hamilton tried to sit up again and succeeded. Eliza placed another pillow behind his back to prop him up. Never a big man, he seemed shrunken somehow in the four-poster bed. His white nightshirt hung loosely on him, and his movements were slow and deliberate, the motions of a man who did not fully trust his limbs to obey his mind's commands.

His mind raced as he regarded his wife's smiling but still worried gaze. The vision of Laurens and Washington was still fresh and vivid in his mind. Had it been real? Or just a delusion manufactured by his fevered brain? Was the country truly headed for a calamity? Was slavery—an institution he had always despised, since witnessing its atrocities at their worst when he was a boy on St. Nevis—going to rip America apart? Or was it all just a hallucination, a fever dream born of his own ambition and desperation?

No, he thought. Something more was at work here than illness and a deranged mind. He could not help but see the hand of the Almighty in this. Even as a child, Hamilton had believed in God. His faith in a higher power had sustained him through his abandonment by his father, the death of his mother, and all the trials of his young life. He might have died many times over during the Revolution, but even as British bullets flew around him, he had always felt a protecting hand shielding him from harm. Even the desperate grief of losing Philip could not have been borne had Hamilton's faith not sustained both him and Eliza during those dark hours.

And the duel! If it had not been for the cry of that osprey, he might not have turned his head, shifting his body slightly as he did. Burr's bullet might have torn through his bowels, killing him slowly but just as surely as if it had penetrated his heart. His life had been handed back to him that day, just as it was being handed back to him again now, as the infection in his body subsided. Why had he been spared, if not to fulfill a higher destiny? And what destiny could be loftier than emancipating a million poor souls from forced labor, rape, and the horrors of the lash?

"You're right, of course," he told his wife as she regarded him curiously. "I must finish getting well. And when I am recovered, I can begin my labors."

"I still have no idea what you are talking about, Alex!" Eliza said.

"My dearest Eliza, best of wives and best of women," he said with a smile. "Your husband must become President. The fate of the nation depends on it!"

"Oh!" she exclaimed, and her expression of surprise and shock was so charming that her husband laughed out loud. He laughed so long and hard it finally triggered a coughing fit. Eliza looked at him with alarm and affection.

"I think that Doctor Hosack should have another look at you," she finally said. "I believe the fever may have addled your brain."

"Well, please let me eat a bite and change into a clean shirt first," Hamilton said. "I feel positively grimy."

"Mister Hamilton!" the family cook, Mrs. Benson, proclaimed from the door. "It is good to see you up and awake, sir! I've made you some chicken soup."

A tray was placed before him, and as Hamilton began to eat, the children came in one by one—Angelica, his oldest daughter, whose mind had been permanently deranged by the death of her brother Philip; Alex Junior; James; John; William Stephen; Lizzie; and even "little Phil," only two years old—all of them anxious to see their father awake and alert again. Hamilton could feel his strength returning as the warm, rich broth filled his belly, and the smiles and laughter of his children buoyed his spirits and filled him with resolve. Whether the vision of Laurens and Washington had truly come from heaven, or from his own fevered imagination, he could not be sure. But the goal set before him was a noble one and achieving it would greatly benefit his country. In the process, he would leave behind such a legacy that his name would never be forgotten.

After two bowls of soup, he lay back and asked the children to leave for a moment. He looked down at his side and gingerly pushed the bandages aside to study the wound from Burr's pistol ball which had nearly wound up killing him, after all. The gash was still red around the edges, but the flesh had closed up, the redness was fading, and it was no longer hot to the touch—he remembered how it had felt like a burning coal stuck between his ribs at the height of his illness.

After resting for a half hour, he asked Eliza to help him up to see if he could stand up. He was a bit wobbly on his legs, but they bore his weight well enough with the help of a cane. He stood long enough to give the servants time to change his bedding, and then carefully sat down on the edge of the bed. He certainly didn't want to do too much, too soon! He changed into a fresh shirt and ran a comb through his hair, and then settled back into his pillows, closing his eyes but not going all the way back to sleep.

"General Hamilton?" a voice interrupted his reverie.

"Doctor!" Hamilton said. "It is good to see you again."

"Words cannot express how overjoyed I am at your recovery," his friend replied. "Your wife was not willing to let me carry out some of the treatments I thought you needed most, but it appears your natural constitution was strong enough to bring you through the crisis after all."

"I appreciate your treatment, and your concern," said Hamilton.

"Do you mind if I look you over?" the doctor asked, and Hamilton gave his assent. Hosack looked at his eyes, felt his brow, took his pulse, and then carefully examined the wound, humming and tut-tutting to himself as he did so. When he finished, he pulled up a chair and sat next to the bed, facing his patient.

"It appears your body has fought off the infection from the bullet wound," he said. "I have seldom seen such a strong reaction to such a minor injury; in fact, I think that your condition may have been an attack of pleural fever compounded by the infection in your side. At any rate, I see no reason you should not be on your feet in another day or two."

"That is splendid news, Doctor, and I thank you for it," Alex replied. "While you are here, I should like to ask you something."

"Of course, Mister Hamilton," Hosack replied. "What would you like to know?"

"Once I recover from my current malady, do you think I will be sound enough of body and mind to resume public life?" he asked.

"I should see no reason why not," the doctor assured him. "Are you thinking of running for office?"

"I am," said Hamilton. "I find that my zeal for public service has overpowered my longing for domesticity."

"You are thinking of the Senate seat left vacant by Ambassador Armstrong, perhaps?" the doctor ventured.

Hamilton hadn't thought of that, but his mind seized upon the notion before Hosack had finished his sentence. He needed a political platform from which to move to the presidency; to establish himself as a vocal opponent to Jefferson's policies, and to organize Federalists throughout the Union to back his candidacy. Jefferson was virtually certain to win reelection that fall; Hamilton simply did not have time to organize a campaign and a political machine in the four months remaining till the election. Besides, General Pinckney had already established himself as the Federalists' standard bearer that fall.

But New York's second Senate seat had been left vacant when Jefferson appointed John Armstrong as his new Ambassador to France. The Republican faction held a slim majority in the state legislature which elected U.S. Senators, but no one knew or understood New York politics better than Alexander Hamilton. He had overcome the opposition of the State's governor, lieutenant governor, and a hostile majority in the State Senate to secure ratification of the Constitution. Getting himself elected as the U.S. Senator from New York should be relatively easy by comparison.

"That is exactly what I was thinking of, Doctor," he said with a gracious smile. "When I have recovered my strength, I shall begin my campaign."

"Give yourself a week or so, General Hamilton," the doctor said. "And keep that wound cleaned and dressed twice daily until it heals over! A relapse might prove worse than the initial infection, since your system will be weakened from fighting it off the first time."

"Good advice, I am sure, Doctor," said Hamilton. "I think I shall begin following it now, if you have nothing further for me?"

"I think that is a capital idea," Hosack said with a smile. "I shall tell your family to let you alone for a while, so that you can sleep."

Alex smiled and settled back into his pillows, but sleep did not come to him for several hours. He had been unconscious or barely conscious for so many days his brain rebelled at the thought of returning to slumber, so instead he planned. Inside his mind, he ran through lists of his political allies, old and new, keeping a running track of favors given and owed, mentally checking off which members of the state legislature he could count on and which would need some wooing. Then he began mentally composing the lengthy newspaper essay which he would use to launch his campaign. Senator Hamilton, he thought, had a nice sound to it, and hopefully it would be a stepping-stone on the path to something even grander: the office of the presidency. Only when he had achieved that office would his real labors begin. He was still smiling when he finally faded off to sleep that evening.

CHAPTER THREE

WASHINGTON, DC—or "Washington City" as most Americans called it in the first decade of the nineteenth century—was a small town, painstakingly hacked from the wilderness over the course of the previous decade by a small army of laborers, slave and free alike. Roughly twenty thousand people lived there in 1804; two-thirds of them were white and free; the rest were blacks, of whom perhaps a fourth were freedmen, and the rest were human property.

A handful of beautifully designed government buildings stood, in various stages of construction, surrounded by clapboard houses, taverns, shops, shacks, and boardinghouses, most of them cheaply constructed of raw, unpainted wood. When Congress was in session, the town's population increased by a third. The streets were made of packed dirt, dry and dusty in the summer and wet and deeply rutted in the winter. The stumps that projected through the packed earth were stark reminders of the dense forest that had covered the site a decade before; they made carriage rides down Pennsylvania Avenue a bumping, jostling nightmare.

But Washington was also a town on the move—people constantly coming and going, Congressmen and Senators dining at the busy taverns, sleeping in the better boardinghouses, living elbow to elbow with tradesmen, workers, attorneys, and occasional travelers from Europe, curious to see how America's experiment in republican government was working out. The President himself often left the Executive Mansion and came down and ate dinner with the locals, usually unrecognized by visitors from out of town.

Ten days after the duel between Hamilton and Burr, the President of the United States sat down to the breakfast table with his Secretary of State, James Madison. The two men had been friends and political allies for over a decade; indeed, Madison had become the President's most trusted aide as well as his closest friend. Thomas Jefferson's red hair had gone gray in his later years, but his face was unlined and youthful still, and his gaze as piercing as ever. His soft voice and courteous manners belied his keen political instincts and comfort in wielding executive power. He had a network of friends, newspaper editors, and sympathetic state legislators who kept him apprised of political developments all over the young nation, and few men were better informed than he.

"Can we somehow hold Hamilton accountable for Burr's death?" asked Madison.

"That would be most difficult," said Jefferson. "Burr shot first, he shot to kill, and Hamilton, by all the dictates of honor, was fully justified in returning fire. Not only that, Secretary Hamilton was grievously wounded and nearly perished from Burr's bullet. His first act on returning from the duel was to go to God's house and seek forgiveness for his deed. Clever stroke, that. I don't doubt Hamilton's sincerity—he always was one who believed in the superstitions of Christianity—but it was also a strong political move. Who can believe he was a cold-blooded murderer when he was so contrite about the deed? Besides all that, the fact that I had already made up my mind to replace Burr as Vice President will be cited as evidence that I agreed with Hamilton's assessment of his character."

"So Hamilton is still a force to be reckoned with, then?" Madison said. "That is most unfortunate. Without him, the Federalists are a motley crew of miscellaneous dissidents. They bicker and fight constantly among themselves. But with his mind and pen to unite them, they could easily become a potent political force in this country again."

"I do not doubt that he aspires to occupy the chair where I now sit," Jefferson said. "He might have been here already, were it not for his personal feud with Adams and his involvement with Mrs. Reynolds."

"Surely the electors would never choose as President a man who is a self-confessed adulterer and a killer on top of that!" said Madison.

"America is changing," said the President, rising and sipping his coffee. "It is a change you and I have worked for, putting the choice for the next President more into the hands of the people and less in those of the political elites. Hamilton will not run against me this fall—it is too soon, and my position is too strong. He will bide his time. I imagine he will campaign for the Senate, or perhaps for governor, in two years, and from there establish a platform from which he can step into the presidency. The people love a man who is willing to defend his personal honor, and who is humble enough to confess his sins publicly and seek forgiveness. In retrospect, threatening to expose Hamilton's affair was a grave error! The 'Reynolds Pamphlet' may have hurt him in the short term, but over time his honesty will be remembered above his indiscretions."

Madison sighed and walked to the window, looking out on the capital city. Washington, DC, was still a work in progress — stumps stuck out of its muddy streets, and half the buildings were unfinished. But the seeds of the Republic had been planted there already and were beginning to bear fruit. What kind of Republic would America become? That was the issue that divided Federalists from the Republicans. Madison and Jefferson had envisioned a nation of productive citizen-farmers, eschewing banks, industry, and great cities in favor of simple, stoic virtues. Hamilton and his followers saw a vast trade empire, with factories springing up across the fertile fields instead of lush green crops, and sprawling cities full of speculation and corruption instead of the simple virtues of country life. It was a vision that repulsed Madison, who shared with Jefferson the view that manufacturing and banking were two of the worst curses ever to afflict mankind.

Jefferson came up behind his friend and laid his hand on the man's shoulder.

"I will admit, Thomas, I had hoped to succeed you in the presidential chair," Madison said wistfully. He had been the guiding genius behind the creation of the U.S. Constitution, and longed to stand at the head of the government that he had helped create.

"You may do it yet," said Jefferson. "But you will have to face Alexander Hamilton as your opponent, and he is a formidable rival — a host unto himself."

Madison smiled, and his overly serious scholar's face lit up and revealed the humorous soul that few but his closest friends ever saw.

"Since your own reelection seems assured, my friend, I can be grateful that I will have four years to prepare myself for the contest," he said. "I respect Hamilton, for all that I deplore his monarchist tendencies. I propose to wage an honorable and clean campaign against him, not the scurrilous avalanche of invective that marked our last presidential contest."

"I said the same of my effort to unseat Mister Adams," said Jefferson. "The problem is that those of us who embrace public life find ourselves equally damned by our friends and by our enemies! It is the nature of our electoral process is that our battles are waged by our surrogates rather than ourselves, so in the end, it matters not how we propose to conduct the struggle. Its nature is determined by those who conduct it for us."

"That is true," said Madison. "I think in a fair and honest exchange of ideas, I might best Hamilton—perhaps! The man is so incredibly prolific. You read the Publius essays, did you not?"

"Your passionate defense of Federalism?" Jefferson said with a wry smile.

"The Federalism we designed in our Constitution was a noble proposition of government," Madison said testily. "I cannot help what those who now bear that name have done to pervert our ideas!"

Jefferson smiled and returned to his chair, taking a long sip of tea.

"I apologize, James," he said. "By all means, finish your thought."

"The rhetoric being used by the foes of the Constitution was wildly inaccurate, but it was gaining a great deal of traction among the masses," Madison explained. "I met up with Hamilton and John Jay, because he had suggested that the three of us combine forces and each write eight or ten essays to be published anonymously, explaining and defending the new Constitution to the people. Jay wrote five, and then fell ill and was unable to assist us further. I wrote twenty-nine essays myself, as it wound up. But Hamilton . . . the man wrote fifty-one essays in the space of six months, Thomas! Some of them he produced in as little as two days, twenty pages or more, and they are flawless! My writing goes through multiple drafts; Hamilton's thoughts spring to the page with instant force and eloquence. It is a shame, really, that his thoughts tend so much towards monarchy. He was a powerful ally once."

"I feel similarly towards President Adams," Jefferson said. "Before politics divided us, we were friends. Indeed, I enjoyed cordial relations with Hamilton until the accursed spirit of monarchy and centralism possessed him. But the powers of the Executive Branch cannot be allowed into the hands of someone so enamored of aristocratic tendencies. So, when the next presidential contest comes, all the means I possess shall be at your disposal. I can think of no one that I would rather entrust this office to than yourself."

"And I will gratefully accept all the aid you can offer," said Madison. "I have a feeling I will need it."

THAT SAME morning, in New York, Eliza Hamilton went to the bedroom to check on her husband and found his bed vacant and his nightclothes draped over the chest at the foot of the bed. Alex had been getting stronger over the last couple of days, and she was not surprised to find that he was up and about again, although she had strictly forbidden him to leave the house for at least a week after his fever broke.

Walking down the hall to his study, she heard the familiar scratching sound of pen on foolscap and peeked in the door to find him seated at his desk, a stack of blank paper on one side, and several sheets already filled with his elegant, flowing script on the other.

"Good morning, my dear Hamilton," she said, kissing the top of his head. "I think this last week is the longest I have known you to go without writing since we met all those years ago."

He smiled and stood, embracing her and returning her kiss, then stretched and yawned.

"I believe I should have gone mad if I was forced to spend another day in that bed," he said, "not to mention that there are things that I must do if I am to achieve my goal. Being ill for a week has already set me back more than I would like. But I am getting hungry. Could you bring me a cup of hot tea and something from the kitchen, my love?"

"I will be glad to," she said. "What is it you are working on?"

He picked up the first sheet and held it out to her. She squinted a bit to read the title—her vision had worsened slightly after she turned thirty.

"*A True Account of the Recent Duel between Vice President Aaron Burr and Alexander Hamilton, as related by the latter,*" she read aloud. "Oh, Alex, is this really necessary?"

"If I am to ask the public to entrust me with high office, I must remove the stain of this affair from my reputation," he explained. "I think the best way to do that is to confront the issue head on and tell my side of the story. The people appreciate candor."

Eliza bit her lip. Hamilton's "candor" had almost cost him their marriage a few years earlier, when he had decided the best way to deal with attempted blackmail was to publish the details of his sordid affair with Maria Reynolds. He had not confessed the affair to her until the pamphlet was on its way to the presses, and the pain of that moment burned her still. Nonetheless, she had eventually forgiven him, as unimaginable as that prospect had seemed at the time.

Now, as she considered his current position and his future plans, his course of action made sense. She knew that Burr's faction—small though it was—wielded a good bit of influence in New York politics, and they had done their best to paint her husband as a murderer. The circumstances of the duel made that effort more difficult for them, and Hamilton's own version of events being published would do much to put the issue to rest.

"I'm sure you have thought this over carefully," she said. "I'll bring you some breakfast so you can continue working on it. But, Alex, one suggestion, if I may?"

"Of course, my love," he said.

"If I were you, I would consult with one or two men whose political judgment you trust. Let them read it, and listen to their opinions, before you make it public," she told him.

"That is excellent advice, my dear, and I had already planned on doing that," he told her, and she smiled before hurrying off to get him some food. He was much stronger, and his color was coming back, but she also knew that when he fell into one of his writing frenzies, he would often neglect both food and drink for hours at a time, and she had no desire for him to relapse.

Alex sat back down and studied what he had written so far. A master wordsmith, he had begun this essay with two goals in mind: first of all, to tell the truth about the whole affair; and second, to tell it in such a way as to show that he had been left with no choice but to act as he did. Overall, he thought that he had struck the right tone thus far, but he was getting to the heart of the story, and as he picked up his pen, he chose his next words with great care.

It is true that my personal relationship with Colonel Burr was generally an amicable one. We had known each other for many years; we served together in the late Revolution, and I knew him to be a man of resolute courage and considerable intelligence. He was a lawyer of rare skill, succinct and persuasive, and his manner was easygoing and encouraged confidence and trust among his friends.

However, Burr's political principles were as ephemeral and ever-shifting as a cloud driven by the winds. At one moment, he was a Republican and a staunch partisan of Mister Jefferson; the next, he was a Federalist, condemning the policies of the current administration and espousing the idea of a dynamic Federal government with authority over the states. But when the Federalists of New York refused to take him back into the fold, Burr became an independent, damning both factions of our American political divide as too extreme to be entrusted with power, while insisting that he himself was worthy of it!

In short, despite his many virtues, Aaron Burr was so enamored of political power that he would do anything, say anything, and become anything in order to achieve it. It is a great virtue of our American system that we allow the offices we have created under our Constitution to seek the men best qualified to hold them; rather than the man seeking the office. A man who openly seeks a position of power is rarely rewarded with it. Burr's oft-demonstrated willingness to prostitute himself to whatever position he thought would make him most appealing to the American people showed him to be a man for whom principles would always take second place to the relentless pursuit of power.

It was for this reason that I opposed his election to the Governor's office, and said, in private circumstances at a dinner with friends, that I considered him to be untrustworthy and unscrupulous. It was these remarks, reported by Charles Cooper in a letter that wound up being published, which prompted Burr to issue his challenge.

Had Col. Burr confined his challenge to my intemperate remarks at the dinner table, I would have been willing to issue an apology and be done with the whole sordid affair. However, he insisted that I retract every negative opinion I had ever expressed of him; to wit, he was asking me to endorse the very

attributes of his public life that first engendered my criticism!
I could not, in good conscience, do this, and informed him so. I
gave him every opportunity to moderate his demands, but he
refused to, and thus the date was set for us to meet at
Weehawken.

As a Christian, I abhor the practice of dueling. While I did, on
a few occasions, act as a second during affairs of honor as a
young man, the older I waxed the more I realized how contrary
to civilized behavior the code of the duel really is. In addition,
seeing my beloved son taken from me in a duel fought over a
simple quarrel between two college boys made me realize all the
more how truly precious and brief our lives are. I would have
done anything to avoid my interview with Colonel Burr;
anything, that is, except the one thing he demanded: to
mortgage my honor and retract statements that were made
based on the purest of principles.

Thus, I made up my mind, if the duel must come, that I would
throw away my shot and not attempt to kill Colonel Burr. I oft
expressed this sentiment to intimate acquaintances during the
days leading up to the duel, and it was still my resolve as I was
conveyed across the Hudson to our fatal meeting point. As we
met, I looked Burr in the eye and could see very clearly that he
had made up his mind to put me to execution that morning. I
had no desire to die, and yet I also had no desire to fire first and
take his life if he repented at the moment of truth. So, I resolved
to let him take the first shot and then respond according to
what he did.

What happened next, I have already related at the beginning of
this essay—Burr's bullet wounded me, superficially I thought

at first, although I was more gravely injured than I first realized. What I saw in his eyes after the gun's smoke cleared and I remained standing was the same hatred that had been there before, compounded by disappointment that I had not fallen. In that moment anger seized me, and I raised my own pistol and returned fire, with fatal result.

So perished the Vice President of the United States, under circumstances that I most deeply regret even now. I am sorry that Colonel Burr is dead, but for all that, I think that I acted in accordance with the dictates of honor; I gave him every possible chance to repent of his evil purpose. I firmly believe that I am innocent in the eyes of the law; as for where I stand in the eyes of the Almighty, that is another matter. All I can do is try from this day forward to live a life of Christian charity and upright character, and to let that life, in both private and public spheres, atone for this thing that I have done.

I certify that everything written above is true and accurate to the best of my knowledge and recollection. I lay this account before the public so that all may know the truth of what transpired between myself and Col. Burr on the morning of July 11, in the year of Our Lord 1804; affixing my signature as a witness to the events of that day.

A. Hamilton.

By the time he was done, the tea was cooling, and the pastry Mrs. Benson had brought him was beginning to dry out. Nonetheless, he drained his cup and wolfed down the small cake. He did not relish the prospect of his narrative about the events of that fateful encounter being debated and discussed in every grog-shop and parlor in New York and beyond, but he knew that if his own version did not guide the narrative, someone else's would.

Eliza came to the door of the bedroom as he finished off the last of the sweet cake, and she gave an exasperated sigh.

"Of course," she said, "you waited until your entire essay was written before eating a bite! Whatever am I going to do with you, Mister Hamilton?"

Alex hugged his wife and planted a kiss on her upturned face.

"What I hope, my dear, is that you will stay around to pamper me, indulge me, and help me rein in the darker angels of my nature until old age renders me incapable of harming myself or others," he told her.

"I supposed that someone will have to keep watch on you," she chuckled. "Oh, my dear Alex, I would be utterly lost without you! I would have perished from grief if you had died."

"You hold yourself in too little esteem, my dear," he said. "You are the strongest woman I have ever known. You have dealt with my own shortcomings, our son's death, our daughter's madness, my own recent illness, and all the demands of our younger children, with unflagging strength and good cheer. I have no doubt that you would have survived me by a half century at least!"

He moved away from her and stepped across the room to his desk. He opened a small wooden lock box and rummaged around for a moment. He turned, holding out a small, folded sheet of paper.

"I want to give you something," he said. "I debated whether or not to destroy it, but I have decided that I will leave that choice to you."

"What is it, my dear Hamilton?" she asked, hesitating to unfold it.

"It is the letter that I wrote to you shortly before my meeting with Colonel Burr, to be delivered in the event that I perished," he said. "You may read it or not, as you see fit. But I wanted you above all to know what was in my heart as I faced that moment."

Eliza looked at him for a long moment, and then slowly, she looked down and unfolded the sheet of paper, carefully reading the short letter Hamilton had written therein. Hamilton closed his eyes—he had no need to look on; those painful words permanently etched in his memory.

This letter, my very dear Eliza, will not be delivered to you, unless I shall first have terminated my earthly career; to begin, as I humbly hope from redeeming grace and divine mercy, a happy immortality.

If it had been possible for me to have avoided the interview, my love for you and my precious children would have been alone a decisive motive. But it was not possible, without sacrifices which would have rendered me unworthy of your esteem. I need not tell you of the pangs I feel, from the idea of quitting you and exposing you to the anguish which I know you would feel. Nor could I dwell on the topic lest it should unman me.

The consolations of Religion, my beloved, can alone support you; and these you have a right to enjoy. Fly to the bosom of your God and be comforted. With my last idea; I shall cherish the sweet hope of meeting you in a better world.

Adieu best of wives and best of Women. Embrace all my darling Children for me.

Ever yours

A H

Eliza slowly sank to the bed when she was done reading, the tears slowly flowing down her cheeks. Hamilton put his arms around her and held her for a long time. Finally, she looked up at him and spoke very softly.

"Think what you like, Alex," she said. "I should have died without you."

CHAPTER FOUR

SENATE ELECTIONS in the early nineteenth century were much different from those held later in American history; the New York election of 1804 was even more so because it was a special election. It had been called by the governor to fill a vacancy left when John Armstrong, the senior Senator from New York, was appointed as America's new Minister to France. The Senators in those days were chosen not by the people, but by the state legislature. This would pose a significant problem for Alex as he sought election to the U.S. Senate that fall, since the elections the previous spring had installed a State Senate and State Assembly that were completely dominated by Jefferson's party. Out of thirty-one seats in the State Senate, only four were held by Federalists; of one hundred State Assemblymen, only seventeen were members of Hamilton's party. Wresting a Senate seat from a legislature dominated by the opposition would be a tremendous struggle— but it was exactly the sort of challenge Hamilton lived for.

Alexander Hamilton's life had been defined by struggle, he reflected as he studied the roster sheet of the 28th New York Legislature. Growing up in the West Indies as a quasi-bastard (his parents were not married, primarily because his mother's vindictive first husband had refused her a divorce, even long after their marriage had crumbled), and then as an orphan, he had faced prejudice and contempt. By sheer determination, ceaseless labor, and intellectual force, he had brought himself to the attention of the island's educated aristocracy; his remarkable gift for numbers and accounting had earned him a position as a clerk and, not long after that, a generous scholarship to go to New York and get a formal education.

Once in the New World he never looked back. He flung himself first into his college studies, and then when the war broke out, into the Revolution. He wrote passionate editorials espousing the Patriot cause, and then joined the militia as a young officer. His organizational skills soon led to his appointment as Washington's chief aide-de-camp; his flowery prose had helped him woo and win the beautiful Elizabeth Schuyler, daughter of one of New York's most prominent and wealthy families. After the war, he'd earned a law degree, and his eloquence in the courtroom made him one of New York's most sought-after attorneys. He'd been elected to the State Assembly, served as a delegate to the Constitutional Convention, and then, in what was thus far the crowning jewel of his political career, he'd been appointed as Treasury Secretary by President George Washington, who recognized that Hamilton's immense talents were desperately needed to help the country resolve its enormous debt crisis.

Those had been the days when his influence was at its peak, as he guided his four-point plan to restore the nation's credit through a disagreeable Congress. He had established the country's first internal taxes, made sure the government could faithfully meet its financial obligations, bound the states to the national government by having it assume their debts, and then created a national bank. He helped determine the location of the United States capitol, as well as being the most important guiding influence on President Washington's approach to government. However, his success came at a price: his former friend and political ally James Madison had been increasingly drawn into the orbit of Thomas Jefferson, the Secretary of State, who viewed Hamilton as an ambitious schemer with tendencies to monarchy.

Eventually, Washington's cabinet members and the Congress had split into two rival camps—the Republicans, led by Thomas Jefferson ("democrats" as their rivals referred to them), and the Federalists, led by Hamilton and John Adams, the Vice President. President Washington tried to remain above the partisan divide, but he usually sided with the Federalists, primarily because he trusted Hamilton's judgment. He also found that Jefferson was so duplicitous that Washington could not consider him trustworthy. Both men resigned from the cabinet before His Excellency's second term was up—Hamilton because he wanted to be close to Eliza after she suffered a miscarriage; Jefferson because he was opposed to Washington's policy of neutrality during the French Revolution.

After Washington declined to run for a third term, Adams and Jefferson had squared off in the first-ever contested presidential election. This put Hamilton on the horns of a dilemma—he despised Jefferson's politics, but frankly, he considered John Adams to be unsuited for the presidency due to his hot temper and erratic mind. In the end, he had supported Adams, but his support was lukewarm and belated, and the new President could not forgive Hamilton for that. Jefferson had finished second in the electoral college and thus became Vice President. The divide between the new President and Hamilton had grown even greater throughout Adams's turbulent term in the White House.

After Hamilton's despised excise tax had sparked a rebellion in Pennsylvania, the Revolutionary French began to bluster and threaten their former ally, Adams had asked Congress to double the size of the nation's tiny army and recall Washington from retirement to be its commander. The former President had agreed on the condition that Hamilton be promoted to senior major general and be appointed his second-in-command. Adams had swallowed his pride and made the appointment, but he complained bitterly about Hamilton to the press, and disbanded the army when the French threat receded.

Then, in December of 1799, George Washington died suddenly, after an illness that lasted less than three days. The loss struck Hamilton like a bolt from the blue; the General had been in excellent health the last time Alex saw him earlier that year, during a quick visit to Mount Vernon. Hamilton had been deeply affected by the loss; he owed everything he had become in America to Washington's friendship and patronage. But despite the thousands of words he had written for and about the First President, Alex had never really taken the time to tell the man what he felt for him. It had been a difficult relationship, to be sure—Washington was stern, demanding, aloof, and rarely let his true emotions surface. Hamilton had toiled relentlessly for the man, and seldom heard a word of thanks. Yet at the same time, Washington was the closest thing to a father that Hamilton had ever had, and he loved the General deeply. Something in him came untethered when President Washington died; it was as if the brakes that kept him from self-destruction had been severed, and Alex was unable to control his pen or his mouth.

By the time the 1800 election rolled around, Hamilton was fed up with America's second President. As Jefferson and Adams squared off against one another that year, Alex authored a pamphlet to be circulated among the leaders of the Federalist Party, entitled *Letter from Alexander Hamilton, Concerning the Public Conduct and Character of John Adams, Esq, President of the United States.* In it he spent some forty pages excoriating Adams as a half-mad, erratic, ill-tempered, and incompetent administrator unworthy of a second term. However, he then spent the last twenty pages explaining that, as bad as he was, Adams was still preferable as President to Thomas Jefferson. He told the Federalist leaders that Charles Pinckney would be the better choice for their country, but if they could not unite behind the South Carolinian, then they should cast their ballots for Adams.

Hamilton had never intended this document to be disseminated to the public; however, a wavering Federalist had handed a copy over to one of Jefferson's supporters, and suddenly Hamilton's essay on Adams was being carried in newspapers all over the country. The Federalist Party shattered into Adams and Pinckney factions, and the split destroyed any chance they might have had of scoring an electoral victory. Furious at Hamilton's screed, Adams was heard to say that he would have been reelected if not for the scheming of that "bastard brat of a Scots peddler, the son of a common whore!" Not only did Hamilton destroy Adams's political career, he had also damaged his own standing as the leader of the Federalist Party. He still had a following, but many Federalists now blamed him for their minority status—and in his heart, Hamilton knew they were right.

However, the drama surrounding the 1800 election was not fully played out yet. Although Adams had been defeated by an electoral vote of 73 to 64, Jefferson had wound up in a tie vote with the man who was supposedly his political partner and vice president, none other than Aaron Burr. This threw the election to the House of Representatives, where the Federalists still commanded a majority until the new Congress took office after the first of the year. Speculation was rife that if the Federalists threw their support to Burr, he might switch his allegiance and continue Federalist control of the Executive branch. Burr did nothing to support this idea, but he did not reject it, either. The election's results were frozen in limbo; the House took vote after vote but remained deadlocked.

Finally, Hamilton, unable to stand the prospect of Burr stealing the election, had circulated among the Federalist Congressmen, sharing his opinion that Burr was too ambitious and power-hungry to be trusted with the nation's highest office. "If we must have a member of the opposition in the Executive Mansion," he told them, "let it at least be one with some pretensions to character." The forty-second ballot in the House decided the election in Jefferson's favor. Thus, Hamilton's greatest rival wound up owing his narrow victory to the man he had spent the last eight years criticizing as a monarchist and a traitor to the principles of the Revolution.

Hamilton's near-death experience had given him a clearer view of his own actions and the thoughts behind them; he recognized now that Washington's death had driven him into a depression that he had not acknowledged at the time. His own actions had sabotaged his political career; attempting to inflict damage on his enemies, he had destroyed himself instead, and imperiled the Federalist Party that he helped create. He was determined to reverse course, but he feared events had progressed so far that the damage could not be undone. Still, there was his dream—or vision, or whatever one chose to call it. The memory of that encounter was still strong, but he had no idea if he had truly been given a glimpse of the other side or if the whole thing was simply a product of his fevered imagination. Whatever it was, it had given him a sense of purpose that he had not felt in years, and he was grateful for it.

All these memories flooded Alex's mind as he stared at the list of names before him. How could he hope to win election to the Senate from a legislature so thoroughly dominated by Jefferson's Republicans? Many of these men he knew, some of them quite well. Not a few of them had been Federalists at one time, before they abandoned the party for various reasons. Some of them would be irreconcilably opposed to him, but there were many he knew could be amenable to persuasion—*if* the President did not apply too much political pressure on them to toe the party line.

Jefferson. It all came back to Thomas Jefferson. Hamilton's only hope of being elected to the Senate was if Jefferson could be dissuaded from opposing his candidacy. Hamilton laughed out loud; was there any way on earth that he could persuade the President not to speak out against him? Long ago, Jefferson had decided that Hamilton was the greatest single threat to America's republican form of government; a traitor to the Revolution that Jefferson had never fired a shot to win! Of all the things about the cool, aloof Virginian, that was what galled Hamilton the most: Alex had risked his life for America again and again on the battlefield, had been wounded in combat, and had sent young men to die carrying out his orders, but Jefferson had wielded a pen instead of a sword, serving as a member of Congress, a diplomat, and a governor of Virginia. The one time a British army had approached the state capitol, Jefferson and his cabinet had fled rather than organize the militia to resist. Hamilton had nearly died trying to free America from monarchy, and Jefferson had the temerity to accuse him of being a monarchist? It was frustrating, but Alex swallowed his resentment.

Few men were more persuasive than Alexander Hamilton, and he was well aware of that fact. He had employed his pen to rally men to the Revolutionary cause, to win support for his policies, and to cast his enemies from office. He was an expert at lobbying; face to face, the force of his personality was hard to resist. But he was about to face his greatest challenge thus far: to persuade a man who had opposed him for over a decade to drop his opposition. But Hamilton knew that he did not stand a chance to be elected to the Senate without talking Jefferson into a stance of neutrality. So, having made up his mind to act, he acted without hesitation.

"Eliza," he called, "could you come here for a moment?"

"Yes, Alexander?" his wife replied. She had been in the nursery, tending to Little Phil, their youngest child.

"I think my strength is recovered enough to travel a bit. Will you be all right if I journey to Virginia and back?" he asked.

"Virginia!" she said. "That is over three hundred miles, Alex! Are you sure that you are well enough?"

"It has been two weeks since the duel," Alex said. "The wound in my side has healed nicely, and I will not push myself to make the journey quickly. But there is something there that I must do."

Eliza studied him, and then smiled.

"My sweet Hamilton," she said. "Have I ever been able to stop you from getting your way? As long as there are no more duels on the horizon, then you have my blessing to make this journey. Who is it you are going to see?"

"President Jefferson," Alex replied. "But there are a couple of people here in New York I must talk to first! I shall return before dark; do not start supper without me, please. Then I shall leave in the morning."

With that, he grabbed his coat, hat, and cane and headed for the front door, leaving his wife staring after him in astonishment.

"GENERAL HAMILTON!" Rufus King exclaimed. "It is a pleasure to see you, my dear sir. I was quite fearful for your health after hearing about your injury in the duel with Burr."

"Thank you, Senator," Hamilton said. King had represented New York in the Senate until quite recently and was the leading Federalist candidate for the seat that Armstrong had just vacated. "I have come to ask you a favor, if you would be so kind as to consider it."

"What might that be?" King asked.

"Are you still planning on running for Armstrong's seat in the Senate this fall?" Alex asked him.

"Yes, I am," replied King. "Someone has got to bear the standard for the Federalist Party, and I already have some experience in the job."

"And how likely do you think you are to prevail in that election?" Hamilton asked him point-blank.

King laughed long and hard at that, and Hamilton joined in. After a moment, King shook his head and looked ruefully at his guest.

"Do you really have to ask?" he said. "The state legislature is completely dominated by our opposition; I am nothing but the designated sacrificial lamb for the Federalist Party."

"Well, if that is the case, how would you feel if I wanted to put my neck on the chopping block instead?" Hamilton asked him.

King's eyebrows shot up, and he beckoned Alex to his parlor. Once they were seated, he poured a snifter of brandy for himself and his guest, and then sat down in the chair across from Hamilton.

"What are you up to, Alex?" he said. "You know as well as I do there is no chance of a Federalist victory, so why would you commit yourself to a lost cause?"

"I don't know that I can win," said Hamilton, "I must be honest with you about that. But I also am not sure that I will lose. Let's be frank with each other, my friend—the Federalist Party is dying. If things continue in their current course of action, we will be a spent force before the decade is out. Some of that is my doing, I freely acknowledge. But what could better revitalize the fortunes of our organization than us stealing a Senate seat out from under the noses of our rivals?"

"Well, no one knows and understands the intricacies of New York politics better than you, old friend," said King. "If you want to seek the office, have at it! I offer you my unqualified support!"

"You're a good man, Rufus, and I will not forget this favor," Hamilton said, tossing down his brandy in two quick gulps and relishing the slight burn of the alcohol going down his throat. "I have a great deal to do before I leave town in the morning, but I will admit I had dreaded this errand. You made this conversation so much easier than I had anticipated. Thank you very much!"

"Will you not stay for dinner?" King asked.

"I shall have you over to my place when I return from my journey to Virginia," said Hamilton, "but I am afraid I cannot linger right now. Adieu, old friend!"

One errand down, he thought as he left King's house. The next would be more difficult and require a bit more diplomacy. He headed down Fifth Avenue and turned right, looking for a small brownstone he had only visited a couple of times before. He located it and knocked on the door, which was answered by a black butler in fine livery a few moments later.

"Good afternoon, sir, may I help you?" the Negro asked him.

"General Alexander Hamilton, calling on Senator John Woodworth," Alex said. "Is your master at home?"

"He is, sir, and if you will wait in the parlor, I will go fetch him for you," the butler said with a bow. Hamilton entered and followed the servant to the study. He studied the books on the shelf as he waited for his host to arrive on the scene. Woodworth, it appeared, was a devotee of Greco-Roman history, and of the law; Hamilton found two entire shelves devoted to legal texts.

"General Hamilton, this is an unexpected surprise," said Woodworth as he entered the room. "I am glad to see you in good health. Are you recovered, then, from your recent ordeal?"

"I am for the most part, I think. Thank you for receiving me on such short notice," Alex said. "I would like to confer with you for a moment regarding a political matter, if I may."

"You realize, of course, that we are members of opposing factions," Woodworth said. "I do not know how much common ground we share when it comes to matters political."

"That may be," Hamilton said, "but at the same time, I believe that there are some matters which may transcend factional interests. If you would, please hear me out before offering your opinion."

"By all means," said Woodworth. "Shall we sit?"

Hamilton sat down in a comfortable chair, a French import, by the look of it, and faced the State Senator. He had known Woodworth for several years and knew him to be a decent fellow, generally given to Republican leanings but also a keen thinker who had shown himself willing in the past to step away from partisan concerns when he felt an idea from the other side had merit.

"I will be as honest, and as succinct, as I can," Hamilton said. "As you know, I was more grievously wounded by Colonel Burr's bullet than I realized at the time of our unfortunate encounter. The truth of the matter is that I nearly died, and I was bedridden for nearly a week even after the crisis had passed. When a man comes so close to losing everything he has, it causes him to reflect. I have served my country to the best of my ability, and I flatter myself to think that my efforts have served the common good to some degree."

"I think gentlemen of both factions now recognize that you did our country a great service in establishing our national credit, even if the means by which you did so were controversial," his host replied.

"Solving the problem was my goal," said Hamilton. "The measures I took I still believe were necessary, but I wish I had explained them better. I now recognize that my more recent actions have not lived up to the standard which I once set for myself. I believe that I still have much to offer my country. Therefore, I have decided that I am going to offer myself to the people of New York as a candidate for the Senate seat recently vacated by the honorable John Armstrong."

"Mister Hamilton, that is noble, but your election is an impossibility!" said Woodworth. "You are a Federalist—in fact, you are the guiding genius of Federalism in America!—and our assembly is overwhelmingly Republican. I admire your achievements, and as an individual I find you to be cordial and charming. But why should I, or any other Republican, cast my vote in favor of a member of the opposition?"

"Because of my experience and my abilities," Hamilton said. "I can do more for New York, and for our country, in the Senate than any other prospective candidate out there. I have an intimate understanding of politics at the national and local level, and I am willing to work with the members of the opposition when it is in the country's best interest. No one else grasps the issues of debt, credit, and finance as well as I do. I have connections in virtually every state, and a fair understanding of the local issues facing them. I want to help this country address some of the most serious issues before us. I know that I can offer some solutions that will benefit the entire nation without harming any one state or section. Surely, sir, you do not think that only you Republicans can come up with good ideas? After all, Secretary Madison was a fellow

Federalist alongside of me not too long ago, and now he has become President Jefferson's right-hand man."

"The term had a different meaning then," Woodworth protested. "I will admit, you make some sanguine points, but surely you realize that President Jefferson will oppose your election with vigor! I do not think there are many Republicans in New York who will go against the will of our own Chief Executive."

"But what if he did not?" Hamilton asked.

"I beg your pardon?" Woodworth asked incredulously.

"Suppose President Jefferson let it be known that he was not opposed to my being elected to the Senate?" Alex pressed him. "Understand, now, I do not expect him to endorse me. But if he said that New York's legislators were free, as far as he was concerned, to vote their conscience without fear of reprisal, do you think I would stand a chance? Do you think some Republican legislators would cross the factional chasm to vote for me?"

Woodworth thought for a moment. He had great respect for Secretary Hamilton's intelligence and abilities, and the man's record of experience was formidable. He was also personally acquainted with a huge number of New Yorkers, especially those of the governing class. Many current Republicans had been Federalists not too many years before. Might they vote for their old political comrade? He had to concede that they might.

"It would be a difficult battle," Woodworth finally said. "But I think it is possible that you might, at the very least, make the race more competitive. However, I highly doubt that President Jefferson would be so indifferent to your candidacy as you think.

The man is convinced that you are the author of most of the political error and mischief in this country."

"That is why I am traveling to Monticello," Hamilton said. "I wish to speak with President Jefferson in person. It has been years since we spoke face to face; I think that it would do both of us good to clear the political air between us."

John Woodworth gave low whistle of amazement. The man had some serious stones, he had to give Hamilton that!

"I wish you the best of luck," he said, "but I frankly think you are going on a fool's errand!"

"It would not be the first," Alex said with a smile. "But I hope that I may surprise you before it is all said and done. Thank you for your time, sir. One last question, if I may?"

"What would that be?" Woodworth asked him.

"Assuming Jefferson does not openly oppose me, would you consider supporting my candidacy for the Senate seat?" he asked.

Woodworth paused, and looked momentarily flummoxed.

"Well," he finally said, "I honestly can't say right now. I would have to see who my party put up to oppose you, but I would at least give you fair consideration."

Hamilton smiled as he stood and made his way to the door.

"Thank you, Senator Woodworth," he said. "This has been a very enlightening conversation."

CHAPTER FIVE

IT WAS SOME three hundred and eighty miles from New York City to Jefferson's Monticello plantation in northern Virginia. Hamilton did not dawdle, but he did not push himself either; he was too conscious of the pain from the healing wound in his side when he exerted himself. It took him twelve days to make the journey, pushing his horse along at a decent clip but not so fast as to exhaust the animal. He paused at commercial stables and switched out mounts twice along the way, knowing that he could pick up his own horse on the return journey. There were several travelers on their way to Washington; some of the time he rode in company with them; at others, he rode on ahead alone, in order to have time alone with his thoughts. It was a mild summer; the sun shone brightly each day, but the heat was not oppressive. Crops were ripening in the field as Hamilton rode past the many farms that stretched across the New Jersey and Pennsylvania countryside. Here and there, along the rivers, sawmills and gristmills plied their trade. Everywhere, whether on a farmstead or in a mill, people were working busily. Every man seemed determine to rise up in society, to better himself, to leave his children something more than he was born into. This was the country that Hamilton had helped build and wished above all to preserve: stable, industrious, profitable, happy, and free.

He knew many people who lived along his route, but he kept his pauses to a minimum, staying at inns and taverns along the way, pausing late in the evening and eating a hot supper before collapsing into a rented bed. Only when he got to Washington, DC, did he allow himself a night at a more expensive establishment, where he got a good hot bath, a shave and haircut, and sent his clothes out to be laundered. Since Congress was not in session, the capital was sparsely populated; building projects dragged drearily on, and the handful of functionaries that ran Jefferson's trimmed-down Federal bureaucracy didn't seem very happy about remaining on the job in the sweltering July heat.

From Washington City it was a short ride to Monticello, where Jefferson had decamped a week or so before Hamilton's arrival in the capital. Hamilton had heard of Jefferson's home, modeled on the lines of a classical Italian villa yet featuring some new architectural details created by Jefferson himself. However, he had never had occasion to visit it prior to this trip. He had to admit, Jefferson's home was a beautiful and impressive structure, its magnificent dome perched atop a hill overlooking the winding Rivanna River. The front portico was striking, both up close and from a distance.

Not far from the house stood a much less splendid row of structures—Jefferson's slave cabins. In the fields that sloped down from the house, slave laborers toiled, hoes in hand, cutting weeds away from the tobacco plants. An overseer, whip in hand, rode around the perimeter of the field at a leisurely pace, watching the workers carefully, ready to punish any who appeared to be shirking their duties. Hamilton watched the Negroes for a long time, deep in thought, pondering both his immediate goal and the long-term vision he had adopted.

He knew Jefferson tolerably well and respected the man's staggering intellect. Hamilton was brilliant in his chosen areas of endeavor and reasonably well-read in many others, but Jefferson's breadth of knowledge was little short of amazing. He knew enough theology to be a seminary professor, enough history and geography to write volumes, enough science to be a member of the Royal Society of France, and enough mathematics to teach at a university. His grasp of natural history was truly impressive; he was a walking encyclopedia of botany and zoology. As a practical politician, Jefferson understood the use of political power, influence, and propaganda as well as any man alive. The only field where Hamilton found him to be deficient was in matters of banking and finance; Jefferson seemingly could not grasp the simplest concepts of economics and was a terrible manager of his own assets. In fact, the President of the United States was a chronic debtor.

But it was Jefferson's selective indifference to the evils of slavery that Hamilton found unforgivable. Jefferson was not blind, or ignorant, to the immorality and baleful influence that slavery wielded over every society that practiced it; he simply lacked the moral courage to do anything about it. The President willingly acknowledged its evil nature in some of his writings, but to Hamilton those passages in Jefferson's various letters and essays smacked of rationalization. He was essentially appealing to the future, saying "See, I knew it was dreadful, but I couldn't really do anything about it." At the very least, the President could have made Monticello a bold experiment in the use of free labor, but instead he relied on the chain and the lash, like every other Southern planter. There were rumors that Jefferson also kept a slave wench as his personal concubine, but Alex did not know if they were true or not.

Hamilton had grown up in the Caribbean, where the presence of slavery was universal and its practice brutal beyond words. Blacks were brought over immediately after being kidnapped from their African villages, often unable to speak a word of English, and shoved onto the auction blocks where they were purchased by the rich planters who owned most of the land on the island. From there they were herded into the sugar cane fields and worked under threat of the lash from daylight till dark. Most field hands lasted less than five years from the time they were sold into labor until they died of disease, exhaustion, and malnutrition. They were flogged for the slightest act of disobedience, and brutally executed if they dared raise their hand to a white man. As a boy, Hamilton had once wandered up on a deep gully behind one of the large sugar plantations; he was shocked to see it filled over halfway to the top with bones from African slaves, denied even the comfort of a decent burial. At the top of the pile was a bloated, stinking corpse dead less than a week; vultures tugged and pulled the putrefying flesh from its bones as a horrified Alex watched.

House slaves in the Indies fared a little better; they were given decent clothes and encouraged to bathe once a week or so. But they could still be raped, whipped, and even killed by their masters at will. Even as a child, growing up in a culture that considered such human bondage not only necessary but profitable, Hamilton had despised slavery. One of the great reliefs of his sojourn to the New World was that he no longer had to witness such horrors daily. Slavery was still legal in New York—something he hoped to change soon—but since plantation agriculture was not practical so far north, most of the slaves in the state were household workers, maids and butlers, and generally better off than their wretched fellow bondsmen toiling in the fields.

Slavery was deeply entrenched in the South. Could Hamilton really do anything about it, even if he did achieve his far-fetched goal of being elected President? He did not know, and in his moments of intellectual honesty, he doubted it. But his dream, or vision, or bout of madness—whatever it was, it had galvanized him. He had been prepared, before the duel, to step into the background of history, to accept that his chance had passed him by, to be content with merely defending his reputation against the base character assassins that sought to destroy it. But now—he felt energized, strengthened, young again! The last time he had felt so driven was when he had ramrodded his financial plan through a reluctant Congress in 1790. Maybe he was tilting at windmills, he thought, but he swore he would do his best to topple them so long as his strength endured.

With that, he spurred his house and rode up the drive to the front door of Monticello. He checked his reflection in the window to make sure his cravat was impeccably tied, then doffed his hat and rang the doorbell. A well-dressed black butler opened it moments later.

"May I help you, suh?" the Negro asked.

"Alexander Hamilton to see President Jefferson," he said, handing the slave his calling card. If the man had any idea who Alex was, his face did not register it.

"I shall inform him that you have come calling," the butler said, and vanished down the corridor. Alex stared up at the beautiful dome rising above him—whatever their political differences, Jefferson was clearly an architectural genius.

Monticello was the most beautiful home he had ever been in, even compared to the palatial residence of his father-in-law, Philip Schuyler. As he admired the beautiful interior, he heard rapid footsteps approaching from within.

"General Hamilton!" President Jefferson sounded a bit flummoxed. "What an unexpected pleasure!"

He looked more surprised than pleased, Alex thought. Away from the capital, the Virginian clearly dispensed with formality. He wore a loose pair of knee breeches, stockings that had obviously not been changed in a day or two, and a pair of faded, worn slippers down at the heel. The top button of his shirt was undone, and his graying mop of red hair was tied back in a sloppy queue. But his eyes shone with intelligent curiosity, and he wore his age lightly, appearing much younger than his sixty-one years.

"A long overdue visit, Mister President," Hamilton said. He knew that he was a persuasive person, and now he turned the full radiance of his charm on Thomas Jefferson. "You and I have labored under misapprehensions about each other for too long, sir. I thought that perhaps it might be time for us to clear the air once and for all. I want to explain myself to you, if I may be so bold."

Thomas Jefferson, Hamilton had discovered long ago, was a man who detested personal conflict. He was always affable, always soft-spoken in person; whenever there was dirty work to be done, he let it be done through the printed word—preferably the words of a loyal and anonymous subordinate. Jefferson had spent more than a dozen years now demonizing Hamilton as the evil genius of the American republic. Alex remembered how, back in the early days of their association, he had often been Jefferson's dinner guest. The hospitable, quiet Secretary of State had encouraged Hamilton to hold forth on his favorite topics, and then had selectively used Hamilton's own words to misrepresent Alex's views on many issues.

He had painted Alex as the serpent in the garden of democracy, the monarchist who had who seduced George Washington away from the purity of his Revolutionary ideas, an ambitious Caesar out to topple the Catonian Republic Jefferson and Madison were fighting to preserve. For a dozen years, he had used Hamilton as a political foil, and Alex had fought back in the press, blasting Jefferson for his hypocrisy and excessive idealism in essay after essay. But now Hamilton stood before the President, smiling and penitent, and for once the sage of Monticello was speechless.

Finally, Jefferson returned Hamilton's smile and beckoned him to follow him into the interior of the house.

"That sounds like a splendid idea, sir," he said. "Please, join me."

Jefferson's study was a small but beautiful room, naturally lit from its multiple windows which were open to catch the breeze on this summer morning. There was a small bench just under one of the windows where Hamilton took his seat; Jefferson sank into a red-cushioned chair next to a writing table that was stacked deep with letters, newspapers, and a couple of books, in addition to an inkwell and a stack of blank paper. A beautifully painted globe sat next to the chair; Jefferson rested one hand on it absently as he cocked his head toward Hamilton.

"First of all, Mister President, regarding the regrettable incident with Colonel Burr, I should like you to know—" Hamilton began.

"Say no more," Jefferson said, "I just finished reading your own published account of those events. As you may know, I personally detest these 'affairs of honor' and would be just as happy to see them abolished forever. That being said, I have not only read your version, but also have three other descriptions; two from Burr's seconds and one from your friend, Nathaniel Pendleton."

"I see," said Hamilton. "Then I suppose I should ask—do you have any questions about what transpired, after reading those accounts?"

"Not really," Jefferson said. "As difficult as it is, politically, for me to say this, I cannot blame you for acting as you did. Colonel Burr was a difficult man, and frankly, sir, not always a trustworthy one. He was a political liability, no matter which faction he attached himself to. You probably know that I had already expressed my desire that he not be renewed in office as my Vice President, I presume?"

"I was aware of that," Hamilton said.

"Then, General, I would let this much be settled between us: I do not hold you responsible for his death. He issued the challenge, he fired first, he missed with his shot, and you did not. I am sorry he is dead; I wished no harm upon him. But, as the Scripture says, 'Whatsoever a man sows, that shall he reap.' He brought his fate upon himself, and the unfortunate affair is ended," Jefferson told Alex.

"If you could express something of that nature to your Republican newspaper editor friends in New York, you should have my gratitude," Hamilton said.

"I cannot answer for the excesses of the partisan press," said Jefferson. "But I will do what I can. But come, sir! Surely your sole purpose in riding nearly four hundred miles to my home cannot be merely to apologize for slaying my Vice President in a duel."

"You are as perceptive as ever, Mister President," said Hamilton. "Shall we cast aside all pretenses, you and I? We are completely alone here; either one of us can later deny anything that transpires in this room. Let us lay aside political vanities and speak, man to man."

Jefferson stared at Hamilton for a long time, coolly evaluating the man who had been his colleague long ago and had been his chief rival for many years thereafter. Finally, he broke into a soft chuckle.

"By God, sir, you really mean it, don't you?" he finally said. "Then let me begin by saying this: although our political ideas have always been wildly divergent, I have never harbored personal animus towards you. In fact, I have always found you to be a fascinating and intelligent person. I accept your proposal, sir. Let us take this opportunity to speak to each other frankly. You want something from me; that much is obvious. Why don't you come out and tell me what it is?"

"I want to run for the New York Senate seat in this fall's special election," Hamilton said. "While I realize that our political differences would forbid something as strong as an endorsement, I was hoping that I could at least make my bid without your open opposition. You have resisted me at every turn since we served under President Washington together at the beginning of our Republic, Mister Jefferson. I believe that your opposition has been rooted in a view of my character and my political positions which is frankly false. I would seek to inform you of my true political self. What is it about me, sir, which you find so objectionable?"

"Your personal character is generally honorable, General Hamilton. My differences with you have always fallen in the realm of politics. To be frank, sir, you strike me as a monarchist," Jefferson said, "or at the very least, one whose political ideals tend towards monarchy. We are a Republic, sir, not a principality. Your vision of America's government would have created a state in which the masses would be eternally crushed beneath the heels of the bankers, speculators, stock jobbers, and manufacturers. In time, we should become no different than the kingdom from which we broke away. We might preserve the trappings of democracy, but true liberty will have been lost."

Hamilton nodded. At least, he thought, Jefferson was being candid. But could he change the man's mind about him in a single conversation? He was not sure, but he was determined to try. He summoned up all of his rhetorical skill and began to speak.

"You mistake me, sir," he said. "No one fought harder to free this country from monarchy than I did. When the officers of the Continental Army met at Newburg to try and persuade General Washington to march on Philadelphia and seize control of the government, I was the one who informed him what was afoot and urged him to direct their discontent in a more positive direction. Had I wanted a monarchy in America, sir, I could have used that moment to push for it! You know as well as I do that most Americans would have gladly hailed Washington as their king, had he wanted such an honor."

"You did your country a service there, no doubt. But what about your speech at the Federal Convention in Philadelphia?" Jefferson asked him. "You advocated a lifelong tenure for the Executive and the Senate. What could be more monarchical than that?"

"The speech!" Hamilton exclaimed, rising from his couch and pacing the room. "That blasted, infernal, everlasting speech! Had I known that the delegates had no intention of keeping our mutual pledge of secrecy, I never would have given it!"

"I am told that it seemed everlasting to your listeners," Jefferson said with a chuckle. "Six hours, wasn't it?"

Hamilton paused and looked at his host, who regarded him with a twinkle in his eye. Finally, Alex laughed ruefully and resumed his seat.

"Thomas," he said softly, "if I may be so bold—you were not there. You were in France, watching the beginning of a wholly different revolution. In America, we were saddled with a government that could not enforce its laws, could not meet its financial obligations, and could not meet even the most minimum requirements of sovereign nationality. We were teetering on the brink of collapse and civil war. As you know, Secretary Madison and I were both deeply concerned about the failure of the Confederation to meet the exigencies of the Union—a concern that was shared by His Excellency, General Washington. That convention represented our chance to save this country from the very results that we have seen unfold in France in the last decade. We wanted to prevent an American Bonaparte, not create one, Mister President!"

"Then why propose a plan that so nearly approached to despotism?" Jefferson asked. Hamilton noticed that the President's voice seemed to denote less mockery and more honest curiosity.

"My paramount object has always been for America to have a government that is stable enough to endure the storms of popular opinion, but at the same time strong enough to protect the liberties of the people," Hamilton said. "I deplore monarchy and have condemned it often enough in my public writings. You know that no one did more than I to ensure the ratification of our Constitution, nor to set the government in operation once it had been put into place. Even that speech that you and Mister Madison have used as a club to buffet me for nearly twenty years was bent to that purpose!"

"I beg your pardon?" Jefferson arched an eyebrow in surprise.

"I was there for the beginning of the Convention," Hamilton said. "I listened as Governor Randolph presented the so-called Virginia Plan, even though I knew it might as well have been called Madison's plan. I will confess, there were parts of it I questioned at the time. Some things even now I think could have been improved on. But it was brilliant, it was so far superior to the flailing and failing Articles of Confederation, Mister Jefferson! Above all, it was practical. It outlined a form of government that could be made to work. I knew right away that it could become the foundation of a government that would bring lasting happiness, prosperity, and liberty to the American people."

"Then why on earth would you present a plan so radically different?" Jefferson asked.

"Because I saw the faces of the delegates when Madison presented his plan, Mister President," Hamilton said. "You have never seen such unrelenting hostility as was expressed by at least half the convention! The delegates from the small states were afraid of being outnumbered in Congress; southern delegates afraid of losing their slaves, northern delegates fearing the taxation power Madison proposed giving to the new Federal government. Everyone seemed to project their worst fears of tyranny onto Mister Madison's proposed plan. As soon as Randolph finished, the room erupted in cacophony! Delegates shouting out their objections, some states threatening to abandon the convention altogether. Then when Paterson of New Jersey presented his own plan the next day, I could see all the small state delegates rushing to support it. His plan not only failed to address the most pressing needs of our country, it also could never have been ratified, since working within the Articles of Confederation, it would have required the unanimous support of all thirteen states."

Hamilton stood and began to pace as he spoke, laying out his case as if he were in a courtroom and Jefferson were the jury.

"I realized that so long as there were only two alternatives, the delegates might not come to agreement. I had already been fleshing out my own ideas for a plan similar to Madison's, but with more elements of stability and continuity woven into it. I essentially took my own ideas and expanded them, rendering them far more radical than I had originally planned. I had thought of a six-year term for the executive, but I expanded it to life during good behavior. I devised a plan that was so extreme that it would make Madison's plan seem like a fair compromise. I did not tell James this because the only way to make such a ploy effective was to let no one know it was a ploy. I allowed them to think that I meant every word, that I wanted to see a life tenure for the Senators and the President. My strategy was effective—the plan I spent six hours explaining didn't receive a single vote; the New Jersey plan was voted down, and the Virginia Plan was accepted as our working model by a majority of the states present."

"Brilliant," said Jefferson. "Whether true or not, it is a remarkable justification for your actions."

"It is quite true," said Hamilton. "My only regret is that those words which I did not mean, which were supposed to remain secret forever, have now been distorted and laid before the public by men who broke the oath of confidentiality, which we all took."

"What would you have done if the convention had accepted your plan as its template?" the sage of Monticello asked him.

"Moderated it, of course," Alex said. "I would have been forced to do so by the demands of the smaller states, regardless. I would have grudgingly given ground until the plan resembled what I originally had in mind. But, honestly, sir, I knew as I spoke that my plan had no chance of being ratified."

"Well, you have answered one of my objections," said Jefferson. "But let me pose another question to you. Why on earth should I stand aside and let a man whose politics differ so radically from my own be sent to the United States Senate, when I could very easily promote someone who shares my ideas for America's future, someone who embraces my political agenda, in your place?"

"Because you owe me," Hamilton said bluntly.

"I beg your pardon?" Jefferson said, aghast.

"You know that you were tied with Aaron Burr in the Electoral College during the last presidential contest," Hamilton said. He knew he was taking a gamble with this tactic, but at the same time, working around George Washington and John Laurens for years had taught him one thing: Southern honor required the acknowledgment of favors done. "You also know that many in my party wanted to throw their support to Burr in hopes that he would cross partisan lines again and embrace a more Federalist point of view in exchange for their support. The House was deadlocked, casting ballot after ballot with no movement in either direction. In the end, my fellow Federalists turned to me for advice. I told them two things: first, that Burr was too ambitious and unscrupulous to be trusted with the powers of the Chief Magistracy; and second, that it was clearly the intent of the electoral college that you should occupy the first place in the land. Burr's equal vote was a mistake on the part of one elector, and they knew that. Mine was the voice that broke the deadlock in the House in your favor, Mister President. It was in my power at that moment to make Aaron Burr our next President, and I chose you over him. I gave you the office you now hold, because I knew that you were a man of principle, even though we disagreed on policy. I am speaking to you bluntly now because we are alone. I would never raise this issue in the public square. But surely your sense of honor will acknowledge a certain obligation?"

"I had not thought of the matter in those terms," Jefferson said.

"There is also the matter of my experience and ability," Hamilton said. "I know New York politics better than anyone else. I understand financial matters better than any man living, and my presence in the Senate would give me an opportunity to serve my country in a way that would benefit all Americans! Would it not be better to have me on the inside of the government working with you, rather than exiled to the wilderness, hurling imprecations at you?"

"You are entirely too enthusiastic for the corruption that money brings into politics, Mister Hamilton," said Jefferson. "The systems you created push our government closer to the British model than to the one our Revolution fought to establish."

"What do you know of fighting, Mister Jefferson?" Hamilton asked, his temper rising slightly. "I came under enemy fire more times than I can count during the war, while you calmly presided over meetings and met with foreign ambassadors!"

"How dare you!" Jefferson snapped, his unflappable calm breaking. "You cannot speak to me in such a manner!"

"No, sir, I can." Hamilton mastered his emotions. "I rode nearly four hundred miles to speak my mind to you, and I am nearly done. You accuse me of loving England when I nearly died from English bullets! The things I copied from Britain's financial system I copied, not because they are British, but because they work! Britain did not become the mightiest nation on earth by adopting flawed policies. I rejected the British system of government and their monarchy, but yes, I copied their financial models because they were practical, for no other reason! And you see the result, Mister President. Our debt is disappearing, our credit is excellent, the dollar is respected around the world, all because of the financial systems that I wrote into existence! Systems, I might add, which you have had every opportunity to tear down these last four years—and have refused to do so.

Because you know as well as I do how well they worked! You are a good man, Mister President, but you are an idealist. I am a pragmatist."

He paused a moment, studying the President closely. Jefferson was watching him intently, but the man's ire had subsided.

"I know you hate despotism, Thomas," Hamilton said. "What you don't seem to recognize is that I hate it, too. You feared that too much industry and business would lead us back to monarchy; I think nothing will more effectively help us elude its grasp. Remember when the French Revolution began? It was led by the sort of people you idolize—workers, tradesmen, farmers, the toiling masses of the kingdom. You thought it would lead France to an enlightened government, to a greater respect for the rights of man, to a new birth of human freedom. But, Mister President, where did their Revolution lead them, after wading through oceans of blood—much of it innocent blood? It led them right back to despotism. Bonaparte might as well be a Bourbon for all the power he wields. He may claim to act in the principles of liberty, equality, and fraternity, but in reality he is just another Caesar."

Jefferson sat in silence, and then stood and looked out his window. The sun was westering in the sky. Finally, he sighed and turned back to face Hamilton.

"You are right," he said. "I was too eager to support the French, and their revolution lacked something, some manner of brakes or moral self-control. I tried to excuse their excesses, but I see now that was a mistake. Perhaps they were not as prepared for self-government as they should have been. Certainly, your conclusion about their current government is correct. Bonaparte has clearly shown himself to be no friend of liberty."

Jefferson sat back down and leaned back in his chair, and then steepled his fingers beneath his chin, surveying Alex calmly.

"I've considered all you have said, Mister Hamilton. You are a man of genuine ability, and it may be that your service to the country has not ended. I cannot and will not endorse you—but I will not openly oppose you. Mister Mitchill is a worthy adversary, and I am sure that you will have your work cut out for you in the coming contest. I will do this much for you, however—I will inform my friends in the press that, despite what they have been led to believe, you are not a monarchist. Beyond that, your fate lies in your own capable hands—and those of New York's state legislators."

The President of the United States stepped forward and stretched out his hand. Hamilton took it, and they shook hands as the light of the westering sun came pouring in the windows of the study.

"Politics is a tiresome topic," said Jefferson. "Why don't you stay for dinner, and I will read you a fascinating letter from Meriwether Lewis about the proposed route for his exploration of the Louisiana territory?"

For the rest of the night, the two men talked of plants and animals and native tribes, of unexplored mountains and rivers, and not another word was spoken about politics. The next day, Hamilton bid his host farewell and began his return journey to New York, whistling a merry tune as he rode.

CHAPTER SIX

IT WAS MID-AUGUST when Hamilton arrived back in New York. Eliza and the children were delighted to see him, and he allowed himself a day to rest and enjoy his family before plunging into the business of winning a Senate seat for himself. More than a month had now passed since the fateful duel, and the furor was beginning to die down. Governor Clinton, a leading candidate for the vice presidency that fall, had pressed the State Attorney General to prosecute Hamilton for murder, but the Grand Jury had declined to issue an indictment. The fact that Burr had taken the first shot insulated Hamilton from legal prosecution; the fact that he had nearly died from the wound Burr inflicted had generated a good deal of public sympathy. As he began to move among the people, Alex found that he was more personally popular in New York than he had been in many years. He might be a son of New York by adoption rather than by birth, but his near death had erased that distinction, and it seemed the people had finally begun to appreciate this orphaned immigrant for the remarkable man that he was. This new public esteem was an asset, and Alex intended to use it for all it was worth.

He was gratified (and a bit surprised) to see Jefferson was as good as his word; a couple of days after his return to New York City, the *New York Herald* had carried a short, open letter from the President of the United States:

To the Citizens and Legislators of the State of New York:

It has come to my attention that the former Secretary of the Treasury, General Alexander Hamilton, has announced his availability as a candidate for the Senate seat recently opened by the departure of John Armstrong to become America's Minister Plenipotentiary to France. The special election for this office will be held this fall when the new state legislature takes its seat in Albany.

It is no secret that General Hamilton and myself differ on a wide range of issues, and this letter is not intended as an endorsement of his candidacy. However, I do wish it to be noted that Alexander Hamilton has been a man of upright character and honorable behavior in all the positions of public trust that he has held. He is a person of considerable ability and personal integrity. While his views on the role of government in the life of our country are far different from my own, I do wish it to be known that the charge of monarchical tendencies, which has been laid at his feet for many years, is erroneous. General Hamilton fought bravely during the Revolution to win our independence from the State of Great Britain; he is a champion of American liberty and a friend of our Republican form of government. Those who have seen him as an agent of royalist designs have seen him falsely; although he favors a broader role for the Federal government in our affairs than I generally do, he is not the man his enemies have made him out to be. If I have played any role in that mischaracterization, I hereby repent thereof.

His opponent, Representative Samuel Mitchill, is a solid Republican and an erudite scholar, with an impressive list of achievements in public and private life. His zeal for the public good is a matter of record upon which I need not elaborate, and since he is a member of my own faction, needless to say, I wish him well. The fact remains, however, that the people of New York are fortunate to have two such well-qualified candidates seeking this trust from the people's representatives; and I doubt not that whichever man is the victor, New York will be well served when the new Senate convenes. Having no desire to unduly influence the choice of the legislators, as President I will not endorse nor will I oppose either candidate. May the blessings of the One who has never yet forsaken our favored land guide the representatives of the people of New York as they choose between these two worthy candidates.

Thomas Jefferson, President of the United States

Jefferson's letter caused a sensation that spread far beyond the city where it was published. It was no secret that the rumors of Hamilton being a closet monarchist had originated with Jefferson, as had whispers of the Treasury Secretary's corruption in office and his secret bargains with speculators and bankers. Jefferson's pet newspapers had used Hamilton as a whipping boy for years, and they had done so with little regard for truth or decorum. Debate erupted across the city and the country as people speculated why Jefferson had taken this new tack and what it might mean. Was he entering into some secret alliance with Hamilton? Had New York's Republicans done something to anger the President, so that he had decided to throw a door open to the opposition party, which was otherwise in decline all across the nation?

New York's governor, George Clinton, an inveterate foe of Hamilton's, was furious with Jefferson over this reversal. Although he was actively seeking to become the new Vice President and was wary of offending Jefferson, he was still determined to do everything he could to thwart Hamilton's candidacy. Their mutual animosity was decades old; Clinton had opposed the adoption of the U.S. Constitution that Hamilton had championed; and then the feud had become personal when Alex had blocked his election to the new United States Senate in 1788. Clinton controlled a powerful political apparatus that had been at war with Hamilton's Federalists ever since that epic battle over the ratification of the Constitution. Two days after Jefferson's letter appeared, Clinton wrote a blistering attack on Hamilton which the *Herald* published as a counterpart to Jefferson's letter. Unwilling to sign his name to the screed, Clinton published it under the name "Cato":

To the People and Legislators of New York:

It should come as no surprise to anyone that the vile murderer of our beloved Vice President, Aaron Burr, now seeks public office once more. ALEXANDER HAMILTON, the self-confessed adulterer, the crown prince of corruption, the architect of the monarchical Federalist Party, may have somehow hoodwink'd our President into believing that he has changed his spots. But we of New York, who have witnessed Hamilton's arrogance and corruption first-hand ever since the ill winds of fortune blew this penniless intriguer ashore here thirty years ago, are united in our steadfast opposition to allowing this would-be American Bonaparte back into public office where he can work further mischief. The stains of corruption are still being scrubbed from the halls of our Republic; why would it behoove us to allow their author back into the halls of Congress to work further mischief? The infamous name of HAMILTON has ever been associated with centralization of power, speculation, stock-jobbing, aristocracy, hereditary power, military despotism, and all the corruption that flows from those activities. We urge the legislators of New York to deny this corrupt bargainer any seat at the table of national government.

In the interests of the people of New York and the United States

–

CATO

A few years earlier, such a blast from the governor would have united all of New York's Republicans against Hamilton—and engendered a strong riposte from the former Treasury Secretary. However, with Clinton leaving to take up his new position in Washington City, his grip on the state's party apparatus was loosening. Ultimately, President Jefferson's word carried more weight than Clinton's did with the people, so Hamilton's window of opportunity was still open—slightly. Hamilton knew that a vehement counterblast from him would push wavering Republicans back into Mitchill's camp. So he bit his tongue and left his quill in its inkwell, determined to use charm rather than invective to bring New York's lawmakers into his camp.

Two-thirds of New York's legislators were from New York City and its environs, so Hamilton had plenty of work to do in his adopted hometown before decamping to Albany to buttonhole the remainder. His first task was to unite all of New York's Federalists behind him. This was not a difficult task—few of them were left in office, and Hamilton had been their leader for a decade or more. A quick round of social calls and probing questions showed that their confidence in him as their chief spokesman had not been diminished by recent events; all were willing to throw their support to his candidacy.

"I don't know what magic spell you cast on Jefferson," Rufus King told him over a glass of brandy late one evening in August. "But that letter stunned New York's Republican faction, I can tell you that! What on earth did you do, Alex, put a pistol on him?"

Hamilton laughed and took a sip of his brandy. He was relaxed and happier than he had been in years. Having a genuine political goal to fight for energized him, and the strong, moral cause at the heart of it filled him with enthusiasm. He was reminded of those first, epic days as Washington's Treasury Secretary, when he had worked sixteen hours a day creating fiscal policy for the new government. But now, instead of fighting for the financial independence and prosperity of a nation, he was fighting for the freedom of an entire people—even if he had not yet revealed that to anyone, not even Eliza. First, achieve power, he thought; and then effect change.

"No, Rufus, I didn't coerce him with anything but words. One thing I learned working for His Excellency all those years is that Southerners take matters of honor very seriously," he said. "Honor is important to any man worth calling a man, but it is sacred to Virginians. I reminded Mister Jefferson of a debt of honor that he had not fully realized he owed me; and he had no choice but to repay it."

"Amazing," said King. "I mean, what he did was not an endorsement, but in places it nearly sounded like one!"

"It was actually far more positive than I thought it would be," said Hamilton. "But I still must convince a dozen state senators and thirty-four assemblymen from the opposition party to support my candidacy, and that is going to be difficult. Some would say impossible—but I prefer merely difficult!"

"Do you actually trust Jefferson, though?" King said. "Could it be that he is simply manipulating you for some underhanded purpose to reveal later?"

"Of course he is!" Alex said with a laugh. "The philosopher of Monticello is a master chess player who always thinks a move or two ahead of his opposition. I shall simply have to think three moves ahead!"

"I have no doubt that you will stand a better chance against him and his cronies than I would have," his friend said, "but I still wonder how you are going to pull this off!"

"I shall start at the top and work down," said Hamilton. "And then we shall see what we shall see!"

Leaving his friend's house, Hamilton quickly made his way down Wall Street and turned right on Fifth Avenue, making his way toward the home of Republican leader John Woodworth. He was admitted to the house and moments later, Woodworth came downstairs, breaking into a rueful grin when he saw Alexander Hamilton standing in his parlor once more.

"Congratulations, sir," he said. "I don't know how you did it, but the whole town is talking about your rapprochement with President Jefferson."

"Well, the President and I are still not friends," Hamilton said, "but I do hope that we are now mere rivals, not mortal enemies. I was grateful for his letter and the sentiments it contained."

"I have always thought our country is better served when our politicians do not try to destroy each other. So, what can I do for you today, General Hamilton?" Woodworth asked.

"Very simple," Hamilton said. "I would like you to support my bid for New York's open Senate seat."

Woodworth's jaw dropped and he stared at Hamilton as if Alex had just made an indecent proposition.

"General," he said, "we already have a perfectly credible Republican candidate in Mister Mitchill. Why on earth should I choose you over him?"

"Let me explain, if you will. Tell me," Hamilton said, "What experience does Mitchill bring to the Senate?"

"He has served two terms in the House of Representatives, and he is a walking encyclopedia of medical and scientific knowledge—in fact, he is one of New York's leading intellectuals and a leading member of the American Academy of Arts and Sciences," Woodworth said.

"He is indeed a knowledgeable man in the natural sciences," said Hamilton, "and if the Senate were a university, he would be an excellent professor. But the fact remains that in his time in the House of Representatives, he has championed no significant legislation and has been relegated to unimportant committees because of his tendency to share his encyclopedic knowledge of everything in longwinded speeches that have very little to do with the issue at hand. In all honesty, sir, I do not question his intellectual abilities or his moral fitness for office—only his ability to create effective and beneficial policies for the people of New York, and the United States as a whole. Mitchill has few political skills other than being an affable and charming dinner guest. He is an altogether decent fellow, but he has shown little talent for actual governance."

"I had not thought of it in those terms," said Woodworth, looking a bit crestfallen.

"Now, then, Senator, what experience would I bring to the office?" Hamilton asked.

"Well, you served with distinction in the Revolution," Woodworth recalled.

"I was the unofficial Chief of Staff to Washington for much of that time," said Hamilton, "and it was my duty to ensure that the entire Continental Army was fed, paid, supplied, and in proper condition to engage the enemy. Given the paucity of our resources, it was a Herculean task. I would much rather have held a field command against the enemy, but I served His Excellency faithfully as a member of his military family for five years."

"True," said Woodworth. "You also were an attorney and a member of the Confederation Congress, were you not, before attending the Federal Convention in 1787?"

"That is true," said Hamilton. "I was also the co-author of the *Federalist* essays and I helped lead the fight to persuade New York's legislature to ratify the Constitution."

"*The Federalist* is a marvelous document," said Woodworth. "I knew you were involved, but how many of the actual essays were yours?"

"I wrote fifty or so," Hamilton said, "out of the eighty-five. One of my colleagues fell quite ill during the process, so I helped finish some of his incomplete efforts."

"I still marvel that you were able to produce so much cogent, organized apologia in such a short time," Woodworth said.

"It is amazing what a man can achieve when he gives up sleep, food, and nearly all human contact!" Hamilton said with a smile. "Refresh my mind, sir, what else do I bring to the table?"

"You were Treasury Secretary for nearly six years," Woodworth said. "Your labors were gargantuan during that time, and you single-handedly reestablished America's credit with the rest of the world."

"And despite the constant accusations of monarchism and self-interest, every single congressional inquiry started by my enemies ended in my complete exoneration," Alex said. "And the charge that I ran America's treasury department for my own enrichment was belied by the fact that I left office almost penniless, after working to the point of exhaustion and illness. Now, sir, I will not embarrass you by asking you to recite my accomplishments any further. You are well acquainted with my life and my career. Let me pose you one final question, then, and I shall leave you to mull over your choice. Leaving aside all questions of party allegiance, which of the two of us is better suited to serve the people of New York, and the United States as a whole, more effectively?"

"You do have far more political experience," the state senator said.

"Then let me simply request this of you—let your vote be cast in the best interest of the people of New York, not the interests of President Jefferson or the Democratic-Republican faction. If you think of it in those terms, sir, I believe your choice will become remarkably clear," Hamilton concluded.

"I must admit, General Hamilton, you have given me much to think upon," said Woodworth. "Before your visit, and Jefferson's letter, I would have told anyone I would as soon vote for Lucifer himself as send you to the Senate! Now I am honestly uncertain who to cast my vote for."

"Let your conscience—and your common sense—be your guide, sir," said Alex with a courteous bow as he left them drawing room. "I shall show myself out."

Over the next month, Hamilton would repeat this visit's theme again and again, in the homes of some thirty state legislators and a dozen state Senators. Some of them, he knew, still viewed him as the devil incarnate, no matter what Jefferson's letter said, but he laid his case before them anyway. Others were open to his appeal and willing to consider him as a candidate on his own merits, regardless of their party affiliation. Many of them had been Federalists at some point in their careers and were willing to sign off on Hamilton as a candidate in the name of their former convictions.

Then there were the ones he had served with in the Revolution, who remembered him as their brave and cheerful captain. Others he had represented as clients in court, defending them against criminal and civil charges, enabling them to keep their property or recover damages thereto. Some he had done favors for during his term as Treasury Secretary; securing government employment, helping them clear customs hurdles, or otherwise expediting their business endeavors. Hamilton was a scrupulous legalist who had made it a point to never break the law during his tenure at Treasury, but his office had enabled him to help many needy people in ways that were completely legal and ethical.

With his encyclopedic memory, there was not a favor he could not recall, not a face he could not put a name to, not a fallen or wounded soldier whose service he had forgotten. He found some way to connect with every legislator he called upon; a link that bound him to that person in a way that at the very least guaranteed him a private audience. By the end of September, he began to think that he might stand a chance of becoming New York's next United States Senator. He had visited the home of every single state legislator who lived in or near New York City; it was time for him to take his campaign to Albany, meeting with several critical members of the Assembly on his way.

The night before he left town, he hosted his friends Hercules Mulligan, Isaac Foote, and Rufus King for dinner at his country home, The Grange. Eliza was happy to see her husband so engaged and energetic again; indeed, his new political activism seemed to have restored his vigor in other areas of life as well. She had not felt so cherished or beloved in years, and she blessed whatever it was in his close brush with death that left him so solicitous of her affections. She smiled as she cleared the dishes from the table and left the men to their political discussions.

"I must say, Alex, your campaign for the Senate is the talk of the city," King said. "Reports have it that you are within a half dozen votes of winning the state senate's approval, and perhaps twice that from securing the necessary votes in the assembly!"

"I knew there was something special about this lad the minute he arrived in New York, still green from seasickness!" Mulligan exclaimed proudly. He was twenty years older than Hamilton, one of New York's most successful tailors. He had remained in the city for six long years of British occupation, serving as a spy for George Washington. He had fitted uniforms for British officers, showing them every bit of respect and confidentiality that they could wish for. As he measured and stitched, he had eavesdropped on their conversations. Then, each evening, he secretly wrote down everything they had said and forwarded the information to Washington by secret courier. To all outward appearances, he was a Tory businessman—so much so that when the Patriot forces reoccupied New York in 1783, his neighbors had been ready to hang him. They were stunned when George Washington made a point of dining with Mulligan on his first evening in the city, praising him for being such an effective agent! From that point until the government moved to Philadelphia, Mulligan had served as the President's personal tailor, and had won the trade of many of New York's most influential families since.

Nowadays he owned three separate stores and had a dozen apprentices working under him, as well as three master tailors. He still kept one ear firmly to the ground and was always ready to forward useful information to his old friend Alexander Hamilton.

"I remember the time you left your musket leaning against the breastworks as we stole six cannons out from under the nose of the British fleet!" Mulligan recalled. "The Royal Marines spotted us and were peppering our position with musket balls. We heaved and strained to get that last cannon up the hill, and then Alex goes: 'My musket!' Day was breaking on us then, but the lad strolled back down to the palisade, snatched up his weapon, and tipped his hat to the enemy sharpshooters as if he were passing them in the park, with bullets kicking up dirt all around him. He strolled back up to us, and we lugged those cannons straightaway back to friendly lines. I tell you, he's a cool one!"

Mulligan looked at Alex and gave him a wink. "The word on the street is that New York's merchants are putting heavy pressure on the legislature to elect you to the Senate," he said. "I think you are going to steal this seat from those Republicans as smoothly as you stole those cannons from the British!"

Isaac Foote spoke up. He was a quiet man, well-spoken and thoughtful, who had supported Hamilton's plans for the better part of twenty years.

"I have an idea, Alex," he said. "You once showed me a letter that the President wrote you after you tendered your resignation from the Treasury. Do you still have it?"

"It is one of my dearest treasures, a keepsake of the great man who authored it," Hamilton said. "Do you know that the last letter Washington ever wrote was addressed to me?"

"Indeed, I do," Foote said with a smile. "I did not know His Excellency very well, but one thing about him I knew, Mister Hamilton, is that he trusted you. He placed more confidence in you than he did in any other minister of his government."

"The kindness and trust that he gifted me with are the greatest honor I have attained in this life," said Alex, "and I would still say that if I were sitting in the presidential chair right now."

"Would you be willing to let me make a copy of the letter I referred to, then?" asked Foote.

"Why would you want to do that?" Hamilton asked, looking over his spectacles at the New Yorker.

"I want to quote it in an essay I am writing, endorsing your candidacy," his friend said. "I think the people of New York need to be reminded just how highly Washington thought of you."

Hamilton thought a moment. The letter was a matter of official record, since Washington had retained copies of all his correspondence. But his copy was a treasured personal memento, and he did not want it to be put to tawdry use. Still, his best hope of the presidency lay in the visibility of a seat in the United States Senate. And if his fever dream was indeed some kind of vision, then Washington's spirit wanted him to seek the nation's highest office.

"I will allow you to make a copy," he finally said. "But I would like to read this essay before you publish it."

"Of course," his friend replied, and Alex walked down the hall to his small study, rummaging through his cabinets of personal correspondence. He was as prolific a letter writer as he was an essayist and always kept a copy of every epistle he sent as well as the ones he received. There were six tall cabinets with five drawers each containing his correspondence, but he had them so well organized that he was able to locate the one Foote wanted in a matter of moments. He lifted it from its folder and studied the President's smooth, flowing handwriting for a moment, remembering the first letter he had received from George Washington in 1776. The hand on this missive was a bit shakier and less firm than those endless missives, orders and requisitions Hamilton had copied for the General during the war, but unmistakably from the same hand. He gently folded the letter and carried it downstairs, grabbing an inkwell and a couple of sheets of blank paper from his desk.

"Excellent!" said Foote. "Pray give me a few moments to copy this out."

The letter from Washington was not terribly long, and Foote did not copy all of it. When he was done, he asked Hamilton, King, and Mulligan to sign off that his copy was true and accurate.

"I will take my leave now, and will have the essay done before morning, Alex," he said, "and if you give it your approbation, I will see it published in every major newspaper in New York City and Albany before the week is out!"

"I look forward to reading it," Hamilton said.

Foote must not have slept much that night, for the next morning while Alex was still eating breakfast with Eliza and the children, a courier brought the finished essay to his house. He read it with interest and a growing sense of enthusiasm, realizing that his friend had hit just the right tone. Hamilton was a master of policy, but the common touch of politics had always proven difficult for him. Every significant office he had ever held had been by appointment, not election. He was a man of great intellect, and it frustrated him that many everyday people simply could not understand his ideas or follow his logic. He recognized that he was going to have to improve his communications skills if he wanted to win the support of the masses.

Foote, on the other hand, was a master of the common touch, and his essay—signed simply as "Tully," (a common reference to Marcus Tullius Cicero, the famous Roman orator)—was a direct appeal to the people of New York. While the legislators chose the Senators, they themselves were chosen by the people, and Foote's masterful composition was a reminder to people and politicians of who really held power in a Republic. It was simply entitled "An Appeal to the People of New York from the Friends of General Hamilton."

In a few weeks our state legislators will choose New York's next United States Senator, it began. *This is a high honor for the chosen candidate, for there are only thirty-four Senators at a time, to represent our nation of nearly ten million souls. As we all know, the Republicans dominate our state assembly at this time, having won a sweeping victory in the elections earlier this year. It is only natural that these men would choose a member of their own faction in this special election to the Senate. However, the question I would pose to the citizens of New York, and to the legislators who represent them and must answer to them in the next election, is a simple one: Who is the best man to represent New York in the United States Senate?*

The Republican candidate, Mister Samuel Mitchill, is a fine citizen and a right knowledgeable scholar; an expert in natural history and medical science. It is not the purpose of this essay to impeach his character in any way, but rather to compare his qualifications for this high office to those of his opponent, General Hamilton.

Many calumnies and damnable lies have been printed in the newspapers about General Hamilton over the last few years; some of them inspired by none other than our current President, Mister Jefferson. Let it be noted that the President himself has now owned up to the error of those assessments of Gen'l Hamilton's character. In place of scurrilous diatribes, let us look calmly at the remarkable career of this man who has offered his skill and experience to the service of the people of our state.

Arriving in America as a penniless student, he cast his lot in with the cause of Independence from the very beginning. As a young captain, he showed consistent courage and inspiring leadership on the battlefield. He stole British cannons when the Continental Army was desperate for artillery; he was wounded during the glorious victory at Trenton; he was elevated to the staff of General Washington and remained as the right-hand man of that worthy leader for the remainder of the war.

He recognized the flawed nature of our confederation and the perilous state of our Union well ahead of many and was a strong voice for the summoning of the Federal Convention in 1787. Once that body's noble work was completed, NO MAN worked harder to assure the ratification of our glorious

Constitution than General Hamilton. But once the new government was elected, who did the illustrious Washington summon to his side? Who did the Father of our Country ask to help him set the Executive Branch in place? Who single-handedly restored our national credit and began regularly paying down our debt? Who established the Bank of the United States on such solid financial footing that even its strongest critics have come to acknowledge its value to our nation's economical well-being?

Many have accused Gen'l Hamilton of using the Treasury's income to line his own pockets; but all we who know him can testify that he left that office as financially distressed as he entered it. In short, every calumny that has been heaped on the head of this worthy gentleman's public service has been proven false; and whatever private blemishes may have stained his character at one time, his public confession and penance have been witnessed by us all.

Some have said that Hamilton's public character is a sham; an act to deceive the nation he purports to serve. But I would invite all who have entertained this notion to read this tribute, written by George Washington himself, to General Hamilton on the occasion of his departure from the Treasury Department: "In every relation you have borne to me, I have found that my confidence in your talents, exertions, and integrity has been well placed. I the more freely render this testimony of my approbation; because I speak from opportunities of information which cannot deceive me and which furnish satisfactory proof of your

title to public regard. My most earnest wishes for your
happiness will attend you. . ."

*Citizens of New York, we who know and love General
Hamilton join with our glorious departed President in
affirming that we place in him every confidence that long
acquaintance can engender. There is simply no other living
soul who will bring to the Senate a similar tale of public
accomplishments, honorable service, formidable abilities, and
personal integrity. We ask that you remind our legislators that
their choice should reflect who can best serve we, the people,
not who will best serve the political interests of any one faction.
The answer to the question "Who will serve New York best?"
can only be answered with one name, that of our dear friend,
fellow patriot, and tireless public servant, ALEXANDER
HAMILTON.*

It still was not easy. Hamilton visited state Senators and
legislators in their homes, in boardinghouses, in roadside inns
and taverns, and by the time the legislature met in November of
1804, he had personally spoken to every single one of its members.
It had been exhausting—in fact, he collapsed into bed each night
as worn out as he had been in many years—but in the end, Alex
knew he had done all he could. His fate was now out of his own
hands. The night before the legislature held its inaugural session,
he ate a hearty supper and then retired to his room in the
boardinghouse where he was staying.

Closing the door, Alexander Hamilton sat in a chair by the
fireplace and pulled his battered traveling Bible from his valise.
He opened it to one of his favorite passages, the Gospel of John,

Chapter Fourteen, and read the familiar words: *"Let not your heart be troubled. Ye believe in God; believe also in me. . ."* He said a simple but heartfelt prayer, and then lay back on the warm feather mattress and pulled the comforter up to his chin. He had done his part, he reflected as he closed his eyes. His fate was now in the hands of God, and of the representatives of the people of New York. He felt a strange peace descend over him as he drifted off to sleep.

The next morning, by a margin of 17-14 in the State Senate and 54-46 in the Assembly, Alexander Hamilton was elected to succeed John Armstrong as New York's next United States Senator.

CHAPTER SEVEN

"WHAT ON EARTH were you thinking, Mister President?"

James Madison was absolutely furious, and Thomas Jefferson was doing his best not to look amused. Madison was a tiny man — at five feet four, almost a full foot shorter than the lanky Virginian he was railing at — and with his thinning hair worn long in the back, overall pale complexion, and cheeks flushed with rage, he resembled a cranky little old lady more than the erudite scholar and consummately professional cabinet minister that he was.

"Hamilton was a spent force," he continued. "He was living in semi-retirement, supporting his brood of brats with his law practice, and out of our hair! Federalism as a political institution had one foot in the grave and the other slipping on the brink, and now its foremost champion has a platform from which to preach the pernicious doctrines of centralization and monarchy to the whole nation. So again, Thomas, I ask — what were you thinking?"

"My dear Mister Madison, please sit down before you suffer a fit of apoplexy," Jefferson said. "Here, have a cup of tea and let us converse like gentlemen. I assure you, my statement about General Hamilton was not the utter capitulation you imagine."

"It certainly appears to be exactly that," Madison grumbled, sitting in the chair across from Jefferson and stirring some sugar into his tea. It was February of 1805, and the President had summoned his cabinet back to Washington in preparation for the swearing in of the new Congress. It had snowed the night before, a thick, wet blanket of snow that coated the young capital city in white. Stray flakes were still drifting down, but the clouds were thinning, and the afternoon promised to be sunny. Here and there the muddy ruts of carriage tracks along the dirt roads of the city cut through the thick white coating like battle scars.

"James, you know as well as I that we both exaggerated Hamilton's political views during the course of our earlier political battles," Jefferson said. "He may be in favor of a stronger government than we thought necessary at the time, but he is not the slavish tool of England we made him out to be. How many of his former positions have we adopted since the Executive Branch came into our trust?"

"I suppose that we have adopted a few Federalist positions," Madison said, "but that is all the more reason to bury Federalism in a grave so deep that no resurrection can reach it! We've taken from it all that is useful; the Federalist Party has no reason to exist."

"I doubt even the formidable General Hamilton can revive the fortunes of his faction," said Jefferson. "The Federalists have been defined more as a party of refusal than reform ever since I took office. People tire of constant resistance to their chosen leaders. But honestly, I felt I owed it to the man to give him some small amount of credit for his accomplishments. You know, I was utterly convinced that his financial system was the devil's work; a complicated ploy to enrich Hamilton and his New York cronies at the nation's expense. So, when I took office four years ago, I ordered my Treasury Secretary to go over the books with a fine-toothed comb, and to write down every single instance of corruption he found for possible prosecution. I also demanded that every one of Hamilton's mistakes and missteps in putting the program together be recorded in detail so that we could reveal his ineptitude to the nation. Do you know what Secretary Gallatin found?"

"Let me guess," said Madison. "No hint of corruption?"

"He called Hamilton's financial program 'the most perfect system ever devised by the mind of man,'" Jefferson replied. "There was no evidence of corruption whatsoever; and the banking and credit scheme was such a brilliantly designed edifice that it could not be undone without dragging America's economy down with it. Needless to say, I buried that report in my files—but I also kept Hamilton's construct in place."

"I still think the nation would be better off if Burr's bullet had struck him in the vitals!" Madison grumbled.

"Burr would have become an even bigger problem had he survived. One more thing in which Hamilton was correct was in his assessment of Burr's amoral character and vaunting ambition. My former Vice President was, in truth, a dangerous man, James. But there is more to it than that. You see, my friend, Hamilton called upon me to repay a debt of honor," Jefferson said. "I could not refuse such a request, but I now regard that debt as paid. Let us be honest—Alexander Hamilton is undeniably brilliant and personally can be quite pleasant. However, he has a remarkable penchant for self-destruction, particularly when he is goaded by outside forces. Think of the Reynolds Pamphlet or his ill-advised literary assault upon President Adams four years ago. Hamilton as a semi-retired, former cabinet minister is free to weigh in against the government at will, but there is not much we can do in return to provoke him into self-immolation. The same tired old charges would lose their potency over time. But, as an active member of the United States Senate, he will be called on daily to debate and comment on policy. His views will be very much in the public eye again. Our allies in the press can needle him constantly, misrepresent his positions, and drag up his past, until he explodes in another avalanche of inky invective. If we wish to see Hamilton become a permanently spent force in American politics, we have to give him a platform from which his self-destruction will be visible to the entire nation. That was why I did not openly oppose his bid for a Senate seat."

"That is deep thinking, Mister President. You were always a master of the chessboard," said Madison. "I hope your prognostication is correct. But I am still worried. You are beginning your second term as Chief Magistrate; I imagine you will step down in four years when it is over. If Hamilton behaves as you have predicted, then all will be well. But what if he should show restraint and fail to respond as he has done in the past? If he does not self-destruct, then I will be left with a most formidable opponent in my quest to succeed you in the presidential chair."

"You worry too much, James," said Jefferson. "One thing life has taught me is that human behavior falls into predictable patterns. Just as the leopard cannot change his spots, even so men will do what they usually do. Hamilton's anger and mania for self-justification will lead him to act intemperately, as he has always done. He will, once more, embarrass himself in the eyes of the nation. Then your ascension to the Executive Mansion will proceed without difficulty."

"I hope you are right, sir," Madison said. "Now let us speak about our payments to France for the Louisiana territory. . ."

Madison was a quiet and patient man with a prodigious intellect and appetite for study. Few men knew more about government than he did, and the United States Constitution was largely his creation. Others had added strokes to his masterpiece, but the final draft adopted by the Federal Convention had followed his general outline far more than it had deviated from it. It had been Hamilton's idea to produce a series of essays defending the Constitution, but Madison had thrown himself into the project with vigor. Constitution, and ironically, Hamilton had been his chief ally in the process. The two men had worked well together, and Madison had a profound respect for Hamilton's remarkable writing ability—armed with a pen, Hamilton truly was, as Jefferson had once put it, "a host unto himself."

But Madison's friendship and political alliance with Thomas Jefferson had caused him to become increasingly disenchanted with Alexander Hamilton. Jefferson had convinced him that Hamilton was a dangerous, intriguing monarchist whose financial systems were designed to reshape America's republican government into a monarchical system—perhaps even, ultimately, to reintroduce hereditary monarchy to America! Some of Hamilton's statements that seemed innocuous enough when Madison first heard them took on a more sinister tone later; when they were reconsidered in light of Jefferson's assertions.

Between the growing influence of Jefferson and the political battles over Hamilton's plan for the Federal government to assume the foreign debt of the states and create a national bank, Madison had come to regard his former friend as the leader of a dangerous and destructive force in American politics. Pen in hand, he had openly opposed Hamilton's policies; and like Jefferson, he had secretly funded scandal-mongering, partisan journalists who had personally attacked Hamilton in scathing and frequently inaccurate editorials.

Now Madison was wondering how wise his course had been. Jefferson had just as much as admitted that the more nefarious charges against Hamilton were completely manufactured for political purposes, and that sat ill with Madison's conscience. He simply did not have Jefferson's talent for duplicity, and he felt a small measure of guilt that he had been complicit in the destruction of an innocent man's reputation.

On top of that, he did not share Jefferson's confidence that Hamilton was done politically. James knew Alex far better than Jefferson did; and he knew that the man was capable of more self-control than the President gave him credit for. The Federalist champion was connected to party leaders throughout the country, although his fortunes had fallen in New England due to his war of words with President Adams. Still, Adams was now a retired, verbose curmudgeon whose political career was done; Hamilton was at the height of his mental and political abilities. He was a potentially devastating opponent; especially for someone like Madison, who was shy and retiring by nature.

Therefore, James Madison was still angry as he left the White House after his meeting with Jefferson that cold, blustery day. Jefferson was his friend as well as his political idol; he felt as if his concerns had been cavalierly dismissed by a man he respected and looked up to. Their relationship was not broken, but at the same time, Madison found that his affection for Jefferson was not as strong as it had been the previous fall. His idol, as it turned out, had feet of clay after all. Thomas Jefferson had truly let James down for the first time in their long association, and his feelings were hurt.

As he tramped down the muddy, trampled snow toward the boardinghouse where he was staying while the Washington residence he had purchased was being finished by builders, Madison drew his greatcoat tightly around his diminutive body. He had never been a big man, and was generally not bothered by his small stature, but on raw days like this he often wished he was a bit bulkier in build. The wind cut through him like a knife, and he missed his sweet wife, Dolley, who was tending their home in Virginia. He was never cold for long when she was waiting at home to warm him! He smiled as he reflected how fortunate he had been to win the affections of his beautiful and gregarious bride. So pleasant was his reverie that he forgot the morning's quarrel with Jefferson and did not see the approaching figure until their paths had intersected.

"Secretary Madison! It is a pleasure to see you again, sir!" Alexander Hamilton said.

"General Hamilton!" Madison was surprised and a bit nonplussed to see the subject of that morning's disagreement standing before him in the flesh. "I had no idea you were in Washington City."

"I just now arrived," Hamilton said, "in preparation for taking my seat in the Senate. A cold ride it was, too! I say, sir, which boardinghouse would you recommend? I'll need lodgings for the upcoming session of the Senate."

"Well, I believe the establishment where I am staying has some rooms yet available," Madison said. "The food there is good and the weekly rent not unreasonable. Why don't you follow me?"

"Splendid!" said Hamilton. "I've already quartered my horse at the stable closest to the capitol, and I'm ready for some food and a hot cup of tea. Would you care to join me, sir?"

Madison looked at his former friend. Hamilton's face was flushed with the cold, but he radiated good will, energy, and purpose. Recalling Alex's lovely wife, Eliza, and his large brood of children, Madison felt embarrassed by the harsh words he'd directed at Hamilton that morning. Whatever his political flaws, the man was a decent fellow, and the world would be a poorer place without him.

"I should be delighted to purchase your meal, General," he said abruptly. "I would enjoy a good, long conversation with New York's newest Senator!"

"Well, I won't take office for a couple of weeks yet," Hamilton said, "but I am very hungry, and I would enjoy a good visit with you, James. It's been far too long since we had a serious conversation. I know that our political views have diverged sharply over the last few years, but that is no reason for us to dislike each other personally."

Madison smiled, an expression that broke the dour planes of his face and showed the essentially decent and kind nature that he often suppressed in order to function in the rough and tumble world of American politics.

"Well said indeed, sir," he told Alex. "I believe the cook was putting on a stew of roasted beef when I left this morning; it should be ready by now. Let us dine together, and then have a nice long talk!"

Hamilton could not believe his good fortune. Madison was a man he had always respected, and it had grieved him that politics had come between them the last few years. He frankly blamed Jefferson for the enmity Madison had shown him and hoped he could mend bridges with his former comrade-in-arms from the battle to ratify the Constitution. Not only that, but Madison was also a Southerner, and if Hamilton's long-term plans were ever to come to fruition, he would need the cooperation of someone from the South.

However, he needed to be careful. Madison was Jefferson's Secretary of State, an active and influential member of the administration. Not only that, he also had, for all practical purposes, become Jefferson's tool in recent years. He would probably be Hamilton's rival for the presidency in four years. Alex could not afford to trust him too freely while that contest loomed in the future. But perhaps he could, at least, make sure that he and his opponent regarded each other with enough respect to keep their rivalry grounded in ideas, not vicious personal attacks and partisan slander. Hardly likely, he thought; candidates had, at best, limited control over what the papers chose to print.

The roast was indeed ready; it had been boiled in a large iron kettle over the fire with cut up potatoes, carrots, and other vegetables, forming a thick, hearty broth that steamed as it was ladled into the bowls the innkeeper provided the two men. There was also a large, fresh-baked loaf of bread laid on a cutting board with a carving knife alongside it. Hamilton cut each man a generous slice, and they sat across from each other at a wooden table whose surface was polished smooth from years of use. The beef was so tender it was falling apart, and for a half hour or so the two men simply enjoyed the food, eating before it could get cold. Hamilton, still chilled and ravenous from several days in the saddle, wolfed down his first portion and then got up and went back for seconds. Finally, he leaned back with a satisfied sigh and looked across the table at Madison, who was nearly done with his own meal.

"I was most glad to run into you so soon after arriving in the city," he said to the Secretary. "It has been several years since we have had a chance to talk."

"It is remarkable, isn't it, Alex, to be sitting here in a city whose very location we decided on over a dinner party some fourteen years ago?" Madison said, leaning back from his bowl. The hot food had chased away the chill of the walk from the Executive Mansion, and he was in a much better mood than he had been before his chance encounter with Hamilton.

"Many New Yorkers were furious with me for bargaining away the capital site," Alex said. "But the Assumption Bill was far more vital to the future of our country than where the seat of government would be. Besides, New York is our principal seaport and the seat of our financial institutions; being the national capital as well would concentrate far too much power in one community!"

"And here I thought you favored all forms of centralization," Madison said.

"Mister Madison, in all honesty, I think you will find my views have, on occasion, been misrepresented in the press," Hamilton said. "Not to mention that my ideas have evolved over time. I do believe that the states need to maintain some sovereign rights, even if the Federal Constitution is the supreme law of the land. You and I have disagreed as to where that line should be drawn, but I do think both of us concur that there should be a line!"

"So tell me, what do you hope to accomplish in your new position, Alex?" Madison asked. He found himself relaxing in Hamilton's company, something he would not have thought possible that morning.

"Well, I am hoping to have a say in the nation's financial policies," Hamilton said. "That position is the most commensurate with my experience. I think I can do the country a great deal of good there. And I should also like to speak out on foreign relations, if possible, although that will depend on the Majority Leader's goodwill."

"Many of my fellow Republicans still regard you as far too friendly to England," Madison said. "You will have to make your case quite strongly."

"Another reason for my early arrival," Hamilton said. "I want to become acquainted with the other members as soon as possible. As far as our relationship with England goes—well, I think time has vindicated me to some extent on that count. The British are our primary trading partners, after all, and we can ill afford to alienate them."

"There is something I have been wondering," Madison said. "Why run for the Senate at all? You have left a mark on our country already, an impressive legacy to your unique genius, through your earlier service. As Treasury Secretary, enjoying the confidence of President Washington, you were free to shape policy at the highest level. As a Senator, you are one of thirty-four men; not only that, you belong to a minority faction. Your influence will be limited and your ability to shape policy will depend on your ability to sway others. You were doing quite well for yourself as a private attorney. Why bother?"

Hamilton drew in a long breath. How much could he confide in this man who was his potential rival? He said a quick and silent prayer for guidance, and then spoke.

"Well, James, I would like to be President someday," he said. "I helped create this Republic of ours, and I believe I could lead it effectively. This two-party system that you and I and President Jefferson accidentally created—I think it is a healthy thing for the country, in the long run. By giving those who disagree with the direction of government a permanent voice, it makes them a part of the system instead of an outside force working to undermine it. My own faction has fallen on hard times, but I would hate to see them die out, or be reduced to impotent critics with no voice in the national discourse. Someone has to keep you Republicans honest and hold your feet to the fire, after all."

"I dislike the tone that opposition has bred in many Federalists," Madison said. "Particularly in New England, their opposition has approached the borders of out-and-out treason and separatism!"

"I actually agree with you," Hamilton said. "The talk of secession in the New England states over issues like the purchase of Louisiana was rash and foolish. I have spoken out in strong opposition to it before and will do so again. I want to move Federalism back to the political center, away from the extremes it has been pushed to in recent years."

"That is a laudable goal," said Madison. "I don't see the need for an opposition party, as you do, but if there must be one, it should operate within the bounds of decency and constitutional government. But I must say, Alex—I plan on succeeding Mister Jefferson in the presidential chair. If you intend to seek it in four years' time, then you and I are going to be opponents."

"I am no fool, Secretary Madison!" Hamilton said with a broad smile. "I know that if it were up to President Jefferson, there is no one he would rather see succeed him. I think that you and I can give the electors a clear choice between two distinct directions, and then leave the decision up to them."

"I'll admit, I would rather face a different candidate," said Madison. "You will be a formidable foe, Alexander Hamilton!"

"Let us make an agreement, Mister Secretary," said Alex, leaning forward across the table.

"What would that be?" Madison asked, arching an eyebrow.

"Politics dictate that we must be rivals for the time being," Hamilton said. "But let us both strive to be rivals only, not enemies. I know that we cannot answer for all the actions and words of the various members of our political factions, but insomuch as it depends upon the two of us, let us keep the contest for the presidency focused on issues and ideas, not baseless slander and personal attacks on each other. You are a man of character and erudition, James, and I know you love our Republic as much as I do, even if our ideas differ. I have no desire to be your enemy."

"What has happened to the ferocious, fire-breathing Hamilton whose pen sprayed invective at all who opposed him?" Madison asked sardonically. "This request does not comport well with the man I have known for the last two decades!"

"That man was slain by Aaron Burr's pistol ball," Hamilton said. "I have been given a second chance at life, both in the private and public domain. I intend to make better use of my days than I have before. I still have strong political beliefs that I will defend in print—but I hope to do so without resorting to the intemperate methods I have used in the past.

Madison studied the earnest figure who sat across the table from him. He recalled his words to Jefferson earlier—that he wished Burr's bullet had struck Hamilton in the vitals—and was suddenly ashamed of himself. This was not a bad man, he thought. Hamilton was a flawed human being, to be sure, who had made mistakes—but he was also a husband, a father, a veteran of the Revolution, and a patriot. He had wondered for a moment if Hamilton's request could possibly be sincere, but now he realized that it was. He recalled how he and Jefferson had often condemned Hamilton in the vilest of terms in their private correspondence and was embarrassed by the memories. He reached across the table and grasped Alex's extended hand.

"Then we have a bargain," he said. "Rivals in politics, but comrades in patriotism we shall be! It will be a pleasure to steer our public discourse away from the unsavory tone it has taken in recent years. Let us drink to our new relationship! Wallace, do you have any of that fine Madeira left?"

The cook nodded and brought them a dark brown bottle of the fine Spanish wine.

"Here you are, Mister Madison, sir!" he said. "Who's your friend?"

"This is the legendary Alexander Hamilton," Madison replied. "General, this is Justinian Wallace, cook and proprietor of the Wallace Boardinghouse and home for wayward legislators!"

"Hamilton?" Wallace's eyebrows drew together. "B'ain't you two enemies?"

Alex laughed out loud at the man's befuddled expression.

"Today, my good man, I have slain my enemy by making him a friend," he said. "Isn't that what good Christians are supposed to do?"

"I weren't under the impression that politics and good Christianity went together!" the man replied, sending Hamilton and Madison into gusts of laughter.

"I should like to rent a room for the upcoming congressional session," Hamilton said. "I will pay in advance, of course."

"Ten dollars a month, with meals," the innkeeper said. "Ye break a window, ye pay for it, and no wimmins!"

Hamilton handed him two five-dollar gold coins with a cheerful smile and nod of agreement. Wallace shook his head at the strange attitudes of educated men, and then went back to cutting up the pork he was preparing to roast for supper.

Madison and Hamilton sipped their drinks and watched out the window as the clouds gathered again and the snow resumed. They talked of family and business and legal cases, and together relived some of the battles and debates of the Federal Convention nearly twenty years before. The snow gently descended on the young nation's capital all afternoon, as night slowly fell, and the two men talked and reminisced together.

Finally, Hamilton stood up and stretched. Wallace had already carried his bags up to the room he would be occupying, and now that his belly was full his eyelids were growing heavy — and having consumed half a bottle of Madeira didn't help much in the battle against fatigue.

Madison was also looking tired, although not as fatigued as Alex. Hamilton was glad to reconnect with his old friend; if he truly intended to lead the nation someday, he would need to have friendships and connections that bridged the partisan divide between Federalist and Republican. Besides which, Madison was simply good company. Alex could not remember a dinner he had enjoyed so much.

"Tell me something, James," he said as they rose from the table. "Do you think that the practice of slavery is really compatible with the ideals of our Revolution?"

Madison heaved a long sigh and looked at Hamilton wistfully.

"Of course it isn't," he said. "I earnestly wish that the Africans had never been brought here, because their presence as human property makes hypocrites of all of us who fought, whether with the sword or with the pen, in the name of liberty. And yet I see no practical way to disentangle ourselves from this odious practice.

There are over one million enslaved Africans in our free Republic today; more in the South than in the North by far, but nearly every state has practiced slavery at some point. I had thought that perhaps, as the land from the Louisiana Purchase is surveyed and sold, the money could be set aside to purchase all the slaves here in America and resettle them back in their ancestral homeland. But the idea did not have enough support to make it through Congress. We in the South are bound to slavery with chains of gold, for it is by their labor that our gold is secured. But a chain binds both ways, and as long as the South depends on slaves to produce its wealth, then we ourselves are enslaved to slavery. Thomas—President Jefferson—once said that owning slaves is like holding a wolf by the ears: you may not like the predicament, but you dare not let go."

"My best friend, John Laurens, said that we could never be truly free while we deny freedom to others," Hamilton said. "Perhaps, someday, we as a nation can find a way to divest ourselves of this peculiar institution. That would be a goal worth fighting for."

"Indeed it would," said Madison. "But I see no practical way to do it."

"Not yet," said Hamilton. "But not yet does not mean the same thing as never!"

With that the two men, still rivals but no longer enemies, bid each other good night.

CHAPTER EIGHT

"THE CHAIR RECOGNIZES the junior Senator from New York," George Clinton growled. He was a longtime political foe of Hamilton's, and it galled him to see his nemesis in the Senate. As Vice President, he had no voice in the legislative body and only voted in the event of a tie, but he still radiated hostility to Alex every time he was forced to acknowledge him.

It was now December of 1805, and the official session of the 9th Congress had just begun. Given the small size of the U.S. government, Congress met for four months out of the year, January through March, for two years at a time. At the end of the second session, the new Congress was sworn in, its officers elected, and then everyone went home until the following December, unless the President called a special session. This rarely happened; no one wanted to be in Washington, DC, during the sweltering summer months when malarial mosquitos came swarming out of the Potomac. Hamilton had spent the summer back in New York, arguing legal cases, meeting with state legislators and the new governor, Morgan Lewis. Lewis was a Democratic-Republican, but as an avowed foe of the Clinton faction, he was more sympathetic to Hamilton than most. The two men had become unlikely friends, considering how often they had clashed in the past.

But now Congress was at last in session, and Hamilton was eager to make his inaugural address as a Senator. He had just received fresh news from Europe that no one else in Washington was aware of, not even the President. The letter had come to him the night before, straight from France, written by Napoleon's foreign minister, Charles Maurice de Talleyrand-Périgord. Talleyrand had fled France during the Reign of Terror and had been a guest in Hamilton's New York home during his time in America. Hamilton admired the wily Talleyrand, although he did not trust him—the man was witty, urbane, and sophisticated, but utterly corrupt. He had served, in turn, the Pope, the King of France, the National Assembly, the Directory, and finally Napoleon Bonaparte, the Emperor of France. A professional survivor, Talleyrand was deeply fond of Hamilton, and had been heard to remark that he considered Alex to be one of the greatest men of the century.

"Mister President," Hamilton said—a title that the Vice President carried only when he presided over the Senate sessions—"distinguished colleagues, and guests, it is an honor to address you today for the first time as a member of this august body. There is much that I could say, and will say in the future, about the political direction of our country and about our esteemed President, Thomas Jefferson. But today I waive those comments in the interest of more pressing news. I have received a letter from France last night which is of grave import for the future of our country and our relations with Europe."

A buzz of excitement swept the room as Senators and guests in the gallery began to whisper. Hamilton had been a harsh critic of the French Revolution, especially during the dark days of the Reign of Terror when the Jacobins had sent tens of thousands to the guillotine. His attitude toward Napoleon was less hostile because the new Emperor of France had been—thus far, at least—more moderate in his policies than the Jacobins. But Hamilton was not generally known as a friend of France, so many of his colleagues wondered how he had managed to gain an inside source of information in Napoleon's Empire.

James Madison was in the gallery, leaning forward to catch Hamilton's speech. Alex had not yet sent him a copy of Talleyrand's letter, but had dispatched a quick note to the Secretary of State that morning, letting him know that his first Senate speech contained information that would be of interest to the President and his cabinet.

"This letter is from a highly placed individual in Napoleon's foreign ministry," Hamilton said, "and it was written some six weeks ago. I received it late last night via post rider and will share its full contents with Secretary Madison later today. But this is the relevant passage I wish to share with you:

> "We just received word from our fleet that there has been a terrific battle off the Spanish coast near Trafalgar. The Royal Navy under Admiral Nelson's command has crushed the French Navy yet again, probably for the final time. Of the thirty-three ships which our Emperor sent forth to contest the English, at least twenty are now known to be sunk or captured. Insofar as I have been able to determine, not a single British vessel was sunk, although there are rumors that Nelson himself was mortally wounded.

> "This loss has scotched Bonaparte's plans to invade the British Isles once and for all. With the losses already incurred to our fleets at Alexandria and Copenhagen, the French people have

neither the resources nor the will to build another armada. As a result, the Grand Army is already being ordered to withdraw from its quarters near the Channel Coast and prepare to march east to meet the Russians, Austrians, and Prussians. With Great Britain supreme on the seas now, our only hope is to establish a comparable superiority on land, something our Emperor is confident of his ability to do.

"Only one thing seems certain at this stage of the struggle: the war for supremacy in Europe will not be a short one. The perfidious English rule the seas, but the Grand Army of France is superior in continental operations. Napoleon is determined to rule or ruin, and at the moment I am not sure which it will be. I would ask our friends in the United States, no matter how they feel about our Emperor, to remember that an all-powerful British Empire is not in the long-term interests of either of our countries. If we cannot be allies, as we once were, we should at the least avoid becoming enemies, for that would only serve the interest of our great common foe. Be vigilant, for if France is crushed, can America fail to follow not long after?"

Groans and cries of dismay greeted the news throughout the Senate floor. While many in the Republican majority were disenchanted with Bonaparte because of his despotic rule, all of them despised the British. Hearing that the indefatigable Nelson had bested France for the third straight time was dismaying to them. Madison was looking at Hamilton with a thoughtful expression, as he sought to evaluate this latest development.

"Esteemed colleagues, in its imprudent haste to dispose of our debts, this administration has sorely neglected our national defenses, especially at sea. Our Navy at this moment is smaller and weaker than it has been since the darkest days of our Revolution. This conflict in Europe has dragged on for a long time and shows every sign of continuing for the foreseeable future. Would it not be prudent to begin rebuilding our fleet at this point?" Hamilton asked the Senate. "When one side enjoys an overwhelming advantage over the other, neutral powers suffer for attempting to maintain their freedom of the seas. I propose a bill to increase our naval fleet to twenty vessels and to double the size of the United States Army for the duration of the war in Europe!"

"Senator Hamilton, I am surprised you are not dancing down the aisle at this news, considering your well-known infatuation with the British," said the new Senator from Ohio, Thomas Worthington. "Surely you don't think your beloved fellow monarchists would use their newfound military power against your adopted homeland?"

"Well, Senator Worthington, it is no secret that I favor good trade relations with England. That is the only sensible policy we can adopt, since two-thirds of our commerce is with the British Isles," Hamilton said. "But good relations are built on a foundation of respect, sir, and no great military power respects weakness! As long as we are indefensible, British and French alike will treat us with scorn and contempt."

Worthington, one of the younger Senators in attendance at thirty-two, sneered at this.

"An eloquent assertion, Senator Hamilton, but could it be you want the army enlarged so that you can place yourself at the head of it once more?" he said. "You strike me as nothing but a would-be American Bonaparte, anxious to recruit a loyal force so that you can win military glory and topple our Republic!"

"I've already had my share of military glory," Hamilton began, but the younger legislator rudely cut him off.

"Leading an army against a bunch of poor farmers who couldn't afford to pay your confiscatory tax on whiskey is hardly glorious!" Worthington said mockingly.

Hamilton's temper flared at this, and he stared the young man down with ice in his gaze.

"What I was referring to, Senator, was leading the last charge against the British redoubts at Yorktown, with musket balls flying around my ears!" he snapped. "While you were still playing with toy soldiers, Senator, I was bayoneting real ones! I've seen enough men die, and buried enough of my friends, that if America never has to fight another war, I will go to meet my Maker a contented man." The Senators applauded this line, for Worthington had overstepped the bounds of Senatorial debate as well as common courtesy with his remarks. Hamilton smiled at the show of support, but then he sighed and began pacing the Senate floor.

"But yes, we did recruit a larger army in the last administration, due to fears of a French invasion," he said. "And we did use that army to put down a dangerous rebellion against Federal authority, and with good reason! If states are allowed to set aside national law at will, if citizens can refuse to obey legislation passed for them by their elected representatives, then sir, our Constitution is but a scrap of paper and our Union is imperiled. My most ardent desire, gentlemen, is for America to be respected and prosperous, at home and abroad. I would see our citizens respect the law and our rivals respect our strength. America has been weakened in the name of budget-cutting and debt paying. While I, too, wish to see our national debt paid off, this was an imprudent step in such dangerous times. I have never favored perpetual debt, no matter how many have said that about me. But if we continue to weaken our defenses in the light of a growing trans-Atlantic threat, then we shall have neither peace nor prosperity. It is time to begin rebuilding our fleet and our armies, even if it means deferring the retirement of our debt."

The gallery erupted in applause, and most of the Senate joined in. Samuel Maclay, the junior Senator from Pennsylvania, turned to Clinton and asked to be recognized.

"The chair recognizes the Senator from Pennsylvania," Clinton responded, and Maclay held up his hands for order. The buzzing conversations died down, and he spoke.

"Fellow Senators, we should thank the Senator from New York for bringing this noteworthy development to our attention," he said. "Mister Hamilton has raised some valid points of concern, and I will support his bill for the enlargement of our fleet and army. We cannot be respected by a country as aggressive and puffed up as the British doubtless are now unless it is our military and naval strength that gives them pause!"

"This is preposterous! I demand to be recognized!" shouted William Giles of Virginia, a longtime ally of Jefferson and critic of Alexander Hamilton.

"The chair recognizes Senator Giles of Virginia," said Clinton wearily. He had never cared for Giles, even though the two were from the same faction of the Republican Party.

"Mister President, the Constitution is perfectly clear on this," he said. "A bill to double the Navy and drastically increase the Army is a spending bill, first and foremost. All spending bills are constitutionally required to originate within the House of Representatives, so Senator Hamilton's request is clearly inappropriate and unlawful!"

Alex looked at his longtime political foe with amusement and waited for his stream of invective to die down before speaking.

"I am well aware of the contents of the Constitution, Mister Giles," he said. "Considering that I was a delegate at the Federal Convention and may have played some small role in the struggle for its ratification!"

The gallery hooted at Hamilton's studied understatement, and several Senators chuckled. Giles was a notoriously irritating windbag who had few friends on the Hill.

"I fully intend to ask one of my colleagues in the House to introduce the bill there," Hamilton said, "but I wished to mention the situation here first, so that our government may be more fully informed as to the nature of the crisis. Far from inappropriate or unlawful, my sincere hope would be that any Senator who became aware of a sudden turn of events in Europe that might affect the destiny of our nation would share the news immediately, as I have done."

The debate continued for another hour or so, with most of the Senators weighing in at one point or another. The majority were against Hamilton's proposal, as he knew they would be, but it was not as big a majority as he had feared. He was pleased to see several Democratic-Republicans taking his side in the discussion, as well as every single Federalist Senator. He needed to rid the Federalist Party of its pro-British label if it was to become a potent force in American politics again, and this day had been a good start to that end. When Clinton adjourned the Senate for lunch, Alex looked up and saw Madison still sitting in the gallery, watching him. He beckoned the Secretary of State to join him as he left the capitol building.

"An impressive speech, Senator Hamilton," the diminutive diplomat said as they met on the capitol steps.

"Thank you, Mister Secretary," Alex responded. "I would have gotten a copy of the letter to you before I shared it, but I had just received it last evening. I shall have my secretary deliver one to you this afternoon."

"Would you walk over to the White House with me, and allow me to show the President your copy?" Madison asked. "I think that the sooner he knows about this turn of events, the better."

"Of course," said Alex. They began walking up the hill together toward the Executive Mansion, and as they did, a clerk from the State Department came huffing down the street waving an envelope.

"Secretary Madison!" he said. "I have an urgent dispatch from our minister in London; it arrived while you were attending the Senate debate, but Mister Johnston thought that you should have it right away."

"Thank you, Miller," said Madison. "And convey my thanks to the Assistant Secretary as well."

The sky was darkening, and a low rumble signaled that the weather was about to take a turn for the worse. Madison looked at the Executive Mansion, still a hundred yards away, and picked up his pace. Fat, cold drops of rain started peppering down from the sky as the two men scurried for the front door.

"I do most of my work over at State," Madison said, "but I do have a small office down the hall from the President's. Let us step in there and read this newest report."

The office was indeed small—a single desk covered with neat stacks of papers, with an inkwell and blank sheets in the center. There was one chair on either side of the desk; Madison took the one behind it and Hamilton sat opposite him.

"It is from James Monroe," Madison said as he opened the envelope. "Ah, here is confirmation of your news from the French!"

He quickly scanned the first page, and then handed it over to Hamilton, who took it without a word. Monroe was a man Hamilton detested; he believed the Virginian was the one who had revealed his affair with Maria Reynolds to the press after swearing to keep it confidential. Hamilton had confronted Monroe so forcefully that they had nearly fought a duel. Monroe denied the charge then and now, but Alex still did not trust the man—while he was plodding, methodical, and largely without imagination, the Virginia diplomat also held grudges with a vengeance. Those same qualities, however, made him an effective minister in London. Monroe was so free of guile his dispatches were usually a word for word report of what others said, with little interpretation or commentary included. Hamilton perused the page Madison had handed over to him.

To His Excellency, the United States Secretary of State, James Madison, from James Monroe, Minister Plenipotentiary to the Court of St. James in London:

The streets of London are thronged with people simultaneously weeping and shouting in excitement at the latest news. For the last six months, England has waited in fear to see if Bonaparte would carry out his threat to invade and depose the King, perhaps installing one of his brothers on the throne as he did in Spain. There were whispers that the entire Grand Army of the French was lying in wait at the Cinque Ports, ready to embark as soon as Napoleon's fleet gained control of the Channel long enough for them to make the crossing. Now it appears that they may have to wait years for another such chance, for the French fleet is mostly at the bottom of the ocean!

On the 21ˢᵗ of October, some ten days ago, Nelson's fleet engaged the French off the coast of Spain near Trafalgar. The one-armed admiral mastered the Gallic navy once more; he managed to use an unorthodox maneuver to rake the leading French vessels with repeated broadsides while taking no fire himself. At the end of the day, twenty-two French and Spanish vessels were either sunk or captured with not one English ship lost. There were, however, several British fatalities, most notably that of Admiral Nelson himself, who was shot through the spine by a French rifleman.

Even as the country mourns the death of its greatest hero, the people rejoice that the fear of a French invasion is no more. Without command of the seas, Napoleon dares not attempt to take his army across the Channel. The British Navy rules the waves once more, and America's policies will need to reflect this reality. The British seem determined to cut off our trade with the French by fair means or foul, and I fear that our freedom of the seas as a neutral power may be endangered by forthcoming pronouncements of the Ministry . . .

Madison took the sheet back from Hamilton and did not hand him the subsequent pages; Alex chose not to press the issue—he was not, after all, a member or even an ally of the administration.

"It appears my missive from France reported the situation with some accuracy," he said.

"Indeed," said Madison. "But it is always beneficial to review news from abroad as seen from both sides in the conflict. I would still appreciate it if you would accompany me to see the President."

"How can I refuse such an invitation?" Alex said, and the two men walked down the hall to see President Jefferson.

The Chief Magistrate was leaning over his desk, perusing a book full of wildlife sketches. Several small samples of fur and a box of bleached bones sat beside the battered volume. He was dressed in an old brown frock coat, frayed at the elbows, and his red hair was down, loose around his shoulders, and liberally streaked with gray. Hamilton reflected how much politics had aged his political nemesis and wondered how he would look after a year in the presidency—assuming he ever got there.

"Good afternoon, Mister President," Madison said in lieu of knocking. Jefferson raised his head and regarded the two men with a quizzical expression.

"Secretary Madison, Senator Hamilton," Jefferson said. "A rather unexpected duet comes to serenade me in my office! What brings you two to my door this afternoon?"

"News from France, Mister President," said Madison. "Hamilton has received an urgent letter from Foreign Minister Talleyrand, and I have just gotten independent confirmation of its contents from James Monroe in London. The British have done it, sir! Bonaparte's fleet is at the bottom of the Atlantic, and there will be no invasion."

Jefferson stood and stretched for a moment, looking thoughtful.

"May I see what Talleyrand wrote you, Senator?" he asked.

"By all means, Mister President," said Alex, handing him the letter. He had left the last page at home; it contained nothing but a few personal words from Talleyrand to his old American friend.

Jefferson read the letter in silence, and then asked Madison for the message from James Monroe. After he had perused them both, he sat down in his chair and looked at both men, his fingertips steepled beneath his chin.

"Well, Senator, I do thank you for sharing this with the administration," he said. "You are a respected authority on foreign relations; what advice would you offer your President?"

"Sir, while I recognize you have made reducing the Federal budget a priority of your administration, I believe that the cuts you have made to our defenses have imperiled our security. With the defeat of the French Navy, the British will be the uncontested rulers of the Atlantic. If we do not have a Navy adequate to our coastal defenses at the very least, our commerce shall be imperiled and our merchant fleet in danger of constant raids by press-gangs," Hamilton said.

"Senator, you have long been an adversary to the revolutionary forces in France, and an advocate of closer relations with the British," Jefferson said. "Will this not be seen as a provocation of your friends in London?"

Hamilton sighed and refused to take the bait.

"Sir, as I just said on the Senate floor, war with Britain would be economic suicide and might lead to the destruction of our government as well," Alex explained. "Good relations with the British are simply common sense for a fledgling nation such as we are. Although I was good friends with many French patriots, I never shared your enthusiasm for a revolution that became a war on the ideas of property, religion, and social order that are the foundations of civilization. Frankly, the course of events there bore out my caution—instead of a stable republic with all the blessings attendant on that best form of governments, the French waded through oceans of blood only to embrace a new form of despotism that frankly is not much better than the one they started with."

"We have trod this ground before, Senator," Jefferson said, "and I have conceded that your position is not without merit. But that is not relevant to the question of increasing our naval strength and how the British will regard such an action."

"Well, I was not done," said Hamilton good-naturedly. "What I was going to say was that the British and French alike respect strength, not weakness. If we continue to weaken ourselves, then neither side will respect our neutrality. I have never heard of a war of aggression that began because its victims were too strong. We cannot hope to build a fleet superior to the largest Navy on earth . . . but perhaps we can build one strong enough to make them think twice about provoking us when the English still have a continental war to fight."

"Such building programs are costly," Jefferson said. "We have greatly reduced our national debt in my first term, and I hoped to pay it off entirely before leaving office. I know you think a national debt to be a national blessing, but I do not share that sentiment."

"I do not favor perpetual debt," Hamilton said, "and those who accuse me of such a policy misunderstand my position. For a new nation, a carefully managed debt can indeed be a blessing, for all those who have loaned us money have a vested interest in our financial success. But an endlessly increasing debt is a chain that binds productivity and ultimately enslaves us to our creditors. That is why I believe our fleet should be funded by the American people, not foreign loans. I know that you detest taxation, Mister President—to be honest, no one who pays taxes enjoys doing so—but if you tell your Republican followers that such a tax is necessary and proper, they will go along with it. In this instance, I think we Federalists and your Republicans must make a common cause in the interests of American sovereignty and welfare."

"What say you upon this matter, Secretary Madison?" Jefferson asked.

"Senator Hamilton made some good points in his speech this morning," Madison said. "We cannot expect the British to respect our neutrality if we continue to weaken our naval defenses. I think the idea is worthy of consideration."

The President nodded, and then put his book of wildlife sketches aside.

"We will have a cabinet meeting this afternoon," he said. "Secretary Madison, if you would join me at two o'clock, I have some matters to discuss with you before the others arrive. Senator Hamilton, would you be so kind as to have a copy of your letter from Talleyrand made for me before then?"

"Of course, Mister President," Hamilton said. "I was already planning to do so."

"Then, if you will allow Secretary Madison to show you out, I have some things I must do to prepare for this afternoon's meeting," the President said. Hamilton and Madison turned to leave, and neither of them saw the venomous glance that Thomas Jefferson shot at them as the door closed behind them.

CHAPTER NINE

"SECRETARY MADISON, why did you bring that man to my office?"

Thomas Jefferson was a soft-spoken man who never raised his voice. Anyone who did not know him well would have thought him to be mildly irritated at worst. But James Madison had been Jefferson's friend and ally for years, and he recognized all the warning signs that others might miss—and he knew the President was furious with him. There were spots of red in his cheeks, the mouth was clenched in a firm, taut line, and his eyes were glittering beneath half-closed lids. Jefferson's normal, easy manner and first-name camaraderie were replaced with icy formality. Madison knew he needed to tread carefully.

"Senator Hamilton received the letter from Talleyrand by post rider late last night," Madison said. "He had the courtesy to inform me in advance of his intent to share its contents with the Senate, so I returned his courtesy by inviting him to come here and share it with you. In my opinion, the circumstances merited such action."

Jefferson heaved a small sigh and began pacing the room, pausing to look at a shelf full of specimens from his natural history collection: fossilized shells, a mastodon tooth, several beautifully flaked Indian arrowheads, and the skull of a huge bear from out west. The President picked up one of the flint points and ran his finger down its sharp edges as he spoke.

"He vexes me, Mister Madison," he said. "For his entire public career Hamilton has been a volcano of uncontrolled emotions. Washington was able to channel his energies into a productive direction, but ever since the death of our beloved first President, Hamilton has proceeded from embarrassment to embarrassment, first alienating John Adams and then provoking Aaron Burr into trying to kill him. I thought that, in the heat of Senate debate, he could be manipulated into self-immolation. But I've been told he fended off several personal attacks today with good-natured ripostes that generated laughter and sympathy. That will not do! And now he has beguiled you into thinking that he is friendly enough to our administration to be invited here into the Executive Mansion on a whim!"

Jefferson returned the Indian artifact to its shelf and fixed Madison with a fiery gaze that the Secretary had never seen before.

"I suppose this is partly my fault, James, for I let Hamilton catch me off guard. The man can be damnably persuasive, and he was so pleasant and sincere in his manner that I let him talk me into sending that letter to the newspapers. It was unwise, I realize that now. But I thought that by doing so, I had paid the debt Hamilton reminded me of. I figured that his election would put him in a position where I could arrange for his permanent political downfall and disgrace."

"If you recall, sir, I told you that it was a bad idea to give him any assistance in winning his Senate seat," Madison said.

"I am well aware of that!" Jefferson snapped. "But look at you! Now that Hamilton has targeted you with his personal charm, you have fallen prey to it like a giddy teenage girl opening her legs to a notorious rake!"

Madison was stunned. Jefferson had never spoken to him in such a tone before, nor in such a vulgar turn of phrase. His own temper flared, and he found himself raising his voice to his beloved chief.

"Hamilton has been more open and fair with me than you have of late, Mister President!" he snapped. "He could have blindsided us with that letter; instead he invited me to the Senate to hear him read it and agreed to provide me with a copy right away. The fact is, President Jefferson, Alexander Hamilton is now a member of the Senate, and his previous service as Treasury Secretary and confidant of George Washington makes him of the most powerful members of that body, regardless of how few other Federalists serve there. We are going to have to work with Senator Hamilton, Mister President, whether we like it or not. It would be wise to cultivate his good will, in my opinion. The best way to do that is to show him a certain amount of respect and courtesy—as he has done to me."

Jefferson's color began to return to normal, and he summoned up a gentle smile for his favorite Cabinet member. Seeing Madison's temper flare was a rare and sobering thing, for he treasured the man's friendship. He wondered what it was about Hamilton that set them at odds with each other so easily. Of course, while he was in Paris, Madison and Hamilton had worked very closely together on the *Federalist* essays; and that collaboration had created a friendship between them that

Jefferson and Hamilton had never shared. Over the next few years, he had pulled Madison from out of Hamilton's orbit, but there was still a residual fondness between the two men that Jefferson had been unable to extinguish. The President did not want to lose his right-hand man and chosen successor, so he decided to tread more carefully.

"I think you are right, James," he said. "Forgive my intemperate outburst; you caught me off guard bringing Senator Hamilton here unannounced. He did indeed do us a courtesy by sharing the contents of his letter from Minister Talleyrand. I am not at all in favor of increasing spending on our military when we are not actually at war, however. Standing armies are always a potential tool of oppression in the hands of any government. Yet, our Navy is indeed weaker than it should be. I had high hopes for using small gunboats as a coastal defense, but it appears they are not going to be as effective a force as I had hoped. Let us put our heads together and see if we can come up with a counter-proposal for the bill Hamilton is no doubt sending to the House at this very moment."

The two men sat on either side of Jefferson's desk, and the President laid a blank sheet of paper down and dipped his pen in the inkwell. For the moment, at least, their quarrel was forgotten—but something fundamental in their relationship was changing, whether either of them realized it or not.

REPRESENTATIVE JOSEPH Lewis of Virginia, a Federalist ally of Hamilton's, had introduced Hamilton's proposal for enlarging the U.S. military and naval forces in the House of Representatives the following week. The Emergency Defense Appropriations Act he created quickly made its way out of committee and to the House floor, where it was vigorously contested. Shortly after the first of the year, Alex had walked down to the House Gallery to listen in on the debate, and he found it as intense as he'd expected.

"This is nothing but a transparent attempt by the Federalist Party to create a military establishment which they can then use to regain the political power the voters in this country have denied them!" declaimed Representative Ezra Darby of New Jersey. "It is the brainchild of that self-same monarchist, Hamilton, who once proposed creating a life tenured President and Senate! Will we allow ourselves to be gulled into forging the weapons of our own destruction? I see you lurking in the gallery, Senator Hamilton, and I know you for what you are!"

Hamilton's temper flared within him, but he tamped it down firmly and simply smiled and bowed to the hotheaded Republican congressman.

"That is the smirk of an overconfident traitor, Gentlemen of the House!" shouted Darby. "Hamilton aims to make himself an American Bonaparte, mark my words!" The House members erupted in shouts of agreement and loud contradictions.

"You are out of line, Representative Darby," said Nathaniel Macon, the Speaker of the House, rapping his gavel for order.

"Mister Speaker, if I may," said Congressman Benjamin Tallmadge.

"The House recognizes the distinguished Representative from Connecticut," Macon said.

Hamilton's smile grew. Tallmadge was an old friend, a comrade from his days in the Continental Army and a veteran of

Washington's staff. He had run the American spy network that Washington kept in the British-occupied colonies throughout the war, and in that capacity had worked closely with Hercules Mulligan.

"Mister Darby, do you think George Washington was a man of sound character and judgment?" he asked.

Darby shot him a venomous glance, for it was political suicide to question the character of America's first President and they both knew it.

"Far be it from me to cast any aspersions on the Father of our Country," Darby finally conceded.

"Well, then, we do agree on something," Tallmadge said. "As you may know, I worked directly for His Excellency during the Revolution. He placed me in charge of some of the most sensitive information regarding enemy activity, and for the last two years of the conflict I was a member of his personal staff. I had a chance to watch George Washington interact directly with nearly every officer in the Continental Army at one point or another, and in particularly with those who were, like me, members of his military family. I also frequently visited the President in Philadelphia and in New York during his terms of office. So, what I am about to say comes from years of personally observing the Father of our Country in action as a general and as President. George Washington trusted Alexander Hamilton more deeply than he did any other officer in the Army, and more than any member of his Cabinet. He certainly trusted Hamilton the Treasury Secretary more than he trusted his Secretary of State— who was that fellow again?" Laughter echoed across the chamber at the reference to President Jefferson, and Darby sputtered furiously. Tallmadge acknowledged the mirth, and then continued.

"What that must mean is that you, sir, are either deeply mistaken as to the character and intentions of Senator Hamilton, or that you hold yourself to be a better judge of character than President Washington himself!" the veteran lawmaker concluded. The House erupted in loud huzzahs; many Republicans joined in, applauding a masterful put-down, even if it was directed at one of their own. Darby demanded to be recognized, and Speaker Macon gave him a minute to respond.

"Mister Tallmadge, even the purest of hearts may be deceived by an artful intriguer. Was not Adam deceived by the serpent in the Garden?" he said. "George Washington was a man of such fundamentally honest nature that he could not perceive the depths of evil lurking in the breast of his faithful subaltern!"

"Oh, so now Senator Hamilton is the devil himself," Tallmadge said with a chuckle. "Please, tell us how he encompassed the fall of man and the temptation of Christ in the wilderness!"

"If not Lucifer, he is certainly one of the devil's minions, Congressman Tallmadge!" snapped Darby. "Look at that infernal financial construct that he put in place, the Bank of the United States! An instrument of oppression in the hands of speculators, stock-jobbers, and Northern manufacturers, to be used against the honest working men of America, our farmers!"

"And yet President Jefferson has chosen to leave Hamilton's entire financial system in place, when he could certainly have torn it out, root and branch," Tallmadge rejoined. "Perhaps you could summon Secretary Gallatin here and ask his opinion of Hamilton's handling of our nation's finances?"

The House hooted again, for it was widely whispered that Gallatin had probed the Treasury Department and the Bank for any evidence of corruption and incompetence and found none.

"This bill is a dreadful mistake!" snapped Darby, "And I will never support it!"

Nonetheless, enough Congressmen did support the bill that it made it through the House of Representatives by a vote of eighty to fifty-five. That meant that it would proceed to the Senate within a week or two, and Hamilton was anxious to throw his weight behind it there. He wanted to return to New York City and hear the latest news from overseas, but he feared to leave the capital lest the bill be brought up for debate during his absence. So instead, he asked one of his Senate pages, an earnest young man from New York named Elijah Cartwright, to make a flying trip on his behalf.

"Find Hercules Mulligan and Gouverneur Morris, and then swing by the Grange and collect any recent mail that has come for me," he told the young man. "It's over two hundred miles, but if you can get there and back in less than ten days, I will pay you fifty dollars for your trouble!"

That was a hefty sum for a twenty-year-old, especially Cartwright, a handsome rake who was cutting a wide swath through the ladies of Washington City.

"Fear not, Senator, I'll be back in nine days!" he said.

"Don't kill your horses, lad," Hamilton said with a laugh. "The girls will still be here when you get back!"

Cartwright had been gone for five days when the bill was first introduced onto the Senate floor. Due to its smaller size, the U.S. Senate was not divided into Committees like the House; other than one select committee on Army regulations, it met in a Committee of the Whole. Hamilton signed on to sponsor the bill, and Samuel Maclay agreed to co-sponsor it. In its final draft from the House, the bill included Hamilton's original proposal to enlarge the Navy to twenty ships; however, it had reduced his request for a six-thousand-man Army to five thousand. Still, it was a vast improvement over the Army's current (and in Hamilton's opinion, scandalously small) two thousand seven hundred officers and men. Even at that, the proposed increase brought out cries of hysteria from the stauncher Democratic-Republicans in the Senate.

"A five-thousand-man Army is a useless extravagance!" declaimed Daniel Smith of Tennessee. "It is too small to be effective against the British, but large enough to effectively enforce whatever despotic measures our government might choose to take against its citizens."

"The last time I looked, Senator, the United States' population was over six million," Hamilton rejoined. "I do not see how a tiny Army of five thousand men could possibly oppress such a large population! General Howe could not do it when our population was half what it is now, and he had over thirty thousand men at his disposal. Besides, is our government not in the tender hands of your own beloved fellow Republican, Thomas Jefferson? Don't tell me you now fear he has designs on your liberties!"

"I would trust President Jefferson with my life," said Smith, "which is more than I can say for you, sir! But, danger to our liberties aside, such a large army would be ruinously expensive!"

"We raised an army of twenty thousand when George Washington was President, and our debt was much more extensive then than it is now," Hamilton said. "We did not break the bank by doing so. Nor shall we now, when our financial status is so much improved, and the force we are raising so much smaller."

The debate went on in the same tone for an hour or more, and then one of Hamilton's fellow Federalists raised his voice and expressed a different concern.

"Senator Hamilton," said Timothy Pickering of Massachusetts, "do you still consider yourself a Federalist?"

"Of course I do," Hamilton said. "Albeit an American first, and a Federalist second!"

"Has it not always been the policy of we Federalists to maintain close commercial ties with England, since that is in the best interest of our country?" Pickering persisted.

"Indeed," said Hamilton, "since England is by far our largest foreign trading partner, to needlessly antagonize the British is foolhardy."

"Then why propose a larger Navy whose sole purpose will be to antagonize England and endanger our trade with them?" the Yankee Senator demanded.

"Mutually beneficial trade relations begin with mutual respect," Hamilton said. "Right now, our Naval strength is so minuscule as to be respected by none! Indeed, with President Jefferson's insistence on scrapping our plans for more capital ships in favor of his beloved tiny gunboats, our Navy is less impressive than it was when John Adams left office! Do you know, sir, that last fall a hurricane picked up one of Jefferson's toy boats and deposited it in a cornfield five miles inland? Indeed, under the current administration, we possess the finest navy ON EARTH!"

The Senate erupted in laughter; it was a good jibe, none the worse for having been used before.

"But precious little good our nautical scarecrows will do us in protecting the coast from the Royal Navy!" Hamilton continued. "The British, as I have said before, respect strength. I do not propose to be their rivals for dominance of the high seas, except perhaps someday in the field of trade. But I do propose that we should be strong enough to make them think twice about raiding our coast. That is not aggression, sir, that is common sense!"

Pickering looked over at his fellow Massachusetts Senator, John Quincy Adams, who arched an eyebrow, and then shrugged. Then he turned his gaze back to Hamilton.

"I pray that the British share your ideas of what comprises common sense, Senator," he said.

By then it was nearing five o'clock on Thursday afternoon; the Senate adjourned not long afterward, and Hamilton made his way back to his rooms at the Wallace Boardinghouse. Eliza had sent him several of his favorite books, his ivory chessboard, and a quilt she had made for him—all to make the place seem more like home. Unfortunately, all they did was remind Alex more sharply of her absence. Still, it was a chill evening, and curling up with a good book before the fire seemed preferable to the noise of the common room.

He was only a few pages into his well-thumbed copy of Cicero's letters when a knock sounded at the door.

"Yes, who is it?" he answered.

James Madison quietly slipped into the room.

"Hello, Senator, I hope I am not causing any inconvenience," he said.

"Cicero has waited nearly two thousand years for my attention," said Hamilton. "Another evening will not offend the great orator. Come in, Mister Secretary!"

"I would have expected to find you perusing Caesar's works before those of old Tully," said the Secretary of State.

"Caesar is a good companion for the warrior," said Hamilton, "and I read deeply of his campaigns during our war for liberation. As a general, he is without peer. But I would sustain our Republic, not destroy it, and Cicero is a fair guide to that object—both in his achievements, and more notably in his failures."

"An interesting observation," said Madison. "I was unable to attend the debates today; how fares your bill in the Senate?"

"We only began debate today," said Hamilton. "I find that there is some support on both sides of the aisle for the enlargement of our Navy, but there is some very stubborn opposition to any attempt to increase our Army's strength. It is frustrating, quite frankly. Some of your Republican counterparts are almost maniacal in their opposition."

"The New England Federalists aren't too fond of your naval proposals, from what I hear," Madison said.

"Well, I hope that we can pass a bill that will, at the least, make our nation more secure at sea than we currently are," said Hamilton.

"Would you believe me if I said that President Jefferson shares your hope?" Madison asked him.

"That does not surprise me," Alex told him. "Jefferson is wise enough to learn from his mistakes, and his naval reductions were ill-timed and excessive. But he cannot publicly support my bill, because of how strongly some in his party oppose it. Am I right?"

"Perceptive as always, Alex!" said Madison. "But I think you will find, as the debate goes on, that some on our side will defect and support your bill—particularly if you are willing to compromise on the size of the land forces."

"Five thousand is a pittance, you know," Alex said. "But perhaps we can find some common ground. I say, how about I send down for dinner and we play a game or two of chess?"

"Capital idea!" Madison said, and they spoke no more of politics that evening, although Madison's king wound up being cornered and forced to capitulate three times in a row.

The next day was spent debating several of the President's judicial nominees, and the Emergency Defense Appropriations Act was tabled until the next week. Hamilton took little part in the debate—he knew Jefferson's nominees would be confirmed and preferred to conserve his oratorical firepower for more important issues.

On Saturdays Hamilton would usually answer correspondence that he had not gotten to during the week, and to write out his plans, proposals, and agendas for the week to come.

He met with constituents, if any had made the dreary journey to Washington City seeking an audience with their Senator (this Saturday there were two; one simply a curious tourist, eager to meet the famous Hamilton; the other a supplicant, wanting a Federal appointment as postmaster in his upstate town). Then in the evening he would socialize with other members of the Senate, getting a feel for how they felt on a variety of issues.

Sundays Alex went to church—a habit he had neglected for many years, but faithfully maintained ever since surviving the deadly encounter with Aaron Burr. Although the details of his vision had faded a bit, he still believed that it was more than just a fever dream. God had spared his life for a reason, and he wanted to make the most of the second chance he had been given. Slavery was often on his mind; indeed, the institution was all around him, since both Virginia and Maryland were slave states and there was a slave market being built in the national capital. Every year, it seemed, the foul institution grew more strongly entrenched, and he knew that he would have to make his move soon, or it would be too late, and the conflagration he had been warned of would be set in stone, irrevocable and deadly, to blight the nation's future.

After church, Alex went on a stroll in the snow outside the city's muddy streets, enjoying the white blanket of peace that masked all signs of human activity in the meadows and forests around the District of Columbia. He returned to his room at the boardinghouse and sat down to write Eliza a long letter, beginning with the news of the week and then settling into several pages of a more personal nature; he offered advice on dealing with the children, suggestions on household economies, and finally spent three pages simply telling his wife how much he adored and missed her. He had already decided that, in the spring, he would purchase a lot in Washington City and have a house erected there; he simply did not want to be away from his wife for four months out of the year if he could avoid it. They could always rent the house out when they returned to New York.

It was nearly ten o'clock when he finally signed his name to the last page of the letter and blotted it. As he folded the ten sheets over and looked for an envelope, he heard the rapid clopping of horse's hooves approaching the boardinghouse. Moments later, rapid steps came pounding up the stairs, followed by a hard, staccato knock at his door. Alex crossed the room and threw the door open to see who was there.

Elijah Cartwright looked more like a snowman than a living and breathing person—his cloak was coated in a full inch of powdered snow, and his hat was almost invisible under a cap of white. He was puffing and blowing and stamping his feet, but his eyes were twinkling with excitement.

"Dear God, boy, I told you not to wear your horses out and I daresay you've killed them!" Hamilton said.

"Only one, Mister Hamilton, and he stepped in a rabbit hole and broke his leg," the Senate page said. "The rest I rode hard as I could but swapped them out often. Mister Mulligan insisted I get this letter to you as quickly as I could—he said it was information you would need to know. He and Mister Morris were actually looking for a way to get this to you when I rode into town."

Hamilton looked at the lad in astonishment. Cartwright had ridden nearly five hundred miles in eight days, in the dead of winter.

"Well, lad, hand me the correspondence and then go down to the taproom and get some hot supper in you," he said. "Beefsteak, terrapin soup, roast duck, whatever you like—get Wallace up to feed you and tell him to send the bill to me. I think you have earned every penny I promised you and a little extra!"

"Thank you, Senator Hamilton, sir!" the page said. "But—if I may be so bold—I would love to know what's in this letter that is so urgent. I nearly froze to death getting it to you!"

"Fine then," said Hamilton, "but you'd better not be sharing it with anyone until I've made it public."

"God forbid!" the young man said.

Hamilton read the cover letter from Gouverneur Morris first, and his eyes widened as he took in what the former Minister to France shared.

Dear Senator, it began.

This letter from Talleyrand arrived by confidential courier early this morning. While I have not read it yet, the man shared some of the news it doubtless relates. Bonaparte has done it again—he smashed the Russians and Austrians at a place called Austerlitz, and the Czar himself is a prisoner of the French! This ends the Coalition of allies the British had assembled against the Corsican emperor, and virtually assures that the war in Europe will drag on for years to come. I had scarcely absorbed the news when your man Cartwright came riding into town; surely Providence must have had a hand in the timing of your young friend! I bought him a fresh horse and paid him a twenty-dollar bonus if he would turn around and leave the very next morning. A likely lad, that one, in my opinion—he didn't demur or ask why, he simply took the letter and swung by the Grange to collect your personal correspondence.

Bonaparte's victory will doubtless be the talk of New York by tomorrow evening, but I daresay no one in Washington City will get wind of it before you, my old friend! Make the most of it and use it to accomplish some good—advice you probably do not need from me! With warmest regards, I remain,

Your obedient servant,

Gouverneur Morris

Hamilton's eyes widened at the news, and despite his eagerness to get to Talleyrand's letter, he read Morris's short note out loud to young Cartwright. The boy's eyes gleamed with pride as Hamilton shared Morris's compliments. But as soon as that was done, Alex broke the seal on Talleyrand's letter and greedily devoured it with his eyes.

From Charles Maurice Talleyrand et Périgord, Foreign Minister to His Serene Highness Napoleon I, Emperor of the French,

To His Excellency Alexander Hamilton, Senator of the State of New York and late Secretary of the Treasury of the United States, Greetings!

Alex, our Emperor has done it! Two days ago, he outmaneuvered the combined armies of Russia and Austria and inflicted one of the most crushing defeats in military history to our Empire's enemies. A full third of the enemies' ninety thousand troops lie dead in the field, while our losses are less than a fifth of the Grand Armee that was engaged. It was as brilliant a double envelopment as could be imagined, Alex! While I still have my doubts about Napoleon's administrative abilities, he is beyond a doubt the greatest general of the age. The Czar of Russia, Alexander the First, is now an honored captive of France, and the Emperor of Austria is retreating pell-mell towards his frontier, sending messages requesting an armistice. I imagine our terms will shatter the moldering carcass that is the Holy Roman Empire once and for all and create a new balance of power in Europe that renders France supreme.

It is my hope that the British will see reason after this latest victory and sign an armistice, but I imagine their naval victory at Trafalgar will keep them confident enough in their naval supremacy to seek new allies for a conventional war on the Continent. Nonetheless, this victory shifts momentum in the Emperor's favor, and the kings of Europe will doubtless scramble to align themselves with him for the foreseeable future.

The United States will need to tread cautiously from now on, my friend. Our great contest has become a battle between an elephant and a whale; each supreme in his own element but unable to enter the other's. That means that economic warfare may replace actual blades and bullets for the foreseeable future, and as a major trading partner of both nations, America runs the risk of being caught in the middle. I do not request any formal alliance, but I do ask that the United States recognize that its interests do not lie in British supremacy on the seas.

I am delighted that you, my friend, are in a position once more to shape America's response to events over here. Use that power wisely, Alex, for the benefit of your own people will, I am certain, also accrue to the interests of France, and to the eventual restoration of peace in Europe.

Many kisses to your fair bride and lovely daughters, and my personal best wishes now and always;

Yours most fondly;

Talleyrand

Hamilton let young Cartwright read the letter, and then spread it out on his desk, where its damp edges could dry out.

"Well, lad, here is sixty dollars," he said. "Go and get yourself some supper and get warm! You've had a brutally long and cold ride."

The boy's eyes widened at the ten-dollar gratuity, and then a gleam of mischief crept into them.

"I know just the person to help me warm up tonight!" he said. "I'll see if I can catch her before she retires for the evening!"

Alex chuckled at the lad's unabashed randiness, recognizing a good bit of his own younger self in Cartwright's eagerness.

"Far be it from me to interfere with the passions of youth," he said, "but on your way out, please have Wallace let Secretary Madison know that I would like to see him—urgently!"

CHAPTER TEN

"NO!" AN ANGRY, raspy voice came clearly through the front door of the stately New England farmhouse known as Peacefield. "John, I will NOT see that man! He is not welcome in my house!"

Hamilton stepped away from the door, having no desire to eavesdrop on the conversation between father and son. He had spent much of his first congressional session renewing his acquaintance with Massachusetts' two Senators. Timothy Pickering was an old friend, a former member of George Washington's military "family," and had always regarded Alex with great fondness, even when they occasionally disagreed on issues. The other Senator was none other than John Adams's son, John Quincy Adams. He was a much harder person for Hamilton to get close to, given the stormy political history between Hamilton and his father, the former President.

Hamilton had doubted that Adams would be able to prevail against Thomas Jefferson in the election of 1800, and so he had thrown his support to General Charles Pinckney of South Carolina instead. When the administration's press outlets had accused him of doing so for petty and personal reasons, Alex had written up a lengthy epistle, outlining his reasons for doubting Adams's suitability for another term. It was this letter, published as a pamphlet under the title *A Letter from Alexander Hamilton,*

Concerning the Public Conduct and Character of John Adams, Esq, President of the United States, that had led to a final and complete break between him and the former President. In Adams's mind, it was Hamilton's treachery, not his own shortcomings, that had led to his defeat that fall, and he had never forgiven Alex for it.

For his part, Alex intensely regretted sending the letter; written at a time when he was still grieving the loss of his political mentor, George Washington, and fearful of the rise of Jefferson, whom he considered a dangerous radical. At that point, Adams had already shown contempt for him on more than one occasion, especially regarding Hamilton's rank and position in the Army. Alex had let his wounded pride and personal rancor get the better of his political judgment. Now he had come to make amends, if possible. He would need the Federalist Party united around him for the election in two years' time, if he was to stand any chance at all of ascending to the White House. Federalism was still strongest in New England, and Adams was its elder statesman. To win the support of the region, he would need to follow the advice that still echoed in his mind from the vision he had experienced as he hovered near death two years before: to "try Massachusetts."

Alex had spent a good deal of the congressional session trying to win the goodwill of John Quincy Adams and had finally succeeded. Quincy was an odd man out; officially he was considered a member of the Federalist Party still, but he had come to side with the administration more and more often of late— especially since New England Federalists had taken such an extremist tone in their opposition. Like Alex, he was a strong nationalist, and hostile to any who threatened to break up the Union over political squabbles.

Hamilton had known the younger Adams for many years, but only as a social acquaintance. Alex had high respect for the man's formidable intellect and broad education; the Massachusetts Senator was fluent in six languages and deeply read in history, law, religion, and politics. Their conversations over dinner at the boardinghouse had been most enjoyable, constantly shifting from topic to topic. But Hamilton had made his purpose plain from the start: he wanted to mend his fences with President Adams.

"I do not think it will work," Quincy told him when Alex first broached the subject. "My father hates you, and he does not give up a grudge easily."

"I have given him reason for that hatred," Hamilton replied. "If nothing else, I would like to make amends for the sake of my own conscience. Your father and I share a strong love of country, and I think both of us would like to see its government returned to more responsible leadership. That will not happen as long as the two leading members of the Federalist Party are engaged in a bitter feud."

"Well, I will do what I can to help you, sir," said the younger Adams. "But I cannot guarantee any good result!"

So it was that Alexander Hamilton found himself standing on the front porch of Peacefield Farm in Quincy, Massachusetts, on a fine summer morning in 1806. He had enjoyed the ride north a great deal; all around he saw business and industry thriving, people busily bustling about, factories under construction, and seaports teeming with ships and commerce. This was the America he had conceived in his mind since the earliest days of the Revolution—a strong, independent Republic whose manufactures and industry would make it, in time, a first-rate power in the world. He contrasted it sadly with his trips through the South, where indolence and luxury were the order of the day, and even the poorest whites shunned hard manual labor as "slave-work."

As Hamilton surveyed the summer morning, the sound of voices in the house tapered off. The conversation inside had lasted for five minutes, maybe a bit longer. Alex remained at the rails of the porch, looking over the fields and farms that surrounded the town until Quincy came back out and tapped him on the shoulder.

"I have managed to talk him into seeing you," he said, "but he is not happy about it."

Alex swallowed his pride and said a quick prayer. He knew the elder Adams would try to goad him into losing his temper, and he was determined not to do so. Then he put on his most charming smile and followed Senator Adams through the doors of the house.

The former President was sitting in a rocking chair by the window, his knees covered with a shawl. Although still somewhat paunchy in the middle, Hamilton could tell that he had dropped some weight since leaving office. His face was deeply lined, and his cheeks still flushed red. His white hair had thinned on top but stood uncombed in a fuzzy halo around his petulant face. He fixed Alex with a glare, and in those eyes, Hamilton recognized the feisty, combative politician who had played such a critical role in America's revolution. Adams's body might be shrunk and withered with age, but he was still mentally sharp and focused.

"Good morning, Mister President," he said. "I am glad to see you looking so well."

"Why?" Adams said. "Why should my welfare be any concern of yours, when you have been my enemy for the last eighteen years? I was having a good morning, until my son told me that you had come to my door. Is it not enough, sir, that you have slandered me and held me up for public ridicule? Why do you come all the way here to trouble me in my retirement? Have you not done me enough injury to satisfy your blackguard's heart?"

Alex sighed. This was not going to be an easy conversation, to be sure! But he had ridden for the better part of two weeks to get here and was determined to see it through.

"You have cut to the heart of the matter, Mister President, as was always your wont," he said with a wry smile. "I am here because I wronged you, sir, and I wish to make amends."

"Wronged me!" Adams snapped. "Well, well, the Father of Lies utters a truth for once! You did more than wrong me, sir, you slandered me! You destroyed any chance I might have had for a second term as President! From the very start you were against me, as far back as 1788! During the time we served together under President Washington, you took every opportunity to slight me and belittle me. Then when we enlarged the Army and asked His Excellency to take command, in case of a French invasion, you somehow convinced him that you and you alone were qualified to be his second-in-command. I do not know what hold you had over the General, Senator Hamilton, but it must have been a strong one, for he insisted I promote you over many men who were your seniors in rank and experience. Then when the French threat dissipated, His Excellency" —Adams made the honorific sound more like an insult—"returned to his beloved Mount Vernon and left me saddled with YOU as the Army's senior general. From there you were free to conspire against me to your heart's content, and conspire you did. Your damnable pamphlet destroyed me, sir. You blackened my name before the electors at the very moment when I was vying for their support, and by doing so you put that Virginian mountebank into the presidential chair!"

Adams had pulled himself up out of his seat as he ranted, waggling his finger at Hamilton and stumping around the room. Then he sighed and slowly sank back down into his chair, picking up the shawl and spreading it over his legs again.

"Now you come to me, saying you wish to make amends. How, sir? Pray tell, how can you give me back all that you took from me?" The raspy voice softened, and Hamilton saw the raw hurt that underlay the man's anger.

"I cannot," Alex said softly, feeling pity for his old nemesis. "Sir, none of us have the power to undo the past. If I could go backwards in time and tell myself never to write that damnable tract, I would do so without hesitation. But what is done cannot be undone. What I should like to do, if you will be so gracious as to listen, is to explain myself to you. For some reason, it seems you and I never have understood each other. Will you listen to me, at least?"

"Listen?" Adams growled. "A fine day when my own son brings the man who ruined me to my door and expects me to *listen* to the bastard brat of a Scots peddler! Very well, Mister Hamilton, state your case. You explain yourself, and I will *listen*."

Hamilton swallowed hard. Of all the slurs thrown his way during his lengthy public career, none galled him more than the aspersions cast upon his birth. His mother, Rachel Faucett, had not been a whore, despite what people said; she had been forced into a loveless marriage at a young age and left her abusive husband behind after five years. But the vindictive John Michael Lavien had stubbornly refused to grant her an annulment, leaving Alex and his brother to bear the stigma of bastardy simply because she was not free to marry the man she loved, James Hamilton, at the time their two children were born.

But Alex was here to make peace, not to take offense. He knew Adams would probably bring up the old slander at some point; he had referred to Hamilton as "that bastard Creole" for years in private conversations, many of which got back to Alex. He might not like what Adams said, but Hamilton needed the old man's good will—or at least, a cessation of hostilities between them.

"Mister Adams, I bore you no ill will eighteen years ago. I admired your courage, patriotism, and tenacity. Even during the Revolution, when you briefly contemplated supporting General Washington's removal as Commander in Chief, I did not take it personally, although I believed you to were gravely mistaken. Your skills as a negotiator were critical in winning a favorable peace treaty for us at the war's end. You were well deserving of the office of Vice President, and I supported you for it. The only reason that I urged some of the electors to cast their ballots for General Pinckney was so that General Washington would be the clear winner of the contest. I feared an electoral tie which might accidentally elevate you to the first rank, when the will of the people and the country had designated His Excellency for that position," Alex began. "Look at what happened with Jefferson and Burr when their electors were careless!

"As we served together under President Washington, I noticed that your love of argument and debate had the effect of bogging down every meeting you were involved in," he went on. "So, when the President began excluding you from meetings of his cabinet, I supported the decision—but it was not my suggestion that he do so! I always respected and deferred to you, sir, during our mutual service, even if I sometimes questioned your judgment and temperament."

Hamilton began pacing the room as he talked, using his most persuasive voice, honed by years of arguing cases in court— although this time, he was trying to convince a jury of one, who also happened to be the plaintiff!

"You say that I must have had some hold on President Washington, Mister Adams?" he started with an interrogatory. "You are correct. My hold on him was no more and no less than this: George Washington trusted me. I was one of a dozen or more military aides-de-camp during the war, and the others were nearly all older and more experienced than me. Yet he put me at the head of them, and he kept me there. He could have chosen any one of three million Americans to be his Treasury Secretary, yet he chose me. He sought my advice and counsel on many matters outside the purview of my department for one reason, and one reason only—he trusted my judgment and knew that I would offer whatever advice I could, based on one criterion only: what was best for our country. President Washington could be a difficult man at times—he was demanding, stern, and not always as grateful as one might wish for services rendered. But he was the greatest man I have ever known, Mister Adams. I am not ashamed to say that I loved him, and that his trust was the highest honor I have ever been given. I did my best never to abuse it."

Adams regarded Hamilton sternly, but did not comment.

"You would not have been my first choice to succeed Washington," Alex continued. "Your years in the vice presidency made me question your temperament. But it was clear that most of the Federal electors favored you, and I considered you infinitely preferable to Mister Jefferson, whose tendencies to Jacobinism and mob rule frightened me far more than your occasional outbursts of temper. I will not lie to you, Mister Adams—I was glad when you prevailed in the election that year."

"I would not have known it, by the way you treated me," the elderly Adams snapped back. "Impertinence and disrespect from the first day I was in office!"

"Respect is a two-way street, Mister President," Hamilton said. "I think both of us had formed negative opinions of each other by that point. You did not like my closeness with your predecessor and resented his choice of me as his military second in command. As for me, I was dumbfounded by some of your decisions while in office. Your absence from the seat of government for months at a time, your fits of anger so intense that they rendered you incapable of speech, your erratic foreign policy towards France—sir, in all honesty I came to wonder if I had done the right thing in supporting you."

"By God, sir, you come to my house and insult me!" Adams snapped. "I should turn you out this instant!"

"Father," John Quincy interjected, "this man is my guest as well as yours! Don't be so ungracious."

"It's all right, Senator," Hamilton said, and then turned his attention to the former President. "Sir, I do not seek to insult— only to explain how things appeared to those of us who were not able to discern your thoughts. In retrospect, your making peace with the French accrued to the benefit of our country. But at the time—by God, sir! Our undeclared war with France was popular with the people and might well have carried the Federal ticket to victory. It seemed to me as if you were deliberately tipping the election to Jefferson. That was why I wrote what was supposed to be a private letter to other Federalist leaders, expressing my reservations."

"Reservations!" Adams snarled, nearly shouting again. "Sir, you eviscerated me! Whether you meant for it to be published or not, published it was! You publicly destroyed and humiliated me, who was lobbying for American independence while you were still scratching at ledgers in whatever God-forsaken Caribbean hell hole spawned you!"

"And I was WRONG!" Hamilton raised his own voice for the first time. "That is what I came here to tell you, Mister President! I should have gone to you first, spoken to you, asked you why you acted as you did. But I was tired, I was hurt, I was still grieving for the loss of my beloved Commander in Chief, and so I lashed out at you in print." He paused, and looked at Adams, who was regarding him thoughtfully. "But can I ask you this, in all honesty, sir? If I had tried to come to you, to ask you about your conduct and your policies at that point in your presidency, would you have even spoken to me?"

Adams gave a long sigh, and seemed to slump in his chair, almost shrinking. In that moment, he looked every one of his seventy years and more.

"Probably not, Mister Hamilton," he said. "I had already come to despise you. I will tell you something, lad. The presidency is sheer misery—splendid misery, but misery, nonetheless. Every action, every word, scrutinized, criticized, and scoffed at! Every action twisted and used against you, the vilest falsehoods imaginable coined about you every day, and presented to the public as facts. Do you know that one of Jefferson's minions in the press accused me of telling General Pinckney to bring back three young Russian girls when he returned from St. Petersburg, so that I could add them to my 'presidential harem'? Now tell me, Senator Hamilton, do I look like the sort of man who would maintain a harem?"

Adams stood up and let the shawl fall away. Hamilton saw the pot-bellied, spindly-legged old man with white hair and a tremulous voice standing before him—and laughed out loud. Adams raised an eyebrow, and then suddenly the ex-President began laughing too, and the two men simply stood and chuckled at one another. Finally, Hamilton spoke.

"Well, sir," he said, "I am sure you could have done them good service in your day, but time does take its toll on us all!"

"I was never the rake that you were reputed to be, Senator," the former President said. "I married the best woman in the world when I was a young man, and I have adored her and her alone from that day to this!"

"I would say that we both married very well," Hamilton replied, "and I wish I was as loyal a husband in my youth as you have been your entire life." He rarely spoke of his affair with Maria Reynolds to anyone, but in showing Adams some trust he hoped that he would earn some in return.

"All we like sheep have gone astray, Alexander," said the former President. "I would like to tell you something that I never thought I would say. Thank you for coming to see me, Alexander Hamilton. I know my ranting cannot have been pleasant to listen to, but I feel as if a particularly malignant boil has just been lanced. My spirits are suddenly lifted, by God! Hatred is an ugly thing, and I am ashamed that I have harbored it towards you for so long."

"I desire nothing but peace between us, President Adams," Hamilton said. "Is that something we can achieve?"

The old man regarded him for a long time, and then slowly he extended his hand. Hamilton took it in his own, and their eyes locked.

"Yes, we can," Adams said. "Let us have peace between us, you and I. Our enmity had been harmful to each of us, and to the country. It is time for us to let it go. Would you be my guest here at Peacefield tonight?"

"I should be delighted," Hamilton said. "I have heard that your Abigail is a legendary cook."

"Indeed, her skills have grown with age," Adams said with a chuckle. "When we first married, the dear girl could barely boil water!"

"This is most splendid, Father!" John Quincy said. "I shall fetch Louisa and we shall join you."

THE MEAL WAS splendid indeed, and whatever reservations Abigail Adams may have felt at having "that man" (as her husband had referred to Hamilton for years) as a guest, she did not let them show. The two Adams men regaled Hamilton with stories of their respective times in Europe, and John Quincy told quite the tale of sitting on the front porch of their house in Boston at the age of eight with a musket on his knees as the Battle of Bunker Hill raged a little over a mile away, determined to dispatch any stray redcoat that dared step into his front yard.

"I believe the lad would have done it, too," the former President said proudly. "I did not raise a coward!"

"You didn't raise a marksman either, Father!" Quincy said. "I probably would have missed at point-blank range. But you, Senator Hamilton—you saw far more combat than my one distant glimpse of a single battle. What was it like, fighting alongside General Washington?"

"Well," Alex said, "unfortunately, once I caught the General's attention, I did most of my fighting with quill and parchment instead of with musket and bayonet! But I do recall one time, after the battle of Brandywine, when His Excellency asked me to ride out on a reconnaissance to see if Howe was trying to outflank us. My comrades and I ran head-on into a British cavalry detachment, and had to board a raft in order to keep from being captured . . ."

It was a fine tale, and entirely true—the craft had been peppered with musket balls, and one of the rowers fell dead, shot through the chest. Hamilton had jumped overboard to avoid being shot himself, and his companions, watching from the river's opposite bank, had been sure he was dead. He had arrived back in camp early the next morning, wet, exhausted, and bedraggled, to find Washington and the rest of the Continental Army's staff in mourning for his presumed demise.

Late that night, Hamilton sat out on the front porch with President Adams, enjoying a cigar and watching the stars shine overhead. The old man was happy and garrulous at first, but as the evening grew later, he began to study Hamilton with an inquisitive look.

"Why did you really come here, Alexander?" he asked. "I know you wanted to make peace, but there is something else on your mind. Go on and tell me; I promise that it will go no further."

Hamilton had not revealed the contents of his vision to anyone, but all at once he felt the weight of his self-imposed mission hanging like an anchor around his neck. So he took the plunge, and told the former President about the duel, and his own near-death experience in its wake, and of the dire warning his dream had revealed.

"I don't know, Mister President," he said, "how much of it was some supernatural visitation and how much of it was my own fevered imagination, but this much I do know—slavery is going to destroy this country if I don't do something about it. I can see it in my mind's eye, like a slow-growing tumor or cancer, sinking its tendrils deeper into the heart of the South year after year. If it is not excised soon, it is destined to tear us apart and consume an entire generation."

"I have often felt the same," Adams said. "Truly our forefathers struck a deal with the devil when they allowed the slave traders to begin doing business in our ports! Well, my lad, you have my support. Whatever influence this old man still has, it is at your disposal. I would never have thought to hear those words come out of my mouth! But still—President Hamilton! It does have a nice ring to it, doesn't it?"

Alex smiled, unable to believe this reversal of fortune.

"Indeed it does, sir," he said. "Indeed it does!" He said a silent prayer of thanks to the Almighty for the success of his mission, and then, just in case he was also listening, he thanked George Washington for sending him on this errand.

"I am going off to bed," Adams said, clapping Hamilton on the shoulder. "Have a good evening, sir, and we shall break our fast together tomorrow. Then there is someone I would like you to meet, over in Quincy."

The old man rose and stumped his way off to bed. Hamilton stepped out into studied the stars for a long moment. The moon had not yet risen, and the clear sky was studded with the shining diamonds of the cosmos.

"I have no idea how you managed it, Alex," said John Quincy, who had quietly stepped out onto the porch. "But thank you. My father has been so bitter since he left office, and much of that bitterness was directed at you. Hearing him laugh with you was a balm to my soul as much as to his."

Alex turned and faced his fellow Senator. Adams was a slimmer, taller version of his father, with broad shoulders and a piercing gaze.

"I feel better about things myself," he said. "Regardless of politics, turning an enemy into a friend is a worthy undertaking. I admire many things about your father, and always have. It is a comfort to have him as an ally."

CHAPTER ELEVEN

HAMILTON HAD to admit one thing—John Adams was a gracious host. The next morning, the entire household rose at dawn. After washing himself and dressing for the day, Alex sat and enjoyed a bountiful breakfast of biscuits, fried eggs, a rasher of bacon, and fresh-picked blueberries. The good cheer of the night before had given way to an easy camaraderie that Hamilton would have thought impossible a week before. The elder Adams was relaxed and garrulous, spinning one story after another, while his son and namesake sat and beamed, watching as his father entertained a man that he had ranted against almost daily for the better part of a decade.

After breakfast, the former President rose and donned his hat, and then retrieved a cane from the hallway, beckoning Alex to join him. Hamilton followed, wondering who it was Adams wanted him to see.

"So, Senator, you believe your life's work is now the abolition of slavery?" the former President asked him.

"Yes, sir," said Hamilton. "I still don't know if what I saw while I was ill was a true vision from the life beyond this one, or a fever dream brought about by my wound, but in any case, it's a worthy cause and I intend to fight for it as hard as I can, for as long as I can."

"If I may make an observation, my young friend," Adams said, wheezing slightly as he set a sprightly pace towards town, "great moral causes are all well and good, but what truly makes men willing to fight—whether it be on the physical battleground, or in the political arena, is when their cause has a human face. Tell me, Senator Hamilton, what is your personal experience with slavery?"

"That question has no short answer," Alex said. "My first experience came as a boy of twelve, after my mother died. She left me her three slaves as part of her bequest to me. They were about all I had, and I made use of their labor because I had little choice. I rented them out to other households to gain enough money to eat. As soon as I was of legal age to do so, I set them free—even as a very young man, there was something about owning another human being that set my teeth on edge. During the war, I worked with my friend John Laurens in his attempt to create an all-black regiment, led by white officers, made up of freed slaves. We were repeatedly stifled by Southern members of the Congress, even though General Washington himself approved the measure. But the idea of an entire regiment of former slaves being given weapons and trained to use them was too frightening for most Southerners to consider. I think many of them would have risked us losing the war rather than lose their slaves."

"I do not doubt it," said Adams. "Here in the north, slaves were always a luxury, an affectation of the wealthy, so it was no great imposition for us to give them their freedom, as Massachusetts did, not so many years ago. But in the South, many depend on slave labor for their livelihood, and it will be much harder for you to persuade men to let go of an institution that lines their pockets and feeds their families."

"I had many conversations with President Washington on this subject," Hamilton said. "He was vexed by the whole issue, and many times I heard him say he wished the first slaves had never been brought here. It seemed as if the longer I was associated with him, the greater his distaste for the institution grew. At the same time, however, he was a Virginia planter and owned three hundred Negroes. He told me that even before the war, he could no longer bear the thought of breaking up families at the auction block. His personal slave, Billy Lee, was with us throughout the entire war, and I know that His Excellency had high regard for his faithfulness and courage. Shortly before I left the administration, Washington told me that he fully intended to free all his slaves in his will, which he did—all the ones that were legally his to free, at least."

"Most interesting, sir. Suppose you are successful," Adams said, "what do you intend to do with these people you have freed?"

"I see no reason why they could not be set to work for wages, and make their lives here," Hamilton said. "I know that there are many who believe that they should be sent back to Africa, or some other tropical clime. Perhaps those who wish to go back should be allowed to do so. But I have never given credence to the idea that Negroes are somehow inherently inferior to whites, and I think with proper opportunities and education that most could acquit themselves admirably."

"You are in a minority in that regard," Adams said. "But I happen to also be a part of that same minority, and I want you to see the reason why here in a moment. Before that, though, I would offer you a few nuggets of advice, gleaned from my own experience. I think that any effort to eradicate slavery must be encouraged at the state level first. If the Federal government tries to force national abolition, much unrest and violence could be the result. You and I both know that the further south one travels, the greater the dependence on slave labor you see. But if you could persuade some of the states of the upper South towards emancipation, it would be a significant first step. Georgia and South Carolina are strongholds of bondage, but I think you could have good success with Virginia and Maryland, if you were cautious and attempted some form of restitution to the slave owners. Perhaps you could also persuade Congress to ban slavery from being established in the new states and territories as well. But above all, be deliberate."

By now the pair had entered the main street of Quincy, and the streets were beginning to fill with busy citizens going about their day's labor. Adams was universally known and respected here; virtually every person they passed tipped their hat and wished the former President a good morning. One or two recognized his companion and greeted Hamilton as well; he was amused at the look of shock on their faces. Apparently, Adams's antipathy to the former Treasury Secretary was well known enough that no one expected to see them strolling down the street together!

Adams led Alex down a side street, and the sound of a hammer busily striking an anvil grew louder and louder. Eventually they paused in front of a blacksmith's shop, where a tall, gray-haired Negro was working on a plowshare, hammering its heated edge into shape. He saw the two white men standing in the door of his shop and set down his hammer, giving a respectful bow.

"Mistuh Adams," he said. "It's good to see you again, suh."

"Good morning, Ajax!" the former President returned. "I have someone here that I would like you to meet. This is Alexander Hamilton, a member of our Senate."

Alex held his hand out, and the blacksmith took it in a grip that was strong, but gentle.

"I am Ajax Smith, suh," he said. "'Tis most good to meet you."

"We here in Quincy like to joke that our blacksmith is both black, and a Smith," President Adams said with a chuckle. "I think you should let this man tell you his story, Mister Hamilton. It is a fascinating tale, and it may give you some food for thought about this mission you have undertaken. I must visit the tailor to see if my new waistcoat is done, and then I shall return to Peacefield. Please join us for the noon meal. Ajax, I leave my friend in your company for now. He is a good man, and you may trust him fully."

With that, the spry old man headed back toward the main street, and Alex was left to size up the man he'd been left with. Smith was tall and broad-shouldered, and his gaze betrayed a keen intelligence.

"If you are willing, suh, why don't you step into mah house and have a cup of tea?" he finally asked Hamilton. "Mah boy Toby can finish up this plowshare."

"I would be delighted to," Hamilton said, and Ajax picked up a bell that sat on the shelf behind his smithy, ringing it vigorously. A young man of twenty or so came in through the back door of the shop.

"What is it, da?" he asked. He had little, if any, of his father's Southern drawl.

"This is Mistuh Hamilton, son, and he is a friend of President Adams," the older man explained. "I am going to take him in the house and have a cup of tea. I want you to mind the forge for an hour; finish out this plowshare and then shape another just like it. Mistuh Bardwell will be pickin' it up in the morning."

"Yes, sir," the youth said. "I shall let you know if I have any problems shaping the iron."

"Come into my house, Mistuh Hamilton—or should I call you Senator Hamilton?" Smith asked.

"I would be perfectly content if you wanted to call me Alexander," Hamilton told him.

"No, suh, it's not my place to call a white man by his first name," Smith said. "That's one of the fust things I learned when I was brought here. You use a white man's given name, you better stick a 'Mistuh' in front of it, if you doan want a whippin'!"

He guided Alexander to the kitchen, where he retrieved two plain but clean teacups from the shelf and filled them both from the pot that was sitting on the corner of the stove. Hamilton took a sip, and then looked across the table at his host.

"Mister Smith," Alex said, "you are a free man in a free state. You can address me however you wish."

The old black man chuckled and looked at Hamilton with a piercing gaze.

"I don't doubt you mean that, Mistuh Alexander," he said, "but suh, you have never been a slave. When they put that collar on you, it's more than just a piece of iron around your neck. It's a chain on yo' soul, an invisible scar that never goes away, even when you leave yo' bondage behind. I been a free man for almost thirty years now, but I still wear it on the inside. The things they done to me—they don't go away, suh, not ever."

"I would be honored if you would tell me your story," Alex said. "How did you come to be here?"

"I was born in West Africa, 'bout sixty years ago, near as I can figger," Ajax told him. "I was a member of the Mende, a large tribe with villages spread all up and down the edge of the jungle. Our village was called Makaha-lorlu. When I was ten, the slave catchers come to our village. They weren't white men, but members of the Ghana tribe that lived on the coast. They had struck a deal with the white folks; they got guns and swords and rum in exchange for slaves that they kidnapped from our territory. The men of our village fought, but several were killed and the rest overwhelmed. I saw my father run through with a sword and fall down; dead as far as I could tell. My mother, brothers, and I were chained together and herded to a place that all of us knew of and feared—a slave fortress on the coast called Elmina."

Hamilton hung his head. As a teenage prodigy in the Caribbean sugar islands, he had managed the books for a large shipping company owned by Nicholas Cruger. He had kept records of the goods Cruger and Beekman traded all over the region—including slaves, purchased from Portugal, who had originally come from Elmina. Even then, he had hated the idea that his employers profited from the horrible Middle Passage, but he had been powerless to do anything about it.

"They kept us in the dungeons of that awful place for weeks," Ajax said. "My brother got a fever and died, and it was three days before the white men came in and hauled his body off. My mother was a pretty young woman; they came and got her most nights and brought her back the next morning, her clothes torn, and her face streaked with tears—and sometimes bruises. Finally, one morning, a ship came. They hauled us out of the dungeon and lined us up, and some rough-looking fellows looked us over and pulled the ones they wanted out of the line. They took my mother and me, but they left my little sister. I never saw her again. When they had about two hundred of us chosen, they herded us into these big rowboats and took us out to the ship. I remember thinking how pretty it was, those great big sails flapping in the breeze, those masts taller than the trees of the jungle. Then the wind shifted and the scent of it hit my nose and I gagged. I was pretty ripe, being locked up in that hot dungeon for three weeks, but that ship put my unwashed smell to shame."

Alex remembered hearing an old sailor on St. Croix tell him as a boy that you could smell a slave ship coming long before you could see it if you were downwind, so strong was the miasma of unwashed bodies, excrement, and despair that soaked into their timbers.

"They brought us onboard and stripped us of all our clothes," the blacksmith continued. "Then they chained us all together and shoved us down below, into that awful smell. The place they put us had such a low ceiling overhead that even at ten years old, I couldn't stand upright without ducking my head. They made us lay down, shoulder to shoulder, almost touching each other, all the way across the compartment. I was in a corner, with the ship's hull on one side and my mother on the other, and a man named Mabuto was just below me, crammed in so close my feet were almost touching his hair. Two hundred people, suh, jammed in there like herring in a barrel, and then they shut the hatch down on us and left us in the dark. There was nothing to do, no place to go, no way to escape. If you pissed, you lay in the puddle. If you shat, you tried to push it out of the way so that you weren't lying in it, but then it got all over yo' hands. Once a day, they opened the hatch and passed down a big bowl of rice and meat. Everyone was supposed to take one handful and pass the bowl down, but we were all starved. Some fought over the food, others took more than they should. My mama and I were close enough to the hatch that there was usually some left in the bowl when it got to us, and we tried to leave some for others. But we were starving by the end of the voyage, and when we got to Charlestown you could count every one of my ribs."

Hamilton was fascinated, despite himself. He had seen slave ships arrive in St. Croix and watched auctions there; he had even bought slaves on behalf of his employers as a young man. He felt a deep sense of shame that he had helped them profit from this hellish business. It must be stopped!

"I don't know for sure how many died, but I do know there were a lot less of us when we finally got to America," he said. "One man, across from my mother, got sick and passed on, and it was two days before they realized he was dead and threw him overboard. God forgive us, we were glad to see them die, for each mouth silenced meant more food for the rest of us! Finally we were unloaded in Charlestown, South Carolina. Of course, I had no idea where I was. They herded us off the ship, and gave us our first real, full meal of hot food since we were taken from our village. They washed us off and gave us some clothes to wear, and two days later we were put up on the block for sale. My mama was bought by some big ole fat man and his wife; I never saw her again, nor heard tell what happened to her. Then came my turn to be sold."

"There was a man in the crowd who had his son with him, boy about my age, and that young lad saw me and pointed. His father bid on me several times, and finally I was sold for the grand sum of twenty-seven dollars. The man's name was Brandon Smith, and his son's name was Lawrence. When they took me off the block, I was skinny, scared, and didn't know a word of English. But they were kind folks, as white folks go. Turned out Mastuh Brandon bought me as a birthday present for young Mastuh Lawrence, and that boy treated me like a pet for a long time. He taught me how to speak proper English, and even started to teach me my letters until his papa caught him at it and gave him a whipping. I can read and write a little bit now, thanks to those lessons. And since I spoke better English than most of the field hands, as I got older, they began training me as a house slave. I was a butler and valet for Mastuh Lawrence as he became a man. When he was twenty, his papa died, and he became the owner of the plantation. He got harder, of course, as he grew up—quit treating me like a pet and made it clear that I was his property. But at the same time, he never beat me and always showed more kindness to me than he did to the field hands. I didn't envy their lot at all, Mistuh Alex. It was only pure chance that I wasn't out there planting and plowing alongside them, and I knew that."

"When I was nearly thirty, my mastuh decided to go north and fight the British and took me with him as his valet. We rode for days and days, and I heard all these white folks talking about how wonderful it was that they would finally be free. I thought that was pure funny, myself, since they was all more free than I was, but I kept my mouth shut. We finally arrived in New York, and Mastuh Lawrence joined up with the Continentals. The war wasn't going so well for the Patriots at that point, and my mastuh was hurt bad covering Washington's retreat at Throg's Neck. I managed to get him to a house that was owned by a Patriot family, and they treated his wounds, but it was no use. He died a week after being shot."

Hamilton remembered the panicked flight across New Jersey in the fall of 1776, when General Howe had inflicted one humiliating defeat after another on the Continental Army before Washington had turned the tide at Trenton. He wondered if he had ever crossed paths with Ajax's former master, and realized it was quite possible.

"On that last day, Mastuh Lawrence was awake, but he was terribly weak. He saw me standing over his bed, and I was crying over him—he was the only master I had ever known, and he was better than most, you see? I honestly had no idea what was going to happen to me next. He looked up at me, and bade me go and get Missus Clements, who owned the house, to bring him a quill and paper."

The old Negro's eyes were misty as he relayed this part of the story, and Hamilton listened intently.

"Mastuh Lawrence looked up at me and said 'Ajax, you have been a good and faithful servant. I go now to a place where slavery is no more, and I have no wish to leave you in bondage. Therefore, in the presence of this witness, I am setting you free. I would urge you to go north, where there are no slaves, so that you may not be forced back into bondage. If you wish, I hope you will take up arms and fight for the Continentals. Perhaps, when this war is over, they will build a country where your people are treated with greater kindness than they have been. That is not for me to know; all I know is, this is the right thing for me to do.' And so he picked up the pen and wrote a few lines on the paper, and asked Missus Clements to sign it as a witness. And just like that, I was a free man."

"We buried Mastuh Lawrence the next day. He had a little bit of gold on him, and Missus Clements gave it to me, along with a little extra from her own purse. She sent me on my way north, but before she did, she spoke to me. 'Ajax,' she says, 'although slavery is legal here, I have never owned a man nor woman, nor do I intend to. I try to be a good Christian woman, and I do not understand how anyone who claims to honor the Golden Rule Jesus gave us can own another human being. Stay free, Ajax, is my best advice to you. Enjoy your life as a free man in some place far from here, where they can never put you back in chains.' I took her advice and fled northward. I didn't know where Massachusetts even was; I just kept asking folks along the way until I got here. I did join the militia and served briefly in the Saratoga campaign under General Gates. I was wounded at Freeman's farm and dismissed from the service, and eventually I found my way here in 1780 or so."

"How did you wind up becoming a blacksmith, if I may ask?" Hamilton queried.

"One thing I found was that, even up here in the free states, many white folks didn't like us Negroes much better than the fellas in the South," Ajax said. "I can't tell you how many inns I was turned away from, how many times I had to defend myself from bully-boys—always afraid I'd get hung for laying hands on a white man, but too proud to give them what was in my pocket just because my skin was darker than theirs. When I came here to Quincy—it was still called Braintree back then—one of the first folks I met was James Finley, the local blacksmith. His boy had joined the Continentals and got hisself killed at the Battle of Brandywine, and so Massuh James had no wife or son. He took a shine to me and asked if I would like to learn his craft, and I said yes, for I had no desire to be a domestic again. He taught me how to work the forge and bellows, and how to shape things out of iron and brass and copper. He told me I was a natural, and in time I became better at smithing than he was. As he got older, he made me his partner, and when he got too old to work as much, I wound up supporting him—the least I could do, since he had given me a trade. I married a seamstress named Anne Beyroud who owned a little shop up the road, and she give me three sons before the cholera took her off five years ago. Mistuh Finley, he died in that same summer, and I been using my forge to support myself and my sons ever since. Folks here have become a might more friendly since I became the only blacksmith in town! President Adams, he is a fine man, sir. He comes into my shop once every week or so and passes the time of day with me just as pleasantly as if I were a white man. All told, Mistuh Hamilton, I have much to be thankful for. I'm a free man with a trade and a house of my own. My boys are all free, and they are right smart young men. Toby is a fine blacksmith, gone be as good as me one of these days! Henry is a tailor—he inherited his mama's skill with a needle, that one did. And James is a sailor on a whaling ship; he's the strongest of the lot and can hurl a harpoon further and straighter than any man on the ship. Yessuh, God's been good to me in my later years."

"What a fascinating story, Mister Smith!" Hamilton said. "Let me ask you something. Would you go back to Africa, if you could?"

"Why on earth would I do that?" the man said. "I've forgotten all but a few words of Mende, my family is all scattered and gone, and the slave catchers still ply their trade all over that region. I have a good life here, and to be honest, I consider myself as American as any white man."

"Do you know what a Senator does, Ajax?" Hamilton asked him.

"Ain't you the folks that make the laws?" Smith replied.

"Correct, sir!" Hamilton said. "What would you say if I told you that I am going to do all I can to end slavery in America?"

"I'd say you be doing the Lord's work, Mistuh Alex, and pray for your success," Ajax said, smiling broadly.

"Here is what I would like to ask you, then," Hamilton said. "What should we do with your people after we set them free? What will they become?"

Ajax thought for a while, furrowing his brow. Finally, he took a long sip of tea and looked at Alex, his keen gray eyes in sharp contrast to his dark face.

"Well, suh, I have actually thought long and hard about that. You see, as I see it, you white folks—you are a lot more grown up than we sons of Africa. You have your engines and your ships and your guns and all your learning, while we still hunt and farm and fish using the same tools and weapons as our ancestors did a thousand years ago. Whether we like it or not, we are like children alongside of you folks. Now that you have brought us here, and taught us your language and your ways, we are your children, whether y'all like it or not. And in answer to your question, Mistuh Hamilton, I would say that we will become whatever you shape us to become. Whether you create us in your own image, or into some dark distortion of what you are—that is up to you."

Alex thought about that conversation for the rest of the day, even over the excellent noon meal that Abigail Adams prepared for the family back at Peacefield. That evening he had a long talk with the former President, and with a couple of the leading Federalist politicians from Boston, who had heard that Hamilton was in town and staying at the house of his former political foe. He shared with them his concerns over the direction slavery was taking the country, and his plans to do something about it. By the time he left Massachusetts, he had garnered several pledges of support and was ready to begin moving toward the next phase of his plan—the presidential election of 1808.

As he prepared to leave Peacefield a few days later, Abigail Adams called him to one side. The matron of the famous family had been rather standoffish during his time there, but now her face was fairly beaming with contentment.

"Senator Hamilton," she said, "I wanted to thank you."

"Whatever for, Mrs. Adams?" he said. "It is I who am indebted to you for your generous hospitality."

"Hatred is a hard burden to bear," she said. "My husband carried it in his heart for many years now, hatred of you, to be precise. The merest mention of your name would sour his mood and any praise of you would send him into fits of rage. It was hard to bear, and hard to watch, for a good Christian man should not harbor hatred in his heart. Coming to him, apologizing to him, and mending your fences with him, as you have done, has taken that load off of him. There is a gleam in his eye and a spring in his step—" She almost seemed ready to say something more but hesitated. Hamilton thought she nearly blushed for a moment. "At any rate," she concluded, "he is a new man, and a happier one, since you came to town. That makes me a happy wife and mother. I thank you for that."

With that, she leaned forward and kissed him on the cheek.

"And as for what you are trying to do for those poor oppressed people in bondage," she said, "I will pray every night for your success."

Hamilton left Massachusetts the next day, ready to go home to Eliza and face the challenges ahead. He felt truly hopeful for the first time since he began his quest. If John Adams, who had hated Alex so much, could become a supporter, surely he could persuade anyone!

CHAPTER TWELVE

1807 WAS A good year for Alexander Hamilton. His trip to New England had brought about reconciliation between that region's branch of the Federalist Party and its New York adherents; he had also reached out through a series of letters to the Southern Federalists, who were grossly outnumbered but still had pockets of strength in some areas, especially South Carolina. Although the Democratic-Republicans still held a strong majority in both houses, Hamilton's tireless efforts had helped the Federalists gain a few seats in both Houses of Congress after the statewide elections were done by midsummer. In the House of Representatives, out of the total of one hundred and forty-two seats, Hamilton's party had gained eight over the previous session, increasing their strength from twenty-six to thirty-four Congressmen. The Senate had been a tougher fight, but two more Federalists had gained seats, and none had lost theirs, which increased the Federalist presence from six to eight. It was a slight increase, but better than the string of losses they'd suffered in the three previous elections.

Congress had begun the year by passing a law banning any further importation of slaves from Africa to the United States. The so-called "Three Fifths Compromise" at the Federal Convention had decreed that twenty years must pass before the trans-Atlantic slave trade could be banned by Congress, although many states had already done so, even in the South. Hamilton strongly supported this bill, but its passage was already virtually guaranteed by President Jefferson's strong approval, so Alex chose not to spend too much political capital on it. He preferred to keep his future plans regarding American slavery concealed until he was in a position to implement them. Still, Hamilton was overjoyed when the bill passed both houses with a minimum of opposition.

After his visit to New England, Hamilton had returned to New York and spent a full two weeks with his family, avoiding political matters altogether. Eliza and the children had often been neglected in previous years, due to the demands of his career. Now he was determined, even in the midst of his new political mission, to make time for them. He read the Bible to his younger children and prayed with them every night, encouraging them in their growing faith. He had long and serious conversations with his two oldest boys, listening to their concerns, offering them council, and encouraging them in their career choices.

He also spent long hours talking and visiting with his oldest daughter, Angelica, named after Eliza's beloved older sister. Angelica had suffered a severe mental breakdown at age seventeen, upon hearing of her favorite brother Philip's death in a duel. She had reverted to a childlike state, her vocabulary and understanding reduced to that of a five- or six-year-old. Despite the fact that she was twenty-one now, she still crawled into her father's lap like a little girl and asked Alex to read to her. Occasionally her eyes showed a flash of understanding as he spoke, but for the most part they remained glazed with a mental fog that completely erased the high-spirited teenager she had once been. Alex kept on trying, though, talking to her patiently and hoping to somehow ease her out of her mental stupor.

But far and away the most enjoyable hours of his homebound vacation were those he spent in Eliza's company. Age had not dimmed the attraction he still felt for his beautiful and intelligent wife, the high-spirited "Betsey" who had caught his eye when he was a handsome young officer on Washington's staff, cutting a wide swath through the young ladies of New York. Hamilton had never regretted marrying her, and he still sought to atone for his affair with Maria Reynolds by showering his wife with attention and affection. In fact, he found himself glad that her middle years had finally arrived; otherwise the inevitable result of their two weeks together might have been another cradle in the nursery! Seven living children were enough for any man, he thought.

All good things must come to an end, however, and as the autumn drew near, public events once more intruded into Hamilton's domestic idyll. The war in Europe was still deadlocked, and one British policy had become a festering sore point in their relationship with the Americans. Desperately short of manpower after thirty years of near-continuous conflict, the British had begun impressing sailors—seizing them and drafting them into service—from American merchant vessels whenever they were shorthanded. Their rationale for doing so was that many of the men they took were deserters from the Royal Navy to begin with, drawn to the American merchant marine by the higher pay and more humane discipline aboard U.S. commercial vessels. How many of those men who deserted were voluntarily serving in the Royal Navy was open to question; but the fact remained that any merchant ship leaving U.S. seaports was liable to be boarded and have crewmembers seized at gunpoint.

Still, merchant vessels were privately owned concerns, and while their owners might protest to Congress, the government was less than eager to stir up trouble with the most powerful nation on earth for the sake of an offended Yankee trader or two. Also, most of the vessels were owned by New England families of Federalist leanings, and the President was a Republican, which made Jefferson even less sympathetic to their losses.

But firing on an American naval vessel constituted an act of war, and that was a line the British had not crossed . . . until June 22, 1807. The USS *Chesapeake*, commanded by Commodore James Barron, was setting sail after a lengthy port visit. Her decks were still cluttered with supplies that had not yet been properly stowed, her guns were unloaded, and she was not battle ready. Less than a day out to sea, British man-o'-war, the *HMS Leopard*, overhauled her and demanded that Barron surrender four sailors who had defected and joined the American navy during the *Leopard*'s recent port call. Barron had refused, and the British vessel had fired a warning shot across the *Chesapeake*'s bow—and then followed it up with a deadly broadside that killed three of the *Chesapeake*'s crew and wounded a dozen others, including the captain. The British were preparing to board the stricken vessel when a second American ship arrived on the scene, the newly commissioned USS *Plymouth*, one of the ships just constructed with funds from Hamilton's naval appropriations bill. She was on her way to conduct gunnery trials off the coast, and her cannon were at the ready. Seeing her fellow vessel in distress, the Plymouth opened fire on the *Leopard* almost immediately.

Caught off guard, the British warship struggled to come about as deadly fire from American cannon raked her deck and rigging. The boarding party rowed desperately to get back to the *Leopard* as the British ship staggered under repeated broadsides and struggled to return fire. After a heated exchange of shot that lasted for the better part of an hour—in which the stricken *Chesapeake* joined after the first thirty minutes or so—the British vessel beat an undignified retreat, with some thirty of her crew dead or wounded.

The *Chesapeake* Incident, as the newspapers dubbed the battle, created a sensation on both sides of the Atlantic. American newspapers crowed over the humiliation of the haughty British, and Hamilton was hailed as a genius for his role in beefing up America's naval defenses. President Jefferson received some praise as well for reversing his policy of downsizing the American fleet, but Hamilton came in for most of the praise, which rankled the President no end. The quick-thinking captain of the *Plymouth*, Elijah Hopkins of Rhode Island, was also feted as the nation's newest military hero.

In England, the unexpected reverse at the hands of the American Navy caused a great deal of anger among the general public, most of whom had never forgiven the United States for winning its independence to begin with. In Whitehall, however, the unexpected clash caused a good deal of soul-searching. The Orders in Council had just been passed by Parliament. This series of trade restrictions on neutral vessels was intended to enforce Britain's blockade of France but had quickly become a festering point of contention with the United States. Now the policy of impressment had further augmented the conflict. The British ministers were arguing back and forth over whether to ramp up the blockade or scale back their demands on France's primary trading partner. In the end, the question facing the Crown was whether they wanted to risk war with the United States, in addition to the ongoing conflict with Napoleon.

Bonaparte, on the other hand, had issued an imperial edict known as the Milan Decree, stating that any foreign vessel that complied with the Orders in Council by stopping in a British port would henceforth be fair game for the French Navy. When it came to foreign trade, the Americans were damned if they did and damned if they didn't!

Britain's new minister to the United States, the Honorable David Erskine, was already en route to his new posting. The new Foreign Secretary, Sir George Canning, sent a courier by the next ship bearing instructions for Erskine to negotiate an accommodation with the Americans if possible. Canning did so, not out of any fondness for the Americans, but rather out of concern for a possible renewal of the old Franco-American alliance. The last thing Britain needed was a war on both sides of the Atlantic!

The Tenth United States Congress was due to convene for its first session of the year in October, and as had become his wont, Hamilton traveled to the capital a month early to get a head start on his plans for the next year. However, this time he would not be staying in Wallace's boardinghouse. He had commissioned the building of a two-story brick home a few blocks from the capitol building, with plenty of room for his family and guests. Alex Junior, now twenty-one, was practicing law in New York after passing the bar exam that spring; his brother James was finishing up his law degree in preparation for joining the profession. But the other five children would be joining Alex and Eliza in Washington City, and all were excited at the prospect, even

Angelica, although she did not seem to understand just how far the journey would be or why they were going.

Eliza and the younger children (as well as Angelica) were making the trip by wagon, along with a couple of household servants, and would take their time along the way, stopping to visit a few old friends. John Church, a lively and active lad of fifteen, and William Stephen, who was only ten but fiercely independent, would be riding ahead with their father to get the house ready. They arrived in Washington City on the third of October after a vigorous thirty-mile ride the last day.

The house still smelled of damp paint and plaster, but most of the furnishings had been delivered, and Hamilton was quite satisfied with its appearance. There was a large dining room and parlor on the first floor, along with a study whose walls were lined with bookshelves on three sides, with a handsome brick fireplace and large windows on the side wall that faced the Potomac. Most of the shelves were still empty, but Hamilton had placed orders at several different booksellers' shops, and Eliza was bringing two crates full of books from his New York residence. All in all, it was a pleasant home away from home, and Hamilton was thrilled at the thought that his work in the new capital would no longer separate him from his beloved wife and family.

He set the boys to work carrying the furniture into the various rooms of the house—most of it had been piled in the front yard or crammed into the parlor—and was enjoying the physical exercise of assisting them. It was a gorgeous fall afternoon, a couple of hours from sunset, and all three of them were struggling to get the massive feather mattress Hamilton had ordered for himself and

Eliza up the stairs when the Senator received his first political visitor of the season.

"Good afternoon, Senator Hamilton!" said a voice from the foyer.

Alex looked over his shoulder and saw James Madison standing there, hat in one hand and cane in the other. He smiled at the sight of his friend and rival framed in the doorway by the slanting light of the westering sun.

"Secretary Madison!" he said. "Forgive me for not shaking your hand, sir, I'm afraid mine are rather full at the moment."

"That's quite all right, Senator," said Madison. "How about if I lend you a bit of assistance?" The diminutive Secretary of State placed his hat on the mantel and leaned his cane on the wall, and then bounded up the stairs to help Hamilton lift the back end of the heavy, floppy mattress. With two people on each end, the job became much easier, and in a matter of moments, the mattress was laid on the bedframe, ready for sheets and blankets to be spread over it.

"Thank you for your help," Hamilton told his guest as they sat on the featherbed to catch their breath. "It's not so much heavy as it is just plain unwieldy and difficult to manage. John, why don't you and William run down to the tavern and fetch us back a chicken or leg of lamb for supper?"

He flipped his sons a silver dollar, and they scampered off together, eager to stretch their legs and explore their new surroundings. Alex smiled as he watched his boys heading out, and then turned to face his guest.

"Well," he said, "what brings the Secretary of State to my home on this fine afternoon?"

Madison hesitated for a moment, with an air of awkwardness that was not normal for him. After a pregnant pause, he spoke.

"The election is a year away, Alex. In all likelihood, one of us two will be the President-elect. We may have our political differences on the proper interpretation of the Constitution, but I do think that it is important for our country to have a consistent message when it comes to foreign policy," he said.

"President Jefferson has not made that easy," Hamilton said. "His hatred of the British and excessive fondness for the French revolutionaries have prejudiced our foreign policy in a way that is contrary to our interests."

"That is why I have come to you without his knowledge," Madison said. "Despite what many say, I am not Jefferson's creature. His friend, yes. His Secretary of State, obviously. But I am my own man, and plan to plot my own course should the electors choose me to succeed him. Part of that course will be to work more closely with those in the opposition in order to strengthen our stances towards the warring powers in Europe. We do not need the British or the French to play Federalists and Republicans against one another to the country's detriment."

"That is an admirable policy," said Hamilton. "And I will pledge to treat you and the other Republicans in government with the same courtesy should the election go my way. We have publicly scourged each other long enough!"

"The new British Ambassador will be arriving in town within the next few days," Madison told him. "I know the demands the

President wishes me to make upon him, in light of the unfortunate *Chesapeake* incident. But I would like to hear your opinion on the matter. What price should we set on continued peace with Great Britain?"

"That is a good question," Hamilton said, "and one that will not admit a brief answer. Let us have a seat and discuss it together."

The family's chairs had already been brought into the house from the front yard, so Alex grabbed two of them and pulled them out onto the expansive porch, arranging them so that the two men could face one another as they conferred. It was a lovely evening; with a light north breeze blowing as the sun settled in the west, and the porch was set far back enough from the road that there was no risk of them being overheard.

"You know that many have accused me of favoring the British overmuch," Hamilton said. "Some have gone so far as to say that I favored a return to the British monarchy itself; others that I desire to set up a copy of it here in America. None of those things are true, of course. No one fought harder than I did to free this country from British rule, and I have the blood of the King's soldiers on my hands to prove it."

Madison squirmed uncomfortably; he was one of the ones who had often accused Alex of being a monarchist and a British sympathizer. In retrospect, he was somewhat ashamed of how far he had let politics color his perception of a man who was a true American patriot—and a war hero in the bargain.

"That being said, England is the world's dominant trading power, as well as the mightiest naval power on earth. I care not,

James, whether the British regard us fondly. But, as a young and militarily weak country, we simply cannot afford to have them become our enemy! Imagine if the British declared war on us, or we upon them, over some mishap at sea. It is true that, right now, they have their hands full with Bonaparte. But in the long term, I predict that he will be crushed. When that happens, if the British are still hostile to us, there is no limit to the damage they could do to our commerce and our coastal cities. It's a short overland march from the mouth of the Potomac to Washington City. Imagine redcoats swarming through our streets, setting fire to our capital, or the British fleet shelling the city of New York and setting it ablaze! I do not think for a moment that we could be reconquered and reattached to the British Empire, but the woe and bloodshed a second conflict with the British would bring on us might set our national growth and prosperity back for decades."

"That is an astute observation," Madison said. "But what about the French? You were friends with Lafayette, and we both know that our independence could not have been won without them."

"I have long loved and admired much about France," Hamilton said. "Because I was fluent in the language, I often acted as an interpreter and unofficial ambassador between Count Rochambeau and General Washington. I got to know many of Rochambeau's officers, and as for Lafayette, he was like a brother to me. Of course, many of the officers I befriended were sent to the guillotine by the Jacobins that you and Jefferson were so enamored of, and poor Lafayette might have shared their fate but for his friendship with our President. That is all immaterial now, but I still think President Washington had it right in his Farewell Address—America cannot afford permanent, entangling alliances with any European power at this time. Free trade with all should certainly be our goal. But we cannot allow ourselves to be drawn into this military cataclysm that is sweeping through Europe."

Madison nodded. He knew, of course, that Hamilton had written most of Washington's last message to the American people. However, he also knew enough of the strange chemistry that had existed between the two men to accept that the address accurately reflected the First President's view of America's diplomatic future.

"So then, what do you think we should do, Alex?" he said. "The British board our ships, they steal our sailors, and they unlawfully restrict our freedom of the seas. As a sovereign nation, we should not allow any power to dictate who we may trade with, don't you agree?"

"In principle, absolutely," said Hamilton. "In practice, however, principles must sometimes bend to practicality. Great Britain is in a life or death struggle with Napoleon's French Empire. It is the greatest military clash in recent history; certainly, the greatest since the Thirty Years' War. Britain commands the seas; America could not hope to challenge her strength were our Navy four times greater than it is. While I certainly believe we should make a principled stand for our rights as a neutral country, I think we should also bow to the reality that those rights may not be perfectly honored during wartime."

He rose and began to pace about as he spoke, warming to his topic.

"As I see it, there are two major points of contention between the United States and the British Empire that could lead us to the brink of war," he said. "The first is the British Orders in Council. The restrictions they place on trade with France are manifestly prejudicial to America's trading rights and to the freedom of the seas. If the British could be persuaded to repeal or at least moderate them, that would be a significant step towards amity between our nations. The second is the policy of impressment of seamen from neutral vessels, especially our own merchant fleet. It is an offense against our national sovereignty and a crime against the American citizens thus forced to bear arms in a fight that is not ours. Its continuance can only result in further incidents like the one involving the *Chesapeake*. What might have happened if there had not been a second warship nearby to offer assistance and drive the British away? An American ship fired on, boarded, its crew fallen prey to English cannon fire, and some of its sailors ripped from under the American flag and forced to serve against their will? There would be a hue and cry for war in this country that the President could not afford to ignore."

"Some would say that such a cry is already in the wind," Madison observed.

"They would be right," Hamilton replied. "But it would be multiplied a hundredfold had the British been victorious. As I have said, those two British policies are the most noxious to America's national honor, as I see it. There are other issues between us, especially near the Canadian border and the forts around the Great Lakes that the British still occupy. But those issues are secondary to the depredations that the British fleet has committed against our maritime interests."

"May I share something with you in confidence?" Madison asked.

"Of course, Secretary Madison," Hamilton said. "I will not hold anything in our private conversations against you if you will return me the favor."

"You have my word on that, sir!" Madison said. "Now, your analysis of the situation is remarkably similar to my own, and that of President Jefferson. Our plan is to push as hard as we can for both a repeal of the Orders in Council, and for a moratorium on impressment of sailors from American ships. Hopefully, the British will be willing to concede on at least one of those points. If they do, then tensions will be eased and both nations can take a step back from the brink of war. However, if the British fail to alter either policy—what next? We cannot afford to declare war, given the state of our military. Even with the enhanced ship-building program in place, we would still look like a gaggle of rowboats in the face of the Royal Navy's full strength."

"I think a considerable increase in the military budget would be in order," Hamilton said. "Congress should vote to increase the Army in size to twenty thousand men and build another dozen warships!"

"Jefferson will not hear of it," Madison said. "He fears the political power of a large army, and the expense of a large fleet."

"I didn't say we should actually build them," Hamilton said. "I said we should vote to build them, a different matter altogether. Preferably, we should do so as soon as the new Congress convenes, while tempers are still hot over the *Chesapeake*. Such a move would impress the British with our resolve; their response would determine whether or not we go through with the plans."

"The President has floated the idea of a complete embargo on all foreign trade should the British fail to see reason," Madison said. "Such an embargo would remove all American commerce from the seas until the British come around. Mister Jefferson hopes that such a move might also compel Napoleon to repeal the Milan Decree, and cause both warring powers to see reason."

"Dear God!" Hamilton exclaimed angrily. "So Jefferson would cut off our trade, not just with the offending French and British, but with the whole world? I tell you, Mister Madison, it never fails to astonish me how a man as intelligent as our President clearly is can be such an imbecile when it comes to matters of trade and finance! Such an action would mildly punish the British while scourging the life blood from America's manufacturing and shipping interests. Does he care nothing for the thousands who would be financially devastated by such a move?"

Madison sighed, weighing how honest he could be with Hamilton. He knew the Alex was a political rival, but despite that, he also had come to have a much greater regard for him over the last year. Jefferson, on the other hand, had lost some of the luster which he once held in Madison's eyes.

The Secretary of State had risked much by coming here, and at this point he decided that if he was in for a penny, he might as well be in for a pound. He looked Hamilton in the eye and told him the truth.

"The President seems to think that only New England shippers would be adversely affected by the decree, and given their implacable political opposition to him, he is not particularly bothered by their economic distress," he said.

"Typical!" snapped Hamilton. "The man is so dedicated to his vision of creating a nation of intellectual farming folk with one hand on the plow and the other holding a copy of Plato's *Republic* that he is blinded to the realities that drive our world. Yes, Boston and Providence are dependent on foreign trade, but so is New York! So, too, are Virginia and the Carolinas. Jefferson is willing to bankrupt half of America to punish the British for their misdeeds. This embargo is a disastrous idea, James. It must not be allowed to go forward!"

At this moment Hamilton's sons returned, carrying a large cookpot wrapped in dishtowels to keep it from burning their hands. As the evening cooled, Hamilton could see the curls of steam coming up from the lid. A delicious aroma tickled his nostrils and set his stomach growling.

"What do we have for dinner, lads?" he asked.

"Boiled ham with red beans and potatoes," said John. "Can we please eat now, Father? We've been smelling it all the way home from the inn, and we're famished!"

"That sounds like a capital idea!" said Alex. "Secretary Madison, please eat supper with us and we can continue our conversation thereafter."

For the next hour politics, British hostilities, and embargoes were forgotten as the four hungry men tucked into the meal with a vengeance. The ham was sweet and tender, the beans savory and rich, and the potatoes had absorbed the flavor of both. The two adults each put away a double helping, and John Church had three. William fell asleep before he could finish his second bowl, and Alex affectionately carried the boy upstairs and laid him out on the big feather bed, easing his shoes off as he did so. He huffed a bit coming back down the stairs; his son was almost too big for Alex to lift anymore.

"John, why don't you go upstairs and read a Psalm before bed," Alex told the older boy, who was yawning loudly. "Mister Madison and I have a few more matters to discuss before I can retire."

"Can't I stay and listen?" the teenager asked.

"Not this time," Alex told him. "Besides, if you nod off, I don't know that I could tote you upstairs like I did your brother, and this couch is not nearly as comfortable as my bed. Go on, now, son!"

John was too tired to argue, so he headed on up, grabbing his father's well-worn King James Bible as he went. Alex watched him go affectionately.

"Your children read the Bible every night?" Madison asked him.

"Of course," said Alex, "as do I. I have always considered myself a Christian, James, but ever since my life was spared three years ago, I have done my best to live every day in a way that God might not regret His decision."

"The President believes that God exists," said Madison, "but he is skeptical of the idea of a personal deity that answers prayers. He sees God as more of the Platonian prime mover than the arch-meddler in human affairs described in the Bible."

"And what do you believe, Mister Secretary?" Hamilton asked.

Madison looked wistful for a long moment, as if recalling some private pain.

"I don't really know," he finally said. "Intellectually, I am more drawn to the idea of an impersonal grand architect who designed this world and set its natural laws in place, then left us in charge of it all. But my heart longs for the God described in the Gospels; a personal Redeemer who can give meaning to this vale of tears which is our earthly journey. I want very much for that God to be real, Alex, but I have a hard time believing in Him."

Hamilton laid a hand on Madison's arm and gave the little man an affectionate squeeze. He could tell there was some deep hurt behind the words the other man had spoken.

"James, my friend, all of our political differences aside, let me tell you this: I have examined the God of the Bible from every angle. Given the evidence of His existence that surrounds us, I can honestly say that if I were sitting on a jury to decide whether or not God is real, my vote would be rendered in favor of His existence," Alex said with conviction.

"Given your legal reputation, that opinion is weighty indeed," said Madison. "Let us discuss the case for divinity another time, however. You were telling me that the embargo plan proposed by Jefferson is a disaster for our nation. I am inclined to agree. But I know the President well, and if the British will not budge, he will put it before Congress, and it will likely pass both Houses. So how can you and I make the British see reason?"

Hamilton leaned back in his chair, steepling his fingers under his chin.

"I think, when His Excellency the new British ambassador arrives in town, you and I should go see him separately," Hamilton said. "You will come in, stern and demanding, making it clear that this insult to the American flag cannot go uncompensated. Lay the administration's demands before him and be inflexible. Then I shall go to him and explain how I believe peace is in the best interest of both our countries and plead with him to see reason and restore amity between our nations. After that, we give him a day or so to reflect on the situation. Perhaps he can go and present his credentials to the President during that time."

"So far, so good," said Madison. "Then what?"

"We go together," Alex said with a smile. "You as the voice of the administration, me as the representative of the loyal opposition. We play off of each other and wring as many concessions as we can out of the man. Between the two of us, we can persuade the British to back down, and avert a war that will be harmful to both countries and beneficial to neither."

"Devious, clever, and possibly an effective solution," Madison said with a grin. "But how on earth can I possibly persuade President Jefferson to let me bring our political nemesis into a confidential meeting between the Secretary of State and the new British Ambassador?"

"That, my friend, I leave to you," Hamilton said. "But I have no doubts as to your resourcefulness! Not to mention, you know the President far better than I, and you stand high in his esteem and confidence. Now, my dear fellow, I am afraid that my eyes are having a very hard time staying open. It has been a long day, and that feather bed is calling my name. Thank you for dining with us, and for seeking my counsel. Regardless of how the election turns out, Mister Madison, I will not forget the consideration you have shown me."

Madison rose and bowed, retrieving his hat and cane from the foyer, and bid Alex a good night. Hamilton watched the little man strolling back up the rutted streets of Washington City, and then headed upstairs. His two boys were sound asleep, William's head resting on his big brother's outstretched arm. There was just enough room for Alex to stretch out on the other side of the bed. Senator Hamilton knelt and said a prayer of gratitude to God for a good day well spent, and then kicked off his shoes, removed his coat, and lay down beside his sons. His eyes were shut within moments, and he fell into a deep and dreamless sleep.

CHAPTER THIRTEEN

"ABSOLUTELY NOT!" Thomas Jefferson's voice was soft, but his anger was plainly written on his normally placid features. "Good God, Mister Madison, have you lost your mind? You want Hamilton to join you in your interview with the British ambassador? Whatever can you be thinking?"

Madison kept his voice calm, but inwardly he was both abashed at the President's reaction, and a little bit angry that Jefferson showed so little trust in his judgment.

"Mister President," he said, "in a year the electors will choose our next Chief Magistrate. Barring any unforeseen developments, either myself or Senator Hamilton will fill that office. If the British think they can get a better deal from President Hamilton than from President Madison, that will motivate them to delay and obfuscate and deny justice to the fallen members of the *Chesapeake* crew. I spoke briefly to Hamilton yesterday, and he and I agree that it is important for America speak with one voice on this issue. If the British know that our demands are not going to change, no matter who the next President is, then they are more likely to resolve the matter quickly—and in our favor."

"That idea is not without merit. But Hamilton is so shamelessly pro-British in his sympathies there is no way he would agree to the hard line that you and I have decided to take with them," Jefferson said.

"Oddly enough, Mister President, I asked Senator Hamilton what he would demand of the British to satisfy the current impasse," Madison said. "I gave him no hint of what you and I had decided on. His position was virtually identical to the one you and I arrived at—they must either repeal or significantly amend the Orders in Council, or permanently renounce impressment. Both actions would be preferable, but if they can agree to even one of them, we can claim a moral victory. If we succeed in achieving some breakthrough there, then we can, perhaps, settle some of the other pressing issues between our nations."

Jefferson looked so surprised that Madison had to suppress a chuckle. The President's eyebrows arched, and his mouth briefly formed into a perfect circle as he softly said "Oh!" After a silence of a half a minute or so, he spoke again.

"Hamilton really proposed the same conditions you and I had agreed to insist on?" he finally asked.

"Virtually the same," Madison said. "He has no interest whatsoever in a war with Great Britain, but at the same time, he cannot abide the thought of America being treated with contempt. He did say that Congress should pass a bill drastically increasing the size of our Army and Navy—"

"Aha!" Jefferson said. "The man is addicted to notions of martial glory; I am sure he wanted to be placed in command of this new army!"

"Actually," Madison said, "Hamilton told me he didn't really want to build the ships or recruit the soldiers, just to give the

British the impression that we were going to do so. Passing the appropriation for them might convince the British we are serious about resorting to force if we must."

"I think the arch-deceiver is working his craft on you, Secretary Madison," Jefferson said. "I cannot perceive any good motive might compel Hamilton to be so agreeable."

"What about simple patriotism?" Madison asked. "Have you ever considered the possibility that Alexander Hamilton might simply love this country he helped create?"

Jefferson looked sharply at his Secretary of State, with several emotions chasing themselves across his face at once. Finally, the President sank into a chair and gestured for Madison to sit as well.

"James, you know that I have sworn before the altar of Almighty God eternal hostility to every form of tyranny over the mind of man," he said. "Tyranny always begins with the concentration of power into the hands of a few. From the moment I met Mister Hamilton, upon my return from France, I saw a dangerously ambitious man whose fascination with banking and manufactures and commerce could have but one result: the creation of an American aristocracy who would lord it over the simple, good-natured farming folk of our nation. Hamilton may not be the out-and-out monarchist I once thought him to be, but his policies will still push the country towards a government far more powerful, far more corrupt, and far more intrusive than any government has a right to be!"

Jefferson paused a moment and took a sip from the cup of coffee that had been cooling on his desk. "You have been my friend, and my closest political ally, for longer than I can remember, James," he continued. "The thought of you succeeding me in the White House warms my heart, assuring me that our Republic will remain in the best of hands when I return to my beloved Monticello. It troubles me to see you becoming so familiar—so friendly even!—with a man as dangerous as Hamilton."

"Your friendship and support mean more to me than I can say, Mister President," said Madison. "And I still hope to succeed you in the presidential chair next year. However, the world is changing all around us. There is no more status quo. Science and industry create new wonders every year, from the French balloon flights that Franklin witnessed in Paris to Mister Fulton's steamboat, and now we see this new proposed device, the locomotive, which will change the world even further! Who knows what will come next? We cannot remain a nation of farmers forever, and I think that our Constitution is strong enough, yet flexible enough, to support a country that is built as much on industry as it is on agriculture. It may well be that Hamilton's vision of our future is a more accurate prognostication than yours or mine."

"I pray you are right," Jefferson said. "About our Constitution being strong enough and flexible enough, I mean."

"I think I am," Madison told him. "But sir, if we have to fight a second war with the British, only thirty years after the first, how far will that set us back? As Hamilton remarked to me, they cannot hope to vanquish us, but they could still do vast damage to our coastal regions. Even the capital would be within their reach! Avoiding war must be our primary objective right now, ahead even of the upcoming presidential contest. Hamilton and I agree on this and want to work together to secure peace. That is not a bad thing for America."

Jefferson stood and paced for a moment, then faced Madison, his feet firmly planted.

"Hamilton has surprised me several times since his near brush with death," he said. "Honestly, I would have thought that his mercurial temper would have brought about his political demise by now. Mayhap he has grown wiser than he once was. Very well, Mister Secretary. If you and Hamilton think you can secure peace with honor from the arrogant British, you have my blessing. But be warned: success or failure, either way, you may have made your path to the presidency more complicated by associating with Hamilton in such a key venture."

"The future of our country is more important than my political ambitions, Mister President," Madison said.

"Just out of curiosity, did you mention my embargo plan to Hamilton?" Jefferson asked.

"I did," Madison replied. "He was not enthusiastic about it, and to be honest, neither am I. I understand your reasoning, but ultimately an embargo would amount to punishing Americans for British misdeeds."

"Well, perhaps if you and Hamilton can make the British see reason, it will not be necessary," Jefferson said.

THE FIRST session of the Tenth United States Congress began with a bang. Passions were still high over the *Chesapeake* incident, and both parties were united in their anger at the British. After the opening ceremonies were done, the House immediately brought up how America should respond to the crisis. Hamilton had consulted with several of the Representatives from his party, and Josiah Quincy of Massachusetts had agreed to be their spokesman. He asked to be recognized as soon as the gavel sounded.

"The Speaker recognizes the distinguished gentleman from Massachusetts," Speaker Joseph Varnum announced.

"Thank you, Mister Speaker," Quincy began. "As we all know, the impressment of American sailors has been an insult to our flag and our sovereignty for a number of years now. Thousands of Americans have been taken against their will and forced to fight, bleed, and die under the British flag. Now we see the ultimate insult—one of our own naval warships attacked by a British man-o'-war! Had the *Plymouth* and her brave captain not been on hand to render aid, the *Chesapeake* might well have been boarded and several of her crew kidnapped. I offer the congratulations and thanks of the House, and of the people of Massachusetts, to Captain Elijah Hopkins and his sturdy crew!"

Cheers and huzzahs greeted these words; Republican or Federalist, the whole country had celebrated Hopkins's victory at sea.

"But it is clear to me now, Mister Speaker," Quincy went on, "that the British do not respect or fear us. Why? Because they regard us as weak! Captain Hopkins may have begun to change that opinion, but I think we need to send a clear message to London that America will not be treated as a second-rate power. Our citizens are not to be a recruiting ground for the naval forces of our enemies! I propose a new appropriations bill to increase the size of the army to twenty thousand men, and to build another dozen warships, just as strong and well-armed as the *Plymouth*!"

The Congressmen sat stunned for a moment. America's entire naval fleet stood at twenty warships, thanks to Hamilton's new ship building program, with three more scheduled for completion in the next year. Another dozen ships would be a huge expense, not to mention tripling the size of the army. But it was the perfect moment to introduce such a resolution: the country was sick of British depredations on its shipping, and exultant that a blow had been struck in return. After Quincy's words had a moment to seek in, Congressman Nicholas Gilman, a Republican from New Hampshire, leaped to his feet to second it. Suddenly the House was filled with clamor as everyone wanted to speak in favor of the new bill. The Speaker rapped his gavel sharply several times to restore order.

"Representative Quincy, have you already drafted a bill incorporating these ideas?" he asked.

"I have, sir, and I have included a series of taxes to help cover the necessary appropriations," he said.

"Then I suggest we refer it to the Ways and Means Committee for a quick and judicious hearing," Speaker Varnum said. "Given the urgency of the situation, I think we can bring it up for a vote by the end of the week."

ON THE OTHER end of the capitol building, Vice President Clinton had just gaveled the senior house of America's legislative branch into session. Once the invocation was said and the new members were recognized, Hamilton stood and asked to speak. Clinton grudgingly recognized his old rival.

"Distinguished colleagues," he began, "this summer's episode at sea underscores once more the peril to America's trade posed by the ongoing war in Europe. As they build up their naval and land forces to oppose Napoleon Bonaparte, the British also extend their dominance over global trade. While I recognize the importance of our trade with England to the health of the American economy, I cannot abide to see my beloved adopted homeland treated with contempt by any nation, however mighty her fleet might be. The British thought that they could fire on the *Chesapeake* and board her at will, kidnapping men who were serving under the American flag and forcing them into servitude in the Royal Navy! They cleave to the notion that might makes right, and that their naval power gives them the authority to deal with the rest of the world however they wish. Well, Captain Hopkins and the crew of the *Plymouth* proved them wrong!"

The gallery erupted with applause, and the Senators roared their agreement. A few New Englanders looked askance at Hamilton's abuse of the British, but popular opinion was with him. He waited for the noise to die down, and then spoke again.

"But, gentlemen, we cannot become complacent. Captain Hopkins and his crew came to the rescue this time, but the fact remains the British have some six hundred ships in their fleet, while we have twenty-three—or will have, when the last few frigates now under construction are launched. Our army numbers less than five thousand. Should the British turn the full fire and fury of their military against us, we would be facing a long and dreadful war against a seasoned opponent," Alex said. "I doubt not that we would eventually be victorious, for our land is vast and our people numerous. But what would be the cost? As Doctor Franklin was fond of saying, an ounce of prevention is worth a pound of cure. Even as I speak, the House is drafting a bill enlarging our Army to twenty thousand men and increasing our fleet by another dozen vessels. I have often remarked that the one thing the British respect is strength. We may not be wealthy enough to match them ship for ship, but a new military building program would, at the very least, show them that we mean business when it comes to protecting our coast. Let us show the British, and the world, that we will defend our flag to the death if need be! For it may be that, if they see our willingness to fight, they will think better of their current policy of endless provocations and insults!"

The Senate applauded Hamilton's motion, and immediately sent to the House for a copy of the bill that Representative Quincy had drawn up. The *Chesapeake* incident had, at least temporarily, smoothed over some of the partisan divide in Washington and created a sense of unity greater than any the nation had experienced since the Quasi-War with France a decade earlier.

ONE SPECTATOR who did not get caught up in the patriotic fervor was the new British ambassador to the United States, Baron David Erskine. Erskine had lived in the U.S. briefly, after the Revolutionary War, and his lovely wife, Frances, was the daughter of an American general, Thomas Cadwalader. He was rare among British aristocrats in that he bore a genuine affection for this young nation; he might deplore the Americans' manners at times, but he admired their ambition, patriotism, and love of liberty. This attitude had set him at odds with the Foreign Minister George Canning, who seemed to have a visceral loathing for all things American and more than once had chided Erskine for "marrying beneath his station."

However, Canning was under pressure from the Prime Minister and from the Prince of Wales to avoid any major conflict with the Americans while the war with Napoleon was still ongoing. Erskine had been ashore in New York for only a few days, discussing the latest developments with the British diplomats in the city, when a fast merchant ship had conveyed a letter from Canning himself with additional orders. It read in part:

> *Given the unfortunate episode involving the HMS* Leopard *and the American vessels* Chesapeake *and* Plymouth, *the Ministry and the Crown have determined that it may be necessary to offer some concessions to the American government to avoid an armed conflict or a damaging trade embargo. While no agreement can be finalized without approval from the Ministry, it may be necessary to offer substantial amendment, or a full retraction of the Orders in Council issued earlier this year. The Americans will doubtless demand a repeal of our policy of pressing sailors into service from their merchant vessels, an alternative which the critical manpower shortage in the fleet should render a last resort only. But for the moment, the Crown considers the preservation of the peace to be of the highest priority. Give as little ground as possible while still satisfying American honor—let that be your guiding policy.*

As Erskine listened to the raucous cheers coming from the Senate gallery every time Britain was denounced, he feared that he might have to give more ground than Canning had authorized. But the thought of preserving the peace with his loud, rowdy, but somehow endearing American friends was an encouraging one. He quietly slipped out of the Senate gallery and made his way to the British consulate and began organizing his thoughts into a written list of proposed negotiating points.

He was not really surprised when he received a notice the next morning that the American Secretary of State was waiting to see him. He knew that passions were running hot throughout the country, and both political factions were anxious to resolve the impasse in a way that accrued to their political benefit. He told his secretary to see the American diplomat in.

Erskine rose as the Secretary of State entered his office. Madison was a tiny man, he realized—they had never formally met, although Erskine had seen him once at a distance before. The American diplomat barely stood five foot four and was so slight in build that Erskine doubted he weighed more than a hundred pounds. But his eyes were keen, his gaze sharp, and his handshake firm. The British minister realized that he was facing off against a formidable intellect—he had read *The Federalist Papers* and knew that Madison had written many of them.

"Baron Erskine," said Madison. "I trust your voyage from England was a smooth one."

"I've traversed the Atlantic several times, Mister Secretary," Erskine said, "and this passage was by far the best in terms of weather. I wish that our political climate was as sunny and agreeable."

"Perhaps we can secure that," Madison said. "This is the message I was instructed to bring from the President of the United States to His Majesty's government: *The attack on the USS* Chesapeake *was an act of war against a neutral country in violation of all maritime law.*

The United States has observed a policy of strict neutrality in the ongoing conflict between the government of Great Britain and that of the French Empire, but we have been repaid only with economic sanctions and now cannon fire. If His Majesty wishes for the United States to remain at peace with Great Britain, then we ask for the following concessions to be made: First, the Orders in Council promulgated earlier this year should be repealed; preferably in their entirety. At the very least the United States merchant fleet must be specifically exempted from the sanctions imposed by them. Secondly, the policy of impressing sailors from American vessels must cease. It is a moral offense for you to force our citizens to bear arms under a foreign flag to settle a quarrel that is not their own, not to mention the act of boarding a neutral flagged vessel and stealing its crew is little more than piracy hiding behind the flag of the British Empire. These are our capital demands; however, if Great Britain wishes to be assured of the good will of the American government above and beyond peaceful coexistence, then the continued occupation of the fortresses near the Great Lakes—which Britain promised to abandon in the Treaty of Paris of 1783—would be a good place to start. Also, a moratorium on the sale of muskets and tomahawks to the frontier tribes, who use them to commit murder and mayhem upon America's farmers and frontiersman, would do much to enhance good will and friendship between our people. I anxiously await the reply of His Majesty's government."

Erskine swallowed hard. The Americans were pressing for more than he had been authorized to give up, and he hoped that Madison was only using them as a starting point.

"This is quite the list," he said. "I am not sure I can yield so many concessions. Will you give me an opportunity to review this in writing?" he asked.

"Of course," Madison said, reaching into his waistcoat and pulling out an envelope. "Take your time and consult with your government if you must, but this issue needs to be settled, the sooner the better!"

"I will do what I can," Erskine said. "I believe that peace between us is in the best interest of both our nations. Thank you for coming to see me so soon, Mister Secretary. Tell President Jefferson I look forward to presenting my credentials as soon as possible."

After Madison bowed out, Erskine sat and read the document the Secretary had left him very closely. It was clear and simple and left little room for negotiation, so he knew he would have his work cut out for him to avoid giving up more than his brief authorized him to yield.

He asked for a cup of hot tea and a poached egg to nibble on as he compared Madison's list of demands with his own list of possible concessions, trying to find a middle ground between the two. Barely an hour had passed since Madison's departure when his personal secretary, a gaunt lad named David Collins, informed him that he had another visitor. Erskine read the calling card and smiled at the familiar name: *Senator Alexander Hamilton, late Major General of the Federal Army, and former Sec. of Treasury, Esquire.*

While he and Madison had been virtual strangers, Erskine had met Hamilton at the home of his father-in-law, General

Cadwalader, several years before. Cadwalader and Eliza Hamilton's father, Philip Schuyler, were old comrades from the Revolution and often visited each other. Alex had been at the height of his reputation that year; his financial plan had restored America's failing credit virtually overnight, and his epic battles with Jefferson over the proposed national bank were the talk of New York. The British ambassador had been deeply impressed with the dapper, brilliant Hamilton and looked forward to seeing him again. He stood to greet his guest as he heard the man's steps briskly ascending the stairs.

"Alexander Hamilton!" he said with a smile. "Or should I say, Senator Hamilton these days! You've created quite a stir, sir. Many are saying you just might be the next President."

Hamilton gave a polite bow. His hair was grayer than Erskine remembered it, and his waist maybe a tad thicker, but his eyes still shone with radiant energy.

"Well, good afternoon to you, Baron! I hope enough people say that over the next year to persuade our electors," Hamilton said. "But that will be as it will be."

"I won't deny, Alex—if I may be so bold as to call you that— there are many in Whitehall who would prefer to see you as the next Chief Magistrate over Madison," Erskine said.

Hamilton raised an eyebrow and smiled.

"Don't breathe a word of that to my countrymen," Hamilton said. "Too many already believe I am an agent of the Crown as it is!"

"So what can I do for New York's favorite son today?" asked Erskine.

"Listen to my government on the *Chesapeake* business," Hamilton said bluntly. "No one is more aware than I am of the importance of having good trade relations with Great Britain, but your captain's foolishness has brought us to the brink of war—a war that will be disastrous for both our countries! We both know that England was in the wrong in this whole affair; a simple admission of guilt and a few gestures of conciliation will accrue to the benefit of both our nations. You do not need a war with America while you are still fighting against Bonaparte and his legions, and America does not need the interruption of our national progress that a war with Great Britain would entail."

"I cannot argue with your summation of affairs," said Erskine. "But have you seen what Jefferson is demanding? It is outrageous; an affront to our national honor!"

"As much as, say, having one of your warships abruptly fired on and nearly boarded by a nation with whom you were not at war?" Alex asked.

"Point taken, Senator," Erskine said grudgingly. "But I do not think the Ministry will agree to Jefferson's demands."

"I am guessing that the two principle demands are the Orders in Council and the issue of impressment?" Hamilton said.

"Have you seen Jefferson's manifesto?" Erskine asked, his eyes narrowing.

"I am not President Jefferson's friend or ally," Hamilton said. "But it does not take a medium to divine the major points of contention between our nations."

"Those are the main points," Erskine said. "There are other issues, but those two are forefront in the President's list of demands."

Hamilton nodded and looked the British Ambassador directly in the eye.

"If you would like my advice," he said, "I think that if you were to yield completely on one point, and partially on the other, and throw in another concession from further down the list of priorities, you might find Jefferson willing to make a bargain. A bad bargain is better than the best war, Baron. I have fought the British Empire once and have no desire to do so again. But just so we understand each other—my loyalties lie with my country, not yours. If it comes down to it, you will find me a formidable foe, whether as Senator or President."

"Since you mention it, Senator—if, perchance, you should be the next President, do you think you might offer my government slightly better terms?" Erskine said.

"When it comes to matters of our national honor and pride, sir, America speaks with one voice," Hamilton said. "You would do better to settle this matter now rather than let it fester for another year."

Erskine nodded. He had not expected any different answer but figured that asking would do no harm.

"Well, Senator, it is a delight to see you again," he finally said. "I thank you for your advice and your candor."

"And it is a pleasure to renew my acquaintance with you, Baron Erskine," Hamilton said. "My wife is still en route to Washington, but I have settled into a new home here in the city. Would you consent to be my guest tomorrow evening for dinner? The boardinghouse down the road grills an excellent lamb, and I would enjoy the conversation. I might invite another guest or two; men whose goodwill would serve you well."

"I should be delighted, my dear sir," said Erskine. "I've heard that the chef here at the consulate is not a very good cook. Rumor has it that his mission in life is to combine the worst aspects of British and American cuisine."

Hamilton winced at that thought, and then gave Erskine a wink.

"I think that I can do your palate more justice than that," he said. "How does six o'clock tomorrow sound?"

"Most excellent," said Erskine. "I shall see you then."

THE FOLLOWING day Erskine had the embassy's carriage, an elegantly appointed vehicle that looked out of place in the rough and tumble, stump-studded streets of the young American capital, take him to Hamilton's home. The house was newly painted and handsome in appearance. Granted, it was comparable to a country squire's summer cottage in England, but Erskine was not as addicted to the trappings of wealth and privilege as his predecessor, Sir Anthony Merry, had been. He could see the oil lamps shining through the windows of the house; as the weather had taken a sharp turn for the cooler that day, they made for a welcome sight. He ascended the steps and rapped sharply on the front door, watching the vapor of his breath hang in the air before him.

Alexander Hamilton opened the door himself, impeccably dressed in formal dinner attire.

"Good evening, Baron Erskine," he said. "Please come in and let me introduce you to our other guests. James Madison, our Secretary of State, you already know. This"—he gestured to a tall, red-headed gentleman at the head of the table—"is President Thomas Jefferson."

Erskine's jaw dropped and remained open long enough that a convoy of flies could have flown down his throat.

"Let's have dinner, shall we?" Hamilton said with a smile and conducted his surprised guest to the table.

CHAPTER FOURTEEN

FROM THE *New York Daily Post*, dated January 5, 1808:

PEACE!!!

SENATOR HAMILTON'S DIPLOMATIC COUP

DINNER PARTY SECURES BRITISH CAPITULATION

A secret meeting between President Jefferson and the British Ambassador, Baron David Erskine, was facilitated by New York's own Senator and favorite son last month. With Alexander Hamilton acting as their go-between, the President and the Ambassador were able to come to an agreement on several issues, most notably the odious Orders in Council, which had brought our two nations to the brink of war even before the dastardly British attack on the USS Chesapeake last fall. While the British ministry has yet to approve the measures, the Baron has placed his personal honor on their endorsement by the Ministry and Parliament. The threat of war has been averted by the diplomatic genius of our beloved Senator and the next President of the United States, Alexander Hamilton!

In the first major concession, the British have agreed to exempt all U.S.-flagged vessels from the Orders in Council of April 1807. This will free American merchantmen to trade with both France and Great Britain, as well as the other nations of Europe, whether they are at war or peace with each other, without fear of interference from the Royal Navy. The issue of impressing American sailors into the British fleet, which has also vexed our relations over the last twenty years, has been settled by compromise. The British may no longer board American ships at will to seize members of their crew for involuntary service in the Royal Navy. However, American merchant captains and ship owners will be forbidden by Federal law from knowingly hiring British deserters. In cases where an American crewman's citizenship is disputed by the British, a joint committee of officers from the American and British navy will hear the evidence and have full authority for binding arbitration.

In one final concession, the British have placed a moratorium on the sale of tomahawks and muskets to the Indian nations along the Canadian border. This will do much to spare the residents of the region the fury of the savage tribes that have ravaged our frontier in the decades since the War of Independence reached its conclusion.

The ongoing British occupation of frontier forts in the Great Lakes region of America is now the last remaining point of contention between our governments. Ambassador Erskine is confident that this issue can also be negotiated now that the immediate threat of war between our nations has receded.

While President Jefferson's administration is scrambling to claim credit for this remarkable diplomatic coup, our sources inform us that the driving force behind it all was our own Senator ALEXANDER HAMILTON, with the cooperation of Jefferson's Secretary of State, James Madison. New York hails its favorite son, who has once again justified the trust our legislature placed in him when they elected him Senator. It is our confident hope that the nation's electors will bestow an even greater trust upon him in the next year.

From the *National Republican Patriot*, dated January 7, 1809:

PEACE AGREEMENT REACHED!
PRESIDENT JEFFERSON'S GREAT BARGAIN
SECRET MEETING AT SENATOR HAMILTON'S HOUSE

Our beloved President has secured peace in our time after a long series of meetings with the British ambassador, David Erskine. Beginning with a secret meeting in the home of his well-known critic, Senator Hamilton of New York, which our sources say was arranged by Secretary of State James Madison, the President and the British Ambassador, Baron David Erskine, came to a series of agreements on the issues that had brought America to the brink of war with Great Britain. Secretary Madison and the Baron drew up a formal document outlining the compromises between our nations, which has

Lewis Ben Smith | 239

now been forwarded to the British ministry with the Ambassador's strongest approbation.

The points of agreement include the exemption of U.S. merchant vessels from all restrictions imposed by the Orders in Council of 1807, and a ban on Royal Navy vessels boarding U.S. ships to impress sailors into service—in exchange for which a new Federal law will impose strict penalties on any American merchant who hires deserters from the British fleet as sailors . . . .

This remarkable resolution of a conflict which might have easily become a war is entirely due to the diplomatic genius of President Jefferson and his loyal Secretary of State, James Madison; some minor thanks are perhaps due to New York Senator Alexander Hamilton for hosting the initial meeting in his home . . .

With the announcement of the new accord between the USA and the British, the presidential campaign of 1808 was launched. Both parties scrambled to claim credit for averting a war; and newspapers on both sides lauded praise on their chosen favorite and did their best to minimize the contributions of the other party. The facts, however, tended to support Hamilton's side—it was hard for the Democratic-Republicans to explain away his hosting the dinner party that had led to the breakthrough. The Federalist Party, which had been teetering on the brink of obsolescence, was once more a major player in America's political arena, with some prominent Republicans defecting to its ranks and many prodigals returning to the fold.

For Alex and for James Madison, it was an awkward season, both politically and personally. It was customary for a man who was being promoted as a presidential candidate to remain publicly indifferent to his chances, and openly campaigning for the office had been looked down upon since the foundation of the Republic. Yet, at the same time, that tradition was fraying. More and more states were allowing a popular vote to determine who their electors would support, and the voters wanted to know why they should choose one candidate over another. An increasing number of them wanted to hear it from the candidates personally; however, any such open appeal to the voters could still be taken by the other side and used against the candidate who made it. Presidential politics was becoming a populist game, but still retained some of its elitist traditions.

In the previous three election cycles, vicious partisan attacks had been the order of the day. John Adams had been vilified as a monarchist, a madman, and a seducer of young women (a mental picture which still made Hamilton shake his head and chuckle), while Jefferson had been decried as a radical Jacobin, a populist demagogue, an enemy of Christianity, and a ravisher of helpless slave women. Since Alex and James Madison had developed a solid working relationship as well as a rekindled friendship over the last year, each of them tried to rein in the worst personal attacks from their party's newspapers. But such efforts at moderation met with mixed success at best: partisan hatred and exaggeration had already become a well-established national tradition.

With the reduced threat from Great Britain, the proposed increases in military spending had been drastically scaled back by the Congress, but in February Alex had a chance to speak out in the Senate on the condition of America's naval fleet, and in the process he addressed the political choices facing the nation that fall.

"It is true," he said, "that our renewed peaceful relations with Great Britain—assuming their Ministry does indeed approve the agreement we signed with Baron Erskine last month—have greatly reduced the chances of a war between our two nations. However, we cannot lose sight of the fact that there is still a titanic struggle going on in Europe, a struggle which will shape the course of the current century. I do not think it would be wise to completely abandon our plans to augment our national defenses, especially with regards to our fleet. A strong fleet is the best guarantor of free commerce—and of a free nation!"

Alex paused, looking over the Senate chamber. He had done his best to make friends of the members there, and he had largely succeeded. There were still a few inveterate Hamilton-haters, and Vice President Clinton was one of them. But Alex could now count on all but the most partisan Republicans to listen when he spoke, and to give his words some consideration. He had worked carefully on this speech for the previous two nights, going over its paragraphs again and again, crafting his prose to hit exactly the right note.

"President Jefferson is a man of prodigious intellect—in fact, he may well be the most intelligent man our young nation has ever produced. But no mind, not even his, can encompass a full understanding of every aspect of human endeavor, unless it be that of our Creator Himself. I have enjoyed many a pleasant evening in the President's company and have heard him hold forth on a variety of topics with remarkable expertise. However, in my long association—and occasional rivalry—with him, both during our mutual service in President Washington's cabinet and since, I have noticed that there are two areas in which Mister Jefferson's mastery of mysteries falls short. One is in the military arena, especially naval armaments; the other is in the field of finance and banking, where I have demonstrated some small expertise. These are critical weaknesses for any man who seeks to be the Chief Magistrate of a great nation, and frankly, the President's shortcomings in those two areas brought us to the brink of war. In his intemperate haste to pay off our national debt—a debt which was already shrinking at a steady rate and would have been gone by the end of the next decade!—the President virtually demobilized our Army and worse yet, in the face of a European war of massive proportions, gutted our fleet!"

Federalist Senators applauded, as did some of the witnesses watching from the gallery. A few Republicans ruefully nodded, others scowled, and one or two jeered Hamilton's jabs at the President.

"Do not misapprehend me," Hamilton continued after a moment. "This is not intended to be an attack on our President, but rather a caution to our nation. The reason for President Jefferson's ignorance of these topics is quite simple—while he has admirably served our nation in many capacities during his long and illustrious career, that service has never been of a military nature. A general who has commanded in peacetime and wartime understands the necessity and use of force on a far more intimate basis than a scholar and statesman, since he has been on both the giving and receiving end of such force! A successful general must be a good diplomat, a strong economist, a strategic thinker, and a political compromiser all at the same time. In a free nation such as ours, the general must be able to work with and at the same time be submissive to the Congress. He must inspire men with his example rather than coerce them through fear, for that is the chief tool of despots. All of these are the reasons why His Excellency General Washington was the indispensable man, not only of our Revolution, but of our Republic's formative years. He combined all the qualities of a great general and a great statesman, and his mastery of those attributes has left both of his successors struggling to live up to his noble example."

Hamilton was on safer ground here, and his fellow Senators applauded his remarks. The reverence for Washington had grown, rather than diminished, in the eight years since the first President's death. People forgot about the ugly political battles and infighting that had marked the great man's second term in office and remembered instead his essential nobility and goodness and love of country, and both parties hailed him as the father of the young republic. But now Alex was coming to the crux of his speech, and once more he silently prayed for guidance.

"Gentleman of the Senate, bear with me for a moment as I speak from the heart. I love this country of ours—perhaps more so than most of you, even. For you see, nearly all of you had the privilege of being born here, in this land that was founded on a love of liberty and natural rights. I was born far away, in circumstances far from comfortable, orphaned and abandoned at a young age. In any other land, I would have been discarded and left to a life of poverty and obscurity. But on these blessed shores I found a home. I found a land that would give opportunity to one like me; to let me rise up and have a voice among the councils of the great. I was allowed to use my meager talents for the betterment of this fair land, and it was and is an opportunity for which I shall be eternally grateful. Nowhere else would a story like my wildly improbable autobiography have been possible! So, when I say I love this land, I love it as only an orphan child can love the parent who adopted them and lifted them from the sink of despair to walk in the broad, sunlit uplands of hope."

The Senate fell silent, and a few of its members even appeared to be on the verge of weeping. Federalist or Republican, one thing they all shared was a common love of country. Hamilton had always been a magnificent orator, and now he was pulling out all the stops as he reached his peroration.

"This fall our electors face a grave choice. They will choose a new President, one who will lead our noble Republic into the next four years of its history! We have survived the leadership of Thomas Jefferson for nigh on eight years now, but that time has not been without great danger and great risk, danger that was exacerbated by the weaknesses previously mentioned. I would simply ask the people of all the states, north, south, and west alike, to charge their electors with placing our nation in the best hands possible. To do that, perhaps they could look to none other than George Washington as their guiding star. Who among us would lead in a manner most like His Excellency? Who has the common experiences of military leadership, financial expertise, skill in diplomacy, and political acumen? Those are the questions that must guide our nation as we choose our next Chief Magistrate. I pray that God will guide each elector as they cast their ballot, and whomsoever they choose, I pray that the same Divine favor that has attended us in all our struggles thus far will rest upon him as well."

The Federalists in the Senate leaped to their feet in a standing ovation as Hamilton returned to his desk; he acknowledged their cheers with a polite bow before resuming his seat. Many Republicans also applauded, although Hamilton's most notable foes looked sourly at the New Yorker. Several newspaper reporters had been in attendance, frantically scribbling down Hamilton's words as he spoke, and they quickly exited after he was done, eager to get the speech into the next day's editions.

Reviews were generally positive in the newspapers of both political factions. Hamilton had never directly referred to his own candidacy, and there was so much common sense and patriotism in what he said that only the most virulent partisans could find fault with the speech. Federalist newspapers in all seventeen states printed the speech verbatim and praised Hamilton's rhetorical skills, while also pointing out that no one met the qualifications he listed for the next President better than the former Treasury Secretary himself. Republican newspapers varied widely in their approach; many praised Hamilton's patriotism while pointing out his various shortcomings and questioning whether he met his own enumerated qualifications to be President. Others blasted the speech as a thinly disguised bid for power that violated the sacred tradition against any man openly seeking the highest office in the land.

In 1808, states chose their presidential electors in a variety of ways. In seven states, the state legislature picked the electors; in ten, the adult male population would vote for them. Six of those states awarded their electoral votes to the winner of a statewide popular vote, while the other four split them according to the winner in each congressional district. It was a complicated process, overall, and a difficult one to track. Since by law the President and Vice President could not be from the same state, any elector who voted for Hamilton would be unable to support Vice President Clinton's reelection. Hamilton asked his Senate colleague John Quincy Adams if he would consider serving in the nation's second office as his unofficial running mate, and the former President's son gladly acquiesced.

Madison was a retiring man by nature, and not very skilled in the hurly-burly of electioneering. He continued to work, quietly and competently, at the State Department, while President Jefferson wrote letters to a wide network of Republican operatives—state legislators, newspaper editors, local officials, and others, promoting the Secretary of State's candidacy. But the formidable Jefferson machine was not the juggernaut it had been in 1804; Hamilton's dazzling successes and the renewed energy of the Federalists pushed back hard against the Republican editorials and speeches.

All eyes were on South Carolina, where the state legislature would be the first to choose presidential electors in October. Once a Federalist stronghold, the state had seen Jefferson win all ten of its electoral votes in 1804, even though the Federalist candidate, Charles Cotesworth Pinckney, had been a native son. But the unpopularity of Jefferson's foreign policy had weakened the Republican hold, and the state was generally considered to be a toss-up in 1808.

Pinckney was a member of the state legislature and was the strongest voice in the Federalist delegation. He was also a lifelong friend and ally of Alexander Hamilton, who had supported both his presidential bids in the past. As the members of the Assembly prepared to cast their vote for the presidential electors, Pinckney rose and asked the Speaker for permission to address the House. After being recognized, he stood and faced his colleagues.

"Distinguished gentlemen of the South Carolina General Assembly," he said. "This is an auspicious moment. We are the first in the nation to choose the Electors who will choose our next President. This is not a time for partisanship, my friends. Federalist, Republican—has not our own President said that they are but different names for 'brethren of the same principles'? Today is not a day to think of parties or patronage or any of the other things that normally dominate our nation's political processes. I would challenge all of us to think of one thing and one thing only as we cast these ballots—and that is, who is best qualified to lead our country during these challenging times?"

"Having been a candidate for the nation's highest office twice, I know full well the passions that can stir us at such moments. But I want to speak to you today, not as a Federalist, nor as a politician, but as an American patriot, a veteran of our Revolution, and as a friend of the men who created this country."

Pinckney stood and began to pace across the State House, his ringing voice carrying to the furthest corner of the chamber. Friends and foes alike were mesmerized by the golden oratory of the famous Revolutionary general and statesman.

"I will speak no ill of Secretary Madison," he said. "I have known him, both socially and professionally, for many years. He is an erudite scholar in the arts of government and a skilled negotiator. If any man can lay claim to the title 'Father of our Constitution,' it is he. I have no doubt that, if elected, he will serve to the best of his ability as our next Chief Magistrate. Indeed, I think he carries more and better qualifications to the office than did his predecessor.

"However," he continued, "I would like to say a few words about my friend and colleague Senator Hamilton. Hamilton is, like Secretary Madison, an expert in law and civics, and has shown himself to be a remarkably skilled diplomat. However, in other areas of expertise, he exceeds James Madison as the noonday sun exceeds the light of the full moon! I tell you, there is no man in America who better understands the world of trade and finance than our former Treasury Secretary. Our public credit was as a moldering corpse, and he breathed into its nostrils the breath of life and today America's notes will carry with any bank in the world. Not only that, no man alive better understands the military arts than does Hamilton. When we served together during the late Revolution, he could, with equal skill, lead a bayonet charge against a British redoubt or tally up the exact amount of money, weapons, and material that would be needed to field the companies, brigades, and regiments that made up our Army. His grasp of such details was truly breathtaking! There is simply no man in America today more skilled in all the necessary arts of governance than Senator Hamilton, and none who would more ably carry out the duties of President of the United States."

He surveyed the House gravely, and then delivered his final argument.

"But, as Senator Hamilton himself suggested, perhaps we should look to our First President for guidance as we deliberate today. I knew George Washington well; like Hamilton, I was a member of his military family for a time, and afterward I was entrusted with a command of my own. I also served as a diplomat during His Excellency's term as President. I had the opportunity to watch him interact with both candidates whom our electors will have to choose between. There is no doubt that President Washington respected Secretary Madison; they were neighbors and conferred often, especially during the early years of Washington's first term. Of course, President Jefferson served alongside Hamilton in Washington's Cabinet, running the State Department even as Hamilton ran the Treasury. One thing I can tell you, my colleagues, from my years of watching His Excellency serve as both commanding General and as President—there is no man whom he respected more, no man to whose judgment he more often deferred, and none who stood higher in his affections than Alexander Hamilton. When the Army was re-formed during the days of President Adams, Washington insisted that Hamilton be named as his second-in-command, even though there were several of us who were his senior in rank. Some were surprised that I was willing to serve under a man who was my junior during the war, but the truth is, I would not question Washington's judgment in so important a matter. I still will not. I firmly believe that if Washington could speak to us from beyond the grave, he would urge you to put your trust in the man he trusted so implicitly. He would urge you to choose electors who would vote for Alexander Hamilton."

After he sat down, the Speaker of the House called on the South Carolina General Assembly to choose their presidential electors. All ten men they picked were pledged to support Hamilton's candidacy. One by one, the other state legislatures charged with choosing their electors also voted—and then, in the first week of November, in the Year of Our Lord 1808, the American voters in the other ten states cast their ballots. Although the individual records of popular votes were not kept after they had been counted, the result was unquestionable. Alexander Hamilton was elected President of the United States by an electoral tally of ninety-nine to seventy. As post riders brought in the results of the individual state elections, Alex realized he had really done it. Now, he thought, the real work can finally begin.

CHAPTER FIFTEEN

IT WAS A gray, gloomy December afternoon in Washington City as James Madison and Thomas Jefferson sat over the dinner table in the East Room, studying the last set of election returns, from Georgia. Jefferson stood and shook his head, then came to Madison's end of the table and laid his hands on the Secretary of State's shoulders.

"I am sorry, James," he said. "I truly wanted you to be my successor as President, and I think you would have acquitted yourself well in the office. I knew it was a mistake for you to let Hamilton have a voice in our diplomacy!"

"Please, Thomas, no less a mistake than your letter, which is what enabled him to win that Senate seat," Madison said with a sigh. "But give credit where it is due—the man helped us achieve peace with Great Britain, at a time when war seemed almost certain. I wanted to be President very badly, but if a generation of young men who might have otherwise perished in battle will now be able to grow old, and live to see their sons grown to honorable manhood around them, then my electoral defeat is a small price to pay."

"I truly thought that Hamilton's self-destructive tendencies would assert themselves once he was in the arena of politics again. He's been so adept at ruining his own reputation in the past,"

Jefferson said. "I do not understand where this newfound discipline of his comes from! I have never seen him so focused, so even-tempered. He was always a man of fiery passions, but now he has become calculating and strategic."

"He is no longer the man we knew," Madison said. "I think that the Hamilton of your cabinet days died on that dueling ground, and the man who emerged has all his genius, but none of his fatal flaws. He is a man reborn, with a new sense of purpose that I do not fully understand."

"I pray that purpose is not the entrenchment of power in the Federal government, at the expense of our individual liberties, and the rights of the states!" Jefferson said. "I fear this man, James. I fear what he might do to our country!"

"I do not share that fear—at least not to extent you do," Madison replied. "I will always have my differences of opinion with our new President, I am sure. But I do not believe he is a man of malign intent. His intentions for our country are good."

"And we all know what road is paved with good intentions!" President Jefferson said. "You see, James, this is how he was able to defeat you. He has managed to somehow convince you of his personal honor and patriotism, and as a result you did not put forward the effort that you should have to defeat his candidacy. Hamilton is the most dangerous man in America, James! You should have unleashed the full might and fury of the press on him, as I did on Adams and Pinckney during my two campaigns."

"You mean I should have maintained a public aura of indifference and disdain for politics, while paying professional vultures to destroy the reputation of a good man?" Madison said sharply. "Thomas, you are an old and dear friend, but at times you are such a hypocrite that I wonder what I see in you!"

"Better the reputation of one dangerous man be damaged than the country fall to despotism!" Jefferson shot back. "You are simply too noble a soul sometimes, James. You fail to recognize that in the service of the greater good, some occasional villainy must be committed."

"And you, Mister President, sometimes fail to realize that just because you want something to be a good thing, does not necessarily mean that it is!" Madison replied. For some reason, everything Jefferson said this evening was grating on his nerves. "Sometimes I think you confuse your desires and opinions with those of the Almighty Himself!"

The habitually mild-mannered Jefferson was taken aback. He had always deplored personal confrontation, preferring to maintain a polite façade even with men he despised. Yet here he was on the brink of a shouting match with James Madison, who had been his closest friend and ally for the last eight years!

"James, I am sorry," he finally said. "This loss has wounded us both deeply, but I would rather lose a thousand elections than see our personal affections diminished. The people have spoken, and their will was not ours this time. But I have spent my life saying that the people's voice should be supreme, and therefore I should bow to their will with better grace. Forgive me my harsh words."

Madison rose and took the President by the hand.

"Of course I will," he said. "It has been a difficult season for us both, but our nation is prosperous and at peace. You left

America a stronger, better country than you found it, Thomas. May the same be said of President Hamilton when his term of office is concluded. Now, if you will excuse me, I feel that I should go and congratulate our President-elect on his victory. Would you care to join me?"

Jefferson shook his head sadly.

"I think not," he said. "I sent him an invitation to come and have dinner with me tomorrow. I think it is important to the nation that there be a certain level of graciousness between us. I would not do to him what Adams did to me."

Both men remembered that after Adams had finally lost the bitter contest of 1800, he had quit the new capital city in a huff, refusing to even attend the inauguration of his successor. Madison appreciated Jefferson's wisdom in wanting to set a better example.

"Well, in all honesty, Thomas, your press treated Adams savagely. I understand his bitterness now," Madison said. "I will give Alex this: he ran an honorable campaign against me. I know he could not control all the Federalist press, but the papers I know to be in his closest confidence focused their editorials on policy differences, not on personal attacks, and I am grateful for that. That is why I urged my own supporters to show similar restraint."

"You are a decent man, James Madison," Jefferson said. "That may be a political liability at times, but it is the thing that has always endeared you to my heart. Go and congratulate our new President-elect, and I will do the same tomorrow."

Madison left the White House with an odd sense of calm. He had grown increasingly disenchanted with Jefferson over the last year; the man's ruthlessness and hypocrisy in the field of politics made it difficult for Madison to respect him as a friend, scholar, and fellow laborer. Now that was done; the President would retire to Monticello, Madison would return to Montpelier, and they could go back to being friends again. Their conversations could center around history, science, philosophy, religion, and nature — not around electoral votes, scandalous journalism, and political strategies that left Madison feeling like he'd just mucked out a stable!

Darkness was falling, but Hamilton's home was well lit, and a reception was in progress. A small picket fence separated the front yard from the street — as did the presence of grass versus the raw mud of Constitution Avenue. Several carriages waited out front, their wheels slightly sunk into the muck, and the crowd had spilled out onto the front porch despite the chill of the evening. Madison paused on the street in front of the Senator's house, watching the happy Federalists as they gathered to hail the man who had brought their party back from the dead. This was a time for Hamilton to be surrounded by his supporters, he thought. He would pay his congratulatory call another evening. He turned away and started to walk back to Capitol Hill, intending to work on some unfinished state papers.

"Secretary Madison!" a familiar voice called after him. "Sir, please tarry! I would be delighted for you to be my guest this evening."

Madison turned and saw Alexander Hamilton standing at the front gate, his hand lifted in a friendly wave.

"I do not think that your supporters would welcome me on this, of all evenings, Alex," he said. "Or, if I may be so bold, Mister President!"

Hamilton beamed at Madison's use of the title and shook his head.

"Not until March, James!" he said. "And even then, I hope that you and I will always operate on a first-name basis. Come on in—anyone who fails to give you a warm welcome will lose their own at my house!"

Taking Madison by the arm, Hamilton conducted him up the steps and into the front parlor. The boisterous crowd grew silent as they recognized Hamilton's guest, and the President-elect spoke up quickly.

"Ladies and gentlemen, allow me to introduce a man that many of you already know—my esteemed opponent in the recent contest of opinion, a man of decency, honor, and patriotism, who has served this country well as Secretary of State—my friend, Mister James Madison!"

The crowd gave a polite round of applause, and Madison bowed, deeply touched by Hamilton's words. Hamilton handed him a glass of wine. John Quincy Adams, his face flushed with happiness, raised his own glass of Madeira.

"To Secretary Madison!" he said. "Our chivalrous foe in politics, our fellow American in citizenship!"

"Give us a speech, sir," said Rufus King.

"Speech, speech!" the Federalists took up the cry.

Madison flushed, and then raised his own glass. The party fell silent again.

"My fellow Americans," he said, "it is an honor to be a guest in the home of the next President. I had hoped that I might be the one hosting such a party this evening, and if I had been, I want you to know that Alexander Hamilton would have been as welcome a guest in my home as he has always made me feel in his!"

This time it was Hamilton's turn to bow, and his guests applauded Madison's gracious words.

"It is a rare presidential contest in which it can be said that the people of America would be well served, no matter which candidate they elect," he continued. "But I believe that 1808 will be remembered as such an election. My friend and former opponent, Senator Hamilton, is a man of strong character, constitutional principles, and the best of intentions. I have no doubt he will be a strong, capable, and effective President. To President Hamilton!"

"President Hamilton!" the guests roared their agreement, and every glass in the home was drained. Madison looked around the room. There was Eliza Hamilton, her face radiant with joy at her husband's victory, their children gathered around, smiling with her. John Quincy Adams, a taller and more robust replica of his father, was quietly talking with Rufus King. Josiah Quincy, Hercules Mulligan, and Benjamin Tallmadge were loudly trying to convince Baron Erskine, the British minister, to join them in a chorus of "Yankee Doodle." Various other luminaries, members of Congress, New York state politicians, and several others that Madison did not recognize crowded the parlor and dining room and wandered out onto the front porch, rotating between the heat of the fireplace and the brisk north wind outside.

"It was good of you to come," said Hamilton quietly in Madison's ear. "I am going to be sending folks home in the next hour or so, but if you would be so good as to linger, Adams and I would like to have a word with you."

Then Alex was off, making the rounds, thanking his supporters, offering words of encouragement and cheer. Hamilton shone in such settings, as if he were a great lord to the manor born. Of no more than middling height, he nonetheless carried himself with a grace and dignity that made every man in the room pale beside him. Madison wondered, reflecting on Hamilton's humble origins, where such self-confidence came from. Was there truth to the rumor that Hamilton's vagabond father had been a Scottish lord? If there was, did that mean true nobility was indeed hereditary?

Madison took his time with the second glass of Madeira, savoring the rich Spanish wine, but also making sure not to overindulge. Whatever Hamilton wanted to talk about, James had a feeling he would need to keep his wits about him. Time passed quickly, and Madison was pleasantly surprised at how kindly Hamilton's friends and supporters treated him. It made him grateful that he had run a civil campaign; one need only to look at the chaos in France over the last two decades to see the dangers of extremism in politics. The time passed quickly, and suddenly he saw Hamilton leap on top of a chair with catlike grace and call for everyone's attention.

"My dear friends," he said, "I want to thank you for all the good wishes and firm support over the last four years. I pray that

God will grant me sufficient wisdom and guidance so that none of you will regret your choice to support me when my time in office is done."

His guests began cheering once more, and Hamilton beamed, looking far younger than his fifty-three years. He held up his hands for silence once more.

"However," he said, "you have eaten all my food, drunk all my wine, and kept my children up far past their bedtimes! I know many of you are staying at boardinghouses here in town, so I will wish you much joy and a comfortable night's rest here in the nation's capital. If I had more room, you would all be my guests this evening, but as it is, Mister Mulligan and Senator Adams have claimed both my guest bedrooms. After March, I will have room enough for all of you to be my guests for the evening, but until I change residences that won't be practical. So, good night to you all!"

There were some groans and protests, but the guests began to file toward the front door, where Hamilton made sure that he personally bade each of them farewell, often with a hearty handshake or a warm embrace. Within a half hour, all of them were gone except for John Quincy Adams and Hercules Mulligan. Hamilton gave a long sigh, and then turned to his wife, Eliza.

"My dear, if you would put the children to bed and bring us a pot of coffee, I would be deeply grateful. I would like to have a quiet conversation with my guests," he said.

"Of course, Alex," she said, and then leaned up and kissed her husband on the cheek. "I am SO proud of you, my dear Hamilton!"

Hamilton broke into a grin that was almost silly with affection, and Madison recognized the look of a man who was deeply in love with his spouse. He'd seen the same expression on his own face in the mirror, when he was with Dolley. How blessed was the man who married well, he thought.

Hamilton grabbed four chairs and pulled them in front of the fireplace; Eliza shepherded the children upstairs and came down a few moments later. She took a coffeepot and set it on the hearth, just close enough to the flames for the fire to keep the beverage hot. Hamilton handed each man a small cup, and then bade his wife goodnight.

"Mister Madison, it was very kind of you to come tonight," he said. "Adams and I have been talking for some time about the State Department and who we would like to head it."

"I am sure that whoever you choose will be more than capable, Alex," said Madison, "and I will be more than happy to meet with them and prepare them for the duties the job entails."

"There is a great deal to be said for experience," Alex replied. "You have provided exemplary service as the President's chief foreign policy advisor for the last eight years. That is why I was wondering if you would like to stay on and continue to serve as Secretary of State during my term of office."

Madison almost spat his coffee back into his cup, so great was his surprise. He swallowed hard, and then tried to think of a reply.

"Sir, I am your friend, but I am still a Republican!" he said. "I doubt your Federalist friends will be impressed with a relic of the previous administration being allowed to continue in yours!"

"That is precisely my reason, James," said Alex. "You know the office better than anyone, you have performed your duties with great skill and diplomatic expertise, and frankly, I need you. I have a great task lying before me, one that will require the cooperation of men of good will from both sides of America's political divide. Your assistance would be invaluable, not just to me as President. I believe that you can help me to save this country from a dreadful calamity that is looming ahead unless something is done to prevent it."

Madison was intrigued, delighted, and doubtful all at the same time. He looked over at John Quincy Adams, a man he had come to know and respect over the last few years.

"What will the Federalists of Massachusetts say to such an appointment, Senator?" he said. "President Jefferson and I have not been too popular up your way."

"Oh, some will complain, no doubt," said Adams. "But the people who really matter will recognize that you have done the job well and should have little issue with your continuing in office. Senator Hamilton and I have been discussing this option for some time, and we are in agreement."

"I must confess that I could not be more surprised," Madison sighed. "I was looking forward to retirement from politics, but I want to ask—what is this impeding calamity you refer to, Alex? And how can I help you prevent it?"

Hamilton looked at the other two men, and then studied Madison with a piercing glance. The jollity of the party was gone, and in its place, James saw a deep intensity that took him aback.

"I will tell you," said Alex. "But first I must ask that everything said for the rest of the evening remain in strictest confidence, from now until the end of my natural life. Can you swear this?"

Madison paused. He trusted Hamilton these days more than he had ever dreamed possible, but what could be so serious, so potentially inflammatory, that Alex would demand such a vow? He thought about refusing, but then he recalled the courtesy and deference that Hamilton had shown him over the last few years, even when they were on the opposite side of a presidential election. In for a penny, in for a pound, he thought.

"Very well, Alexander Hamilton, I swear not to divulge your words for as long as you live, unless you release me from the oath in person," he said.

Hamilton smiled and looked at Mulligan and Adams.
"I told you he was a good man," he said to them, and then turned back to his bewildered guest. "Now, James, I am going to tell you a story. As you well know, I was gravely wounded in my duel with Vice President Burr four years ago—so much so that I nearly died. As I lay there with one foot in both worlds, I saw a vision. How much of it was real and how much was my own fevered brain at work, I cannot say. But what I can tell you is that everything I have seen since has pointed towards its fundamental truth. America is headed for a brutal civil war, a cataclysm that will destroy an entire generation and change the country forever—unless it is prevented. And it can only be prevented if the cause of the conflict is removed now, before it can take root any further."

Madison arched an eyebrow. A vision, he thought with wonder. Hamilton had never struck him as a mystic.

"And what is the cause of this terrible conflict that lies ahead?" he asked.

"Slavery," said Hamilton. "America will rip itself in two over slavery, and hundreds of thousands will die. Unless we stop it! So the primary focus of my administration shall be to work for the national abolition of slavery, or at least, to see it abolished in so many states that it will die of its own accord in the remainder."

"Alex, that is—that is the most preposterous thing I have ever heard!" said Madison. "And has it slipped your mind that I am a slave owner myself?"

"But you recognize the evil of it, don't you?" Alex said. "Slavery in America makes a mockery of everything we claim to believe in! And besides, the fact that you are a planter is the reason I want you! The most common objection my friend Laurens used to encounter when he tried to free the slaves to fight for our cause during the Revolution was that Southerners could not survive without slave labor. I need you to help me prove otherwise!"

"How would I do that?" Madison said, intrigued despite himself. "Assuming that I agreed to go along with this harebrained scheme at all?"

"Free your slaves," Alex said. "Ask them to work for wages. Pay them well, treat them well, and see what happens to your harvests. Offer them incentives for hard work and self-improvement. I have long believed that wage labor by free men is superior to slave labor in every way. The slave works because he is forced to, and therefore does the minimum that he can get away with, as an act of defiance against those who deny him his freedom. The free man works to better his fortunes and those of his family. I think you will see record harvests if you offer the right incentives to your workers."

"I don't know, Alex," Madison said. "I have always regarded slavery as a moral evil, a veritable cancer on our land, to tell the truth—"

"Then work with me to end it!" Hamilton said. "Help me erase this blight from our beloved country! If you lead, Virginia will follow. And if Virginia were to abolish slavery, then rest of the upper South may follow suit. Once that is done, it will increase the pressure on the Deep South to join the rest of the nation in doing away with this pernicious practice."

"You do make a compelling case," Madison said.

"James," Alex said earnestly, "we were both delegates in Philadelphia. You and I, and those other fifty-odd men in there, we created America! You know that even then slavery was the serpent in our garden. Remember the words of John Randolph: 'This infernal slave trafficking is the curse of heaven upon our land!' We deferred doing something about it, in order to get South Carolina to go along with the Constitution. We coddled the viper instead of casting it forth. Now is the time that we can rectify that error. The fate of our nation, and the lives of millions of men yet unborn, both black and white, hang in the balance. I need you, Secretary Madison! I need your support, and I need your moral leadership. Federalists cannot do this alone; they will need the support of conscientious Democratic-Republicans as well. Will you help me?"

Madison furrowed his brow and thought for a long time. Deep down, he knew Alex was right. Every time he saw the black laborers toiling in the fields at Montpelier while a white overseer supervised them on horseback, whip in hand, his conscience had pained him. He had rationalized, and made excuses, and lied to himself about the situation for long enough. Some things were worth fighting for, he realized. Human liberty was one of them — and that meant liberty for ALL humans, black and white. When the history of America was written a century hence, which side of that history would he stand on?

Slowly he extended his hand toward Alex, who took it with a broad smile.

"You have my support, President Hamilton, and you have my service for as long as you wish it. I am in, by God!" he exclaimed.

Hamilton embraced him, and the two others joined in their congratulations.

"Well then," Alex said. "We have much to discuss. Have another coffee, gentlemen. It's going to be a late night."

CHAPTER SIXTEEN

"SENATOR HAMILTON, welcome to the Executive Mansion," Thomas Jefferson said, opening the door for the President-elect. "I hope you will be as happy living here as I have been."

"I know you had hoped that the next occupant would be someone other than myself, Mister President," said Hamilton. "But I thank you for your gracious welcome. May the nation never have cause to regret that I lived here."

"May that be true of all our successors!" said Jefferson. "I must say, Senator, I thought that your campaign against Secretary Madison was conducted with decency and dignity. You comported yourself well, as did he."

"I have a great deal of respect for Secretary Madison," Hamilton said, "as well as a personal fondness for him. I refused to slander him just to gain votes."

"He expressed similar sentiments about you," said Jefferson. "Politics is an ugly business, Senator. In my own career, I did what I felt I must do, for the good of the country and to preserve the liberty of our citizens, but I would be lying if I said I relished it. I am glad to be leaving it behind me forever. Philosophy, history, the natural sciences—those will be my fields of study and debate after this March! Now, allow me to show you around."

Jefferson proved to be a consummate host, showing Hamilton every room in the White House, and explaining what functions were generally held where. Alex was fascinated, listening to the soft-spoken third President as he described the intricacies of the President's House to its next occupant.

Alex could not help but notice the presence of slaves in the White House. The maid, butler, and cook were all of African descent, and they bowed and scraped whenever Jefferson entered the room. Hamilton wanted to ask about them, but he waited until the tour was done and Jefferson led him to the dining room. A red-headed woman of middle age was seated at the table with them; the family resemblance was undeniable.

"This must be your daughter," Hamilton said, bowing politely.

"I am Martha Jefferson Randolph," she said. "My family and close friends call me Patsy."

"I am delighted to make your acquaintance," Hamilton said. "I am sure that you are a great aid and comfort to your father."

"It has been my privilege to be his hostess here at the White House," she said, "when my own family responsibilities allow. But we are happy to have Father returning to Virginia, where we will be neighbors once again."

The meal was delicious—a roasted ham, basted with honey glaze, served with potatoes and terrapin soup as an appetizer. After they were done, Jefferson's daughter brought them a pot of coffee and left the two men to talk privately.

"Mister President," Hamilton said. "These domestic servants that work in the White House—what exactly is their status?"

"Those are my people," Jefferson said. "They are my property, and I will take them with me back to Monticello when my term expires. But if you wish to find servants to replace them, there is a slave auction on the first Saturday of every month, two blocks down from the capitol. I could make inquiries, if you like."

"Absolutely not," said Alex. "There will be no slaves in my White House. I will hire free men and women to work here, out of my own pocket if necessary."

Jefferson raised an eyebrow at this.

"Well, of course that is your choice, but it is far more economical to pay once and have labor for a lifetime than to pay someone every month, and have them free to run off whenever the fancy strikes them," he said.

Hamilton fixed the President with a steely gaze.

"You have written more eloquently about the blessings of liberty than any man of our age, Thomas Jefferson," he said. "And yet in that simple sentence you just belied every word of it. How can you believe that liberty is the natural condition of humanity, the first inalienable right endowed by our Creator, and then deny it to your fellow humans based on simple economics?"

"It's not that simple," Jefferson said.

"Of course it is," said Hamilton. "Either all men are created equal, or they are not. Either all men deserve liberty, or none do."

Jefferson sighed and ran his hands through his hair, now far more gray than red. For a moment, he looked like a man approaching eighty rather than his early sixties.

"I have often and fervently wished, Mister Hamilton, that these poor benighted Africans had never been brought to our shores," he said. "Slavery is a vile institution, and its presence here does indeed make a mockery of our love of liberty! But what else can we do? We cannot ship a million Africans back to their dark continent, nor can we rob the wealthiest class of the southern half of our nation of their property without recompense, and we certainly cannot turn savages free to live among us as equals!"

"Mister President, I intend no disrespect," Hamilton said. "But I have seen free black men fight in the Continental Army with all the courage and resourcefulness of whites. I have seen free blacks laboring hard and honestly and supporting themselves and their families. How do we know that they cannot live amongst us in a state of liberty until we try that option? You assume that the black man is an inherent savage who can never be civilized. I believe that that he can be. At the very least, I believe that freeing these Africans who were brought here against their will, and then keeping them here among us as a free people, working for wages, is an experiment worth trying."

Jefferson leaped out of his seat looked at Hamilton in astonishment.

"So that is it!" he said. "For four years I have marveled at your discipline, your focus, and your drive to succeed me in this office. I have wondered at how the self-destructive streak that was so plain in you before the duel seems extinguished and replaced with a deadly intensity. Now I see the goal you have carefully hidden from us all. You intend to free the slaves!"

The President slapped the dining table with his palm as he uttered that last sentence, his face flushed with emotion. Alex slowly nodded.

"I tell you this in deepest confidence, Mister President, as one elected executive to another," he said. "Slavery is going to tear this nation apart and plunge us into a deadly fraternal conflict if it is not abolished. I believe this as surely as I believe that there is a sun in the sky and a just God in the heavens. As a nation of free men, we will endure forever, but if we persist as a nation half slave and half free, our country will die by suicide!"

Jefferson slowly sank back into his seat, his piercing light blue eyes focused on Hamilton's dark violet ones.

"You may create the very conflict you seek to avert by forcing the issue," he said. "The South is utterly dependent on slave labor."

"But what if they did not have to be?" Hamilton said. "What if we could show that free black laborers are more productive and economical than slaves?"

"That's preposterous!" said Jefferson. "Everyone knows slave labor is more effective and economical than paying wages."

"Everyone assumes so," replied Hamilton. "What I want to do is prove that assumption false."

"How?" Jefferson asked. "I cannot imagine that any Southerner would go along with such an irrational scheme!"

"Secretary Madison has pledged to help me in this," said Hamilton. "He will conduct the first great experiment at Montpelier. Then I intend to enlist the aid of a few other friends I have in the South. If they all show positive and profitable results with free labor, then we shall demonstrate that slavery is not economically necessary. Sir, you have an enormous following. You are a much-loved leader in the South and have been for thirty years. You could help us greatly by conducting a similar experiment at Monticello! You and Madison are good friends; you could be even greater partners in the cause of human liberty if you will join us in this noble effort."

Jefferson paused, deep in thought for a moment. Hamilton could see that he was struggling with conflicting emotions. Finally, the President shook his head.

"I am sorry, Senator Hamilton," he said. "I believe that there is some truth in what you say, and I also believe in your sincerity on this issue. But for a variety of reasons, some of them deeply personal, I cannot aid you in this endeavor. However, I do share your belief that it is a noble effort. Therefore, I will not oppose you—neither publicly nor privately. But I will speak no more of this."

So, it was true, Hamilton thought. Jefferson would probably never own up to it, even under the pain of torture, but at that moment Hamilton had no doubts about the old rumors regarding Jefferson and his slave-concubine Sally Hemings.

"Have you given thought to the composition of your cabinet?" Jefferson asked, shifting the topic. "A President is only as good as the quality of his advisors."

"I have decided on most of them," Hamilton said. "I think I shall ask Benjamin Tallmadge to serve as Secretary of War. He has excellent military experience and I trust him deeply. For Treasury, I am thinking of asking Oliver Wolcott to return to the department as its head. He was a worthy successor when I left the office, and we worked well together when he was under my supervision before that. For Attorney General, I am hoping to persuade John Jay to come out of retirement."

"What about the Secretary of State?" Jefferson asked. "You are going to have a hard time finding a replacement as competent and brilliant as James Madison has been in that capacity."

"I know," Hamilton said, allowing himself the smallest of smiles. "That is why I have asked him to stay on in that capacity."

For the second time during their conversation, Hamilton saw the President of the United States look utterly flummoxed. Jefferson swallowed hard and finally spoke.

"And Secretary Madison has agreed to this?" he asked finally.

"He has," Hamilton said.

"Well, I can't exactly criticize your choice, then, can I?" Jefferson asked ruefully.

"It would be rather difficult, wouldn't it?" Alex said with a smile, and then began to chuckle at Jefferson's discomfiture. The President looked mildly offended at first, but then he, too, began laughing, and the former political enemies ended their luncheon with smiles and best wishes.

FOR THE NEXT week, Madison and Hamilton spent nearly every day planning how to create an effective system of free labor for Montpelier, Madison's plantation. Hamilton applied all his knowledge of economics and human nature into crafting a system that would do away with bondage and coercion, but still motivate the workers to excel. Alex had been reading up on the subject for several years, as he planned the task his long-ago vision had laid upon him. Ever since he was fourteen, when he had been asked to serve as bookkeeper for a large seafaring trade, Alex had possessed an uncanny ability to juggle and manipulate numbers in his head. But he was more than just a skilled accountant; he also had intuitive grasp of how money worked, how it could be manipulated, invested, and traded to make more money, and how the intricacies of commerce could be utilized for maximum profit. He and Madison argued, debated, and discussed for days on end the best way to turn Montpelier into a thriving agricultural concern using only free labor.

As for Madison, the more time he spent in Hamilton's company, the more respect he gained for the President-elect. He had always known that Alexander Hamilton had a quick intellect and a greater understanding of finance than almost any man alive; what he had not realized was just how far-ranging Hamilton's mind was. Alex had a remarkable grasp of history and philosophy, and a passion for human liberty that was surprising coming from someone that many (James included) had thought to be a monarchist. Hamilton had a far greater enthusiasm for manufacturing and shipping than Madison, who was an agriculturist at heart. But, as Alex explained, the ability to produce manufactured goods would render America finally and completely independent of Great Britain, and the regulatory clause of the Constitution would enable the government to ensure that American factories did not become the squalid hellholes that Jefferson had witnessed in Manchester and Liverpool. Agriculture and industry, working together and freed from the chains of chattel slavery, would make America one of the greatest powers on earth in the century to come, Hamilton explained.

More than any financial philosophy, though, what stood out to Madison was Hamilton's passion for emancipation. The President-elect believed that America's entire future hung in the balance of his efforts. Madison had been a reluctant convert, to be sure, but the more time he spent in Alex's company, the more revulsion he felt at the institution of slavery he had supported for so long, and the more eager he became to have a part in its end. When he finally headed back south, the fire of zealous abolitionism was burning in the heart of a Virginia planter. Madison was eager to begin his great experiment.

TWO WEEKS LATER, James Madison stood at the front door of his Montpelier plantation and looked across the fields. He had tried to move away from growing tobacco, which had been the staple crop of his father and brothers, because it was so hard on the soil. His farms now produced corn, wheat, and cotton on a rotating basis, with some fields planted in peas, which put nutrients back into the soil. He had divested himself of much of his family's vast properties, but still controlled over two thousand acres of farmland, and owned a hundred and twenty-five slaves to work the land and serve as his domestics. He had asked his overseer to summon them all to the front yard of his estate to address them at nine o'clock that morning.

"They are all gathered now, I think," said Rufus Jenkins, the plantation overseer. "What's this all about anyway, sir?"

"You're about to find out," Madison said.

He walked down the steps and stood before his assembled slaves, who were watching him curiously. Some held looks of barely concealed resentment; others dread. He smiled slightly, and then began, projecting his voice as best he could.

"Good morning," he said. "I hope this day finds you all well. I have called you here to make an announcement—a very important announcement, in fact. However, I would ask you to continue listening after I have made it, for there is much I would discuss with you."

Now curiosity overtook all other emotions on the rows of black faces before him. Here goes, he thought.

"From this day forward there will be no more slavery here at Montpelier. I am emancipating each and every one of you. You are free men and women, effective today!"

Madison heard a hundred throats gasp at the same time, and after a pregnant pause, the Negroes began cheering. Some fell to their knees to give thanks; others tried to crowd forward to take him by the hand. He shook their hands, but then retreated up the porch so that they could all see him better.

"Now then," he said, "please LISTEN!" He raised his voice sharply on that last word, and the crowd fell silent, although there were still expressions of joy on most of their faces, now mingled with curiosity.

"Being free men and women, each of you are at liberty to leave Montpelier and never return—if that is what you wish. However,

I would ask you to consider what I have to say next before you decide. I would like each of you to stay here and work for me as paid employees. You would be doing the same things that you do for me now, except that there will be no whips, no coercion, no threats. You men will be paid four dollars a month for your labors, and two for women. You will still have your same quarters to live in—although you may improve your cabins as you please, using your own time and money to do so. Your meals will still be served as they are now, but again, if you wish to purchase more food, or better food, collectively or individually, you may do so. Let me be clear, however—I am paying you to work, and so I expect you to work. Anyone who refuses to perform his duties will be dismissed from my employ and sent on their way—I will not support idlers! The plantation's fields will be divided into smaller plots, with a dozen workers assigned to each lot. I believe that men who are working for pay will work more industriously and productively than men forced to labor against their will. You will compete to see whose plot has the best yield. If I am right, I expect to see improved harvests from this point forward. If my plantation prospers, you will have a share of that prosperity. The three plots with the highest yields will receive a bonus at harvest time. If we have an abundant harvest all around, after bills are paid, additional bonuses may come from the remaining funds. Last of all—as long as you are here, on my plantation, I can protect you. The South is not always a safe place for free Negroes. There are unscrupulous men who will kidnap you and sell you back into slavery if they find you wandering. You can make the journey to the North, if that is what you wish, but you will still have to find work there to support yourself and provide for your families. I know some of you are married and have children. You may need to discuss your decision as a family. Others may wish to think on what I have said before deciding. I will say one more thing—if you stay here and work for me, you will be proving something to the watching world. You will prove that a plantation that uses free labor and pays its workers can be just as profitable, if not more, than one which uses slaves. If we do that, other planters may follow suit. We may start a wave of liberation which will roll across the South and eventually set all your people free! So, think on that, too, before giving me your answers. There will be no more work assigned today. Reflect on your choices, together and separately, and let me know what you decide. Thank you!"

The former slaves cheered their diminutive master, and Madison gave them a courtly bow before retreating into the house. Rufus Jenkins followed him, his face flushed scarlet.

"By Jehovah, Mister Madison, have you lost your mind?" he said when they were alone. "You have just bankrupted yourself, and me in the bargain! Paid nigger labor? What are you thinking? There won't be a darky left on this plantation in a week!"

Madison fixed his foreman with an icy stare.

"You will not speak to me in such terms," he said. "This is my choice, and I think you may be surprised what Africans prove themselves capable of when properly motivated. Now, Mister Jenkins, I want you to retire to your quarters and stay away from these people! I do not want the slightest hint of fear or coercion to drive their decision. They are free, whether you like it or not, and I want them to debate their future without you staring over their shoulders."

The overseer glared at Madison but did as he was bid, stomping out the door in a huff. Madison watched him go, making sure that Jenkins walked to his own modest overseer's cabin and not toward the slave quarters. Then he walked back to his study. He had ordered a huge stack of certificates of manumission printed up while he was in Washington, in preparation for this step. He now pulled down his plantation ledger and began meticulously copying the name of each slave he owned onto a certificate. Male and female, young and old, he wrote in their names and then signed and dated each certificate, blotting the damp ink and adding the finished papers to a stack. It was laborious work, and as Madison neared the end of the task, he was startled to see that it was late afternoon. He repaired to the kitchen and pulled an apple from the barrel in the pantry. It was wrinkled but still sweet, a remnant of the previous fall's harvest. He was returning to the study to finish the certificates when he saw a figure standing at the door. It was Nero, one of the lead field hands—a tall, strong thirty-year-old who had been born and raised on the Madison family farms.

"Good evening, Nero," he said, opening the door for the former slave. "I was just signing the papers for you and all your companions. Please come in."

Nero followed Madison and stood awkwardly in front of the Virginian's desk, his tattered wool cap in his hands. Madison reflected how odd this must be for the man and spoke to him in a patient tone.

"Have you come to tell me something?" he said.

"Yassuh, Marse James," Nero said. "I'se sorry, I jest trying to figger out how to say what I come to say."

"Part of being free is being able to say what's on your mind, so why don't you try that," Madison said.

"Aw right, suh, if dat's de way you want it," the Negro said. "You see, me an' the othuh folks don't mind workin' for you as free folk. You'se been a good massuh, and treated us fair nuff. But we'se decided dat we all gone take our chances elsewhere, suh, no disrespect intended. T'ain't you dat's de reason."

Madison suppressed a groan. So Hamilton had been wrong after all. He was ruined, financially and socially! How could it have gone so drastically wrong? But he kept the smile fixed on his face and looked Nero in the eye.

"What is the reason for this decision, then, if you do not dislike the idea of working for wages here?" he asked.

"It's dat Jenkins, the slave driver," said Nero. "He be rapin' our womenfolk. He doan do it when you here, but de minute you head out to Washington City he take a diff'rent one ever night! Sometimes two a night. Young, old, it doan matter to him. Any woman fight him, he have her whipped. Any man of us threaten to tell you, he have dem whipped. It doan matter to him if we be slave of free, he still gone be rapin' our womenfolk ever time you gone. If we really free, we doan hab to put up wi'dat no mo'."

Madison stared at the man's face and saw no hint of deception there. Jenkins, a serial rapist? Like all Southerners, Madison knew that female slaves were often used by plantation owners or their employees for sexual purposes. His own brothers, when they were teens, had a pretty mulatto that they had dallied with from time to time. But James himself had always looked down on such behavior and had never tolerated it on his property. But he had also noticed the loathing with which his Negroes always regarded Jenkins. In a rush of humiliation, he understood why. He had allowed this to happen by his own willful blindness. Suddenly, he was filled with a growing fury—and in that fury, he had a burst of inspiration.

"Come with me, Nero," he said. "We are going to deal with this."

Nero's eyes widened with fear, but he dared not disobey his former master. He dutifully followed the diminutive Secretary of State across the yard to the slave driver's cabin.

"Jenkins, come out here now!" Madison called. Muffled oaths came from inside the two-room cabin, and a few minutes later, Jenkins stood at the door, red-eyed, cradling a whiskey jug in one arm.

"What is it now?" he asked, looking confusedly from Madison to the tall Negro standing behind him.

"I am told that you have been systematically forcing yourself on my female slaves when I am not in residence," Madison said. "Is this true?"

Jenkins's eyes widened for a moment, and then he shook his head.

"Of course not! I wouldn't dirty my bed with a nigger wench!" he said.

"Lie to me again and I will make sure no plantation in Virginia ever hires you!" Madison snapped. "Is it true? Did you force yourself on these slave women?"

The slave driver heaved an angry sigh and glared at Nero.

"Of course I did," he finally said. "Every overseer does! It's one of the unwritten benefits of the job! Half the plantation owners do it too—at least, the ones who are big enough men to do the deed!"

Madison's temper blazed; he leaped up the steps and grabbed the much taller man by the collar, yanking him forward and hurling him headlong into the dirt of the footpath. James thanked his lucky stars that he had grown up in a houseful of rowdy brothers, so that he knew a thing or two about taking a bigger man by surprise. Jenkins slowly rose to his feet and turned to face his employer.

"You have one hour to clean out this cabin and get off my property," Madison said. "Take your things and go, and do not dare have the temerity to ask me for a reference! In fact, I'd move a few counties over before looking for a new job, because I intend to inform my neighbors what a wretched man you are. If I ever catch you on Montpelier or any of my other properties again, I will have Nero here horsewhip you within an inch of your life. Am I perfectly clear?"

"You'd let a nigger whip a white man?" the foreman asked in astonishment. "What kind of madness has possessed you?"

"A foul-tempered, vengeful type," said Madison, "if I ever see your face again!" Inwardly he was smiling; he doubted that he could order such a thing without consequences in the South, but Jenkins need not know that.

"Fine, fine," said the former overseer. "Give me a few moments to grab my things, and I'll be gone for good!"

"You'd better be," said Madison. "Nero, follow me."

They returned to the house, and Madison poured himself a glass of wine. He looked at the former slave, and moved by some strange impulse, he took down a second glass and poured it also. He knew he was crossing some strange Rubicon, but disciplining Jenkins had filled him with elation.

"I thank you for bringing this matter to my attention," he said. "Perhaps now some of your comrades will be willing to stay on. Here, have a drink with me."

Nero stared at his former master, aghast.

"Suh, I 'preciate the kindness, but it's not my place to be drinkin' wid de likes of you!" he finally said.

"Join me just this once," Madison replied. "I want to ask you something. Are you willing to stay, with Jenkins gone?"

Nero's brow furrowed in thought for a moment, and then he spoke.

"He a bad man, Marse James, and I shore be glad he gone," he said. "But one overseer is pretty much like another, as I sees it. Whoever you hire to make us work, he likely to treat us de same."

"Free men don't need an overseer," Madison said. "Or, to call them what they truly are, a slave driver. Free men have a supervisor, true, who inspects their work, hears their grievances, and serves as a go-between with their employer. But he doesn't wield a whip over them, nor does he have the power to molest their women and then force their silence with threats of flogging!"

"An' who you gone find to do a job like dat, down here in Virginia?" Nero asked. "All we have down here be slave drivers!"

"I was thinking of asking you to do it," Madison said. "You'd be paid a couple dollars extra a month, and you would supervise the work of your people. You'd also move into Jenkins's cabin, since he won't be needing it anymore."

"I'm not entirely sure dat I be wantin' dis, Marse James," said Nero.

"The alternative is to bring in a white man from another plantation," Madison said. "Or to nominate another one of you former slaves. Can you think of one of your comrades who would be better suited to the job? I asked you because you are the one that was chosen to come and talk with me. It seems your people trust you."

Nero forgot himself at this point and sat down for the first time since entering the house, his head in his hands. He kept looking up at Madison, as if to make sure the offer wasn't some form of elaborate trick. Finally, he took a drink of wine and spoke.

"Let me talk wid de othuhs," he said. "An' I give you my answer den."

An hour later he returned and told Madison that he would be willing to serve as the supervisor for the freed laborers of Montpelier. In the end, only three slaves chose to leave for the north—an older couple and their thirteen-year-old daughter, who had been raped and beaten several times by Jenkins.

"Dis place is bad juju for her," said her father, Donald. "De wife an' me, we be willin' enuff to stay here, but so much bad has done happen' to our girl, we jest wants to get her away from it as far as we can."

Madison gave them their papers and some money for passage to New York, with a letter of introduction to one of Hamilton's friends. He knew that the vast port city had entire neighborhoods of free blacks and hoped they would find a place there for their daughter to grow up and heal.

Nero moved into Jenkins's former cabin and proved to be an excellent supervisor. Madison spent a good part of the winter teaching him to read and write, so he could keep the plantation's books with a minimum of assistance. As he walked among the cabins of his former slaves, he was satisfied to see a buzz of energy about them. Men and women went about their daily chores with a bounce in their step and smiles on their faces. At the end of January, he gathered his workers about them and distributed their first pay to them—silver dollars for each, and a five-dollar gold coin for Nero. It was a chill morning, and the gray clouds promised snow sometime soon. Madison handed out the coins from a large bag, and Nero put an "X" by each name to show that person had received his first wages. After they were all paid, Madison turned to a small bonfire that he had asked the new supervisor to light for him.

"One last thing," he said. "Nero found this as he was cleaning out the cabin where your former overseer lived."

He held up a bullwhip, its business end stained deep black with the blood of the slave driver's unfortunate victims. The former slaves blanched at the sight of the hated instrument.

"We have no more need of such things here," Madison said. "So let us be rid of it!"

He cast it into the fire, and as he walked into the house, the free men and women of Montpelier began to sing and dance around the fire.

CHAPTER SEVENTEEN

THOUSANDS OF people crammed into Washington, DC, to witness the swearing in of America's fourth President. All of Alex's children were there to witness the joyous moment, as well as every member of New York's congressional delegation and most of its state legislators. Partisan lines aside, it was a moment of great pride as America's most populous state saw her first President take office. Massachusetts came out in force as well, excited to see a native son assuming the second office in the land. Even former President John Adams had descended from his Peacefield farm to see his son take the oath of office as Vice President.

Thomas Jefferson wrote a moving and eloquent farewell address which was published in all the leading Republican newspapers; the departing President took the high road and urged his political followers to give Hamilton a chance before passing judgment on him. His closing lines were a moment of rare honesty from one whose political career had featured so many moments of duplicity:

> *Mister Hamilton and I have found ourselves on the opposite sides of nearly every political struggle of the last twenty years, and I will be the first to admit that I had hoped to be succeeded by his opponent, Secretary Madison. However, in all candor, I*

will also admit that I often mistook our differences of policy for differences of principle; and that on more than one occasion I attributed to him motives that were alien to his patriot's heart. I have come to know Hamilton better in these last four years, when he has ably represented New York in the United States Senate, and I have found him to be a man of character and decency, who loves this land no less than any Republican. In short, I was wrong about him, and I wish to confess it here for all my countrymen to see. President Hamilton and I may yet disagree on many matters of policy, but in leaving this office, I cannot but wish him well, and pray that the same divine Providence which has favored our land from the beginning will guide his words and deeds, that America may become greater, freer, and more virtuous as well as more prosperous under his administration.

As the morning of his inauguration drew closer, Alex worked feverishly on his address to the nation. A brilliant and rapid-fire writer, he knew that this speech would set the tone for his entire presidency. Alex had always loved the high drama of the courtroom, priding himself on his ability to sway a jury with a symphony of words carefully woven. On the Senate floor, he had further polished his literary and oratorical skills, speaking to a room full of men who often had more experience and education than he did. He also drew on his reservoir of experience as a cabinet secretary, when he had spoken in a room with only five other men in attendance, using his words and indomitable will to win the President and his fellow cabinet members over to his point of view.

But at this moment, Alex would be speaking to the entire nation. Federalists, Republicans, common folks, captains of trade and industry, and masters of huge Southern plantations alike would either hear him in person or read his speech in their local newspapers. He had no wish to cause a panic; however, he also recognized that it was time to reveal his guiding purpose to the people he had been elected to govern. He expected to encounter bitter and entrenched resistance to his plan of emancipation, especially in the Deep South. He also knew that the Republicans and more extreme Federalists would be watching like hawks to see if he intended to assert a more vigorous role for the Federal government in shaping national policy at the expense of the States.

Even with all these concerns pressing in on him, Hamilton still felt a great sense of optimism and hope. Against all odds, he had triumphed. He had risen from obscurity and poverty to become an officer by virtue of his quick wits and heroism on the battlefield. He had, by dint of sheer ability, earned a place in the cabinet of the new nation's President. He had survived scandal and disgrace, and the bullet of a rival hell-bent on killing him. He had revitalized a dying political party, and against all odds he had been elected to the United States Senate. He had helped avert war with Great Britain and received the grudging thanks of a President who had once despised him. And now . . . he was about to take the oath of office as the President of the United States! As he lay down to sleep the night before his inauguration, he remembered his beautiful, brilliant, fiery-tempered mother, and wished that she could see him now; her little Alex standing at the pinnacle of power. He thought of his recently deceased father, a man with whom he had longed to reconnect throughout his adult life, and hoped that he, too, would be proud of his son's achievements. Other faces flickered through his dreams that night; he saw Laurens and Lafayette, Washington, and Henry Knox, all his companions, some still living, others gone on ahead in death.

He woke just before dawn the next morning, and the first face that greeted his eyes was that of Eliza, her rich brown hair spread out on the pillow next to him, a soft smile on her lips.

"Are you well, my love?" she said. "You were talking in your sleep, calling out so many different names!"

"I am feeling wonderful, my dear! I am happy, confident, and full of energy this morning," he said. "We have a momentous day before us, but before it begins, come here and let me show you how wonderful I feel!"

He caught her in his arms, and time stood still for a while.

An hour later, Alex stood before the mirror, buttoning his coat. Like Washington and Jefferson before him, he chose to dress in American-made fabrics, a coat woven in Boston and trousers and stockings from New York, accompanied by a pair of polished leather shoes from a cobbler in Virginia. As he adjusted his cravat, Eliza came up to him and kissed him firmly on the cheek.

"If you are as good a President as you are a lover, our nation shall be well served indeed, husband of mine!" she said, and Alex kissed her one more time.

"You had best get dressed, my love, you have a breakfast to attend with the wives of the Congress!" he said. "And you have been enough of a distraction already this morning!"

"I don't recall you complaining," she said with a wink, but retreated to her closet and began pulling out the lovely navy-blue formal dress she had purchased in New York before their journey to Washington a month before.

Alex had been invited to dine with the Congressmen and Senators that morning before riding to the White House to meet President Jefferson—they had agreed to ride to the capitol building together in the same carriage to show that the unity of the nation transcended partisan differences. Speaker of the House Joseph Varnum, along with outgoing Vice President Clinton, were waiting to walk Hamilton to the large outdoor pavilion that had been set up to host the meal. It had rained the day before, and the streets were muddy, but no rain or snow fell throughout the day on March 4, 1809. The air was cool but not chilly, and Alex smiled and exchanged pleasantries with both men as they made their way to the head of the table.

"I must give you credit, Senator Hamilton," said Clinton. "We've been at odds since the day you became Treasury Secretary, but you are the most indestructible man I have ever encountered! I wrote you off as a spent force at least a half dozen times, but like Lazarus, you refuse to stay in your grave. I will not lie and say that I like you, sir, but I do wish you well."

"I will accept your good wishes with a grateful heart, and return them fourfold, Mister Vice President," said Hamilton. "Today is a day for clean slates all around! Let our past enmities be put aside as we forge a new path forward, for our nation and ourselves."

Clinton gave a curt bow, and then Speaker Varnum stepped up to the podium that had been set at the head of the table. The buzz of conversation died away as all faces turned to the venerable Massachusetts politician. Varnum was only a few years older than Hamilton, but he carried them heavily—his hair was white, and his face deeply lined, but his voice was firm and clear as he addressed the assembly:

"Distinguished colleagues, Senators and Representatives alike, it is my great pleasure to introduce to you the next President of the United States, Senator Alexander Hamilton of New York!" he said with a flourish. The legislators applauded, and Hamilton gave a courtly bow. Varnum continued: "Sir, we have come to respect and esteem you as a member of our Congress, and now we look forward to working with you as you go to head the Executive Branch of our government. At this time, we would invite you to say a few words before the Chaplain of the Congress blesses our meal."

Hamilton stood and surveyed the membership of the outgoing 10th United States Congress, joined by the newly elected members of the 11th Congress. While the Republicans still held a majority in both houses, the Federalists had increased their numbers in both houses to a respectable minority.

"Lawmakers of the United States Congress," he said, "on this occasion I address you as my colleagues for the last time. It has been a distinct pleasure to work with you, whether directly, as with my fellow Senators, or indirectly, as with my friends in the House. We have accomplished much together, and much remains to be done. As I take control of the Executive Branch of the government for the next four years, I am keenly aware of the brilliance of our system, which created three coequal branches to stand as perpetual watchdogs on each other, guarding the liberties of our people. I have much to say to you, and to the American people, and I will begin saying it shortly, as I stand to take the oath of office. But what I will ask of you, our Congress, is simply this: do not let the good of your party or faction stand in the way of the good of the country. Remember that you are elected to represent the people, as delegates of their will, and stewards of the rule of law. What matters in the end is not whether we are good Federalists or good Republicans, but whether we are good Americans. I will always strive to be worthy of that noblest of titles, and I pray that you will do likewise. Now, let us refresh ourselves as we prepare for the tasks of the day!"

At that point Chaplain Obadiah Brown stood and intoned a solemn prayer of gratitude for the food and blessings for the new President and the nation he would lead. Brown was a tall, garrulous man, pastor of Washington's First Baptist Church. He was a bit radical in his theology for Hamilton's taste, since Alex favored a more liturgical brand of Christianity, but he was also a witty, engaging fellow and an excellent conversationalist, and his prayer was eloquent and heartfelt.

When the invocation was done, the hungry politicians dove into a delicious breakfast. Platters were piled high with rashers of bacon, ham, and sausage; eggs were available in a half dozen different styles, and there was a variety of nuts and some small, sweet apples that had survived the winter with their flavor intact. There were also biscuits and pastries aplenty, with various sauces and gravies. When the meal was done everyone pronounced themselves fortified and ready for the day.

Hamilton made a point to circulate to each Senator and Congressman and speak a few words; many of them were old friends or rivals, and even the most hostile critics tried to be civil on the auspicious occasion. One young man made a strong impression on Alex; he was a tall, sparely built Kentuckian with an unruly mop of hair, a high, aquiline nose, and piercing eyes.

"Henry Clay, Congressman of Kentucky's Second District," he said in a deep voice with a rolling Southern accent. "I will admit, sir, that I favored Secretary Madison over yourself, but your remarks earlier were candid and refreshing, and I have deeply studied your record as Treasury Secretary. I think our country will be in good hands during your tenure, and as long as your policies do not violate my conscience, you can count on my support."

"I thank you for that, Representative Clay," Alex said. "And I hope that my policies will always withstand the test of conscience."

After bidding farewell to the Congressmen and Senators, Hamilton rode his horse down the ankle-deep mud of Pennsylvania Avenue to the Executive Mansion, where President Jefferson awaited his arrival.

"Good morning, Mister President," said Hamilton cordially. "I cannot tell you how grateful I am that you have chosen to attend my inauguration and lend your good will to the beginning of my presidency."

"It is the least I could do, after the honorable struggle for office has been decided by the will of the people," Jefferson said. "If you are as happy to be entering this House as I am to be leaving it, then you are the happiest of men!"

He escorted Hamilton inside, to the President's personal office space. The walls were bare, save for a framed copy of the United States Constitution, and the desk was freshly cleaned and polished. Neatly positioned in the center of the desktop was an ivory-colored envelope with Hamilton's name written on the outside in Jefferson's flowing script.

"I have left you a letter to read, after I am gone," Jefferson said. "It's mostly advice on small things regarding the office, and some personal thoughts on your agenda."

"I thank you for your courtesy, and I look forward to reading it," Hamilton said.

"My personal effects are packed up and will be gone by tomorrow," Jefferson said. "One of your sons came by last night and asked about having your bedding delivered this morning, so I went ahead and had the linens stripped after I got up. You are in for a long day, my young friend, and it would not do for you to have no clean sheets and warm blankets awaiting you at its end."

"You are the soul of courtesy, Mister President," said Hamilton. "I hope that you shall come back sometime as our personal guest, after we have time to get settled in."

"I think the best thing that I can do for you, and for our country, is to step away from the national stage, and return to the simple life of a farmer," Jefferson said. "You have been chosen by the people to lead this country, and the last thing you need is me hanging about like a pastor who has resigned the pulpit but still sits in the front row every Sunday, exciting comparisons among the congregation!"

"You are a wise man, Mister President," Hamilton said. "I do pray that you will reconsider supporting me in the supreme object of my presidency, however. Your voice would carry great weight."

Jefferson looked at him wistfully.

"You seem so certain of your purpose," he said. "I fear the consequences of your crusade, even as I recognize its essential justice. I am reminded of something that Doctor Franklin was supposed to have said in a certain secret meeting—that while I do not approve of all parts of this plan, I am not sure I shall never approve them."

Hamilton was well aware of the letter that Benjamin Franklin had addressed to the members of the Federal Convention in 1787, even though he had not been there when it was read, on the day the final vote on the Constitution was taken.

"Well then, President Jefferson, I pray that my plan will stand the test of time as well as the work of our convention has," he said.

As the two men spoke, they had been donning their outer coats and heading toward the front doors of the White House. A carriage was waiting, and the driver assisted the two Presidents, one outgoing and the other incoming, as they took their seats. It was a short ride up the hill to the rear entrance of the United States Capitol Building. A platform had been erected at the top of the front steps, and a huge crowd stretched out on the green sward that sloped down the hill from the majestic building towards the Potomac River. Hamilton took his seat next to President Jefferson; former President John Adams sat further down the row, looking on with pride as his son was sworn in as the nation's Vice President.

John Quincy Adams spoke only briefly after taking the oath; he was not a longwinded public speaker, and he had also told Alex that he did not want to overshadow the presidential address in any way. In a matter of moments, the Vice President's role was concluded, and Chief Justice John Marshall, a longtime friend and political ally of Hamilton's, stepped up to administer the presidential oath of office.

"Senator Hamilton, will you repeat after me," Marshall said, and Alex nodded. For a moment silence fell over the vast crowd, and Hamilton's high, clear voice echoed in the cool March breeze.

"I, Alexander Hamilton, do solemnly swear that I will faithfully execute the office of President of the United States, and will to the best of my ability preserve, protect, and defend the Constitution of the United States, so help me God!"

Hamilton then bent and kissed the Bible on which he had sworn the oath of office, and the crowd broke into loud cheers. Alex shook hands with the Chief Justice and bowed to his two predecessors. Then he gave Eliza a quick wink and a smile, seeing the pride beam from her lovely face. That done, he turned to face the multitude that had come to witness him taking office. The crowd fell silent, waiting to hear what the new President would have to say. Alex knew that those most distant from the capitol steps would be unable to follow his words, but he had already seen to it that over a hundred copies of his address were printed up, waiting to be distributed to newspapers in all seventeen states. Alex closed his eyes for a second and prayed for guidance, and then he spoke.

"Fellow citizens," he began. "Members of the House and Senate, Justices of the Supreme Court, Presidents Jefferson and Adams, Vice Presidents Adams and Clinton, honorable officers of our armed forces, governors, state legislators, and all others who have come to honor our country this day. It is with the deepest sense of humility that I stand before you as the fourth President of the United States. I am sensible of the honor that the nation has done me, and I shall always strive to be worthy of it. I should also like to pay homage here to those who have gone before us, who no longer dwell in the land of the living; to my many brave comrades of the Revolution who perished under enemy fire, men like Hugh Mercer and John Laurens. Most of all, I should ask us on this occasion to honor the memory of the first holder of this office, the Father of our country, His Excellency, President George Washington."

The crowd applauded at the mention of the first President's name, and Alex paused a moment. The breeze had died down, and it appeared that his voice was carrying well. A good thing, he thought, for now he was coming to the meat of his inaugural address.

"As a nation, we began by declaring that all men are created equal," he said. "It is one thing to enunciate such a noble principle, and another to practice it. But my presence here, today, preparing to assume the duties of Chief Magistrate, is evidence that we meant what we said in those founding statements. America, as many of you know, is not the land of my birth. I came here at the beginning of our Revolutionary conflict, a poor student from a distant and destitute land, with few connections and not a penny to my name. But I fell in love with the words of our Declaration of Independence the first time I heard them, and I love them to this day. For this country enabled me to raise myself up, to come from poverty and anonymity and take a seat at the councils of the great. I fought for that noble declaration, and fight for it still. I have served America as a soldier, as a delegate to the Federal Convention, as a Cabinet Secretary, and as a Senator. Now, through your electors, you, my fellow citizens, have entrusted me with the highest office in the land. As a man who began with nothing, how can I be anything other than eternally grateful to the nation that has done so much for me?"

Once more the crowd applauded Hamilton's words with great enthusiasm. He waited for a moment, and then resumed speaking.

"During the war, while I served on the staff of His Excellency General Washington of immortal fame, there was one man who was closer to me than any other. He was more of a brother to me than my own blood brother; and his friendship was the strongest bond I had made with another human being since the death of my mother when I was but a child. I am speaking of my dear departed friend John Laurens, son of the honorable Henry Laurens of South Carolina. John and I could not have been more different—he was the son of a wealthy planter with everything to lose; I was a penniless immigrant with everything to gain. Yet our love of liberty made us brothers, and but for his tragic death in a meaningless skirmish at the very end of the war, he might well be standing where I am right now."

The crowd was now dead silent. Laurens had been loved by many, but he had also been in his grave now for over twenty-five years. Many wondered why Hamilton would bring him up on this occasion.

"John Laurens was a true son of liberty in every sense of the word, and one thing that vexed him deeply was the fundamental hypocrisy that lay at the heart of our founding principles. We claimed boldly that all men are created equal, and yet in practice, we denied that principle every day by our practice of slavery. John and I had many deep conversations on this subject, and one of his most deeply held beliefs was that those who deny liberty to their fellow men deserve it not for themselves. He planned to devote his life to the abolition of slavery when the war was ended, but alas! It was the war that ended him instead."

There was scattered applause, but there were also some glares from the Southern delegates. Laurens had been courtly and charming, but his views on slavery were considered heretical by many of his friends, and even his family.

"Like most of you, I loved the memory of Colonel Laurens, but I had disregarded this passion of his—at least, for a time. But as I grow older, and I hope at least a bit wiser, I see the rightness of his convictions more clearly year by year. Are we indeed to be the land of the free? Is liberty as precious to us as we claim? Then how can we systematically deny it to our fellow human beings, simply because of an accident of birth or skin color? Do we truly deserve to be free when we sell women and children at the auction block?

"No one is more sensible than myself of the limitations our Constitution places on the Federal government, my fellow citizens. Indeed, I helped craft some of those limits, over twenty years ago. No President, no Congress, has the power to force emancipation on any state or individual. What we cannot do, we will not do, but I swear before you today, in the presence of God Almighty, and all of you, and all those who have gone before us to stand in His presence, what we can do, we will! In the places the Constitution grants the President and Congress the authority to act, we will act. And beyond all of that, this high office that I assume today is a powerful pulpit from which to preach the gospel of liberty to our nation, and to all nations, and that is what I will do!"

Although many Southerners continued to stare at the new President in shock and thinly veiled hostility, the vast majority of those present were caught up in Hamilton's rhetoric, and that last line evoked a storm of cheers from the crowd. Hamilton smiled and continued.

"John Randolph of Virginia spoke truly when he said: 'This infernal slave trafficking is the curse of heaven upon our land!' My friends, I believe that slavery is a curse that will bite us deeply if it is not curtailed and ultimately abolished. I recognize that the people of the South are deeply dependent upon slave labor, and I would not see them impoverished. That which needs to be done must be done with patience, and the greatest respect to the rights of property as well as the right to liberty. All I ask is that every American, whether northern or southern in his residence, recognize with me that slavery is a danger to our nation, and that we must work together to find a way to eliminate that danger. It will be a slow process, I fear. State by state, perhaps even district by district. But let us go forward together, my friends, in the name of liberty, in the name of Republicanism, in the name of Federalism, and in the sacred name of America! Let us call on each other, and on our nation, to live out the words of our founding creed, that all men are created equal, and that they are endowed by their Creator with certain unalienable rights, and that chief among these are life, liberty, and the freedom to pursue happiness and prosperity, for ourselves and for our children. Let these be more than words on a page, to be recited on the Fourth of July. Let them truly become principles we live by, principles we govern by, and principles we apply equally to all men!"

Even the most diehard Southerners were swept away by the power of Jefferson's words, quoted by the man who had once been his nemesis. The crowd rose to their feet and cheered, and Hamilton stood, basking in the moment. Finally, the people grew quiet, and Alex gave his conclusion.

"Eight years ago, my predecessor said that we are all Federalists, and we are all Republicans," he said. "We have not always practiced those noble sentiments. But I would like to make it known that I stand here today, not as the President of the Federalist faction, or the Republican faction, or the growing Democratic faction. I was elected to be President of all Americans, and that is what I shall strive to be. I know that the needs of the country are great, and that no one man can begin to meet them all. But I do ask each of you, even if you oppose my plans, to do so in a spirit of patriotism and good will for our nation. Let us work together when we can, and when we reach points of disagreement, let us not allow our differences on policy to undermine our broad agreement on principle. Let the rights and liberties of our people be our north star, our sure point in a changing world, and I am sure that we shall not sail too far off course in our quest to build an empire of liberty that shall be the envy of the world! Now with a deep humility in the face of Divine Providence, let us move forward together towards our common goal."

With those words, Alexander Hamilton concluded his address and bowed deeply to the crowd. Even as he retreated into the capitol building to prepare for his first reception, the buzz of voices raised in earnest debate and conversation grew and swelled behind him. President Hamilton's war on slavery had begun.

CHAPTER EIGHTEEN

FROM *The Washington Federalist*, March 10, 1809

HURRAH FOR LIBERTY!
PRESIDENT HAMILTON'S BOLD CRUSADE

In his inaugural address, our new President has declared a second American Revolution to fulfill the promise of the first. Proclaiming his desire to establish "an empire of liberty," Alexander Hamilton pledged his administration to the policy of first containing, and then ultimately abolishing, chattel slavery in America. It is a controversial stance, to be sure, but it raises a worthy question that has plagued America since our foundation—is slavery compatible with a Republican form of government? We have long given an affirmative answer to this query, justifying it by claiming that Africans are an inferior order of being, inherently savage and unable to function or live within a free society of white Christians. And yet when one travels to Massachusetts and elsewhere in New England, one finds free blacks who are thriving tradesmen and day laborers, living industrious and peaceful lives, and raising their children up to do the same. This would certainly seem to belie that claim.

However, supposing that these free black men are the exception, and that the majority of their people are the savages that slaveowners claim them to be, there remains another question: do we have the moral or legal right to enslave others simply because they come from a society more primitive than our own? Does might make right?

For most of human history, the answer to that question has been an overwhelming affirmative. However, it has also been assumed since creation that servitude is the natural condition of the majority of mankind; that kings and emperors have a divine right to rule over other, lesser mortals. In America, we have prided ourselves on turning that notion on its head, proclaiming to the world that we are done with kings and despots forever. Perhaps it is time for us to teach the world another lesson—that the powerful need not prey on the weak; that slaves and masters are no more natural and necessary than kings and czars. We wish President Hamilton the best in his noble crusade; and to our concerned friends in the South, we remind you that the President has pledged himself to be limited by the powers delegated to him by the Constitution, to be mindful or the rights of property as well as the principles of liberty. We trust that he will keep his word and urge that you do the same.

From *The Charlestown Courier*, May 11, 1809:

HAMILTON'S WAR ON PROPERTY
OUR NEW PRESIDENT'S SINISTER
DECLARATION OF LIBERTY:
WILD AFRICANS AMONG US!

President Hamilton—a name and title that should reek in the nostrils of every Southern Republican—wasted no time in showing his true colors! In his inaugural address, he declared war on the prosperity of the South and the social order of the entire nation by pledging his administration to the abolition of slavery, and worse yet, to allow "liberated" African savages to live among us, assuring us that our knowledge of their brutal nature, born of long experience, is mistaken and that they will become a peaceful and well-ordered class of paid laborers. To the everlasting shame of our state, he dared invoke the name of one of our most precious martyrs of the Revolution, John Laurens, as the inspiration for his sinister scheme.

In a single blow, the President has declared war on the very foundations of the South's economic prosperity and has presented our nation with a nightmare scenario from the lurid imagination of a fevered novelist. What next, Mister President? Since we are going to free these savage beasts to live among us, are we going to grant them citizenship? Will we see Negro voters, Negro legislators, perhaps a Negro President? Will you see these dusky barbarians defile the fair-haired daughters of the South as their mad shrieks break the very clouds? Will you see our plantations in flames, our fields untended and unharvested, and grass growing in the streets of our fair cities? For those would be the least of the evils wrought by your horrible plan. Make no mistake: the abolition of slavery will be the end of the South as we know it, and therefore the end of America!

For years, Southern Republicans have strived to warn the nation of the boundless ambitions, corrupt practices, and moral depravity of Mister Hamilton. Despite our best efforts, this libertine, monarchical duelist has now been elected to our nation's highest office. Let the nation now bear witness that our assessment of his character was correct! We do not know which is more shameful; that a man of Alexander Hamilton's character could be elected to the presidency, or that so many good and decent Southerners, including Secretary Madison, should be so deceived as to his nature and intentions. Well, now both have been made clear.

The battle lines have been drawn, men of the South! A war for the survival of white America is looming, and all that we hold dear—Christianity, patriotism, and the purity of our race—is at stake. Let the President be warned: this attack on our way of life will not stand!

One peculiarity of nineteenth-century American government is that once the new Congress was sworn into office in March, they almost immediately went into recess until late May. This odd custom gave Alex time to study the impact of his inaugural address, and to begin using the influence of his office to win converts to his cause. One of his first targets was the Governor of Virginia, a rather cranky old curmudgeon by the name of John Tyler. Sixty-two years of age and looking a decade older, Tyler had been an opponent of the Constitution during the Virginia debates on ratification but had eventually been won over by the success of Washington's presidency. He did not care for Hamilton but let himself be persuaded to visit the White House as a guest of Secretary Madison on this fine April morning.

Hamilton knew that Virginia was critical to his efforts. Home to two of America's Presidents and of the last great battleground of the Revolution, Virginia was the most influential state of the South. Where Virginia led, the South would follow—or at least, a few other Southern states might do so. No longer as dependent on slave labor as the lower South, Virginia's voice still counted heavily among its fellow slave states. Not for the last time,

Hamilton thanked God that James Madison had joined him in his effort. Madison might be small in stature, but his influence in Virginia was enormous, and his friendship with Jefferson still counted heavily in his favor.

As he waited in the President's office, he walked around and looked at the artwork he'd chosen to adorn his walls. A bust of Washington stood behind his desk on the right, a reminder to all who visited of the link between America's first and fourth Presidents. Hamilton regarded himself as Washington's heir in many ways; he hoped to complete the work that His Excellency had begun by truly uniting the states of America in a bond that regional loyalties and interests could not break. On the left, there was a bust of John Adams, whose goodwill and energetic letter writing campaign had helped Hamilton carry New England in the 1808 election.

Across from his desk, flanking the door, there were two busts: one of Jefferson and one of Benjamin Franklin. Jefferson was there to remind Hamilton of the opposition he'd overcome in order to reach the high station he now occupied, but also to help him remember that political foes need not be enemies. As for Doctor Franklin, he was there simply because Alex admired his creative genius, his art for compromise, and most of all his wry and occasionally earthy sense of humor.

On the wall to the right, there was a framed portrait of Alex as a young officer in the Revolution, wearing the uniform of a New York artilleryman and leaning against an earthwork. Across from it on the opposite wall, there was a painting of the British surrender at Yorktown. While Washington and General Benjamin Lincoln dominated the foreground, Alex was visible in this painting also, mounted on a horse behind the Commander in Chief.

Finally, framed copies of the U.S. Constitution and the Declaration of Independence rounded out the room's décor, hanging on the walls next to each of the paintings from the Revolution. Alex had chosen and positioned the pieces very carefully, so that all who visited his presidential office would be reminded of those who had held it before, and the military and political conflicts that had created the country. Alex was proud that he had played a role, both in winning America's independence and shaping its government, and wanted his visitors to be aware of that. Radical he might be, but America itself was a radical experiment; and one that was far from concluded.

On his desk lay a bound copy of *The Federalist,* and his well-thumbed King James Bible. Ever since his brush with death, Alex had made a point of reading from it twice a day and remembering to thank God for the many blessings He had bestowed. Alex surveyed his office one last time, straightened his collar, looked at his pocket watch, and listened for the sound of footsteps coming up the hallway. At the stroke of ten, exactly on schedule, he heard the footsteps of two men approaching. He opened the door before they could knock.

James Madison was dressed in his usual severe black, but his expression was less grave than of old, and the wrinkles around his mouth betrayed his newfound habit of smiling. He and Alex had grown closer during the months since the election, and Madison was excited about continuing his role as the President's chief diplomat and confidant.

John Tyler was tall, white haired, and slightly stooped, with a long, aquiline nose. He wore a small pair of spectacles perched at its bridge which magnified his watery blue eyes and gave him the look of a slightly drunken bird of prey.

"Governor Tyler, so good of you to come!" Alex said. "Please, both of you step on in and have a seat. I will have the butler bring us some tea."

"Thank you, Mister President," said Tyler, slowly settling into one of the padded guest chairs across from the President's desk. "A bit of tea would go down nicely."

Madison took the other chair, perching on its edge, his keen eyes darting back and forth between the two like a bird's. Robert O'Malley, the new White House butler, brought in a silver tray with a teapot and three cups, along with a sugar bowl. Hamilton waited until all three cups were poured, and then after O'Malley left, he spoke.

"Governor Tyler, I have invited you here because you wield enormous influence in Virginia, and in the South overall. You are one of the most respected statesmen of the region," Hamilton said. "I will tell you, sir, in strictest confidence, that I believe slavery will have deadly consequences for our Union if it is not placed on the path to extinction. Every year its baleful influence grows, and its tentacles sink deeper and deeper into the Southern economy. In another decade, the South will be too deep in its thrall to let it go, without a bloody civil war. But if Virginia leads, the South will follow—and if you, sir, take a lead, then Virginia will follow you. Secretary Madison has already made the shift to paying his field hands and liberating them from bondage. I would like for you to join in the effort."

Tyler leaned forward, rubbing his gnarled knuckles under his chin.

"Sir, as much as I respect your passion on this subject, I think you are unnecessarily alarmist. I see no danger in the perpetuation of slavery; it's been here for nigh on two hundred years! Why should I court economic ruin?" the governor asked.

"You would not be," said James Madison. "I will admit, I was skeptical of President Hamilton's plan, but I emancipated my Negroes in January, and they are working harder than they ever did while in bondage. I don't have to keep an overseer; one of their own arbitrates all disputes and keeps them on task. My fields were plowed and planted in record time; I may have my best harvest in years! Even deducting the money I am paying my workers, I stand to make a handsome profit on my fields this year."

"Working harder? How the devil did you manage that?" asked Tyler. "My overseer stands over those lazy devils all day long with a whip and they still move at a snail's pace!"

"Of course they do," said Madison. "Why should they work harder when their only reward is more work? My strategy was simple: I treated them as if they were white men whom I wanted to do a job, rather than cattle who have no minds of their own."

"Preposterous!" snapped Tyler. "Everyone knows blacks are little more than animals! They are incapable of understanding liberty, much less enjoying it."

"Then why is Secretary Madison's new strategy working so well?" Hamilton asked. "Sir, indulge me for a moment, if you will. Ever since I arrived in America as a penniless seventeen-year-old immigrant, I have found myself thrown into the company of Southern planters. Washington, Laurens, Jefferson, Secretary Madison here—I've watched all of them struggle to balance their accounts in war and in peacetime. One thing I have seen is that all of you, regardless of how many acres and how many Negroes you own, all struggle to turn a profit, and most of you are deep in debt."

"I resent that, sir, my debts are a fraction of the total value of my holdings," said Tyler.

"But not of your profits, are they?" Hamilton asked. "The South counts wealth in land and slaves, not in profits, or money in the bank, or interest rates. Will you concede, sir, that I know a bit about how money works?"

"Obviously," said Tyler. "Your work as Secretary of the Treasury established that beyond all doubt. I opposed your financial system, but having seen it work out in practice, I am willing to concede that I was wrong."

"Then let me explain why your system consistently turns out more debt than profit," Hamilton said. "The heart of all commerce is labor and capital. We use labor to create capital, but we must expend capital to acquire labor. Now, in the North, we pay our workers. Those who shirk their duties are dismissed from employment, but those who excel are given opportunities to advance themselves and become something more than they are. Paid laborers work harder and more conscientiously because they want to advance themselves. Now, the South takes the attitude that, because slave labor is cheaper, it must be more efficient. And it does look that way on the surface—you pay for a slave one time and have his labor for the rest of his life. Pair him with a female, and you get more laborers for free, right?"

"Precisely!" said Tyler. "Some of the slaves on our plantation have been there for three generations now."

"Here is the weakness," said Hamilton. "The labor you get is resentful and inefficient. What motivation is there for the slave to excel at anything? He is consigned to a lifetime of bondage, with little or no hope of ever receiving his liberty. His children will likewise be consigned to a life of toil. He has no power over his own body, or his own family. His wife can be sold away, or simply taken and ravaged at will by any white man on the plantation."

"By God, sir, what are you insinuating?" demanded Tyler. "I have never touched a slave woman!"

"Are there any mulattoes on your plantation?" the President rejoined.

"Well, yes, I don't control who my slave women choose to breed with," said Tyler uncomfortably.

"Neither do they," said Hamilton. "I suppose that they do get to choose their husbands sometimes, but the fact is no slave woman is free to refuse the favors of any white man who wants her. Nor is her husband free to protect her from her ravishers. Would you, Governor, give your best effort to a master who allowed your wife to be raped by any white man who came along? Who regarded your children as his personal property, to buy or sell or flog as he sees fit? That is the weakness of slave labor—and it is why nearly all you Southern planters are career debtors."

"I never thought of it that way," said Tyler.

"Are you a Christian man, sir?" asked Hamilton.

"Well of course," the Governor said. "I have been a deacon in my church for years."

"The greatest rule ever laid down for mankind came from our Lord and Savior Himself," Alex said, "when he told us to 'Do unto others as you would have them do unto you.' Sir, in a million years, would you want anyone to treat you the way these hapless Negroes are treated on a typical Southern plantation?"

Tyler thought hard for a minute, and finally laughed out loud.

"I suppose not, sir!" he finally said. "By God, I never looked at our system like that before. It really is not a very Christian thing, is it? But then why does the Apostle Paul tell slaves to be obedient to their masters?"

"The purpose of the Gospel was to change men's hearts, not their laws," said Hamilton. "But when enough hearts are changed, the laws will follow. Slavery cannot coexist with Christ's golden rule forever. Will you help me, sir? Will you help rid America of this injustice, and in so doing make our world a bit closer to the place God intended it to be?"

Tyler rose and took the President by the hand.

"I will, sir!" he said. "If Secretary Madison would be so kind as to share with me how he has done all of this, I should be most grateful."

"Why don't you come with me to Montpelier," Madison said, "and I will let you see my system in operation. President Hamilton was kind enough to draft a plan of action that has proved most effective; I shall be glad to draw you up a copy. As a matter of fact, sir, since we have some time before Congress convenes, why don't you come, also? We have known each other for over twenty years, and you have never once been a guest in my home! I am sure Dolley would welcome you and your lovely wife."

"I haven't left the city since December," said Alex. "I should be glad for a chance to get away for a bit. And I have no pressing business to attend to at the moment, so there is no reason I cannot come. I will inform Eliza, so she can begin to prepare the children for the journey—if that is all right?"

"Absolutely!" said Madison. "I have always wished that my wife and I could have children, but that has been denied us. My stepson, John, is seventeen and lonely; it will be good to have your energetic brood running around the place!"

"And, perhaps if the two of you could consider it together, I would love the chance to meet with some of your friends and neighbors who might be inclined to support my free labor proposal," the President added.

"Capital idea!" said Madison. "They can see for themselves how well things are working out on Montpelier. Indeed, I shall let Nero know what is at stake before that week. One thing I have realized is that these people are not stupid. They know that their performance may help win freedom for their fellow Africans, and that is a further incentive for them to excel."

"You actually shared your plans with your workers?" Tyler asked.

"As I said, when I made up my mind to do this, I decided that I would treat them as if they were white men," Madison said. "And thus far, I have not regretted that decision."

"Remarkable!" said Tyler. "I would like to hear more about this."

Hamilton smiled as the two men excused themselves, and he could hear their voices echoing down the White House corridor for some time after they left his office.

LATER THAT evening, a hundred miles away at Monticello, Thomas Jefferson lay in bed, watching as Sally Hemings prepared to join him. Theirs was a complex relationship; Sally was his slave, but she was also almost certainly the half-sister of his long-dead wife, Martha. Martha's father was a well-known Casanova who had showered his attentions on any woman who caught his eye, slave or free. One of those women had been Sally's mother, a slave on his plantation.

It was Sally's resemblance to his beautiful spouse that first drew Jefferson to her, when she had joined his household in France as a teenager. Shortly after his return to America two years later, he had taken her to his bed, unable to bear the agony of loneliness anymore, but bound by his promise to his dying wife that he would never remarry. Oddly enough, Jefferson, the most thoughtful of men, had taken this sixteen-year-old girl as his concubine without any forethought. She was his property, he wanted her, and so he took her. It was an impulse that had become a habit, which then slowly grew into a marriage in all but name.

But he had thought long and hard about their relationship since then. Sally was quite intelligent, and in many ways the equal of any white woman—hardly surprising, since she was three-quarters white and could have passed as a white woman in any northern city. Their children looked no different than the sons and daughters of many of Jefferson's white Virginia neighbors, but the stigma of their one-eighth Negro ancestry made them slaves for life, just as Sally's nearly invisible African heritage made her

Jefferson's legal property. Jefferson the idealist recognized the fundamental hypocrisy of his being a slave owner while professing to be a champion of liberty; Jefferson the moralist despised himself for loving a woman whose love for him was not a matter of choice but of obedience—if she loved him at all, which he sometimes wondered. Did slaves ever truly speak their mind to their masters? Did Sally devote herself to him in the most intimate of ways because she cared for him, or simply because he required it? Such thoughts vexed and tormented him, and yet he could not resist keeping her near him.

The former President watched as she blew out the lamps and brought a single candle to their bedside, then slid into the bed next to him as she did most nights when Jefferson was not entertaining guests. He stared at her face, slightly lined with age but still far more youthful than his—hardly surprising, since she was nearly thirty years younger than him. Sally turned and studied his face in return, a quizzical expression on her face.

"Is there something on your mind, my dear?" he asked, unfailingly polite as always.

"Master Thomas," she said—which was how she had always referred to him. Her speech was clear and fluent and devoid of Negro dialect, having been raised as a house slave. "Is it true that your friend Master Madison has freed his slaves?"

Jefferson sighed. Madison's plantation was only thirty miles from his own; he supposed it was inevitable that word should spread of his friend's bold experiment.

"It is true," he said. "Our new President has persuaded Madison to join his crusade against slavery."

"I see," said Sally, and for a long time said nothing.

"My dear Sally," said Jefferson, "you do know that you are more than just a slave to me, don't you?"

"Yes," she said. "You're a good man, Master Thomas, as far as white men go. You've treated me very gently through all these years, even when I was young and so very scared that first time."

"You were afraid of me?" Jefferson said, stunned. He had never seen himself as frightening to anyone. "I would never have hurt you."

"But you could, at any time," she said. "Even now, when I have been by your side twenty-five years and borne you five children, you could still send me to the auction block tomorrow if you wished. That is the world I live in, my dear Master. You're not a wicked man, far from it! You've always been kind and decent. But it is a wicked world, and this system you and I live on opposite sides of is a wicked system."

In all their years together, Sally had never once spoken to him so plainly about her feelings. Jefferson wondered why she chose to do so now, but then he grasped it and understood.

"You are wondering if I will join Mister Madison and set all of my people free, as he has done, aren't you?" he asked.

"I'd be lying if I told you otherwise," she said. "I am sorry, Master Thomas, if I have said too much. I'll leave if you want me to."

He placed his hand on hers, and gently lifted it to his lips.

"No, dear Sally," he said. "You may stay, and I am not angry at you for speaking your mind. You must think me a dreadful hypocrite, to talk so much of liberty while denying it to you and your children."

"It's not my place to think that," she said.

"What would you do if I set you free?" he asked. "Where would you and our children go?"

"Where else is there for me?" she said. "Mister Madison's slaves stayed because he offered them justice and fair wages. I would stay, because I don't know of any place where I would be treated better. But—" She fell silent, leaving the thought unspoken.

"Go ahead, Sally," he said. "It appears we are being completely honest with each other, perhaps for the very first time in all our years together. Don't stop now."

Sally flushed slightly, something Jefferson found deeply endearing. Finally, she spoke very softly.

"It would be good if I could stay here as a matter of choice, rather than a matter of duty," she said. "And that is all I will say. Do you want me tonight, Master?"

"Stay here and sleep beside me," Jefferson said. "That is all I want this time."

She did as she was told—as indeed she had always done. But Thomas Jefferson stared out the window for many hours that night before sleep finally took him.

CHAPTER NINETEEN

ALEX WAS excited as he and his family prepared for his first trip outside Washington since taking up residence in the Executive Mansion. Of course, traveling as President, even in the political off season, was not quite the same thing as traveling as a civilian, or even as a member of the Senate. For one thing, he found that staying in taverns was a thing of the past. No matter where he traveled, local dignitaries were anxious to host him and his family. The President's two oldest boys, Alex and James, were in New York, busy at their studies, and the fragile Angelica had remained at their new home in Washington City in the loving care of the family's cook and nursemaid, Mrs. Benson. Angelica was showing signs of mental recovery; she still mostly possessed the mind of a child, but occasionally she would come out of her fog and speak like an adult.

The other children—John Church, William, Lizzie, and Little Phil—were all excited to accompany their parents on the journey, and they rode behind the President in a sturdy carriage. Hamilton had brought Elijah Cartwright along—his Senate page was now the President's personal secretary, and he was as conscientious and dutiful during work hours as he was wild and carefree by night. Eliza Hamilton regarded Cartwright with a certain exasperated indulgence, much as Martha Washington had looked upon Alex during his days as a randy young officer in the

Continental Army. (It had been a standing joke among Washington's military "family" that she had named her feral tomcat "Alex.")

The only other man in the party was Thomas Jefferson's former secretary, Meriwether Lewis, who had led the famous exploration of the Louisiana Purchase and was now back in Virginia after a brief and unhappy stint as territorial governor. He had written Hamilton during the interim between the election and inauguration, asking to be relieved of his duties and complaining of arrears in promised reimbursements from the War Department. Hamilton had discussed the matter with Benjamin Tallmadge and recommended that Lewis be paid the full amount, despite reports from the Territorial Secretary Frederick Bates, who claimed Lewis had been profiteering from the Indian trade. Hamilton knew Bates slightly; he regarded the social-climbing young lawyer as somewhat shady, and his allegations against Lewis had been lacking in proof. Lewis, a melancholy soul at times, was deeply grateful for Hamilton's intervention and had agreed to escort him on his ride through Virginia, since Lewis's family was from there and he had some legal matters to attend to regarding the family estate.

Although senior Virginia Senator William Giles remained an outspoken political foe of Hamilton's, the newly elected Senator Richard Brent was a far more reasonable sort. Nominally a Democratic-Republican, he had still made a point of reaching out to Hamilton after the new Senate was sworn in and unlike many, had not been appalled by Hamilton's anti-slavery sentiments. Since his home was just across the Potomac, not far from Washington's old Mount Vernon residence, he invited the President and his family to stay as his guests on their way to

Montpelier. His plantation was small, and devoted to the growing of fruit trees, so his personal investment in slavery was smaller than that of many Virginians—he owned a half dozen household slaves, and another twenty who worked in his orchards. He also had several children about the age of Hamilton's younger ones, and the two men watched indulgently while the youngsters romped about the yard playing tag and chasing a small pony that Brent had purchased for his daughter.

"Mister President, from what I have read of your wartime career, your opposition to slavery was rather tepid when you were younger," said Brent, puffing contentedly on a cigar. "Why have you chosen to make it such a focal point of your presidency?"

Hamilton watched as little Phil and Lizzie began a contest to see which child could throw an acorn the furthest and smiled, and then turned to his host.

"The older I got, the more I saw the injustice of slavery," he said. "Even before my unfortunate affair of honor with Colonel Burr, I had taken a lead role in its abolition in New York. But as I hung between life and death following my injury, I gained a new clarity on the issue. If we allow the North to continue to develop its economy without slavery, but leave the South dependent on it, our one nation will gradually become two. And as the sections drift further and further apart, their positions on all issues will diverge further and further. Slavery itself could well become the flashpoint of a terrible civil war that will rend our nation to its core. But there is still time to prevent this awful circumstance! If we can persuade most of the Southern states to leave slavery behind, to embrace free labor, to develop manufactures as well as agriculture, then our nation may yet grow together to the point that we live up to the name we optimistically bestowed on ourselves in 1776."

"You are a persuasive man, Mister President," Brent commented. "I will do what I can to support you, but I don't think I can afford to pay my Negroes for their labor."

"I've been thinking about that," said Hamilton. "You see, most people who favor the abolition of slavery have also favored sending these people back to Africa—even though many Negroes have been here for three or four generations and have long forgotten their tribal customs and languages. I propose freeing them and keeping them here as a paid laboring class, and perhaps, over generations, elevating them to the level of citizenship. I think we could persuade the Virginia Assembly to create some sort of financial incentive for planters who voluntarily free their slaves, at least during the transition. I believe that if you follow the plan which I sketched out for Secretary Madison, in a short time you will find your profits increase to the point that you will have no problem meeting your payroll. Most people, white or black, recognize that labor is a necessity of life—as long as they are free to enjoy the fruits of their labor."

"Well, I suppose we shall see about that," Senator Brent rejoined. "The proof of the pudding is in the eating, as they say— speaking of which, I believe it is time for dinner!"

So it continued as Hamilton made his way south; some of the men he stayed with were receptive to his ideas, others were openly hostile, but nearly all extended their hospitality and were willing, at least, to listen. One other thing that he noticed was the intense scrutiny he received from the slaves working in the fields.

They did not put aside their labors, but he could see them watching curiously as he made his way to the various plantation houses, and he wondered how much they knew of him and his plans for their liberation.

President Hamilton was staying at the plantation of James Breckenridge, a Federalist member of Congress who had served with him in the Revolution at the siege of Yorktown, when a remarkable incident happened. He was only one day's ride from Montpelier, and Breckenridge had agreed to accompany him to Madison's home the next day. The children had retired after a hard day of riding followed by an excellent supper. Alex and Congressman Breckenridge were enjoying a brandy on the porch when they heard approaching footsteps and turned to face the twilit path to the front porch.

An ancient Negro stood there, barefoot, his hat in his hand. His face was deeply lined and his hair snow white, and he looked very nervous.

"Cicero, what are you doing here?" Breckenridge asked, not unkindly. Like many Southern planters, he had a paternalistic attitude toward "his people."

"Marse James, is this be Pres'dent Hamilton?" he asked.

"Yes, Cicero, he is. Now why don't you go back to the cabins?" Breckenridge said.

"I will, suh," the old man said. "I jes' wanted to see him fo' myse'f. An' I wanted to tell you somethin', Massah, if I may."

"This is rather irregular, Cicero, but I will listen," said Breckenridge.

"We heard 'bout what Massuh Madison did wiv his slaves jes' down de rivuh," he said. "An' we heard dat it be Pres'dent Hamilton who put him up to it. Me and de uthah slaves, we been talkin'. Iffen you was to free us, suh, and put us to work for wages, we promise we give you de bes' work you evuh seen in yo' life! Jes' give us a chance, suh, and we will show you what we kin do!"

Breckenridge furrowed his brow, and then gave a wry smile.

"That's all well and good, Cicero, but you do realize that you just pretty much confessed that you and all the others are not giving me your best, don't you?" he asked.

The old man hung his head and nodded, but Hamilton had seen enough.

"Cicero, thank you for coming forward," he said. "That took great courage. Now why don't you let me and your master talk for a bit?"

"Yassuh, Mistuh Pres'dent, suh!" The old man bowed deeply and shuffled off.

"You see, James, that is exactly what I am trying to tell you and all the others!" he said once the slave was out of earshot. "No slave ever gives his best effort—why should he? His only reward for his toil is more toil. I hope you will consider giving these blacks a chance, as the old man said, to show you what they can do!"

Breckenridge looked thoughtful, and then shook his head and gave a rueful smile.

"I may have little choice now," he said. "For all his deferential attitude, I think old Cicero was sent to put me on notice."

"Don't be too hard on them," Hamilton said. "It took a lot of nerve for that old fellow to approach us like that."

"I've always tried to treat my Negroes with a measure of kindness, as the Scriptures teach us," Breckenridge said, "for we too have a master in heaven."

"Indeed, we do," said Alex. "And I believe, in the end, that human bondage is one of those things that goes against the deepest tenets of the Christian faith. How can we love our neighbor as ourselves and then sell him on the auction block? Would we have any man do that to us? I hope, sir, that you will join me in forging a new future for America."

"I'll give you my hand on that, Mister President," said Breckenridge, and the two men left the front porch and headed upstairs.

FORTY MILES away, at Monticello, Thomas Jefferson was having a restless night. Unable to sleep, he had put on his slippers and dressing gown and gone downstairs to his library, where he had pulled out his original draft copy of the Declaration of Independence. He knew the words by heart, but on this night, he read them over and over: "We hold these truths to be self-evident, that all men are created equal. . ." Then he looked at his shelves, where the familiar names on the spines of his books glowed faint in the candlelight—Plato, Aristotle, St. Augustine, Locke, Montesquieu, Rousseau, and Hobbes—all the great voices of philosophers from the past. It seemed to him that the theme of liberty ran like a golden thread through all of them, sometimes dingy and muted, sometimes blazing like the noonday sun.

All his life, he had wished to be remembered as one of their number, a thinker who had "sworn eternal hostility to every form of tyranny over the mind of man," as he had proudly said not so many years ago. But right now, he felt more like one of the tyrants he condemned than a champion of freedom. Ever since his conversation with Sally a few weeks before, the fundamental hypocrisy of his life loomed larger and larger in his mind. Thomas Jefferson, proud defender of liberty, who owned over two hundred human beings, ruling their lives with a despotism that George III could only dream of. He recalled something he had written over twenty-five years before: "*The whole commerce between master and slave is a perpetual exercise of the most boisterous passions, the most unremitting despotism on the one part, and degrading submissions on the other.*" He recognized the truth of it, and his complicity in its wrong, today just the same as when he had written it long before, but how could one man change the way the world worked?

And yet, he told himself, that was exactly what Hamilton was attempting to do. The man he had long condemned as a monarchist and champion of despotism was in fact more sincere in his devotion to freedom than Jefferson himself. It was a harsh truth that kept the former President awake long past his normal bedtime.

"Master Thomas, are you all right?" Sally Hemings's voice startled him out of his reverie.

Jefferson groaned under his breath. Ever since their conversation a few nights before, he'd avoided Sally's company. The sight of her was a stark reminder of the moral dilemma that was eating at him.

"I'm fine, Sally," he said. "I just can't seem to sleep lately."

"Would you like some hot tea, or perhaps a brandy?" she asked.

"Perhaps some tea with milk and sugar," he said. "And then, if you would come sit with me, I would be grateful."

"Of course, Master Thomas," she said, and curtsied as she left, as proper as ever. An outside observer would never guess from the exchange that she had borne him five children.

Of course, that was part of the conundrum that was gnawing at Jefferson's guts as the clock struck midnight. He had two sets of children; one set would live their lives as free women, able to marry whom they chose and inherit property and enjoy equal standing with any other citizen; the other set, unless he chose to alter their fate, would be auctioned off like cattle when he died. It was a deeply unjust system; but it was also the way of life he had willingly followed for his sixty years on earth even as he recognized its evil.

But the more he reflected on it, the more he realized that perhaps it was not too late to balance the scales. To think that of all people, it was his archnemesis Alexander Hamilton who had forced him to open his eyes! Thomas Jefferson was a devious man when he had to be, and a ruthlessly effective politician, even though he had regretted the meanness of his tactics at times. But his political career was done; he had served for eight years in the nation's highest office and retired from it with honor. He had little to lose now. He could retire to his life as a quiet Virginia planter, and continue to reap the profits from the labor of his slaves—but then he would die knowing he did nothing when others were taking a stand for liberty. Or he could speak out and do something to help rid the country of a deep moral wrong. As he thought, the choice slowly became clearer in his mind.

"Here you are, Master Thomas," said Sally, setting a cup of warm, sweet tea down before him, then cautiously drawing up a chair beside him. She had sensed the distance between them over the last few days but did not know what it boded.

Jefferson looked at her, this beautiful woman who, but for an accident of birth, might have been the matriarch of any proud Southern clan. She was only one quarter African and, with her olive skin, could easily have passed for a European from Spain, France, or Italy. He saw the uncertainty in her eyes and smiled.

"Do you know what this is, Sally?" he asked her, pointing at the Declaration.

"Yes, Master Thomas," she said. "That is the declaration you wrote, that freed your people from the British."

"You are right," he said. "But do you know what it actually says?"

Sally closed her eyes for a moment, and then began to recite, haltingly at first, but then with greater confidence: *"When in the course of human events it becomes necessary for one people to dissolve the political bands that have connected them with another, and to assume, among the nations of the earth, the free and equal station to which the laws of nature and of nature's God entitle them, a decent respect to the opinions of mankind dictates that they should declare the causes that impel them to this separation. We hold these truths to be self-evident, that all men are created equal—"*

"Sally, that is quite remarkable!" Jefferson said proudly. "I did not know that you had memorized all of that."

She hung her head shyly.

"They are good words," she said. "I am proud that it was my master that wrote them."

That last sentence cut Jefferson more deeply than anything she could have said, and in that flash of self-awareness, he made up his mind.

"Oh, my dear Sally," he said. "If I truly lived up to those ideals, I would never have willingly borne the title of 'Master.' How can I espouse such beliefs and live the way I do? I am the prince of hypocrites!"

Sally Hemings looked at Jefferson, and for a moment the mask of the subservient concubine slipped, and he saw the real woman beneath. There was anger there, but he also saw, to his immense relief, that there was real love as well.

"You didn't ask to be born a master, any more than I asked to be born a slave," she said. "Both of us have done the best we can in a bad situation."

"Perhaps so," he said, "but no more. I will not own any man— or woman—ever again! Do you hear me, Sally? I am setting you free."

Her eyes widened, and suddenly she threw her arms around him in an embrace more passionate than any they had shared before, even in the most intimate of moments.

"I knew it!" she said. "I knew that you had a good heart, if only it could reach through that enormous brain of yours enough that you could hear it speak! Thank you, Master Thomas, thank you!"

"Never call me that again," he said. "I will be just Thomas to you from now on—if you wish to speak to me at all. And whether you choose to stay with me or go and make your own way in the world, there is one thing I want to tell you right now that I have never told you before. I love you, Sally Hemings. I have loved you for all these years, even though my pride and my attachment to custom forbade me from saying so."

"I have always been fond of you for your kindness," she said. "But tonight, for the first time, I can truly say that I love you also. Oh, Master—I mean, Thomas—can I go and tell our children?"

Thomas Jefferson stood and took her by the hand.

"We shall both tell them," he said, "but would you be willing to wait till the morning?"

For the first time in twenty years, Sally Hemings followed Thomas Jefferson to bed of her own free will.

TWO DAYS LATER, at Montpelier, James Madison looked nervously into his dining room, President Hamilton standing at his shoulder. Around the table were some twenty members of the Virginia General Assembly; eight state senators and twelve assemblymen, as well as Governor Tyler. Madison had extended the invitations carefully; each of these men had great influence in the legislature, and if they could be persuaded, they could swing many votes in the upcoming session.

It was a warm May evening, and Madison's workers were still busy in the fields. The Secretary of State thanked the God he was not sure he believed in that the weather had been exceptionally kind thus far this spring; his crops were lush and green, and the year gave promise of a record harvest. Nero—or Nero Madison, as he had taken to proudly calling himself—made sure that the former slaves were all busy about their duties as the Virginia grandees assembled to hear the new President.

Madison looked at Hamilton, who was fairly quivering with nervous energy. He smiled back at his chief—Hamilton's enthusiasm was infectious, and Madison could not help but share it.

"Are you ready for this?" he asked the President.

"One moment," said Hamilton. "Please pray with me."

Madison nodded, and Hamilton bowed his head. Despite the softness of his whispered words, the passion behind them was evident.

"Almighty God," the President prayed, "you gave me my life back when it might well have been lost. You spared me for this moment. Lord, I pray that if what I experienced was truly a vision from you, that you would bless me today and give my words the power that can only come from you, the power to shatter the hardest of hearts and animate them with a love of liberty, and a love of their fellow men, even those they regard as less than men. In the name of Jesus Christ, amen!"

It was a powerful prayer, and even the skeptical Madison was moved by it. But once it was done, Hamilton squared his shoulders and bounded through the door with the energy of a man half his age. The guests stood and applauded as Madison said:

"Gentlemen, the President of the United States, Alexander Hamilton!"

Hamilton gave a deep and courteous bow, then went around the table and greeted each guest by name. Most of them were known to him, although a few were strangers. Madison had told him their names as they watched the carriages arrive from the upstairs window, and Hamilton was equally gracious to them all. After he had made the rounds, he took his place at the head of the table.

"My dear Virginians," he said, "I want to thank you so much for accepting Secretary Madison's invitation to come here and listen to me tonight. Let us thank his gracious wife, the lovely Dolley Madison, for the hospitality of her home!"

There was polite applause, and Mrs. Madison, who was standing beside her husband, curtsied to her guests.

"Virginia occupies a place dear to my heart, and to the heart of every true American," Hamilton said. "When our country needed leadership, Virginia has faithfully provided it—on the field of battle, in the lofty realm of ideals, and in the White House itself."

He was interrupted by another round of applause and paused for a moment to acknowledge the guests' courtesy.

"Now it is time for Virginia to lead once more," he said. "Secretary Madison, Senator Brent, and Congressman Breckenridge have already pledged to join the growing number of Virginia planters renouncing slavery and moving to a system of paid labor instead, giving their Negroes the true dignity of working for their daily bread instead of laboring for another without recompense. You can see the result in the fields of Montpelier—diligent work, motivated not by the threat of the whip but by the promise of just compensation!"

He looked around the room and saw that the smiles had faded on a few faces, while others regarded him with intense curiosity and, in some cases, encouraging nods.

"This is more than just an idle interest of mine," he told them. "I believe in my heart of hearts that the perpetuation of chattel slavery in America will set the stage for a dreadful conflict that will break this noble Republic of ours and consume a generation! You may think me alarmist, but is it a chance we are willing to take with the lives of our children and grandchildren? Would it not be better for them to grow up in a land where our love of liberty is played out by how well we treat the least among us, rather than in a land of pretense and hypocrisy? Can we truly live out the words of our creed, that all men are created equal, when we buy and sell our fellow human beings like cattle?"

"Well said!" Richard Henry Lee, the former governor and a member of the State Senate, spoke up. "I have often thought that our founding creed was invalidated by our love of human bondage."

Hamilton nodded; he knew Lee was currently in deep financial trouble and appreciated him attending the meeting anyway.

John Randolph of Roanoke spoke up next, raising a point that many around the table felt.

"Sir, I agree with you in sentiment, but how can you seriously recommend that we free these savages to walk among us? The physical, moral, and intellectual differences between black and white will forever forbid them living together on a footing of full equality!" he said, and a smattering of applause greeted his remarks. "I have long held that two races cannot occupy the same territory without one becoming a slave to the other."

"I believed that, too," said James Madison, "but then I looked at the difference in my Negroes when I freed them and offered to pay them for their labor. They are more diligent, more thorough, and indeed far more intelligent than I ever gave them credit for. Give them the opportunity to live and work in liberty, and you might well be surprised by how civilized they become!"

"Thank you, Secretary Madison," Hamilton said. "Gentlemen, we have created a Constitution in which the states, although subservient to the Federal government in some regards, still retain their rights and sovereignty under its provisions. I cannot compel Virginia to free her slaves, although I can, as an individual with some influence, offer those of you who choose to do so every bit of financial and administrative assistance at my disposal.

"But that is why I began as I did, asking Virginia to supply the moral and political leadership that our nation needs on this sensitive issue. Where Virginia leads, the South will follow—most of the South, at least. If the Virginia legislature could vote a system of compensated, gradual emancipation into place, and show their fellow slave states that such a plan could work, we will set forth a mighty current of liberty pulsing through the nation that will change our destiny! Will you help me, gentlemen? Will you breathe out liberty with the fire of Patrick Henry and the courage of George Washington? Who of you will help America live out the words of its creed?"

Hamilton raised his voice as he hurled his last argument to the gathering, but the answer which came in response was in a soft-spoken Southern drawl.

"I will," Thomas Jefferson said as he slipped into the dining room from the far door, where he had been quietly listening since the gathering began.

Every head in the room swiveled towards him, and for once it was Hamilton who stared in open-mouthed shock at the former President, whose face broke into a rare grin at Alex's surprise.

"Like all of you, I was skeptical, even hostile, when President-elect Hamilton first revealed his emancipation plan to me several months ago," he said. "But I have thought long and hard on his words since our last meeting, and in the end, I cannot deny their essential justice and logic. As long as we continue to buy and sell our fellow humans at the auction block, we cannot truthfully call ourselves a free people. Yesterday morning, I freed every slave on Monticello, and following the guidelines Secretary Madison has used so effectively here at Montpelier, I hired them all back as my workers. A few chose to go north and find their fortunes there; I gave them their papers and wished them Godspeed. I cannot tell you what a profound relief I felt when I made that announcement! Gentlemen, that which is right is not always easy, and that which is easy is rarely right. I know many of you harbor grave misgivings about President Hamilton's plan, if not about President Hamilton himself. He and I have fought many a battle in our day, but on this issue, I tell you with all humility, that he was right, and I was wrong. Mister President, I am with you. Let us proclaim liberty to the captive and justice to the oppressed together!"

"NO!" a sharp voice sounded from the end of the table nearest Jefferson. George Fitzhugh, a physician from Prince William County recently elected to the legislature, stood up, red in the face. Fitzhugh was well known for his passion and eloquence in the Assembly, and for his conservative views.

"How can you seriously propose freeing Negroes to walk among us as equals?" he said. "They are beasts of burden, no more deserving of freedom than a pig or cow or donkey! Their understanding is that of a child, and they are incapable of enjoying liberty. They need masters to control and, when necessary, restrain them. Set them free among us and they would either be ground to powder, incapable of competing with white laborers, becoming a permanent impoverished underclass with no master to protect them—or else they will master us through brute force and animal cunning and our roles will be reversed! The barbarians will be the masters and the educated men their slaves! I will take my wife and my little Georgie and leave this state forever rather than see those animals freed to run wild among us!"

Hamilton opened his mouth to respond, but Jefferson shot him a look, and the President deferred to his predecessor.

"Mister Fitzhugh," Jefferson said, "do you really believe the black man is so far inferior? Do all of you believe that?"

Half the room nodded vigorously, and the former President swallowed hard and looked around the table at each man before continuing.

"Then why do we sire children on their women?" he said. "No man in his right mind would breed with a beast of burden, but every plantation in the South boasts a large mulatto population. Don't look so outraged, gentlemen, I am as guilty of it as any of you. For the last twenty years I have used a woman whom I should have loved and cherished instead, simply because her grandmother was a Negro slave. Her skin is nearly as light as mine, and her intellect is a rival for that of most white women — and some white men!" — here he shot a mischievous glance at Fitzhugh before continuing — "that I know! This is a topic of which we are all aware, but have refused to discuss publicly — and yet each of us know it invalidates the claim of Mister Fitzhugh, and those like him, who insist Negroes are little better than animals!"

The room fell dead silent; even James Madison stared openmouthed at the former President. Jefferson threw his head back and gave a soft laugh.

"I've lived a lie long enough!" he said. "If these people are equal enough to bear our children, then they are equal enough to share with us in the perils and blessings of liberty. Nearly every man in this room voted to support me for President — most of you did so twice! Now I ask you to support me, and to support my successor, by lending your support to the noblest of enterprises — the elevation of a race we have long despised to their birthright of liberty."

Thomas Jefferson slowly walked to the front of the room and stood next to Alexander Hamilton, two Presidents side by side, the elder towering over the younger by more than half a foot.

"Who is with us?" he asked.

Eighteen of twenty were.

CHAPTER TWENTY

TWO WEEKS later President Hamilton was back in Washington, preparing for the first session of the Eleventh United States Congress. Most of his cabinet was also back in the capital, except for Secretary Madison, who had remained home to attend to business matters for a couple more days after Hamilton left. Eliza and the children were returning with Madison and his wife, moving at a more leisurely pace. The President, having successfully sold his plan to the most influential men in Virginia, was ready to move on to the next phase—limiting slavery in the areas controlled by the U.S. Congress, namely the Federal territories, and also trying to come up with a way to render financial aid to those planters who wished to convert to paid labor but lacked the capital to do so.

Attorney General John Jay was the most reluctant of all Hamilton's cabinet appointments, not for political reasons, but because he had left public office behind in 1801 and retired to his family farm. However, he and Hamilton were warm friends and shared a common aversion to slavery, and Jay's vast experience—delegate to the Federal Convention in 1787, Chief Justice of the Supreme Court, special commissioner to England, and Governor of New York—made him one of the most experienced legal and political minds in America. Simply put, Hamilton needed him, and had used all his powers of persuasion to lure Jay back into public office.

Jay was sixty-four years old, tall and almost entirely bald by 1809, his fringe of remaining hair solid white, with bright blue eyes bisected by a long, aquiline nose. He was an impressive orator and a brilliant courtroom debater, and the Congress had confirmed his appointment as Attorney General unanimously back in January, during its lame-duck session. He and Hamilton had been friends for decades, and after overcoming his initial reluctance to leave retirement, he had been at the new President's beck and call.

"It sounds as if your visit to Virginia was quite the success," said Jay after seating himself across from Hamilton's desk. "I was astounded to see Jefferson come over to your side, but his aid will be invaluable. Virginia, the first Southern state to abolish slavery! I never would have thought it."

"I have seldom been more surprised by anything in my life, or more delighted," Hamilton said. "Jefferson and I have been rivals for decades, but I have always contended that he was a man of principles, even if at times I thought them wrong ones. You should have seen their faces when he brought up the issue of black concubinage! I knew it existed in the South, but I had no idea it was so widespread. For him to not only speak of it, but to acknowledge his own participation in it—I thought one or two of them would collapse from apoplexy on the spot!"

"What do you intend to do next?" asked Jay. "One state is a step in the right direction, but if you truly intend to put slavery on the course of ultimate extinction, then you cannot stop there."

"That is why I summoned you," Hamilton said. "I require a formal legal opinion from the Attorney General of the United States. Under our Constitution, Federal territories are administered by Congress, are they not?"

"That is correct, sir, although under the terms of the Northwest Ordinance, they are allowed a measure of self-government once they hit the necessary population threshold. Even then, however, Congress still has extensive power over their territorial legislatures," Jay said.

"I wish to propose to Congress a measure that shall bar slavery from all existing territories," Hamilton said. "Thus we can confine slavery to the states where it already exists, check its further spread, and place it on a course of ultimate extinction."

"You may have some difficulty in the Southwest Territories," Jay said. "Slaveowners from Georgia and South Carolina have already emigrated to many of them and brought their chattels with them. I do not think a blanket prohibition covering all territories would be able to get through Congress."

"What about the Louisiana Purchase?" asked Hamilton. "Those vast territories west of the Mississippi are largely uninhabited and unregulated. Do you think a ban on slavery there would have a chance of getting through the House and Senate?"

"I'd say the odds are much better. By leaving South Carolina and Georgia the territories between their borders and the Mississippi to expand into, you could mute their objections and probably bring states like North Carolina, Kentucky, and perhaps even Tennessee on board. But in the end the short-term gains they would make would be counterbalanced—we would be allowing three or four new slave states into the Union while barring slavery from a dozen future states!" Jay said, warming to the idea.

"I think that the language should also include future territories west of the Mississippi," Hamilton said. "The Spanish Empire is crumbling; the northern parts of Mexico may choose to join the United States at some point. We should eliminate the possibility of those territories being admitted as slave states."

"Free men, free soil, free markets, and free labor!" said Jay. "My dearest friend, as much as I hated to leave my farm, it is worth giving up my bucolic life to be part of such a great venture!"

"We need to be sure to proceed within the bounds of the Constitution," said Hamilton. "I spent a good part of my life being accused of being a monarchist! Do you think you could prevail upon your successor, Chief Justice Marshall, to render an opinion on the legality of the legislation once it is drafted?"

"Since we are sure to be challenged on it, that would not be a bad idea," said Jay. "Who do you want to introduce the bill in the House and in the Senate?"

"It would be good if we could prevail on a Southerner to sponsor it in at least one house of Congress," Hamilton commented. "I shall speak to Senator Brent of Virginia. He is supportive of our measures thus far."

"I'll begin writing out a draft of the legislation out for your review," Jay replied.

"Excellent!" Hamilton said with a smile. "Let's try to have the draft completed before Congress convenes next week, so we can place it in the hands of our legislative sponsors."

"I will have it on your desk tomorrow, sir," Jay assured him with a smile. "And I'll have several Congressmen lining up to co-sponsor it in the House!"

"You're going to be an invaluable asset to my administration, John," Hamilton said warmly, rising to clasp his old friend by the hand. "Thank you again for leaving your retirement to be a part of it!"

The Attorney General bowed and made his exit, and Hamilton sat and began working on notes for his address to Congress. Washington had addressed Congress directly on more than one occasion, as had John Adams. Jefferson, a poor public speaker due to his soft voice, had denounced direct speeches to Congress as "monarchical" (his favorite term for anything he disliked, Alex mused) and simply sent written messages to be read out by the clerk of the House.

Hamilton, on the other hand, was a dynamic public speaker who relished debate and discourse, and he had decided before taking office that he would revive the tradition Jefferson had abandoned. He'd been tinkering with this first address for some time, but was getting ready to produce a more polished, possibly final, draft. However, he'd only written a couple of paragraphs when a knock at the door interrupted him.

"Yes?" he said, a bit irritated at the interruption.

"David Lenox here to see you, sir," came Cartwright's voice.

Hamilton leaped up with a smile on his face. Lenox was the Director of the Bank of the United States, and Alex had wanted to see him for some time.

"David!" he exclaimed. "How good of you to make the trip from New York on such short notice!"

"Thank you, Mister President," the banker replied, shaking Alex's hand firmly. "I missed your inauguration, but I wanted to be on hand for the opening of the new Congress anyway. When I heard that you wished to see me that simply gave me one more reason to make the trip. Now, what can I do for you, sir?"

"First of all, the bank's charter expires in two years," Alex said. "I want to urge the Congress to renew its charter early so that there is no uncertainty as to our financial future. The bank has been a national blessing, restoring our credit and helping promote prosperity by encouraging manufactures and entrepreneurs."

"I could not agree more, Mister President," Lenox said. "You gave many gifts to this country during your tenure as Treasury Secretary, but none has given more back to the country than the national bank."

"Thank you, sir," Hamilton said with a smile. "Your operation of the bank has been smooth and without errors. But I have another idea for a way that the Bank of the United States can benefit the country, one which, in time, may become its greatest legacy."

"What would that be, Mister President?" Lenox asked, genuinely curious. Hamilton's financial genius was legendary among those few Americans who understood economics.

"As you know, the great crusade of my presidency is my campaign against slavery," Hamilton said. "I have invited Southern planters to liberate their Negroes and hire them as paid workers, believing that such a policy will increase the productivity of their farms and raise prosperity throughout the region."

"A noble concept, sir, but how can the bank aid it?" Lenox wondered.

"As you well know, sir, slavery is a notoriously cash-poor system. Despite their vast wealth, if measured in land and slaves, most Southern planters have little ready money and many are deep in debt," Hamilton explained. "The main reason for that is the weakness of the system itself. Slavery generates a false prosperity that measures wealth in human bondage, not in actual capital. The main complaint I heard, even from planters sympathetic to our goal, is that they lack the money to pay for labor."

"If you can explain finance to a Southerner, sir, you are a better man than I," Lenox exclaimed. "Most of them seem to think of we bankers as warlocks and economics as some form of forbidden dark magic!"

Hamilton laughed out loud.

"That is one of the many reasons why I respected President Washington so much," he said. "He understood his lack of understanding in that area and was willing to listen to my expertise. Few men in this world, Lenox, actually know what they don't know! That fact alone made Washington indispensable. What I propose is that the bank set up a special fund to provide low-interest loans to any planter who wishes to convert to paid labor. The loans should carry little risk, since I do believe that the Negroes will work much more efficiently as free men than they did while in bondage. The bank will make a small profit on interest from the loans, but more importantly, it will be assisting in the liberation of an entire people to enjoy the blessings of freedom!"

"That's a very good idea, Mister President," said Lenox. "I imagine it will not have a great many subscribers at once, but as the truth of your free labor principles is demonstrated in the fields of the South, more and more men will sign up. Liberty will spread, harvests will improve, their profits will rise, and perhaps some of these Virginia grandees will be able to pay off their other debts!"

"Excellent! If you are willing to endorse the idea, that will not only help the progress of my program of voluntary emancipation, it will also help extinguish some of the lingering hostility to the National Bank in the South, and ease the process of renewing your charter," Hamilton explained.

"All three members of our governing board are in town for the opening of Congress; I will meet with them tonight and present your proposal. Do you have a more detailed outline written out, to make sure I describe it correctly?" Lenox asked.

Hamilton grinned and reached into his desk drawer, pulling out six sheets of closely written foolscap he had worked on the day before.

"This formal proposal outlines recommended interest rates, duration, and an estimated rate of defaults and returns, based on my observations in Virginia," he said, "along with a rough estimate of how much the loans will cost the bank in the short term. I tried to anticipate any questions the board might ask."

Lenox looked over the neat, flowing script and gave a low whistle of amazement.

"This was not something you thought up overnight, was it, Mister President?" he asked.

"I've been planning this for five years," Hamilton said. "I've wrestled with the problem over and over, and this is the result of that work."

"I believe you," Lenox said. "May I take this with me to study?"

"Of course," said Hamilton. "I already had another copy made, so that one is yours. Thank you again for coming all this way to see me, Mister Lenox."

"My pleasure, sir. Is it true that you plan to address Congress in person?" he asked.

"It is," said Hamilton. "I was working on my address just now, in fact."

"Then I shall show myself out and let you get back to it," Lenox replied.

Alex spent the rest of the afternoon and evening working on his address, occasionally pacing about the room and reciting parts of it aloud, listening to his own words for effect. Mrs. Benson had cooked up a savory venison stew for him and Angelica to enjoy together, and to his delight, Alex found that his damaged daughter was almost her normal self this evening. He kept the topics of conversation light and humorous, and she responded with a little of her old saucy nature from the days before her brother's death had stolen her sanity. But after a half hour of conversation, she began stumbling over words and retreating into her childlike self. Saddened by her relapse, Alex led his daughter to her bedroom and read a simple Bible story to her. She was sound asleep by the time he was done, and he kissed her forehead before leaving her to slumber.

The next day was Saturday, and Alex left the White House, accompanied only by his faithful secretary Cartwright, visiting the boardinghouses where many of the returning members of the House and Senate stayed during the congressional session. He greeted many friends old and new, and renewed his acquaintance with some of the newly elected members. All of them were full of questions about how he intended to put the anti-slavery principles he had outlined in his inaugural address into action, and he assured them that he would reveal his intentions soon.

Representative Clay of Kentucky was fascinated by Alex's initiative, and asked the President if they might meet over supper to discuss it. Clay had served for a single year in the U.S. Senate previously, and now was one of the rising stars in the House of Representatives. Hamilton bade him come to the White House that evening, figuring that an ally from the new western state might be an asset in the coming session. Clay had a youthful enthusiasm that reminded Alex of himself when he had first stepped in as Treasury Secretary, all aflame to solve America's financial headaches overnight at the ripe old age of thirty-four.

Alex returned to the White House about four in the afternoon and spent some time with his daughter, then drafted a letter to the British ambassador, Baron Erskine, requesting a meeting to discuss England's suspected role in fermenting unrest on the frontier. While planning his assault on slavery, Alex was also concerned with the constant turmoil in the Indiana territory. The governor, William Henry Harrison, was obsessively concerned in trying to wrest the best farmland in the territory from the tribes that controlled it, and the Indians, especially the Shawnee, were putting up a stubborn resistance. Hamilton did not want a war with the Indians distracting attention from his domestic agenda, so he had already warned Harrison to deal more fairly with them, especially regarding tribal lands. But Alex was also concerned that the British, who were still not fond of the upstart American republic, might take advantage of the turmoil in the west to make more trouble for the new President and the nation he led.

After revising his words for the third time, Alex decided he was done and laid the letter aside. He was tired, but also excited at the prospect of the weeks and months ahead. He had been President for just over sixty days; there were still so many things to be done! As he changed clothes for supper—it had been a warm day and he'd walked all over town, working up quite a sweat— he thought about the train of events that had led him here. Ever since the day of his duel with Burr, Hamilton recognized that he was living on borrowed time—no, he shook his head, that was not the right phrase at all. He'd been living on gifted time—a life that should have ended, handed back to him by the Almighty. He was determined to make the most of that gift with however much time he had left, spreading not just the idea of liberty but its practice to as much of his country as he could. Every man needs a purpose, he thought, and he had found his.

He headed down to supper with a cheerful smile on his face, looking forward to spending a pleasant evening with the young Congressman Henry Clay. Something about this man, so energetic and excited for America's future, struck a chord in Alex.

America needed such men, he thought, men who rose from humble origins to better themselves and their country.

It proved to be a delightful evening. Clay was a wonderful raconteur and had a store of jokes and funny stories that made Alex laugh harder than he had in ages. But in between the light conversation, the two men also shared their vision for America.

"Compromise is the key to prosperity and tranquility," Clay said. "In every political conflict each side's argument holds some merit. Our legislators must make every effort to weed out the narrow sectional and partisan measures and find common ground that promotes the common good."

"That is a sound principle," Alex said, "but I do believe there are also times when one must make a stand. Not every issue need be a hill to die on, but there are nonetheless moments when the man of conviction must say to evil: 'Thus far shall you go and no further!' That is why I have made my campaign of emancipation the centerpiece of my presidency. Slavery is a cancer, my young friend, and we must find a way to excise it or it shall slay our great Union."

"You do know that I am a slaveowner; do you not, Mister President?" Clay asked with a sardonic smile.

"I am not surprised," Hamilton said. "Most Southerners of any substance are. But that does not change my opinion of the institution itself."

"Nor does it mine," said Clay. "Although I try to make the most benevolent use of it possible, it is still an inherently wicked system. Many of us feel that way, truthfully—slavery was not an institution we asked for, but one we were born with, and we try to make the best of it. I tried hard to keep slavery out of Kentucky when we sought statehood ten years ago, but I was voted down. Still, I am most interested in your program of converting plantations from slave labor to paid labor. Do you really think it is economically and socially feasible?"

"Well, Mister Clay," Hamilton said, "I've watched slavery my whole life; I was surrounded by it from birth. Slave labor, in my humble but correct opinion"—he gave a wink to show that he was half jesting—"is the least efficient labor system ever devised, because there is simply no incentive behind it other than fear. Fear will drive a man hard in the short term, but over time we become inured to it and find ways to resist. The slave's life is one of passive protest; he will do the least possible amount of labor to avoid the lash and not a hair more. But give a man freedom and the opportunity to better himself; clothe his work with the dignity of fair compensation, and he will strive harder so that he may raise himself up and bequeath his posterity a better life than he had. That, my friend, is the universal human urge—to make a better world for our children than the one we grew up in."

"Well said indeed, Mister President!" Clay exclaimed. "If you will show me how to make the transition to free labor on my plantation, I would like to join your crusade."

"I've actually written a tract on the subject," Hamilton said, "because so many people are asking me about it. I will be publishing it through the Federal printing office and disseminating copies free to anyone in the South who desires them, starting next month. But I may have an early draft in my desk that you can borrow, if you don't want to wait."

"I'll be here in Washington till the spring session expires," said Clay, "so I will be happy to wait. I will tell you the truth, Mister President. I was a strong partisan of President Jefferson's, and I campaigned hard for Secretary Madison to succeed him. But the more I see of you, the more convinced I am that the right man won the election. I will do what I can to persuade the people of Kentucky to abolish slavery. Even if I can't do that, I can probably persuade some of our leading citizens to give your system a try. At first, we may simply be leading by example, but if your ideas work out as well as you think they will, I think in another year or two the legislature will be willing to take up the issue. When they do, I'll be your man. We may disagree on other topics of politics, but I am convinced that in this, you have the right of things, and I will stand with you."

On that amicable note the two men parted, and Alex went to bed happy with his day's work. The next day was Sunday, and he attended the morning service at St. Paul's Episcopal Church, one of the oldest churches in the region. The pastor, Matthew James Milam, was a powerful and eloquent speaker who was a known political enemy of President Jefferson. His text for that Sunday was from the Gospel of Luke, the fourth chapter, verses sixteen through twenty-one: *"And He came to Nazareth, where He had been brought up; and as was His custom, He entered the synagogue on the Sabbath, and stood up to read. And the book of the prophet Isaiah was handed to Him. And He opened the book and found the place where it was written,* **The spirit of the Lord is upon me, because he has anointed me to preach the Gospel to the poor, He has sent me to proclaim liberty to the captives, and to give sight to the blind; to set free those who are oppressed, and to proclaim the favorable year of the LORD.** *And He closed the book, gave it back to the attendant* *and sat down; and the eyes of all in the synagogue were fixed on Him. And He began to say to them, Today this Scripture has been fulfilled in your hearing.*"

Reverend Milam then proceeded to deliver a strong sermon that was both political and spiritual; reminding the audience of the great principles of the Christian faith and questioning whether the practice of slavery was truly compatible with discipleship of the Lord. Yet, at the same time, he did not openly espouse the President's initiative nor denounce it; instead he called on the conscience of the individual believers in his audience. It was, all things considered, one of the most inspirational messages Alex had ever heard, and he warmly shook the parson's hand when the service was over.

After church, Alex returned to the White House to continue working on his address to Congress. It was nearly five o'clock when he heard the rapid pattering of several sets of footsteps coming down the corridor outside the President's office, and the door was suddenly thrown open.

"Papa! We're home!" cried Little Phil, now a sturdy seven-year-old. John Church, William, and Lizzie came crowding in behind them, and the President embraced his children and showered them with kisses.

"Save some for me," came Eliza's voice from the door, and Hamilton struggled through his children's arms to include his wife in the family embrace.

"My darlings," he said, "I am so glad to see you all again! This big old house is far too quiet without you all. Welcome home!"

Little Phil looked around the President's office and sighed.

"This really is our home now, isn't it?" he said. "It's nice enough, but I miss New York sometimes!"

"We'll be heading back there when Congress recesses for the summer," Alex promised. "Washington is our home only while I am President. When my term is done, we shall be going back to our old place for good."

"It is a nice big house," William said. "I like having a room of my own!"

"Go on up and unpack your bags, children," Eliza said. "I want to talk with your father for a moment, and Mister Madison needs a word with him as well."

With a few grumbles of protest, the four children headed up to put their things away and say hello to Angelica, who was waiting shyly at the head of the stairs for her exuberant siblings. Eliza stepped up and embraced her husband, more gently but no less passionately than their children had.

"It is good to be home," she said. "Mister Madison was a delightful traveling companion, and he has some news for you. I'll let him inform you, and then perhaps we could all have a family dinner together—and then we can put the children to bed and have some time to ourselves!"

With that, she gave him a lingering kiss that left little doubt what that time together might involve, then stepped into the hallway and headed up to the residence. Cartwright, always handy, carried her bags up for her, and Hamilton turned and found James Madison waiting in the foyer of the White House.

"Good afternoon, James!" said Hamilton. "I want to thank you for returning my family to me safe and sound. Eliza said you were a wonderful traveling companion."

"It's hard to be otherwise, in such charming company," Madison said. "Your children are a delight. I do wish my stepson showed as much promise as your boys do. He is altogether too fond of strong drink, even at his early age."

"That is unfortunate," said Hamilton. "It's been the ruin of many a good man. So, Eliza says you have some news for me."

"That I do," said Madison, taking a seat across from Hamilton's desk. "I received an urgent letter asking me to stop by Monticello on my way back to Washington City. No hint as to any reason, just an earnest plea from Mister Jefferson to come and see him. I sent word that I would be traveling in company with your family, and he returned that they were welcome as well. So, we all dropped by Monticello the day after leaving Montpelier and found the place in an uproar. Before we ever arrived, I passed Reverend Jameson, the local Anglican minister, riding along in a perfect snit. He barely said good morning do me, despite the fact that I have sat through his boring sermons on multiple occasions. But after he settled down a bit, he looked at me and said: 'If you are truly a friend to Mister Jefferson, you must talk some sense into him! I think he has lost his mind.' I queried what on earth he meant by that, but not one more word would he say, so we rode on in some anxiety."

"Jefferson is one of the most level-headed people I know," Hamilton said. "I wonder what the good reverend was so upset about?"

"I'm getting to that," said Madison. "When we arrived, Jefferson's daughter met me at the door, and it was obvious she'd been weeping. I asked her whatever was the matter, and she just shook her head and told me her father was waiting in the garden. More perplexed than ever, I wandered out back and there was Thomas Jefferson, dressed in his finest coat and tie, and at his side—that slave woman of his, Sally Hemings! He crossed the yard and took my hand with the warmest of smiles, and then he asked me to be an official witness to his wedding."

"By Jove!" said Hamilton. "He's actually going to marry her?"

"Not going to, already did!" Madison said. "That's why Pastor Jameson was so upset—the President had asked him to perform the service and he had refused, so Jefferson invited a local Quaker elder to do so! It was a lovely, simple ceremony. Afterward, Jefferson told me that he had long ago promised his wife on her death bed that he would not remarry, because she did not want their daughters to be raised by a stepmother—apparently her own stepmother had treated her horribly, and she did not want her girls to be abused as she had been. But, as Thomas explained it, he felt he had upheld that vow by raising their girls to adulthood as a single father, and now he was now free to marry the woman who had captured his heart years ago. Patsy was quite upset, but she told me later her father had informed her that the situation was not without precedent. Cato the Elder had married one of his freedwomen, in the days of the Roman Republic."

Hamilton laughed. "Leave it to Jefferson to find a supporting example from classical antiquity," he said. "I wonder how his neighbors will feel."

"I'm sure they will declare him utterly mad!" Madison commented.

"Is he, do you think?" Hamilton responded.

"If he is mad, then may all the world go insane as he did!" the Secretary of State replied. "He seems happier, calmer, and more satisfied with life than I have ever seen him. It's almost a miraculous change. Jefferson was always quiet and thoughtful; those qualities are still there, but now matched by a surpassing joy."

"The blessings of liberty," Hamilton mused. "Well, may God bless them both! And may America experience a similar happiness when slavery is but a sad memory for us all."

"I'll drink to that, by God!" Madison said, and Hamilton called for a bottle of Madeira.

CHAPTER TWENTY-ONE

THE HOUSE of Representatives' chamber in the still-unfinished Capitol Building was quite a bit bigger than its actual membership merited; it had been constructed with future growth for the Union in mind. Therefore, on the rare occasions when a joint session of Congress was called for, the Senators joined their colleagues in the lower house of the national legislature. So it was on May 23, 1809, that President Alexander Hamilton stood at the Speaker's podium and looked out at the elected representatives of his country.

Thirty-four Senators and one hundred and forty-two members of the House looked back at him; many were supportive, a few were hostile, and many more skeptical. For eight years Thomas Jefferson had avoided addressing the Congress in person, and as a result, many junior members had never heard the President speak to the national legislature. Those who had been there since the early days could recall President Washington's occasional addresses, which had become rarer as time went on. The first President had a soft voice, and his ill-fitting dentures made extended public addresses an exercise in discomfort. His successor, President Adams, had addressed Congress on a couple of occasions. He was a better public speaker than Washington, but his mounting unpopularity and irascible nature had caused him to eschew direct meetings with Congress after his first two years in office.

By 1809 ten years had passed since a President directly addressed the national legislature. Hamilton loved addressing crowds; Eliza once told him he had a preacher's passion, a trial lawyer's mastery of facts, and a professor's desire to inform his listeners. He had worked tirelessly on this speech, honing his phrases more often than was his wont, concerned that he must make the most of this first, priceless opportunity. Dressed in a fine black frock coat and cravat made by one of Hercules Mulligan's apprentice tailors, he cut a dignified figure as he rose to speak.

"Legislators of the United States," he began after the Speaker of the House introduced him. "Congressmen, Senators, distinguished guests, and citizens of America, I want to thank you for this opportunity to speak to you directly. The Constitution says that the President may, from time to time, report to Congress regarding the state of the Union. Although my time in this office has been short, I asked to speak to you today to share with you the deepest concerns of my heart for the future of our nation, as well as to address our current state of affairs."

A smattering of polite applause rose from the Federalist members, but the majority simply sat and waited, curious to see what the new President had to say.

"In many ways the state of our Union is stable, prosperous, and growing," he continued. "Our population continues to increase at a rapid rate; our Western territories are flooding with settlers as the axe and the plow convert the primeval forests to farmland. Of course, this expansion stirs up conflicts with the land's first inhabitants, and the reports of Indian raids on our frontier are troubling. While we wish to protect the pioneers, who are the vanguard of our nation's growth, a decent respect to the principles of justice requires that we cannot simply run roughshod over the rights and territories of those who were here before us. I would ask that our territorial governors deal fairly with the chiefs of the Indian nations, and that they rein in the runaway abuses of speculators and swindlers who would steal lands promised to the Indians in solemn treaties. I have always said the first duty of society is justice, and if we do not show justice to these primitives that our nation's fortunes have committed to our care and protection, then how can we claim to be a just nation?"

This sentiment was met with another round of applause, primarily from the members who represented the eastern states. The western legislators' reaction was more mixed; a few clapped politely while others scowled. The greed for land was strong, and most of them held the Indians in contempt.

"In terms of foreign relations, America is at peace with our neighbors and trading partners. Thanks to my wise predecessor's negotiations with Great Britain, the odious Orders in Council that promised to paralyze our trade have been rescinded. American citizens may no longer be impressed into service in the Royal Navy, yet deserters from His Majesty's fleet are being legally repatriated with due regard to their civil rights. The war that has convulsed Europe for nearly two decades now goes on, and the times ahead there are troubling and uncertain, but America has successfully maintained the neutral course so wisely laid out for us by our first President, His Excellency General Washington. The United States are safer, more prosperous, and freer for having avoided foreign entanglements!"

This brought Hamilton a standing ovation from the Congress; his generosity toward Jefferson for an entente that had been largely due to his own efforts, combined with his praise for Washington, reminded the Congress of the qualities that had won him the election. Alex bowed deferentially as the applause continued, then spoke again as it died down.

"But the state of our Union is nonetheless imperiled," he said. "It was my perception of this peril that drove me to seek out the high office I now hold and averting it will be the primary focus of my presidency for the duration of my tenure. Many do not see slavery as a danger to the peace and prosperity of our Union, but I tell you all, in all seriousness, that if left unchecked, it will lead to a crisis that may destroy our Republic and bring all our Founders' great work to naught."

There was no applause at this, only looks that ranged from genuine curiosity to boredom to outright hostility.

"Let us, for the moment, disregard the morality of enslaving another human being altogether," he continued. "Men have argued and will argue over the perceived justice or injustice of slavery ever since the first load of Africans was sold in Jamestown nearly two hundred years ago. Personally, I would not be a slave, so I will not own a slave. But it is my observation that most men will not change their minds about a deeply held moral belief, no matter how many facts and arguments are marshalled to prove that they are wrong. So let us look at the issue of practicality, my fellow Americans. Let logic and rationality guide us in this discussion."

Hamilton leaned forward and surveyed the members of the Congress with a keen eye. This was the passage that he had worked on for weeks, trying to drive home a message that every person there would understand.

"Ever since the founding of our Republic, we have watched as the Northern states exponentially increased their wealth and productivity at a rate far greater than their Southern counterparts. Not that the South is impoverished, but its rate of economic growth is far slower. Why is that? Are Southerners inherently lazier, or more financially deprived, than the residents of the Yankee states? Of course not! While I have made my residence in New York since coming to America as a teen, it has been my privilege in war and peace to serve alongside men from Virginia and the Carolinas, and I know that they are diligent and hard working. Yet the Southern states are left further behind economically, year after year. Why?

"One thing I hope that all of you will acknowledge is that I have been gifted with a unique understanding of financial matters. It was this gift of mine that led General Washington to appoint me to his military family—not for my prowess on the battlefield, although I fought as hard as any—but because I understood the financial and logistical needs of an army. He called on me again, at the establishment of our government, to use my skills to help restore America's credit and start our Republic on firm financial footing. Many opposed my ideas, but the financial systems I created have stood the test of time, to the point that even my political foes refused to tear down that which I had built. So I speak to you today, not just as your President, but as a man whose economic vision extends further than most.

"Slavery is what holds the South behind, my friends. Slavery is the most deceitful economic system on earth. It gives the appearance of short-term wealth while delivering long-term debt and poverty. No slave ever gives his best effort to his master—why should he, after all? There is no reward for his toil, whether it be industrious or indolent. A slave works hard enough to avoid the lash and no harder. But a free man who has personal liberty and the right to enjoy the fruits of his labors—such a man will labor long and diligently, in hopes of raising himself to a higher station in life and leaving his children a brighter posterity. I have challenged many of my slave-owning friends to join in a great experiment, freeing their slaves and then hiring them back on as paid laborers. This requires a hefty original investment, but the results thus far have confirmed everything I just said—free men work harder, are more productive, and do not have to be guarded with whips and dogs to keep them from running away! As its virtues are demonstrated, I believe simple economic self-interest will impel many of you to join in this great national experiment. Time will show us all that wage labor is a sensible, profitable, and viable alternative to chattel slavery.

"That is why I will always reject the idea proposed by some, that emancipation of our black slaves must be accompanied by their immediate colonization in some remote part of the earth. Not only do I reject as false the contention that Negroes are inherently savage beings who cannot remain on our shores as freemen without turning on our citizens, their removal would create a dearth of labor that would reduce the South to permanent penury. Let them remain among us as free laborers who can advance themselves through the dignity of work, and in time their culture will advance and blend with our own! It will not be an overnight transition. I have no plans to try to establish these freemen as full, equal citizens—that will be a matter for the states to decide, over time. But I do believe that a doorway to some form of citizenship should be left open for future generations. I urge the individual citizens of the South to make this effort, to shift your work force from slave labor to free men working for wages. I have authored a pamphlet outlining how to make this transition work, and it will be available as a free publication of the Executive Branch for any citizen who wishes to have it!

"Likewise, I would urge the legislatures of the Southern states to begin debating this issue in earnest. I have already met with members of the state legislature of Virginia and have been promised that they will introduce a bill for the compensated emancipation of all slaves in the state during their next session. To assist in this, I have met with David Lenox, the director of the Bank of the United States, and urged him to introduce a system of low-interest loans to help indebted Southern planters make the transition from slave labor to wage labor with a minimum of economic distress. I would have no man say that he would free his slaves, if only he could afford to!"

Hamilton's words were sinking in. He saw glances being exchanged, and whispered comments made, as he worked his way through these critical passages of his speech. After announcing the bank's loan program, he saw several members stand and applaud, slowly joined by more and more, until most of the chamber was on its feet. Even a few members of the South Carolina delegation were on their feet, although their reactions seemed more forced than the others.

"Many of you greet these words with skepticism, and some, I can tell, with outright hostility," Hamilton said. "Why should we change, you ask me? Slavery was a good enough system for our fathers and grandfathers; why should we not maintain it? Let me tell you what it is that I fear, my friends. You see, my desire to see our slaves set free springs not only from my love of liberty and my moral convictions. As I said at the beginning of this address, its primary source is a fear of the great peril the maintenance of chattel slavery represents to our future."

Hamilton drew a deep breath and said a silent prayer as he prepared for the conclusion of his speech, mustering all his powers of persuasion and asking God that they be enough.

"If slavery continues, and if it can spread into our federal territories as the nation continues to grow, it will continue to exercise its baleful influence everywhere that it takes root. Planters will live like aristocrats in their manors while struggling with crippling debt generated by the very nature of the system they have chosen; meanwhile, the Northern states, with their diverse economic interests in shipping, manufacturing, and merchandise as well as agriculture, maintained by free labor, will grow wealthier and more prosperous with each passing year. In time, the North will come to resent the economic backwardness of the South, and the South will regard with contempt the wealth and prosperity of the North. Northerners will blame slavery for the relative poverty of the South, and for its reluctance to embrace manufacturing and industry; Southerners will become more defensive of their domestic institutions, and more violently resentful of progress. This nation cannot endure permanently half slave, and half free. We will gradually become two separate nations, with separate economies and political systems, bound together under one Constitution, but each side becoming more hostile to the other over time. And eventually, a spark will ignite those hostilities into a bloody conflict that may consume a generation of Americans and sow bitter seeds of hatred and divisiveness stretching into the future as far as my limited gaze can see."

The Congress was silent; the grim picture the President had painted with his words was taking shape, even in the minds of the most resistant. Would it be enough? Hamilton prayed that it would, and then he continued.

"I am a mortal man, not a prophet or seer. Yet in my bones I believe this prediction is true. We have it in our power to change our course as a nation, to stop this horror before it is upon us. I ask you, as the nation's lawmakers, is it not worth the risk? At worst, we have liberated a group of people who are shamefully oppressed and mistreated and freely given them the same blessings we fought a Revolution to achieve. Surely a just God cannot but reward a nation that shows such charity to those who have been placed in its power! And at best, we will have prevented a dreadful future conflict and saved a generation from the holocaust of war. It is a great change that I ask this nation to undertake, but if we show the same courage and steadfastness that we showed during the Revolution, I have no doubt that we can do this. And when we do, we will finally, fully realize the truth of the creed that we embraced at the birth of our nation— the truths we hold to be self-evident, that all men are indeed created equal, and that they are endowed by their Creator with the inalienable rights of life, liberty, and the pursuit of happiness. Join me, work with me, and help America fulfill the promise of its founders!"

As his final words echoed through the House chamber, the members of Congress came to their feet and applauded vigorously. The guests in the gallery also stood, and Alex bowed deeply. He knew that much of the enthusiasm was feigned, but he also felt he had reached some people. Would it be enough? That was the question that plagued him as the applause died down and he resumed his seat. The Speaker of the House dismissed the session, and the President made his way through the Senators and Congressmen, shaking hands and accepting their congratulations.

"A brilliant address, Mister President!" said Henry Clay. "It will be an uphill battle in Kentucky, but I will do what I can to aid you."

"Thank you for that, Mister Clay," said Hamilton. "I will need all the help that I can get!"

John Taylor of South Carolina was less impressed.

"A pretty speech, sir," he said, "but it will be a cold day in hell before the people of South Carolina assent to the destruction of their way of life!"

"Time is a great condenser of things," Hamilton said. "Even the people of South Carolina may change their minds eventually."

"I wouldn't count on it," Taylor said, and with a curt bow he walked away.

THE PRESIDENT'S speech was widely reported in newspapers throughout the Union, and the coverage was generally favorable, at least in the North and in the Upper South. South Carolina and Georgia remained implacably opposed to Hamilton's plan, but many slaveholding states were willing to at least consider his proposal. And as the news spread, many individual planters decided to take advantage the bank's new "Liberty Loan" program.

In the fall of 1809, as promised, the Virginia State Legislature proposed a Manumission Act, which pledged to eliminate slavery within the state over the next decade and offered a compensation fund for all planters who would voluntarily free their slaves. The debate was fierce, but ultimately the act passed by a margin of nearly two to one. Maryland, smaller and less dependent on slave labor than Virginia, proposed a similar act in its own legislature which likewise passed by a large margin. Delaware, still technically a slave state but not dependent on plantation agriculture, simply abolished slavery, with no compensation and little fanfare. Most of the state's slaves were domestics, not field hands, and the conversion to paid labor proceeded simply.

In Kentucky, the governor asked the state legislature to debate the subject, but the bill died in committee. However, led by the example of Henry Clay and a few others, many individual Kentucky planters decided to experiment with making the shift to paid labor. North Carolina's legislature did not act, but they did vote to take up the subject of emancipation in the next year's session after seeing how things progressed in Virginia and Maryland. As in Kentucky, many planters decided on their own to give free labor a try, taking advantage of the national bank's loan program to make the transition.

Indeed, in nearly every Southern state, at least a few slaveowners, inspired by reading Hamilton's address, or perhaps pricked by their own consciences, decided to convert to free labor. In the Deep South, such men were pariahs—indeed, in South

Carolina, a wealthy eccentric named Charles Rankin announced that he was freeing his slaves and converting to paid labor. He might have been spared, but he insisted on traveling to neighboring plantations and urging their owners to follow suit. When this failed, he tried to bring up the topic of emancipation among the slaves themselves. This proved too much, and an angry mob descended on his plantation and lynched him, then sold his freedmen back into slavery in an auction lit by the fires that consumed Rankin's home.

Such episodes were mercifully rare, and as fall came, the accuracy of Hamilton's prediction became plain. The plantations that had converted to free labor experienced, on average, twice the yield of those who still relied on slaves. Madison saw his profits increase almost threefold over the last several years' average, and he was able to pay off several nagging debts and give his laborers a generous bonus. He had gone from being a reluctant convert to Hamilton's plan of emancipation to one of its strongest supporters, and over the winter he toured the South, speaking in public assemblies and urging his fellow planters to join the administration's great experiment.

Another movement also began to spread throughout the South, this one involving the slaves themselves. Word of America's new President and his plans for their liberation had spread like wildfire from one plantation to another, and many blacks did what Senator Brent's Negroes had done—they chose one of their number to approach their masters with an offer to work harder and longer in exchange for their freedom. For some slaveowners, this was the final impetus they needed to embrace free labor, and they responded as Brent had. For others, this was a sign of just how pernicious and destructive Hamilton's plan was; several slaves were flogged for daring to bring it up, and one sadistic South Carolina planter had the messenger hanged before the entire slave workforce of his 15,000-acre plantation.

But despite the fierce opposition to emancipation by diehards, black resistance to slavery began to grow. Plantations that refused to move to free labor saw their yields fall, and more of their equipment damaged. Very rarely could a culprit be found for these shortfalls, but overseers throughout the South complained that Hamilton's pernicious ideas of liberty were sabotaging their way of life.

Before dismissing for the summer, Hamilton's allies in Congress introduced the Louisiana Territory Act of 1809. The bill set the stage for dividing up the vast territory into potential future states, and appointed provisional governors for each unorganized territory, but its most controversial measure was found in its final article: "Neither slavery nor involuntary servitude, save hard labor imposed after conviction of criminal charges in a trial by jury, shall exist in the Louisiana Territory, or any territories the United States may acquire in the future, to the west of the Mississippi River."

Debate over the Louisiana Act was ferocious, with the opposition led by the formidable Senator John Gaillard. Urbane in his manners and amiable in his temperament, he was nonetheless implacably opposed to the emancipation of the slaves. However, he expressed his opposition with a humor and dignity that often led his opponents to underestimate him—until he drove his point home with an elegance and logic that left them scrambling for a reply.

"What will be the end result of liberating the million or so Negroes who live among us?" he asked during the Senate debate. "And what can be the goal of preventing Southerners from spreading their way of life, their livelihood, to these new territories except to force us to bow the knee to the Executive's dire will? Of course, they tell us, we do not dream of making Negroes citizens. They shall live among us as a permanently lower caste of free laborers, no longer to bow to their masters, but nor yet free to exercise the same liberties as a white man. How long will that last? How long will our *free* laboring class be content with wages only? What will come next? Negro voters? Negro legislators? Racial intermarriage that will defile the flower of Southern womanhood with the savage seed of Africa? Emancipating slaves will not be the end, my friends! How long will it be, after President Hamilton's plans are realized, before we see a dusky African face looking out the windows of the White House? For that day will come, if we take this step, make no mistake! And when it comes, then we will see our roles reversed. They shall be the masters, and we, the slaves. But not if we can nip it in the bud! Let the Federal territories be open to all, North and South, and open to whatever labor system men choose to practice! Do not suffer the South to be betrayed with a kiss, my friends!"

It was Nicholas Gilman of New Hampshire who stood up in the Senate the next day to give the reply to Gaillard's speech. With a polite nod to the Vice President, he took his stance on the Senate floor and locked eyes with his South Carolina counterpart.

"What will be the end goal of liberating a million Negroes from bondage, my esteemed colleague asked us yesterday," he began. "The answer is simple. They will be free! No longer will they have to fear being sold away from their wives and children, nor being flogged for failing to work too hard, or for trying to run away, or for simply looking at their master in a way that displeases him. They will be free to work for wages at the plantation where they were once enslaved, or free to seek their fortunes everywhere. Senator Gaillard spins wild fantasies out of the air in an effort to blind you to the fundamental issue of this great discussion: is it right for a nation founded on liberty and equality to not only allow but propagate the vilest form of human bondage ever conceived? Negro legislators, Negro voters, interracial marriage—although why the mixing of the races should be of concern to men who have sired thousands of mulatto children throughout the South is beyond me! Even the specter of a Negro President; all these things are a distraction, designed to outrage you and provoke you into opposing a bill that will not abolish slavery in a single state that does not choose to do so. All this act will do is make sure that future states which join the Union will do so as free states, peopled by free men, working for just wages. The Federal government lacks the power to force emancipation on any state and has no intention of doing so. We do not intent to take your Negroes from you, Senator Gaillard; only to make you see the wisdom of letting them enjoy the same blessings of liberty that you do. Where that will lead us in a hundred years, who can say? But what it will do in the here and now is further the cause of American liberty, hasten the peopling of the West, and increase our nation's prosperity. What Senator Gaillard and his ilk truly fear is not some dusky face looking out of the windows of the White House a century or more from now; what they fear is that the Administration's policies will show their system to be as morally bankrupt as it is financially unprofitable! They fear that the people of the South will have the scales fall from their eyes and see that they have been deluded into embracing a system that is as unprofitable as it is immoral!"

The outcome was uncertain; however, Hamilton received help from an unexpected ally a week before the vote. An open letter from Thomas Jefferson appeared in several newspapers in Virginia, Kentucky, and the Carolinas; from there it was quickly reprinted nationwide. Southerners were still reeling from their political darling's defection, and even more for his taboo-breaking marriage, but this final public appeal from the former President was more than some could stand.

> "To the citizens of the United States, particularly my fellow Southerners," it read. "It has been my deepest honor and highest privilege to serve you, as a member of the Congress, as a governor, and as your President. My successor is a man whom I spent much of my political career opposing with all my might and main on many issues. My public life has ended; I have retired to pastoral pursuits and have no intent of ever standing for public office again. But being thus freed from the chains of political leadership, I now see with a clearer eye than ever before. Our pretentions to liberty were laid on a false foundation; we cheered human freedom while denying it to an entire class of mankind. President Hamilton is not only right in his opposition to slavery; he is pursuing his goal of emancipation in a legal and constitutional manner. I admire that he refuses to constrain any state to act against its will, but he makes a valid point that Federal territories are under the governance of Congress. Banning slavery from the Louisiana Purchase is a legal and constitutional act, provided it is approved by a majority in both Houses of Congress. But more than that; it is the right thing to do. It is a long-overdue act

that will set those future states aside for the cause of freedom and liberty. I am now an old man, and I have no political axe to grind these days, except for a profound wish that America continue to chart its course in the direction of greater freedom for all men, white and black alike. I urge all those who have supported me in the past, and who bear me any affection or political allegiance, to cast your vote in favor of this bill."

It was close, but with Jefferson's entry into the debate, the Louisiana Territory Act passed through Congress by a margin of nineteen to fifteen in the Senate, and eighty-five to fifty-seven in the House. The western boundary of the slave states would now end at the Mississippi River. President Hamilton signed the bill into law on June 27, 1809, the day before the Eleventh U.S. Congress adjourned for the summer. Afterward, Alex and his family returned to New York for an extended stay. He felt a sense of profound relief; his work was well begun.

CHAPTER TWENTY-TWO

"HAPPY NEW Year, Mister President!" James Madison's cheery voice startled Hamilton, who was focused on a letter from London.

"James!" Hamilton straightened with a smile, stepping around the desk to warmly embrace the Secretary of State, whom he had not seen since the previous November. "It is good to see you again. I hope your Christmas was enjoyable?"

"Very much so," the diminutive Secretary replied. "But it is good to be back in Washington again—we have much to do. Indeed, I bring you some news of interest from the South."

"And I have news from London that might interest you," Hamilton replied. "To be honest, I need your diplomatic expertise, but first tell me your news."

"South Carolina has filed a lawsuit against the Louisiana Territory Act," said Madison, "claiming that it violates the due process clause of the Fifth Amendment."

"Chief Justice Marshall did render an unofficial opinion that the act was constitutional," said Hamilton.

"So he did," Madison replied. "But the attorney arguing the case was eloquent enough that a Federal Judge agreed to refer him onward to the Supreme Court. An unofficial opinion from the Chief Justice is not legally binding. If the Court agrees to hear the case—and I imagine they will—we must be prepared to fight it out."

"John Jay is a masterful attorney," Hamilton said. "His breadth of experience is second to none, and he is a first-rate orator. Who is arguing the case for South Carolina?"

"Some youngster named John C. Calhoun," Madison told him. "My cousin said he heard him plead the case in Federal District Court and was deeply impressed. He said Calhoun may be young, but he is very well educated and a brilliant debater. Jay may have his hands full!"

"Then we need to be sure and prepare him for the trial," Hamilton said. "A shame, really, that my office precludes me from stepping into the ring. I'd love to argue the government's case myself!"

"Well, I've never seen you in the courtroom," Madison said, "but I well remember your fire and fury at the Convention! Of course, oral arguments before the Court are limited to one hour, not six."

Hamilton laughed out loud at that jibe, and Madison grinned in return.

"I was a bit intemperate in my youth," the President acknowledged. "But you must admit my grand design for an overly conservative Republic made your Virginia Plan seem much less radical by comparison!"

"That it did," said Madison. "And I've often wondered if that were not your intent all along!"

Hamilton gave him a sly wink at that, and then changed the subject.

"What other news from the South do you bring?" he said.

"North Carolina is planning to bring up a compensated emancipation bill modeled on Virginia's in the upcoming session of their legislature," Madison told him, "but I am not sure if they will have the votes for it to carry."

"We will need to make sure that our allies there have a counteroffer to put on the table that will leave the door open for future emancipation, then," said Hamilton. "We are playing the long game here, my friend, and must always need to have a fallback position prepared. We will not win every battle."

"I agree," said Madison. "Carrying Virginia and Maryland both was a great victory, but we cannot rest on our laurels. Have you heard from Representative Clay and our allies in Kentucky?"

"Not lately," Hamilton said. "My last letter from Clay was penned in November. He is trying to draw more legislators over, but it is a struggle. Many in the state are fanatically attached to slavery."

Madison nodded. "A number of Virginia diehards have emigrated to South Carolina and Georgia in advance of emancipation," he said, "including George Fitzhugh and his family, whom you met last spring. They would rather relocate hundreds of miles than live in a state that doesn't allow human bondage! I imagine that the fall congressional campaigns in those states will be centered strongly on opposition to emancipation."

"You are probably right," Hamilton said. "I do not think South Carolina will ever voluntarily emancipate its slaves. But if we can isolate slavery to a small handful of states, and thus keep the upper south and west from growing dependent on it, my hope is the cancer will be effectively quarantined. Eventually, like all wicked systems, it will be poisoned by its own venom. If, on the other hand, we allow half the country to remain shackled to the peculiar institution of the South, then the consequences I so dread may yet come to pass. Never forget, my friend, this is not an idle pursuit. The lives of a generation yet to come stand in the balance of our decisions!"

Madison sighed. He knew that Hamilton was utterly convinced that a terrible civil war over slavery would come if he failed, but James was not so certain of that bleak forecast. Nevertheless, he had discovered within himself a passion for abolition that was focused, not on preventing some possible future evil, but in the simple moral justice of the act itself. Since freeing his slaves, Madison was happier and more content than he had ever been—as if some guilt he was barely aware of was expiated, and a cloud lifted from his vision. He laughed and joked more often, and barely remembered these days how badly he had yearned to occupy the seat Hamilton now held. More than anything, he had come to love and appreciate the genius of the man he served under and was happy to ease the burden of the office when he could. Hamilton had become as close a friend as Jefferson had ever been to him, and James Madison felt blessed to have known two such remarkable men.

"When will the Supreme Court hear the oral arguments for South Carolina's lawsuit?" Hamilton asked him.

"Probably late February," Madison said. "They have not yet published their docket, but that is the usual timeframe."

"I want you there as an observer, since protocol forbids me from attending," Alex told him. "Do you still have the gift of abbreviated writing you used to record the Federal convention?"

"It's called shorthand," Madison said, "and yes, I can still do it. I presume you want a full transcript of the proceedings?"

"Exactly so," Hamilton replied. "It sounds as if this Calhoun fellow is going to be a worthy adversary for our Attorney General."

"It should be a grand courtroom duel," said Madison. "I actually look forward to watching it. Now, what was it you wanted my advice about, Mister President?"

"I have two letters here," Hamilton said. "One is from our new Minister to Great Britain, Nathaniel Pendleton, and the other is from the former French Foreign Minister, Talleyrand. Both express a concern about the same subject. Here, read for yourself."

He handed the two letters to Madison, who studied them in detail. Talleyrand's was in French, a language Madison was reasonably fluent in, but still took him a bit longer to process than Pendleton's short and elegantly worded missive.

Dear President Hamilton, Talleyrand's letter began,

It is with a heavy heart that I write you. The master that I have served for several years now has plainly revealed himself to be an autocratic tyrant of the worst order, as his vindictive treatment of our former allies in Austria has shown. I resigned my seat as foreign minister not long after the peace agreement was reached between America and Great Britain, but I retained a seat on Bonaparte's ruling council and have many operatives still active in the Foreign Ministry. It is evident that he drives for the dismemberment and perhaps even the dissolution of the Habsburg Empire, and is still fighting desperately to keep his brother Joseph on the throne as King of Spain, a move which has generated bitter warfare on the Iberian Peninsula. Napoleon is a genius on the battlefield, no doubt, as his many victories have shown, but the man is a petulant child who tolerates no rivals and brooks no opposition. He is skilled in the arts of war but incapable of maintaining peace. His own shortsightedness will no doubt bring down the Empire he has forged and him with it, if he learns not more wisdom than he has now.

But what I write to you about, my old friend, is not Continental affairs but rather the future of the United States. Bonaparte has been furious with America ever since your rapprochement with the British a year and a half ago. He has issued a decree from Milan that the French Navy is to attack all American ships on sight. It is my opinion that he had hoped to pull the United States into a war with Great Britain, and since that failed to happen has become enraged at what he calls "American treachery." However, he cannot strike at America directly, since the U.S. remains France's only real ally, and because of the affection so many Frenchmen feel for America. Instead, I think that if he can stabilize Joseph's grip on the Spanish throne, he may well use Spain to wage a proxy war *against the United States. Spain's New World Empire is crumbling, and her Navy is antiquated, but still, a Spanish foray into an undefended America harbor could do great damage, and the Indian nations of the American South could be coaxed into setting the frontier ablaze, and then retreating into Spanish Florida.*

Whether any of these things will come to pass is far from certain, but for the sake of our old friendship—and in the hope of rekindling a new relationship between our countries when the current unpleasantness has passed—I urge you, Alex, to keep your eyes peeled to the South! With Bonaparte's encouragement, I fear you may find the Spanish up to no good.

With respect and affection I remain,

Charles Maurice de Talleyrand Périgord,

First Prince of Benevento

Madison gave a low whistle when he finished the document. Hamilton nodded in silent agreement, and then handed him the letter from Pendleton. The Secretary of State studied the neatly penned missive with a growing sense of foreboding.

Dear Mister President, the American Minister wrote,

The battles on the Iberian Peninsula continue to seesaw back and forth, with neither side able to hold an advantage for long. French Marshal Soult inflicted a devastating loss on the Junta's General Juan Carlos de Areizaga at the Battle of Ocana, inflicting some 20,000 losses while suffering only 2000 casualties of his own. Del Parque has abandoned Salamanaca, but at the same time, irregular forces and local militias continue to harass and attack French forces whenever circumstances allow, causing the Bonapartistes to engage in horrific atrocities against the civilian population in reprisal.

For the moment, Joseph Bonaparte is in firm control of the government of Spain, and I have heard through several unofficial channels that his brother is urging him to make some demonstration against the United States to show Napoleon's displeasure at our rapprochement with the British. King Joseph is reluctant to do so, since Spain's military weakness, combined with its badly divided government, leave her in a poor position to start a new conflict. But since when have any of Napoleon's brothers been able to refuse the Emperor of France anything he wishes?

I know that many factors go into the government's foreign policy decisions, but it seems to me, my dear old friend, that prudence would dictate that we should guard our Southern frontier closely in the near future. Things in Spain could change any time; a few British victories by General Wellesley, who is a remarkably skilled soldier, could eliminate the threat altogether.

I have observed since my arrival in Great Britain that there seems to be more goodwill towards the United States these days; reports of your efforts against slavery are quite popular with the British public, and the abolitionist movement here is gaining strength daily. The tensions of two years ago have receded greatly, and I think our chances of war with the British are less than they have been in many years.

On a personal note, Mister President, I thank you for this assignment—my wife loves London, and I find that serving as

America's Minister here is a most pleasant duty. Give my best to Eliza and the children and assure Secretary Madison that a much more detailed report of the developments I have briefly recounted above is on its way, if it has not yet arrived.

Sincerely and respectfully,

Nathaniel Pendleton,

Minister Plenipotentiary from the United States to the United Kingdom of Great Britain

"It seems that your French friend and our ambassador both perceive the same danger to the United States," Madison said when he was done. "Do you really trust Talleyrand?"

"No further than I could throw one of your wife's delicious apple pies underwater," said Hamilton. "He is the most self-interested person I have ever met. But he does hate Bonaparte, and I have no doubt that in this instance, he is telling the truth as he perceives it—especially since Pendleton, whom I do trust, confirms his testimony."

"So then, what do you propose to do?" Madison asked.

"What was the name of that militia general from Tennessee—the one who was in the Senate for a couple of years?" Hamilton asked.

"Andrew Jackson?" Madison said. "Hot-tempered fellow, but a fierce fighter. He trounced the Indians last year during the Creek uprising."

"I'm going to suggest that the Southern governors call out the militia for duty along the Florida border," Hamilton said. "I'll put him in command. If the Spanish should try anything, they will have a bunch of ferocious Tennesseans to contend with."

"I think the presence of a couple thousand roughneck frontiersmen on the border will probably make the Spanish pull their claws in pretty quickly," Madison said.

"And if not, we'll be in position to counter any move they make," Hamilton said. "Let's also order several of our new frigates to Savannah and Charlestown, in case the Spanish decide to attack from the sea. You know, I've often thought that Florida would make a good addition to the Union—although if it should come to that, we'll need to devise a way to keep slavery out of the new territory."

"Perhaps so," Madison said, "but maybe we can solve this without violence. We could make an offer instead to buy Florida outright from King Joseph—and from the Junta as well! If one government of Spain will not sell us the territory, perhaps the other one will."

"And whichever agrees to the sale, it will be difficult for the other to take the territory back by the time the long battle for Spain is over," Hamilton finished his thought. "I think Joseph is our best bet—after all, selling territory to the United States is a family tradition, and his government is in desperate need of money. Draft the necessary letters, Mister Secretary, and let us see how it goes!"

The two men conferred for a bit longer, and then Madison excused himself and returned to his office. Hamilton watched the Secretary of State leave the President's office with a bounce in his step and a smile on his face. He reflected on how many of his fellow Federalists had tried to talk him out of retaining Madison's services. Alex was glad he had stuck to his guns; Madison was doing a splendid job and the two men had developed a solid working relationship.

In fact, politically, America's young two-party system was undergoing a profound change. More and more members of Jefferson's coalition, especially in the North, were moving toward Hamilton's revived Federalist Party. They called themselves Federal Republicans, to distinguish themselves from the partisans of John Adams, but in their ideas and policies they were leaving Jefferson behind and gravitating toward the President. Most of the original members of the Federalist Party had fallen in step behind Hamilton, although a few felt he had gone too far in courting the other side and were pushing back against his leadership.

In the Deep South, however, opposition to Hamilton was becoming stronger and more defined. Led by Congressmen like John Gaillard and Virginian planters who had moved to the Deep South, like George Fitzhugh, this group referred to Hamilton as "King Alexander" and did their best to portray him as a power-mad dictator anxious to suppress the rights of the South while imposing a nightmarish vision of black equality and racial intermarriage. This opposition had not yet coalesced into a political party, but they were moving steadily in that direction. Hamilton regarded them with caution, but they were too disorganized to pose any real danger to his political plans thus far.

Congress had convened for its winter session in late November, and then taken a month-long recess for the Christmas holiday. Now the Senators and Representatives were converging on the capital for the second half of the session. 1810 was an election year, and most of the House members were planning to stand for reelection, as were most of the incumbent Senators whose terms ended that year. As a result, the debate in both Houses of Congress was largely devoted to political grandstanding and eloquent speeches for the consumption of voters back home; little urgent business was being debated and no major bills were under consideration. Hamilton signed a few minor pieces of legislation over the next month and hosted several dinners for the legislators in the White House. The North Carolina legislature was going to commence its session on February 1, and Alex had dispatched a couple of observers to keep him informed on the progress of the Emancipation Bill.

Alex also took the time to invite his old friend Senator Joseph Anderson of Tennessee to dinner one evening to sound him out on the issue of emancipation. He had known Anderson for many years; the Senator had fought bravely in the Revolution, seeing combat at the Battle of Monmouth and fighting under Hamilton's command during the siege of Yorktown. Anderson was a strong-willed free thinker who had opposed Alex in the past on some issues, but he had also bucked Jefferson's proposals on occasion. He was a quintessential Tennessean—brave, tough as an old tree stump, and physically strong. Frontiersmen respected those attributes and would not vote for a man who did not display them; Hamilton respected these qualities also.

But Anderson had not supported the Louisiana Purchase Act the previous session, and he showed little interest in emancipating his slaves.

"Why should I free a bunch of ungrateful savages so they can run off and leave me destitute?" he said. "Your talk of a looming civil war is alarmism, pure and simple. Tennessee folk love the Union; they just want to be left alone by the Federal government. You've had some good ideas in the past, President Hamilton, but this one is a right clinker!"

"My dear Senator," said Alex, "if I cannot sway you on the grounds of morality, can I at least urge you to look at the economic rewards of paid labor? Results have been pouring in for the last six months now, and every plantation that freed its slaves has seen increased yields and productivity!"

"So you say," said Anderson, "but let's be honest, we're only a year into this policy. Will those profitable returns continue, or will the Negroes revert to their savage nature, and their long-established traditions of laziness and dishonesty? In a decade, if your system is still yielding such wonderful results, I might consider freeing my slaves. But I will not be party to any Federal measure that coerces the people of Tennessee to free their slaves against their will!"

"I have already said, on more than one occasion, that what I cannot do, I will not do," Hamilton said. "It is not within the power of the Federal government to force a state to alter its domestic institutions against the will of its citizens. But I will hold you to your word, Joseph—if in a decade emancipation continues to show itself a profitable alternative to slave labor, then I'll ask you to free your own Negroes and start paying them!"

"Fair enough," said Anderson. "So tell me now, old friend, when was the last time you heard from Lafayette? I still owe that French scoundrel a duel for seducing my sister!"

"He's had a rough few years," said Alex, "but his fortunes seem to be improving . . ."

A long-term commitment was better than none, Alex thought after his dinner guest left. He only prayed that his predictions would continue to come true, that paid laborers would prove to be as productive and profitable as he hoped. In the end, he thought, economic interests would move me to act long before moral considerations would.

By mid-January, all of Washington City had heard about the upcoming court battle over the Louisiana Purchase Act. Hamilton's supporters were cautiously confident, while the opponents of emancipation were almost giddy with excitement. Much of the conversation centered on the young South Carolina attorney who had been chosen to argue the case before the nation's highest court. When John C. Calhoun arrived in town on the twenty-fifth of January, he was thronged with curious visitors, anxious to see what the designated champion of Southern institutions was like. Hamilton decided to give the man a day or two to recuperate from his long journey, and then invited him to the White House for dinner.

The twenty-eight-year-old attorney arrived at the stroke of seven, impeccably dressed in a formal black frock coat, white gloves, and a neatly tied cravat. Calhoun was indeed an impressive figure—tall, broad-shouldered, with a shaggy mane of black hair combed straight back. He had a deep Southern drawl and piercing light brown eyes, and his expression was one of ferocious will moderated by the slightest hint of a smile.

"Mister Calhoun," Hamilton said as his guest was ushered in, "it is a pleasure to have you as my guest this evening. Allow me to introduce James Madison, my Secretary of State, and your soon-to-be opponent in the courtroom, Attorney General John Jay."

Calhoun gave a courtly bow and surveyed the three men with an amused air.

"Thank you, Mister President," he drawled. "I begin to know how Daniel must have felt when he was dropped into the lion's den."

"Please be at ease, sir," Hamilton said. "It has become an axiom of mine that political differences should not become personal. In fact, one reason I invited you here is so that you can understand that I bear you no ill will, despite the differences of policy between us."

"And what might be your other reasons for this unexpected invitation, if I might be so bold?" Calhoun asked.

Hamilton laughed; the man's directness was refreshing in a town where intentions were so often masked in shallow social pablum.

"Plain old curiosity, primarily," he said. "There are hundreds of attorneys in South Carolina; why would someone as young and inexperienced as you be chosen to argue a case before the highest court in the land?"

"I'm told I have a gift with words," Calhoun said, "and my legal credentials are second to none despite my youth."

"A prodigy, eh?" Hamilton said. "Perhaps you and I have a few things in common after all. Well, let us sit down and enjoy this fine meal together. Did you know Henry Laurens, Mister

Calhoun? His son was my closest friend and boon companion during the Revolution."

"I was only ten when he left this vale of tears," Calhoun said, "but I have known some of his family. They are fine people."

O'Malley, the White House butler, began dishing out supper to the guests—steaming bowls of clam chowder for the soup, followed by a platter of grilled beefsteak and roast chicken, with potatoes, carrots, and fresh onions on the side. The four men tucked into the meal with enthusiasm, and the conversation that followed was centered on mutual acquaintances and a few war stories from the older men, which Calhoun, born in the last year of the Revolution, listened to with keen interest, his eyes glittering as Hamilton and Jay related their experiences at the Battle of Trenton.

Calhoun was a consummately courteous guest, but despite several subtle attempts to draw him out, he refused to comment on his errand or any other political matter. At the end of the evening, Hamilton showed him to the door, impressed despite himself with the South Carolinian's reserve. He returned to the dining room and poured a glass of wine for himself and his two cabinet officers.

"What do you think, John?" he asked after he had resumed his seat.

"That is one intelligent and earnest young man," Jay said, "and I think he is going to be a formidable courtroom opponent. But constitutionally, the law is on our side. I think his appearance in the Court is aimed at building a political following more than any realistic hope of victory."

"John Marshall is a bit of a wild card," said Hamilton. "No one is more Federalist in his sentiments, but he has also been a defender of slavery in the past. I would not presume to tell you how to argue the case, old friend, but I will urge you to argue it well!"

Jay favored the younger man with a grin.

"I don't do half measures, Mister President," he said. "If the Court can be swayed, I will sway them, rest assured!"

"Well said!" Hamilton replied, and shook his hand warmly. "Thank you for coming tonight."

"Always a pleasure, Mister President," John Jay replied, and headed for the door. Madison lingered behind for a moment.

"So what did you think of our young attorney, James?" asked the President.

Madison's brow furrowed, and he slowly shook his head.

"I don't like him, Alex," he said. "Despite his outward courtesy, I sensed something dark and almost fanatical about him. I've never had this feeling before, but I swear a shadow moved across my vision when he entered the room."

Hamilton smiled and clapped his friend on the shoulder.

"You worry too much, James," he said. "Leave your work at your desk and go home for the weekend. Enjoy some of Dolley's fine cooking and get some rest. I am confident all will be well."

"You're probably right, Mister President," Madison said. "I shall see you on Monday. Have a good night."

After Madison left, Hamilton stepped back into his office and went through the bundle of letters that had been dropped off by the post rider that afternoon. Most looked routine enough, but one caught his eye—the return address was Monticello, Virginia, and the handwriting was unmistakably that of Thomas Jefferson. He used his pocketknife to cut open the envelope, and extracted a short note which he unfolded and read.

Dear President Hamilton, Jefferson wrote;

There was a time in my life when the thought of writing those two words together would have filled me with fear and revulsion. As you well know, I believe that centralized power in a corrupt government is the source of many of mankind's woes. I believed, sincerely enough, that you were the champion of everything I loathed, and I devoted much of my political career to thwarting you whenever I could. I still think that in the great battles of the founding of our Republic you often took positions which lent themselves to the centralization and corruption that I feared. Because of that I believed that you yourself were corrupt and ambitious to the extreme; I convinced myself that you were a monarchist, a profiteer, and an aspiring aristocrat.

Upon assuming the Executive Office, I began to discover how mistaken I was. Your financial system was a work of genius, a benefit to the country, and it created far less opportunity for corruption than I had imagined. Still, I thought, the system may not be corrupt, but the man himself undoubtedly is. Yet, as I have watched you handle the reins of power over the last year, I have been forced to the conclusion that I was wrong, not just about your political designs, but about your character as well. Your passion for liberty exceeds mine, because it was not corrupted with the base alloy of hypocrisy, as mine was. You are, sir, an American patriot and a constitutional leader. Seldom has being wrong afforded me more personal pleasure!

Politics breeds bitterness, and our rivalry was not a friendly one during my public career. But as I grow older and sense the dissolution that is to come—as it will, eventually, for all of us!—I find myself wishing to end my earthly existence on terms of peace and friendship with all men, especially those whom I have wronged. And I did wrong you, sir—I slandered you, I accused you of things I knew to be untrue, and I encouraged the publication of shameless rumors and falsehoods. For this I would seek your forgiveness, and while your friendship is perhaps too much to hope for, I would like for there at least to be no further ill will between us. You are a good man, Alexander Hamilton, and I am only sorry it took me so long to realize that.

Sincerely yours,

Th. Jefferson

Alex shook his head in wonder, and as he left the Executive Office, he could not help but grin. He knew that his task was still in its early stages, and that there was much left for him to achieve during his presidency. But if he could win the approbation of a man who had once been his bitterest political enemy, then perhaps an American Civil War was not as inevitable as he had once imagined it.

CHAPTER TWENTY-THREE

"ALL RISE," the solemn voice of the Clerk of the Supreme Court intoned. "The Supreme Court of the United States is in session, His Honor the Chief Justice John Marshall, presiding."

There was a rustle of clothes as everyone in the room stood, from the attorneys before the bench to the spectators in the gallery. James Madison had an advantageous position in the front row, along with a quill and a stack of foolscap. He was more nervous than he would care to admit; if the Louisiana Territory Act was declared unconstitutional, half of Hamilton's work (and his) toward abolishing slavery would be undone.

After the usual opening preliminaries, the Clerk announced the first case on the docket, *South Carolina vs. the United States*, regarding the Louisiana Territory Act of 1809. Chief Justice Marshall, an imposing figure in his black robes, summoned the two attorneys to the bench.

"The Court has thoroughly reviewed the documents in the case and has allowed the plaintiff and the defendant each a half hour to make their oral arguments," he said. "After hearing your arguments, we will move on to the next case until all oral arguments for the day have been heard. Then we shall deliberate on our verdict, which will be announced on the first day of May.

Do you each understand the rules of procedure for the Supreme Court of the United States?"

"Yes, Your Honor," both attorneys said together.

"Does either side have, at this time, any further documents to be submitted as evidence in this case?" Both men answered in the negative, and Marshall continued. "Very well, the plaintiff shall be allowed to go first. Mister Calhoun, the floor is yours."

The young South Carolinian strode to the center of the courtroom and courteously bowed to the gallery, then turned to face the bench. Madison dipped his quill in the inkwell and prepared to take down what he said—reminded, as he did so, of those endless summer days in Philadelphia, over twenty years before, when he had frantically scribbled sheet after sheet full of shorthand notes, trying to record the entire proceedings of the Federal Convention that created the Constitution.

"Honorable Justices, ladies and gentlemen, and officers of the court," he began. "I stand before you today on behalf of the citizens of South Carolina, to challenge a monstrous injustice perpetrated by this administration in the name of morality. President Hamilton, in an effort to force his twisted misapprehension of justice onto the unwilling citizens of my fair state, has conspired with his allies in Congress to strip away what is, perhaps, the most important of all inalienable rights—the right of a man to own what is his; the cornerstone of America's economic system—the very existence of private property."

The rich Southern drawl filled the courtroom, melodious to the ear, as Calhoun slowly paced back and forth in front of the bench like a great cat confined in a small cage.

"The question this court must answer in its decision is a simple one," he said. "Are we a nation governed by emotions and moral considerations, or are we a nation governed by laws? Are we to be subject to other men's concepts of right and wrong, or to the Constitution our Founders created?" He paused here and looked at Madison with a wry smile. "In the end, is the role of government to do justice, or to enforce the law? While most would say that the desirable thing is to do both, there is a problem with the concept of government acting according to a sense of right and wrong, a problem self-evident in the short-sighted restrictions placed on property rights in the misbegotten piece of legislation referred to as the Louisiana Territory Act."

He reached into his breast pocket and pulled out a folded over piece of paper, holding it up before the court.

"This is a copy of the Bill of Rights to our Constitution, the first ten amendments, added to the main document by the very first United States Congress," he said. "It is a list of personal and corporate freedoms so sacred that even the Federal government, with all its sweeping legal powers, may not violate them. I would argue that these ten amendments are perhaps the single most important part of the Constitution, because unlike the body of the document, which tells the three branches of our government what they may do, these amendments sternly warn our government of what it may NOT do—they act as the watchman on the walls, telling the creeping forces of tyranny 'Thus far may you go and no further.' It is my contention that the Louisiana Territory Act violates these sacred rights, and thus violates the Constitution itself, and therefore must be declared null and void by this court.

"The Fifth Amendment to the Constitution, in the relevant passage, clearly states: *'nor shall any citizen be deprived of life, liberty, or property without due process of law.'* Honorable justices, I would put it to you today that a man's slaves are, in fact, his property, no different than his farm, his carriage, his plow, or any livestock that he may own. Slaves have been legally recognized as a form of personal property from the most ancient of times, from the time of Abraham through the Roman Empire. Slavery is sanctioned in Scripture, in law, and tradition as an integral part of human society. Even in Eden, where only two were created, one was proclaimed subordinate to the other! How is it then that now, suddenly, at the dawn of the nineteenth century since Christ walked among us, President Hamilton has discovered a new order of morality that is somehow higher and more perfect than that ordained by God Himself? That, you see, is the danger of ignoring the law in favor of popular morality! For men's standards of right and wrong will vary from place to place and age to age; to submit our property to another's moral standards is nothing but submission to tyranny, pure and simple. In fact, doing so amounts to economic slavery for those who so submit. We must let ourselves be governed by the LAW, not by popular passions of the Yankee mob, nor by the whim of an executive drunk on power and self-righteousness!"

Calhoun was at the top of his form now, his voice thundering across the courtroom, and every eye was on him.

"If slaves are indeed property, then restricting them from the Louisiana Territory amounts to robbery on a massive scale. The honest slaveholding gentlemen of the South are prohibited from settling in these newly organized territories unless they agree to leave the source of their wealth and prosperity behind. That is unfair, discriminatory, and tyrannical! It is the same kind of meddling governmental interference in our private concerns that sparked our Revolution. The people of the South respect the rule of law; we respect the Constitution of the United States and our elected leaders. But if we are to be despoiled of our private property and our wealth in the name of *morality*"—he fairly spat the word out by this point—"then perhaps, as did the patriots of 1776, we shall be forced to seek other means by which to achieve the justice which should be ours under the law."

He tossed the copy of the Bill of Rights on the table before the bench and turned back towards his seat. Pausing with one hand on the chair, he fixed each of the seven justices with his steely gaze.

"It is up to this court to make the final determination," he concluded. "Are we to be governed by the laws we have established for our Republic, or by the whims of a moralizing politician? And if you open that door, what else may come through it? What will it cost us to shut it again, and to tell the intrusive, tyrannical dictates of the Executive Branch, 'Thus far shall you go, and no further'? It would be far better, far safer, to shut the door on this dangerous notion now, gentlemen, than to face the disastrous consequences of choosing short-sighted moralism over the rule of law!" Calhoun bowed to the court once more, resumed his seat, and said quietly: "I rest my case!"

"Thank you, Mister Calhoun," Marshall intoned solemnly. "The Court will now hear the defendant's case, argued by the Attorney General of the United States, John Jay."

Madison watched keenly as John Jay slowly rose and took his position before the bench. Calhoun's argument had indeed been masterful, if occasionally redundant, and he was curious to see how Jay would counter the South Carolinian. The former Chief Justice was an imposing figure; almost completely bald but for the fringe of white hair surrounding his scalp, taller than average, with a hawklike nose and striking blue eyes. The lines around his mouth revealed a predisposition to laughter, but his expression was grave. Chief Justice Marshall studied him curiously, recalling that Jay had been re-nominated as Chief Justice in January 1801 by President Adams. The New Yorker had declined to serve a second time in that office and John Marshall had been Adams's second choice. But for Jay's decision, their roles might well have been reversed this day.

"Justices of the Court, distinguished guests and witnesses, and all the officers of the Court," he said. "I would like to begin by thanking Mister Calhoun for that fine demonstration of the very kind of emotional moralizing that he warns us against so eloquently. Denunciations of tyranny, accusations of theft, veiled threats of insurrection, the specter of anarchy, along with a few classical and Biblical references—it was a fine speech, long on style and short on legal substance! In that respect, it did not differ too greatly from the arguments behind South Carolina's frivolous lawsuit against the government of the United States."

Associate Justice William Cushing, a former colleague of Jay's on the Court and its most senior member, snorted slightly at Jay's opening riposte, and Marshall shot him a stern look. Jay continued, with a gleam in his eye and the hint of a smile playing around the corners of his mouth.

"What this case is really about, my friends, is not about the rule of law against the popular notions of morality—or unpopular notions, as Mister Calhoun would doubtless term them. It is a simple matter of legal jurisdiction, nothing more. Does the issue of property weigh in? Yes, it does. This case is about the right of the owner of a piece of property to control what is allowed to happen on HIS property—or in this case, the right of the United States Congress to determine what is allowed or forbidden on the property of America's Federal government. Allow me to emulate my esteemed opponent by quoting the United States Constitution: *'The Congress shall have power to dispose of and make all needful rules and Regulations respecting the Territory or other Property of the United States.'"*

Jay paused for a moment, holding out his own copy of the Constitution.

"From the beginning of our Republic, the Congress has been granted the right to determine whether or not slavery is allowed in Federal territories. Even before our current Constitution was ratified, the Northwest Ordinance of 1787 declared that the Northwest Territory would be permanently closed to slavery, while the Southwest Territory would be open for slaveowners to expand their holdings. The right of the Congress to make this pronunciation was not challenged or even questioned at the time; it was naturally assumed that such power belonged to our National Legislature. Indeed, it was with this precedent in mind that those of us who met at the Federal Convention that produced our Constitution—I am dreadfully sorry, Mister Calhoun, but I believe you were too young to attend those proceedings!—that we granted Congress the power to administer the Territories." There was some tittering at this; Calhoun had been five years old at the time of the Convention. "Not once since then has congressional jurisdiction over the territories been challenged in court—until now!"

Jay walked over to Calhoun's table and picked up the copy of the Bill of Rights his opponent had dropped there. He held the two documents up, one in each hand.

"The heart of South Carolina's case is simple enough—Mister Calhoun would have us believe that the Congress closing certain territories to slavery is an assault on the protection of private property enshrined in the Fifth Amendment. The flaw that damns this premise is simple enough—not a single South Carolina slaveowner will be stripped of his property by implementation of the Louisiana Territory Act of 1809. Our government is, in fact, being sued for stealing property it has no designs on whatsoever!"

Jay stacked the two documents neatly on the corner of the table, and then he turned to face the Justices.

"It is already well-established law that states have the right to abolish slavery within their borders; Pennsylvania and Massachusetts did so long ago, New York and Virginia more recently," he said. "The states are able to do this because their legislatures have the power to create law within their borders. Federal territories are not yet states, so the Congress stands in lieu of a state legislature for them and has the same authority over them that a state legislature has within its jurisdiction. So, for Congress to declare certain territories closed to slavery is not, in the eyes of the law, one whit different than the state legislature of Massachusetts voting to abolish slavery within the borders of that state. I ask the Court to consider—did South Carolina protest Massachusetts's decision to get rid of slavery? Of course not; even Mister Calhoun must recognize that the Massachusetts legislature has the authority to do so. Did he call it an act of theft from the people of South Carolina? No, he did not, for it was no such thing. Neither is the Louisiana Purchase Act! Even the slaveowners who resided in the territory at the time of the act's passage will not lose their property, since that would violate the prohibition on *ex post facto* laws found in Article I, Section 9 of the Constitution. The law simply forbids any further transportation of slaves into the territory—and requires that children born to slaves within the territory must be legally emancipated upon reaching their majority. No one will lose any property as a result of the act, unless they voluntarily choose to relocate to the Louisiana Territory after the act's passage—in which case, the incurred loss will be as a result of their own action, not that of the government."

Madison nodded and smiled to himself as his quill flew over the page. It was a brilliant rebuttal of Calhoun's position, one that Hamilton would have been proud of.

"Justices of the Court, if a Quaker invites his neighbor to dinner, but insists that his guest leave his sword and pistol at the doorstep, he is not stealing from his guest, he is merely asking that guest to honor the rules of his house during the time of his visit," Jay concluded. "The guest is free to take up his weapons again once he has left his peaceful neighbor's dinner party. South Carolina's argument, that the Louisiana Territory Act of 1809 violates the due process clause of the Fifth Amendment, is devoid of constitutional merit. Established law and precedent show that Congress acted in a legal and constitutional matter when the act was passed last year. I would therefore ask the Court to dismiss South Carolina's claim as specious and unconstitutional; otherwise we shall see the ridiculous prospect of any one state, at any time, being able to undo the passage of any law passed by the

United States Congress or by any other state's legislature, simply by falsely claiming that it violates their private property rights. The government rests its case."

With that he returned to his seat, and Chief Justice Marshall stood, calling the court to order.

"I wish to thank the attorneys for both plaintiff and defendant for their clear and concise declarations of their clients' cases," he said. "At this time, I would like to declare a short recess before we hear the oral arguments for the next case."

Jay stood and gave Madison a wink, then turned to John Calhoun and extended his hand.

"That was a fine effort, sir, an excellent presentation of a badly flawed case," he said.

Calhoun's hand remained stiff at his sides; the copy of the Constitution crumpled in one of them.

"I will not shake your hand, sir, for you have humiliated me!" he snapped. "Were it not for the respect I hold for you as one of the founders of our Republic, I would challenge you to meet me on the field of honor!"

With that, the South Carolinian wheeled away and stalked out of the courtroom.

"That insolent puppy!" Madison said in shock and anger. "By God, John, if you were a dueling man he would be in trouble!"

Jay shook his head slowly, and then laughed.

"My dueling days are long done," he said. "I was never so happy as when New York barred the barbaric practice. Still, had he spoken to me in that tone thirty years ago, I probably would have put a pistol ball in his breast!"

"Thirty years ago, Mister Calhoun was nothing but a gleam in his father's eye," said Madison, chuckling. "Ah, the impetuosity of youth! Well, that was a fine defense, my friend. Let me buy you an ale, and then we can tell the President how things went."

Hamilton was indeed pleased when Madison read him the transcript that of the Attorney General's defense; he was even more intrigued with Jefferson's shorthand writing system and asked if Madison would teach it to him. Over the next few weeks, as they waited for the Court's verdict to be handed down, they met up for an hour each evening so that Alex could practice the abbreviated script. The President was a quick study and picked up the new way of writing in no time.

"By God, sir," he told Madison, "I wish I had known about this thirty years ago! Perhaps my right hand would not look two decades older than the rest of me!" He held up his hand by way of explanation, and Madison saw the swelling of arthritis beginning to show in the President's knuckles.

"Or you could have just written a bit less," he said, and Hamilton laughed out loud at the comeback.

"What would be the fun in that?" he said.

Those early months of 1810 were fairly non-eventful; Napoleon's forces remained engaged in a slow and deadly war of attrition on the Iberian Peninsula, but the tide seemed to be slowly turning against the French dictator. Hamilton's offer to purchase Florida from one or the other of Spain's governments had been sent, but it seemed unlikely that a reply would arrive before

Congress adjourned in May. In North Carolina, the legislature debated the issue of compensated emancipation throughout its entire session but remained deadlocked.

However, on the brighter side, more and more planters in the upper South were making the shift to paid labor by freedmen, and the results were overwhelmingly positive. Diehards did all they could to foil the system, however, even going so far as to threaten freed slaves if they caught them unattended, and occasionally firing barns and fields on neighboring plantations that had emancipated their chattels. The Governor of Tennessee was threatening to call up the militia at harvest time if the lawlessness continued. Hamilton deplored the violence and suffering, but public sympathy in the North was on the side of the emancipators, and even in the South some of the moderate planters were exasperated by the violence and stubbornness of the fanatical slaveholders.

Meanwhile, a mixed force of militia and regulars commanded by General Jackson had assembled in Georgia and begun marching southward. By late April, five thousand American troops, evenly divided between regulars and volunteers, were mustered along the Florida border, and Jackson set them to work building a string of outposts up and down the frontier to keep an eye on the Spanish in Florida. The largest post was named Fort Hamilton, in the President's honor.

A couple of weeks after the showdown in the Supreme Court, Attorney General Jay showed the President a letter he had received from John Calhoun, who was staying in Washington until the Court announced its verdict.

Dear Mister Jay, it read;

I would humbly beg your pardon for my ill-tempered and boorish outburst in the courtroom. Frankly, sir, while I have enjoyed great success before the bar in my native state, I have never received such a drubbing as you gave me before the Justices that day! While I still hope that the Court may take South Carolina's side in this controversy, the fact is that I felt like a schoolboy in the presence of an Oxford don by the time you were done making your case. My pride was stung, and I spoke in anger words that I should not have said. You are a legend of American jurisprudence, and rightly so. I hope you will wink at the faults of my youth and intemperance and understand that I wish you nothing but life, long health, and prosperity. Regardless of how strongly I disagree with the position that you and this administration have taken on the issue of slavery and the rights of private property in general, my rudeness was inexcusable. Again, I beg your pardon. I have the honor to remain,

Your ob'dt servant,

John C. Calhoun

"Well, that's certainly a shift in temperament!" Hamilton exclaimed. "I wonder what that young fox is up to now?"

"Trying to get himself elected to Congress, I'd wager," said Madison, who had followed Jay into the President's office. "He's been hanging around the Hill every day since the trial, watching how the House operates, and bending the ear of every member of the Southern delegation—looking for endorsements, according to rumor. I am sure that they told him that insulting the first Chief Justice of the United States and current Attorney General was not an effective way to win support!"

"I wouldn't be surprised if the people of South Carolina cheered his words," Hamilton said. "That state seems to have become the epicenter of resistance to our efforts. You know, Charlestown was settled by rich planters from Barbados a hundred and fifty years ago, and that blue-blooded arrogance which is still rampant on those accursed islands soaked into the soil there early on. I imagine that South Carolina may remain a bastion of slaveholding long after the rest of the Union has rejected human bondage once and for all!"

Madison nodded in agreement.

"It is truly remarkable that your friend Laurens, whom I only had the privilege of meeting once, should have somehow developed the hatred for slavery that he expressed so frequently, coming from that background," he said.

"John Laurens was a remarkable man," Hamilton said, "my dearest friend and companion during the war. He was more of a brother to me than my own blood brother was. His passion for liberty was truly remarkable, and I have no doubt that had his reckless courage not cost him his life in that stupid, futile skirmish at the war's end, he might well occupy the office I now hold—and probably be doing a better job of it!"

John Jay laid a companionable hand on the President's shoulder.

"Sir, I've had the privilege of serving three Presidents," he said. "You are doing a fine job in the office, and I will tell you this much, Alexander (if I may be so bold as to address you so)— George Washington would be very proud of what you have done—and what you are doing!"

Hamilton looked the Attorney General in the eyes, and Jay could see that he was blinking back tears.

"Nothing you could say, sir, could make me happier," the President said, "and I pray God that it is true!"

A few weeks later, Madison and Jay were in attendance as the Supreme Court announced its verdict on the four cases it had heard during its session. Calhoun was also present, and he made a point of coming over to shake the Attorney General's hand. Jay hesitated a moment, but then took the olive branch.

"Once more, I apologize for my harsh words, sir," Calhoun said in his finest Southern drawl, but Jay could see there was still an angry glint behind the smile that greeted him.

"Your apology is accepted, Mister Calhoun," he said. "Let us say no more of the matter."

"All rise!" the bailiff announced. "The Supreme Court of the United States is now in session, the Honorable Chief Justice John Marshall presiding."

The attorneys and witnesses stood, and the seven justices filed in. Jay was shocked when he noticed that his old friend William Cushing looked markedly frail and thin; his appearance had deteriorated markedly in the few weeks since the Court had heard the administration's arguments. The Attorney General prayed that Cushing would recover soon, but he also knew that the Associate Justice was getting on up in years and might soon go the way of all flesh. He made a mental note to begin drawing up a list of Supreme Court nominees for the President to consider, if worse came to worst.

"You may be seated," said the Chief Justice. "The Court is now prepared to announce its decisions on the cases heard during this session. The verdicts will be announced in the order that the cases were heard. Therefore, we shall first pronounce judgment in the case of South Carolina vs. the United States, regarding the Louisiana Territory Act of 1809. While Mister Calhoun presented a strong argument regarding the rights of private property and due process, as they are enshrined and protected in the Fifth Amendment, Attorney General John Jay's defense of the government's position has convinced the Court that South Carolina's case is without merit. The right of the Congress to legislate for the territories is clearly defined in the Constitution, and the right of legislators to restrict or abolish slavery within the states and territories subject to their jurisdiction is well established in both law and precedent. Therefore, by a margin of five to one, with one abstention, the Court finds in favor of the United States government. South Carolina's complaint is dismissed without prejudice. A full text of the court's ruling, as well as Justice Todd's dissenting opinion, will be published in the court's official proceedings, and will be available to the public next week. Case dismissed!"

Madison grinned broadly and wrung Jay's hand, and several spectators, friendly to the administration, applauded. The Chief Justice demanded order in the court, and so the attorneys and observers spilled out into the corridor where they could talk and celebrate without disrupting the proceedings.

"Congratulations, sir!" Calhoun's voice sounded behind them. "I am afraid you have schooled me in the art of persuasion, Mister Attorney General."

Jay shook the young Southerner's hand warmly.

"The law and precedent were on our side, sir," he said. "You did the best you could with the flawed position your state took."

"Perhaps so, sir," Calhoun said, his eyes glittering with venom behind the smile. "But I think that the whole nation will, in time, regret this ruling. South Carolina depends on slavery, and you seek to destroy it! Strip away a man's livelihood, sir, and he becomes desperate. And desperate men do desperate things."

"The President has no wish to force emancipation on South Carolina, or on any other state," Jay said. "I wish you could understand that. He seeks to persuade, not coerce."

"And when all our neighbors have been 'persuaded'—by which you mean, bribed!—what then, sir? How shall South Carolina endure when our property can run away in any direction? This is a dark day for the future of our Union," Calhoun said, and shook his head. "So enjoy your victory for now, Mister Jay. You will rue this day before all is said and done."

Madison and Jay watched in quiet wonder as the tall young South Carolinian stalked away.

"I think I preferred him when he was rude!" Madison whispered.

CHAPTER TWENTY-FOUR

IT WAS SUNDAY night, and President Hamilton was seated at his desk, reading his Bible. Congress had adjourned and gone home for its summer recess, and Washington City had emptied quickly thereafter. Alex and his family had returned to New York City, and there Hamilton enjoyed the first extended period of rest since he had taken office a year and half before. The Fourth of July was coming up, and New York was planning a huge celebration to honor its favorite adopted son as well as the thirty-fourth anniversary of America's Declaration of Independence.

Across the nation, candidates were gearing up for the congressional elections coming in the fall, and Hamilton's Federal Republicans were picking up support in the northern and middle states. In South Carolina, Georgia, and Tennessee, the old Jeffersonian Republicans, who now called themselves the Democratic Whigs, were vigorously denouncing Hamilton's policies (especially emancipation) and gaining a large following.

Alex was pleased with the progress of his drive for emancipation thus far. He had managed to persuade three slave states to manumit their Negroes, and North Carolina was still debating the issue. Kentucky was split, but he still had hopes that the legislature might eventually come around. That left South Carolina, Georgia, and Tennessee as the holdouts. He had some hopes for Tennessee, but the other two were intractable in their opposition. More importantly, though, the Louisiana Territory Act had drawn the line at the Mississippi River. The remainder of the Southwest Territory, which was located between Georgia, South Carolina, and the Mississippi, might still incorporate as slave states, but Hamilton was determined to prevent that if he could.

But would it be enough? This was the question that haunted him; had his efforts tipped the scales enough to prevent the catastrophic war that his vision had foretold? Was the vision even real? He still asked himself this occasionally, usually deep in the night when he was awake alone with his fears. He believed that it was, and the course of events over the last six years had confirmed its reality in his mind, but still, he sometimes doubted—hence his devotion to the Scriptures during his moments of solitude. God had given him a second chance at life; he believed that with all his heart. He wanted to use that chance to do God's will, and he sought to find that will through the Word of God.

"It was for freedom that Christ set us free; therefore stand as free men and do not be subjected again to the yoke of slavery," Paul had written to the church at Galatia. It was a passage Hamilton had first heard during the Revolution as a young man, when the Americans used it to justify their rebellion against the British crown. He knew that Paul was speaking of spiritual, not physical, bondage, of the superiority of grace over the law. Yet at the same time this simple declaration of liberty in Christ never failed to set his heart racing. What would come of his own efforts in the eternal scale of things, he could not know in this life. But what he did know in the here and now was that tens of thousands of men who had once been bought and sold like cattle were now laboring for

wages, freed from the yoke of slavery, and his presidency had accomplished that.

Was it enough? He prayed that it would be, but he also knew that his work was not done. Alexander Hamilton was determined to continue fighting for all he was worth, for as long as he could, to secure freedom for as many as he could.

The President read a bit further, and then bowed his head in prayer. Once he was done, he stood; his strength was restored, and his resolve renewed. He decided to slip down to the kitchen for a warm cup of tea while he waited for Eliza to return from their neighbor's house, where she was helping a new mother who was struggling to raise a sickly baby.

Alex had just stirred in a nice mix of honey and lemon into his tea when he heard a sharp knock at the front door. He wondered who was coming to call so late in the evening on a Sunday as he strode down the front corridor of the Grange, his Manhattan country home and the only house he had ever designed. He was surprised when he opened the door and beheld his visitor's face.

"Cartwright!" he said. "What brings you to New York? I figured you'd be down in Virginia visiting your sweetheart."

The Casanova of Capitol Hill, as Henry Clay had jokingly named young Elijah, had fallen deeply in love with the eldest daughter of a Virginia attorney named Nicholas Carroll, and had finally forsaken his pursuit of every female he encountered for a lonely quest to with the approval of his dear Lily-Beth's father. Carroll was not at all sympathetic to Cartwright's lovesuit, and Hamilton had even gone so far as to write a letter supporting his young aide. Cartwright's clothes were dusty and sweat-stained, and his normally well-combed hair was plastered to his forehead with dried sweat.

"Secretary Madison received a visit from the Spanish Ambassador," the young man said. "He wanted me to deliver this letter to you, with his own comments attached. He said it is a matter of some urgency."

"And you responded with your usual alacrity," Hamilton said. "I appreciate your willingness to be a courier! Are you hungry?"

"I've been in the saddle for ten days straight," Cartwright replied. "I believe I could stand to eat a bite and sleep for a day or two!"

Alex smiled and clapped him on the back.

"Well, then, go down to the kitchen and tell Mrs. Benson I said to feed you until you can't eat any more, and then our guest bedroom is yours! If you don't come out in two days, I'll check in and make sure you are still breathing."

Cartwright grinned, that crooked smile that had set ladies' hearts fluttering from New York to Richmond, and then nodded.

"I appreciate it, sir!" he said. "And I'll have you know, Mister Carroll has finally given permission for me to marry Lily-Beth!"

"Well done, lad!" Hamilton said. "Now, if you'll take a word of advice from an old man, be a faithful and loving husband to her, even when temptation is great. And, if you should ever stray, don't publish the fact in the newspapers until AFTER you have crawled to her for pardon!"

Cartwright's eyebrows shot up at that; Hamilton very rarely alluded to his past indiscretions, much less joked about them. But the President had become quite fond of him, he knew, and he also recognized that beneath the jest was good advice.

"My tomcatting days are done, Mister President," he said. "None of those other girls measure up to my Lily-Beth."

"Good lad!" said Hamilton. "Now go refresh yourself, and I will see what Mister Madison has to say."

Hamilton retrieved his cup of tea and took the letter to his study, where he opened it. There were two letters inside, as Cartwright had said; one was in Madison's familiar, flowing script; the other was written on rich vellum with a more angular, bold penmanship.

Dear Mister President, Madison wrote.

I hope you are enjoying your summer in New York. I stayed on in Washington for a bit after you left, since my path home is so much shorter than yours. That turned out to be a good thing; just before I left I received visits from two different Spaniards. As you know, America has declined to receive an official ambassador while the Spanish crown is in contention between King Fernando IV and Joseph Bonaparte. Nevertheless, Luis de Oniz has been here for a year now, unofficially representing the Bourbon monarchy and the Junta that supports it, and Jose de la Garda has recently arrived, representing the interests of King Joseph.

By all accounts the war on the Iberian Peninsula is still deadlocked, with most of the Spanish people supporting King Fernando but three French divisions keeping Bonaparte's grip on the throne secure for the moment. In all honesty, King Joseph is friendlier to the United States and would be a more congenial ruler for our national interests, but it remains to be seen whether he can win over the loyalty of a large enough body of the Spanish people to remain in power. For the moment, he is seen as an agent of the kind of radical political change that conservative, Catholic Spain has feared and loathed for centuries.

Our offer to purchase Florida has provoked interest from the Bonapartist faction and outrage from the Bourbon side, as we thought it might. While Señor de la Garda would not commit King Joseph's offer to paper, this is what he authorized me to tell you: **His Majesty recognizes that the current difficulties in Europe have complicated Spain's ability to retain control of Florida, whereas the proximity of the United States to that territory would make American control much easier to enforce and maintain. The current governor of East Florida, Enrique White, is loyal to the Junta and hostile to American interests. His stubbornness makes it difficult for any permanent understanding to be reached, but King Joseph is willing to entertain America's offer as long as the President understands that the current Governor of Florida will not recognize the legality of any such transaction. Should some unfortunate incident along the border render it necessary for American forces to enter Florida and seize control from the governor, it would of course be regrettable—but it might also make future accommodation to American interests easier to secure.**

That is not to say King Joseph desires any such thing, but is merely offered as an observation.

As you can see, Mister President, Napoleon's penchant for intrigue and double dealing is apparently a family trait! While I would not presume to dictate policy to you, I feel that I now know you well enough to guess your mind on this. America does not beat up her neighbors and rob them of territory—with the purchase of the Louisiana territory, we have more than enough land to contain our growing population for decades to come! Still, having a territory the size of Florida controlled by a reactionary European nation hostile to our interests is hardly an ideal state of affairs, as this missive forwarded by Señor Oniz makes clear:

To His Excellency President Alexander Hamilton of the United States, from the Cadiz Junta fighting for the restoration of Spain's rightful monarch, His Serene Majesty King Fernando Francisco de Paula Domingo Vincente Ferrer Antonio José Joaquín Pascual Diego Juan Nepomuceno Januario Francisco Javier Rafael Miguel Gabriel Calisto Cayetano Fausto Luis Raimundo Gregorio Lorenzo Jerónimo de Borbón y Borbón-Parma, Greetings.

It was the privilege of the Spanish Crown to fight alongside the Americans and the French in your virtuous rebellion against the perfidious British, and Spain has always sought to be a good neighbor to our American friends. However, no amount of goodwill can overlook a blatant attempt to intrude on our sovereign territory, and I have been authorized by the Junta to inform the

American government that we will regard any incursion into Florida as an act of war. Do not mistake our current internal divisions for weakness or lack of resolution; if America moves on Florida, Spain will respond with all the fury of righteous indignation. When the current conflict in Spain is resolved, King Fernando may be willing to discuss the future of Florida, and of Spanish-American relations, through normal diplomatic channels. But any attempt by the United States to take advantage of current disorder will be met with force. If we are mistaken and have misjudged America's intentions, then please accept our humble apologies for the tone of this message. But it is better to be forceful and leave no room for misinterpretation than to use the polite language of diplomacy and be ambivalent in our meaning. With fondest regards and good wishes for the peace and prosperity of America, I remain, Luis de Oniz, Minister Plenipotentiary from the Spanish monarchy to the United States of America.

As you can see, Mister President, the Junta are not going to accept any bargain that we may proffer on the subject of Florida, and the long-term prospects for King Joseph are not sanguine enough to merit concluding a treaty, in my opinion. As always, I will defer to your judgment in this matter, but it seems to me that, short of an actual Spanish incursion into U.S. territory, our prospects for legally acquiring Florida from either faction are dim. Of course, events on the border could change those prospects at any time, but I am sure you will agree that we must not be the ones to precipitate or encourage such an incident. If blood must be shed over Florida, better that *first blood be drawn by our enemies, so that it can never be said that America is governed by thieves and bullies.*

I hope this letter finds you safe and well, Mister President, and that your Fourth of July celebration is a joyous and happy one. God bless you and keep you, and may He favor our beloved country with your leadership for years to come!

Your obed't servant,

J. Madison, Sec'y of State

Alex read the letters through carefully, and then read them again. He had feared it might come to this—two governments battling for the control of a country on another continent held part of America's destiny in their hands. The acquisition of Florida, and the abolition of slavery there, would be a potent blow in his battle for nationwide manumission. Certainly, he thought, if he did not acquire Florida, a later administration, one that did not share his opposition to slavery, might do so. Then the whole bloody chain of events he sought so desperately to prevent might be set in motion once more.

Yet, at the same time, he recognized Madison's wisdom. America cannot become a bully, he thought, brutally attacking weaker neighbors just because it craved their territory. Whatever happened regarding Florida must come because of Spain's actions, not his! The border was well guarded now, and he had issued strict orders for the American forces there not to cross over into Spanish territory unless it was to retaliate for an act of aggression. In the meantime, Hamilton decided, a public statement regarding the situation there might be in order. He had been invited to speak at the Fourth of July celebration dinner at Columbia College, where he had attended classes a lifetime ago and now served on the board of regents. What better occasion to reassure both factions in the Spanish conflict that America was not going to steal their territory?

As Hamilton filed the letters away for future reference, he heard Eliza's quick, pattering steps in the front hallway.

"Good evening, my love!" he said merrily. "How is little Jimmy Sanders faring today?"

"He is still small and weak," she said, "but he's finally started suckling properly and isn't crying as much. Poor Jane is still worried sick about him, but I think he may pull through!"

Hamilton pulled his still-beautiful wife close to him and kissed the top of her head, smelling the sweet scent of her hair. He remembered the intense grief they had shared at the loss of Philip, as well as the stillborn child Eliza had borne him shortly after the Revolution, and he prayed that the Sanders child would recover and grow up healthy and strong.

"I know you were a great comfort to her, sweetheart," he said. "She is as blessed to have such a friend as I am to have such a wife!"

Eliza tilted her head up and kissed her husband fondly. He returned the kiss and said: "Come on upstairs, my darling, and I shall draw you a bath."

For the rest of the evening thoughts of Spain, Florida, and slavery were banished from his mind.

The next morning Alex woke up early and left Eliza sleeping while he crept downstairs to begin writing his speech in the stillness of the early morning. However, as he reached the bottom of the stairs, he was surprised to hear soft, feminine laughter echoing from the library. None of his children were normally early risers, so he poked his head through the door to see who was awake.

Angelica, his eldest daughter, was sitting on one of the padded reading chairs, leaning forward, facing Elijah Cartwright, who was spinning an elaborate story for her amusement.

"And as I scrambled out of the window with my trousers in one hand and a pistol ball whistling over my head, I decided that enough was enough!" Hamilton's secretary said. "No amount of female affection was worth being gunned down by an irate member of the House of Representatives! I made a vow to God as I ran for my life, half expecting the next pistol ball to hit me between the shoulder blades, that if He would send me a good and virtuous girl, my days of seduction were over and done! Lo and behold, it was two days after that when I met my Lily-Beth, and I have faithfully observed that vow ever since!"

"Oh, Mister Cartwright," Angelica said, in a perfectly normal tone of voice, "You are truly an example of the redeeming power of love—and the curative properties of gunpowder!"

"Perhaps it was a bit of both that made me mend my ways," Cartwright said with a chuckle.

"Just mind you don't relapse with my daughter!" Hamilton said, stepping into the room with a smile.

"Papa!" Angelica sprang up and hugged him. "Mister Cartwright was just entertaining me with stories of his former evil ways. He was a most delightfully wicked man, was he not?"

Alex was stunned. Angelica very rarely came out of her shell around anyone other than her immediate family, but here she was, as vivacious and full of life as she had been before Philip's death stole her mind. He made up his mind to do nothing to break the spell that Cartwright's silly anecdotes seemed to have cast over her.

"Well, lad, why don't you tell her about the time you rode from Washington to New York and back in the dead of winter to bring me news of the latest battles in Europe?" he said. "I know you probably had an adventure or two on the way that you didn't relate to me at the time!"

"Well," Cartwright said with a sheepish grin, "there was this one innkeeper's daughter who owned a magnificent sorrel mare that she was very reluctant to rent to a young courier on a vital mission, so I . . ."

Hamilton and Angelica sat and listened for more than an hour as Cartwright narrated one salacious story after another, implying more than he told, but telling enough to make Hamilton's daughter giggle and blush while her father watched with a bemused expression. Eventually, Angelica held up her hand and the young secretary fell silent.

"I've been very selfish," she said. "You were looking for something to eat and I started listening to your stories and never did fetch you any food. Father, would you like me to bring you both some breakfast? I heard Mrs. Benson stirring in the kitchen, I am sure she has some biscuits and a rasher of bacon cooking."

"That would be delightful, my dear," said Alex. "Elijah and I will be in my study."

He gestured for the lad to follow him, and Angelica headed off to the kitchen, humming a sprightly tune.

"I am so sorry, Mister President, I know she is fragile and she's hardly ever spoken more than a word to me, but this morning I greeted her and she asked after me, and the next thing you know we're chatting like old chums!" Cartwright explained nervously. "I meant no harm, sir!"

"Do not apologize, my boy," Alex said. "She retreated into her own grief when her brother Philip was killed nine years ago and has only recently started to revert to her old self again. You are the first person outside the family she has had an extended conversation with since her illness began. You have my leave to tell her bawdy stories all day long if it has this effect on her!"

"Well, sir, I did sanitize the details a good bit," Cartwright said, blushing furiously. "I would not want it said that I corrupted the President's daughter!"

"I'd say you've done more good than harm," Alex told him, "and I thank you for it!"

By the time Angelica returned with a pot of coffee and two plates piled high with ham, eggs, and fresh biscuits, she had regressed a bit—she was still aware and called both of them by name, but some of the light in her eyes had died back, and her vocabulary was more like that of a little girl than of a young woman. However, Alex was happy to observe she did not retreat all the way into her mind, and when Cartwright smiled at her, she still giggled. Alex was so happy with her progress that he set to speechwriting with a much lighter heart than he had brought downstairs with him that morning.

A FEW DAYS later, on the Fourth of July, Hamilton rose to address the faculty and student body of Columbia College. The quadrangle was spread out with dozens of tables, and on the speaker's platform Hamilton was flanked by the Governor, both New York's Senators, and all fifteen of her Congressmen. The front tables were crowded with state legislators, dignitaries, and journalists, all of whom were holding their notepads, ready to report on Hamilton's address to their readers. He already had his speech printed up and ready for delivery to the seventeen state capitols and the appropriate foreign embassies. He had polished his words carefully and was excited to finally be able to deliver his address. He sat patiently while Benjamin Moore, the president of the school—the same pastor he had spoken to on the fateful afternoon of the duel six years before—introduced him to the assembly.

"Few men have more nobly redeemed a second chance at life than our beloved President, New York's favorite son, America's heroic patron of liberty and justice, Alexander Hamilton!" Moore concluded, and the audience stood to its feet and applauded as Alex made his way to the lectern, dressed in full academic regalia.

"Honored guests, distinguished visitors and alumni, students, fellow citizens, and all others here assembled, may I begin my remarks by wishing all of you a happy and blessed Fourth of July, when we celebrate the declaration of our independence and the establishment of our republic of liberty!" he declaimed in his clear, strong voice. The audience nodded and clapped in approval, and Hamilton waited for silence to fall before continuing.

"Thirty-five years have passed since I first set foot on this campus," he said, "a penniless immigrant sent to get an education by the charity of friends and neighbors in the distant islands where I was born. It was here that I fell in love with America. It was here that I first heard the immortal words of our Declaration of Independence, at a time when the realization of that independence was very much in doubt. It was here that I volunteered to serve in the New York militia, and it was only a few blocks from here that I received my baptism of fire in the first battles of our Revolution!" As he spoke, his mind raced back to those heady, danger-filled hours of his youth. "Not far from here I caught my first glimpse of the man who would become my commander, my general, my mentor, my friend, and my President, the Father of our Country, His Excellency George Washington!"

As he knew they would, the crowd surged to its feet at the mention of Washington's name. More than a decade after his death, the first President's hold on the hearts of the people was stronger than ever. Alex paused again, and when the applause had died down, he resumed.

"It was also not too far from this beloved campus that I nearly perished six years ago, from a wound sustained in a foolish quarrel with a dangerous man. I am not proud of the events surrounding that deadly duel, and it is my honest wish that they had never transpired. But after my brush with eternity, I made up my mind that I would devote the remainder of my life to one great and overriding cause, the very cause of our Revolution, the holy cause of human liberty! We began our journey as a nation by declaring that all men are created equal, but even in the room where those immortal words were penned, we knew that they were unfulfilled. How can we call ourselves a free people when we continue to hold our fellow sons and daughters of Adam as property? I know that slavery has always existed—its defenders constantly remind me of that fact! What of it? Have not murder, theft, and adultery always existed? Does the mere antiquity of a practice somehow guarantee its morality? If we are truly to live out the words of the noble creed that Thomas Jefferson, a man with whom I warred for the better part of two decades but am now proud to call my friend, penned for us on this auspicious day thirty-four years ago, then we must rise above such pale and petty justifications for something we all know in our hearts to be wicked! I would remind everyone here that I have sworn a sacred oath before Almighty God to preserve, protect, and defend the Constitution of the United States. I will not seek to exercise powers that document does not grant to the presidency, but I will do as much as I can, as long as I can, with all the might and main that I possess to free every slave the law allows me to, and to persuade others to act in the cause of emancipation where I cannot. As long as I am in possession of this splendid pulpit, I will preach the Gospel of Liberty to the American people and challenge them to live up to the promise of our founding declaration!"

Not all New Yorkers were as enthused about emancipation as Alex was, but the fervor of his voice and the joy of the occasion were infectious, and the crowd came to its feet again, applauding the orphaned immigrant who had risen to the nation's highest office. Hamilton waited, enjoying their acclaim but also knowing that they were clapping as much for the nation and its anniversary as they were for his own unorthodox ideas.

"Thomas Paine challenged us, in his tract *Common Sense*, to receive the wretched refugee known as liberty as a guest to our shores, and to prepare, in time, a refuge for all mankind," he continued. "I believe that God has ordained America to shine the light of liberty bright and clear in a world darkened by despotism, monarchy, and the wicked anarchy of perpetual revolutions. Liberty, equality, and fraternity are noble concepts, but unless those who proclaim them also practice them, they can become just another mask for despotism and tyranny! The United States must show the world that there is a better path to tread, a path that rejects the archaic concept of the divine right of kings without enthroning the passions of the mob, a government where liberty is both restrained and expressed through the rule of law," he said. The audience grew quieter, and some men leaned forward in their seats, recognizing that something more than rhetoric was being expressed.

"America must reject the notion of conquest and plunder," Alex continued. "Providence has blessed us with an abundance of territory, so that we as a nation can turn from the course of territorial aggression that has plagued so many kingdoms, empires, and republics across time. Through treaty and purchase, America now holds enough land to house our children and their children and their children's children! So, I here commit my administration and the course of our country to a policy of peace with our neighbors, good will to all nations, and neutrality in Europe's endless cycle of wars and revolutions. I make this declaration to France, to England, to Russia, to Spain, and to all the other nations of the world: America has no quarrel with you. We have no desire to conquer your territory, to depose your monarchs, to fight your revolutions, to sway your counsels, or to further your conflicts. Peace with all nations is our desire and will be our policy!"

The crowd rose once more and applauded Hamilton's words, which echoed the sentiments of Washington's Farewell Address, the most beloved American document written since the Bill of Rights. Hamilton smiled, remembering how he and Washington had labored together over the first President's final message to the American people.

"But I would also remind all the nations of the world, our neighbors both far and near, whether they wish us good or ill," he said, "that our desire for peace and neutrality is not born of fear or weakness. We would have no conflict at all, but we will also stand ready to fight any who do not respect our borders or our freedom on the high seas. America longs for peace, but America will also draw the sword if we are forced, in order to defend the lives, liberty, and property of our people, and in to reject any incursions into our national territory. It is my fondest prayer that I will never have to ask Congress to declare war on any nation, nor to use deadly force against any foreign foe. Let us commit ourselves to a national policy of peace, of charity towards our neighbors, but also of strength and resolution in the defense of our sacred liberties! That was the vision that drove us to seek our independence all those years ago, at great peril to life and limb. The scars my fellow veterans and I bear on our bodies are a reminder of the cost of liberty, as are the stones raised in memory of our loved and lost, fallen in defense of our lives, our homes, and our freedoms. May their sacrifice never be in vain, and may generations yet unborn raise a glass to freedom on this sacred day, the day of American independence, and may all our posterity be born as free people in a free land, and citizens of a free Republic!"

The journalists scrambled to record the words of the President as the crowd rose to its feet to cheer his words. Hamilton hoped that his message to the world would be received and understood everywhere, but especially in the capitals of Europe's troubled kingdoms during their long and desperate war with France.

CHAPTER TWENTY-FIVE

THE MID-TERM elections of 1810 brought good news for Hamilton. His Federal Republicans, an amalgamation of old Federalists and Jeffersonian Republicans who had switched their allegiance to the new President, swept into strong majorities in both the House and the Senate. With eighty-five seats in the House and twenty-two in the Senate, Hamilton now had enough support in the legislative branch to implement his policies without spectacular floor battles—assuming he could keep his faction united behind him.

As Madison and others had predicted, John C. Calhoun had been elected to the House of Representatives from South Carolina, and despite his youth, his golden oratory rendered him a formidable critic of the administration. The faction that elected him, the Democratic Whigs, had attracted an odd coalition of Jeffersonian Republicans and disgruntled, pro-slavery Southern Federalists. There were also a handful of Representatives who rejected both the newer factions and still styled themselves as simple Federalists or Republicans. Henry Clay of Kentucky was expected to be the new Speaker of the House, to Hamilton's delight—he looked forward to working with the genteel, gregarious frontier politician. Alex was already working on various legislative proposals to further limit the spread of slavery once the new Congress got down to business.

It was now January of 1811, and Hamilton had come back to Washington City to witness the swearing-in ceremonies. He was hosting a grand ball at the White House to celebrate the newly arriving lawmakers and to bid farewell to those who had been defeated for reelection, or who had simply chosen not to seek another term. It had been a mild winter thus far, unlike the brutally cold weather of the previous year. Travel back to Washington City had been easier and quicker than normal, and Hamilton was upstairs at the White House, preparing some remarks for the upcoming gala, when James Madison knocked at his door.

"Good evening, Mister Secretary!" Hamilton exclaimed, turning to face him. Madison had arrived in town shortly after he had, and they had lunched together earlier in the day. Now, however, the Secretary's face was flushed with excitement, and he was fairly bouncing on his feet as he stood in the doorway.

"What on earth is it, man?" Hamilton asked him.

"Urgent news just arrived from down South, Mister President!" Madison exclaimed. "The Florida frontier is ablaze with conflict!"

Hamilton rose quickly, pulling out a map of the Southern United States from his desk drawer and unrolling it as he beckoned the Secretary of State forward.

"Tell me everything," he said.

"I had three letters arrive by post rider an hour ago," said Madison. "All were dated within a two-week span of each other, so I read them in order. Do you want me to summarize, or read for yourself?"

Hamilton smiled, despite the tension of the moment.

"You ought to know me well enough by now not to ask," he said. "Let me see them!"

Madison handed Hamilton the bundle of letters, and the President unfolded the top one. It was in a scrawling hand, difficult to read in places, with frequent misspellings, but its message was clear enough.

> *Fort Hamilton, Georgia*
> *Maj. General Andrew Jackson, Cmdt.*
> *Nov. 4, 1810*

Mister President,

At two o'clock yesterday afternoon, the soverren borders of these United States were violated by forren invaders from Spanish Florida. A mixed force of Seminole Indians, runaway slaves, and uniformed Spanish soldiers about two hunnerd or so in number crossed over the boundary line and attacked a nearby settlement called Macon's Crossing. There was a considerable loss of life, sir, as the men were caught out in the fields bringing in the last of the cotton harvest and most were killed where they stood. One young man was shot clean through the chest with an arrow, and had swooned from the pain. He regained conshusness in time to see the Spanish soldiers setting most of the houses on fire; a number of women and children were already screaming in the grasp of red savages. Recognizing he could do them no good in his bloodied state, he caught a horse that was running from the carnage and rode straight to the fort, where I interviewed him. My men and I immediately saddled up and rode for Macon's Crossing.

We were too late for most of the people there; we recovered three dozen bodies, most of witch had been scalped and mutilated in typical red savage fashion. We did rescue three survivors; one man who had been grievously wounded and left for dead, and a young woman and her son, who had hidden in a root cellar and avoided captivity. She said that at least twenty women and children had been taken captive by the band of marauders, who left Macon's Crossing, following the river eastward towards the next settlement.

I then left a physician and a squad of soldiers to guard the survivors and set out in pursuit of the marauders, who had about a day's head start. I decided to ride ahead with the two hundred cavalry I had brought to see if we could ketch up in time to save the unsuspecting settlers at Jonastown, the next settlement downriver, leaving three hundred infantry to bring up our rear, under the command of my capable young Captain, Winfield Scott.

Our horses were blown by the time we rode up on the town, but we had made up enough time to exact vengeance, if not prevention. Most of the buildings were already on fire, and many of the menfolk were dead, but the savages and their Spanish allies were still in the midst of their sack and plunder. I ordered my men to dismount and fix bayonets, and we descended upon them like the wrath of the Eternal! We killed fully half of the raiding force, including six Spanish soldiers in uniform. One of them, a captain, was carrying a letter that appears to be from the Spanish governor of West Florida, that old rascal Vincente Folch. Sergeant Polk, who speaks Spanish, translated it for me; it is an order for the commandant of Fort

Pensacola to send a detachment to "chastise the Americans who encroach on the sovereign borders of New Spain."

Given that our national territory has been invaded by these foul creeturs, I consider that a state of war exists, and I am ordering my men to march across the border and take Fort Pensacola in retribution. I'll hang that rascally commandant meself to exact justice for the poor settlers whose bodies we buried. I shall send a fuller report after we have engaged the enemy,

Respectfully and obediently yours,

A. Jackson, Major General, Commanding

Hamilton let out a low whistle as he finished reading the letter. "Apparently the Spanish have chosen to ignore my olive branch," he said. "Very well, on their heads be it!"

"Read on," said Madison. "It gets worse."

Alex quickly unfolded the second letter from General Jackson and began reading.

Ft. Pensacola, West Florida
Major General Andrew Jackson, Acting Cmdt.
Nov. 10, 1810

Mister President,

I gave pursuit to the band of Spanish brigands who had invaded Georgia and tracked them across the border into the swampy land east of Pensacola. I expected them to make for the fort, but instead they tried to turn south and east to flee down the peninsula. We cornered them when I sent a flying cavalry patrol under Capt. Scott to cut them off at the coastline, and a short skirmish caused the rest to lay down their arms. Once they were taken into custody, their commander, a Major who gave his name as Antonio de la Paz, explained to me that the orders to cross the border and attack our settlements was delivered to him by a Captain Raul Vega, who had fallen in our initial fight at Jonastown. Vega had insisted that his orders were direct from Governor Folch, which puzzled the major, cense he thought Folch was under directives from Cadiz not to provoke our country.

This was a confounded puzzlement to me, because the last communications we had received from across the border indicated that the Spanish were anxious not to stir up trouble with us while there was still a civil war going on between the Junta and the Bonapartiste king. But innocent blood had been shed on American soil by the agents of a foreign power without a declaration of war, so I reckoned justice needed to be swift and brutal. After a tribunal conducted before my officers, it was agreed that the leaders of the Expedition be hung and the enlisted men executed by firing squad. De la Paz was mortified by our decision but bore it like a man, stating that if he was destined to die for his country, then the method really did not matter to him.

At this point events took a new turn. We heard the whinny of horses approaching, and even as we were building our gallows, a force of Spanish cavalry came riding up from Pensacola. They demanded to know what we were doing on their side of the border, and I sent a note back asking why their soldiers had been ordered to attack our settlements in Georgia. Their captain returned that he knew of no such orders, and at this time I met him under a flag of truce. His name was Martin Perfecto de Cos, and he was as arrogant a son of a bitch (your pardon, Mister President, but I am a man of blunt speech!) as I have ever met. I related how De La Paz and his men had raided and burned two towns and murdered several dozen U.S. citizens, and Cos insisted that Governor Folch had not ordered this and did not know anything about it. He demanded to take de la Paz and his men into custody, and I told him that they had been condemned by a military court martial and were going to be hanged higher than Haman!

Cos broke off talks at this point and returned to his soldiers, and I ordered my men to stand to arms as we prepared for the executions. Turned out that was a good decision, because moments later the Spanish troops came charging at us. We fended them off with a generous dose of lead and a sharp bit of skirmishing, then finished our executions and moved in pursuit of them. I regret to say, though, that about half the captive marauders escaped during the confusion, including Major La Paz.

After this, I took a day to let my horses rest and gather supplies, then marched eastward. Cos met us outside Pensacola two days later with a larger force, but I had sent post riders across the border commanding the rest of my garrison to ride south posthaste. Another hunnerd men joined me just before we met the Spanish forces, and as it turned out, we needed every one of them. Cos had thrown up a hasty rampart in front of the city, with three brass six pounders and one twelve pounder. I knew a frontal assault might not succeed aginst such strong defenses, but fortunately many of my Tennesseans were riflemen. I used ropes and pulleys to lift them up to the tops of the tallest trees that were within the range of their weapons. I had two men straddling branches, re-loading and handing rifles to my sharpest shooters, and they laid down such fast and accurate fire that the Spaniards could not man their cannons. After a half hour of sustained rifle fire, I ordered my men forward. Cos was screaming at his troops to fire the cannons, but my riflemen kept the fire up hot and heavy, and the Spanish could not git off more than a couple of cannonballs before my men were at the foot of the ramparts. From there it was just hand-to-hand work, and my men were well armed with tomahawks, daggers, and flintlock pistols. After twenty minutes of the hottest fighting I've ever seen, Cos struck his colors and surrendered. I'd lost eighty men killed and another two-dozen wounded, but there were fully three hundred dead Spaniards along their rampart.

After Cos and his men laid down their arms, he conducted me to the governor's home in Pensacola, where I met Vincente Folch, Spanish governor of West Florida, for the first time. He told me he was visiting Pensacola after a group of American filibusters tried to set up a separate government here last year, only to be driven out by Spanish troops. Folch is a courtly old soul, Castilian Spanish, with a good command of English, despite his thick accent. I presented him with the letter bearing his name that we found on the body of Captain Vega and demanded to know why he had ordered an armed invasion of the United States. Folch denied writing or signing the letter and showed me numerous documents he had written to demonstrate that the letter I recovered from the marauder's corpse was not in his hand.

Mister President, I am no diplomat; I'm a simple soldier and farmer in the middle of affairs that have proved to be bigger than me. America was attacked, and I responded, and I know my response was right and proper. But the Governor in whose name the attack was made has no knowledge of the order, and I have no idea who was behind this!

I am taking Governor Folch back across the border with me as a hostage until this can be sorted out. He will stand as surety for the good behavior of the Spanish troops in West and East Florida, and perhaps Governor Matthews will be able to figure out what is going on—I've dispatched a post rider to him asking him to meet us back at Fort Hamilton. I hope, sir, that you will not find fault with my actions, as all I have done has been directed at defending the honor and integrity of the United States.

Your obd't servant,

Andrew Jackson, Major General, Commanding

Hamilton paused for a long time, reading this missive over and over again. Rogue Spanish troops, attacking on forged orders from a governor who disavowed them? Who then had planned the incursion? Was it the Junta, or agents of King Joseph? Madison watched him curiously, and when Alex nodded, he handed the President the third letter.

Ft. Hamilton, Georgia
Nov. 16, 1810
Captain Winfield Scott, Acting Cmd't

Dear Mister President,

I know that it is highly unusual for an officer as junior in rank as myself to be addressing a letter to the Commander in Chief, but circumstances have left me as the senior officer at this post, and I am also the only person who knows all of what has transpired since that fateful morning when word first arrived here of a Spanish raid on Macon's Crossing. I have so much to relate that I hardly know where to begin, but I suppose the most pressing news is this: General Andrew Jackson and Major Sampson, my two superior officers, are both dead.

I took the liberty of reading General Jackson's two dispatches to you after his death, so I would know where to begin my narrative, and if in so doing I overstepped my authority, please accept my apology. As you know, we invaded West Florida in response to an armed raid on two American settlements that left forty men dead and created dozens of widows and orphans. After the battle General Jackson described in his last letter, we decided to march north and west, back to Georgia, taking the Governor of West Florida, Vincente Folch, as a hostage, both as a safeguard for the good behavior of his troops, and also hoping to figure out who ordered the raid, since it was evident he had not. Folch was not pleased with this decision, but did not actively resist it, either. He told Captain Cos not to resist us as we left Pensacola last Thursday, and with General Jackson and Major Sampson riding at our head, we marched out of the city heading north and east. The roads in West Florida are narrow, sandy dirt trails surrounded by thick woods, and our column was strung out over a mile as we neared the American border, just west of Georgia. I had ridden to the rear to help get our baggage train moving as one of the wagons had broken an axle, and after overseeing the repair I was riding back up to report to General Jackson. I topped a small rise and saw the vanguard of our Army a few hundred yards in front of me.

Jackson and Sampson were riding along at an easy pace, their vigilance perhaps relaxed due to the proximity of the U.S.

border. A squad of cavalry, some twenty-five strong, rode directly behind them, guarding the carriage that held Governor Folch. The rest of the cavalry was trotting behind them, followed by columns of infantry and militia, and the three wagons bearing our wounded men. All told, we were returning to American soil with some three hundred and fifty soldiers, several dozen wounded men, and some fifty bearers, cooks, and other noncombatants. Only a few miles remained between us and the safety of American soil when the ambush occurred.

As I said, I had topped a rise and could see our entire force of armed men ahead of me. I paused a moment to survey the sight, and to take a drink from my canteen before spurring my horse onward, when suddenly I saw both General Jackson and Major Sampson reel in the saddle. Sampson fell right away—I later found that a musket ball had hit him square in the head, killing him instantly. General Jackson was obviously hit, slumping in the saddle but his hand still gripping the reins. It was a couple of seconds after seeing them struck—and a dozen of our cavalrymen as well—that the rattle of musketry actually reached my ears. I drew my flintlock and spurred my mount frantically, ordering the infantry to come behind me with muskets primed and ready to fire. A second round of musket fire came pouring into the vanguard as I rode towards them, and at this point General Jackson fell from his horse, shot through the chest twice. Then I heard the war cries of echoing through the trees as a mixed force of Seminole Indians and Spanish soldiers came charging from the forest that had concealed them.

What followed was a short and bloody fight. The Spanish and Indians tried to cut their way through our surviving forces towards the governor's carriage, but I managed to rally the troops for a charge that drove them off thrice. Governor Folch leaped out of the carriage—whether to join his would-be rescuers or order them to stand down, I do not know—and fell moments later, shot through the neck. I do not know which side fired the shot that felled him; the air was humming with musket balls by that point. I am not sure how many attackers there were, but after a half hour or so of heavy fighting, they broke off and fled, leaving about seventy dead on the ground behind them; we also took ten of them alive. How many wounded they dragged away, I do not know. Being caught by surprise, our losses were slightly higher—some twenty men fell in the initial ambuscade, and another eighty or so were killed or wounded in the battle that followed. One of the enemy dead was the same Major de la Paz who had avoided the hangman's noose a few days earlier. According to one of the prisoners we took, he was determined to avenge his earlier embarrassment by rescuing the governor, and overruled Captain Cos, who warned him that the governor had forbidden such an attempt.

We brought the bodies of our dead, and that of Governor Folch, who had conducted himself with great dignity and honor throughout this whole affair, back across the border with us. General Jackson and Major Sampson, and the rest of our fallen, were buried with military honors this morning at Fort Hamilton, and Governor Folch was given a grave site not far from theirs.

I cannot even begin to imagine the diplomatic ramifications of this chain of events, Mister President. While General Jackson may have acquired a reputation over the years for being impulsive and hot-headed, I think that, from the start, his *actions were completely legal and proper given the provocations and outrages he was confronted with. Nonetheless, the two highest-ranking American officers in Georgia are now dead, the Spanish governor of West Florida has died in U.S. custody, and I think it safe to say that a state of war exists on our southern border. I have written to Governor Matthews asking him to call up the state militia, and I have also written to General Wilkinson in New Orleans asking him to send as many regulars as he can spare to shore up our defenses. I am doing all I can to place our frontier in a state of readiness, because I imagine that this conflict is far from over. I am sorry to be the bearer of such dreadful news for our country, and I hope that my actions meet with your approval. I did the best I could to extricate my men from a dangerous situation and get them safely to a defensible position while showing due respect to our fallen. Please, sir, send someone senior to me to take command here, for I fear I am out of my depth altogether. But until such an officer arrives, I have the honor to remain,*

Your obedient servant,

Captain Winfield Scott, acting Commandant,

Fort Hamilton, Georgia

"Good God!" said Hamilton. "This is grave news. Like it or not, James, we are at war. This was not what I wanted—it's a bother and a distraction from our mission, but that is beside the point now. I am going to have the entire Congress as my guests tonight; I will have to change my prepared remarks. We'll need to convene a special session of Congress, of course. Now that we are at war, we will make Florida ours, and we will make the Spanish pay for this outrage!"

"I wonder. . ." Madison began a thought, and then fell silent.

"Go on, out with it, sir! I asked you to stay on because I value your advice and your opinions," Hamilton said.

"I just wonder . . . if Joseph Bonaparte's signature is not attached somewhere at the end of this strange story," Madison said. "He pretty much stated that a border incident would make it easier for us to seize control of Florida."

"Well, if he thinks that I am going to pay him anything for the territory after such a provocation, he is dead wrong!" Hamilton said. "Whether it was him, or the Junta, or some malign third force, Florida is now forfeit to us, and we will pay not one cent in tribute to those who shed innocent American blood!"

"Wise policy," Madison said. "I will say this young Scott fellow sounds like a good soldier."

"He does indeed!" Hamilton said. "Reminds me a bit of myself at his age. I think I shall promote him to Colonel and leave him in command of Ft. Hamilton; he has conducted himself with skill, courage, and decency. Now, James, if you would be so kind, I have much more to do this afternoon than I thought I would. If you would inform the other cabinet members, I would like to meet with all of you after tonight's reception, which I fear is going to be cut short."

"Of course, Mister President," said Madison, and then left, closing the door behind him, and thanking the Almighty that he was not the one making the decisions that would send young men to their deaths.

CHAPTER TWENTY-SIX

THE SPANISH-AMERICAN War of 1811 was formally declared by a special session of the United States Congress on January 20. Both Spanish envoys to the United States angrily denied that their faction had any knowledge or complicity in the attacks on Georgia, and both were ordered to leave the country after a brief audience with the President. Then, in consultation with Secretary Madison and Secretary of War Tallmadge, Hamilton prepared his war message, paying careful attention to the wording. Rather than an open-ended declaration of war on both contending governments of Spain, the message called for "a vigorous war upon those hostile forces in Spanish Florida who have attacked the United States, up to and including the governor of East Florida and whosoever may have ordered him to carry out these attacks."

There was some grumbling about the imprecise nature of the message from Hamilton's diehard critics, especially from William Giles of Virginia, who still regarded Hamilton as a greater to America than any foreign potentate.

"Why are we declaring war if we do not know who is responsible for these attacks?" he blustered in the Senate. "Would it not be more prudent to arm our frontier and order our diplomats to find out who ordered this assault?"

Hamilton's old friend James Anderson of Tennessee thundered back: "What does it matter who ordered the assault? We know whence it came—that swampy den of Spanish iniquity known as Florida! Our southern frontier will not be secure until Florida is in our hands for good! American blood has been shed on American soil by a foreign aggressor; let us root them out and deny them a place of refuge! General Jackson must not have died in vain!!"

Both houses voted firmly in favor of the declaration with huge majorities; only a handful of Democratic Whigs voted against it. Armed with a strong declaration of war, with public opinion outraged by the attacks on the frontier and the death of the popular General Jackson, President Hamilton and Secretary of War Tallmadge planned a quick and decisive campaign.

The senior officer in the South at the time was James Wilkinson, a hoary old veteran of the Revolution whose combat record was as dubious as his unauthorized diplomatic activities were suspicious. He was widely known in the army as the general "who never won a battle or lost a court martial." Tallmadge had been quietly investigating Wilkinson for the last year, and shortly after the Spanish attack, he confided to Hamilton that his suspicions about Wilkinson had been confirmed: the highest-ranking officer in the American army was a spy for the King of Spain, sending regular coded reports to the Viceroy in Mexico City.

"Can you prove this?" the President asked.

"Not conclusively," said Tallmadge, "but the circumstantial evidence is convincing."

"I can't have a Spanish spy running a war against Spain!" Hamilton snapped. "However, he has powerful allies in Congress; I can't summarily dismiss him either."

"I think he should be posted to the Canadian frontier, to make sure that the British don't take advantage of our Southern dilemma to stir up trouble with the Great Lakes Indian tribes," Tallmadge said. "Wilkinson's long experience and advancing years make that sort of assignment more appropriate for him than a vigorous campaign in the malarial swamps of Florida."

"Who is the best candidate to replace him?" Hamilton asked.

"Well, young Scott has the makings of a fine field commander, but he is too junior to be placed over an entire campaign," the Secretary said. "Colonel Jacob Brown was just promoted to Brigadier General of New York's state militia. He's an experienced soldier with a strong head for tactics, and he is loyal to you and to the country."

"Excellent choice!" said Hamilton. "I've known Brown for years; he even worked for me briefly during the threat of hostilities with France, back in '98. Let us send him south on a fast ship to New Orleans with orders to relieve General Wilkinson. We can require Wilkinson to return to the north on the same vessel; that will get him out of Brown's way—and keep him from betraying our strategy to the Spanish!"

"That, sir, begs the question: What is our strategy?" Tallmadge said.

Hamilton turned to his desk, where a map of Florida and the Gulf Coast was unfurled. He lifted several pieces from the chessboard sitting in one corner and placed one in St. Augustine, in northeast Florida.

"This is the seat of government," he said. "With the death of Folch, the governments of both East and West Florida now rests upon Enrique White, the Spanish governor of East Florida. My plan is to send an army of five thousand men straight across the border and make a forced march to St. Augustine by early summer, seizing White and forcing him to cede control of Florida to us. I will place another five thousand troops west of New Orleans, near the line of the Sabine River, in case the Spanish governor of Texas decides to march north and cause us any trouble. Moving armies in the springtime is difficult, with muddy roads and rain-swollen rivers, but I want us to march as quickly as we can. While the armies are en route, I will order four frigates to the Florida Coast and three to Louisiana, to interdict any Spanish warships that may be arriving."

"That seems to be a solid plan," Tallmadge said. "With any luck, we can secure Florida by midsummer."

"That is my goal," said Hamilton. "As near as I can reckon, there are fewer than five thousand Spanish troops in all of Florida, and they are scattered throughout the province. Even as our troops march, I have dispatched messages to both King Joseph and the Junta that supports King Ferdinand, demanding to know who was responsible for ordering the attack on America. Given the death of General Jackson and the innocents in Georgia, the United States will demand that control of Florida be permanently ceded to us in exchange for peace. If either government proves amenable to this prospect, the U.S. will suspend further hostilities and recognize that government as the legitimate government of

Spain. If they prove recalcitrant, then our forces in Louisiana will march to San Antonio and we will take Texas from them as well!"

"From what I have heard, there are rumblings of deep discontent in Mexico against Spanish rule," said Tallmadge. "The revolutionary priest, Father Hidalgo, may be dead, but his followers have been in Louisiana, trying to recruit Americans for filibustering expeditions to free Texas, and then Mexico, from Spanish rule."

"I had not anticipated being a wartime President," Hamilton said. "But if that is my lot, I want to be a successful one! However, I have not forgotten the vision that drove me to seek the presidency. I need to meet with Speaker Clay and discuss some political issues that this conflict has brought to the fore. Please begin drafting the appropriate orders for raising and recruiting the necessary forces and putting our chosen commanders in place."

"Yes, sir!" said Tallmadge. "Exciting, isn't it? I feel like we're back in the Revolution again."

"Except we're the politicians and not the soldiers this time," said Hamilton. "A shame, really. I'd rather be in a tent planning an assault on the enemy than stuck here, two thousand miles away, letting someone else win all the glory!"

Not long after Tallmadge left, Henry Clay knocked at the door of the President's study. Hamilton greeted the Speaker of the House warmly.

"Thank you for coming, sir!" he said. "I need to discuss the funding of the war with you. Sending out the number of troops this campaign will take is going to be expensive."

"Fortunately, your wise economic policies have blessed us with a full treasury," said Clay. "We should be able to make the initial expenditures without having to go further into debt, although if the war should stretch out for more than a year, we will have to start borrowing."

"It's a good thing that we re-chartered the Bank of the United States, then," said Hamilton. "If we must borrow, I'd rather it be from our own people. Foreign debt should always be a last resort."

"Isn't that contrary to your original position on the issue?" Clay asked.

"Somewhat," said Hamilton. "When I became Treasury Secretary, we were already saddled with a huge national debt, over half of it owed to foreigners. For a fledgling country, that was indeed a national blessing, since it meant that all our creditors had a vested interest in our success. But I also made it a priority to pay down the foreign debt first, to avoid excessive entanglement in European affairs. Now that the foreign debt is mostly gone, I'd like to keep it that way."

"Sensible," Clay commented. "Well, I shall meet with the Budget Committee I've formed, and we shall put together an appropriations bill based on the guidelines you sent me. If this war is as short and successful as we hope, no borrowing at all will be necessary."

"One more thing," said Hamilton. "I would like you to insert a proviso somewhere in the appropriations bill for the war and try to guide it through the House with as little fanfare as possible."

"What would that be, Mister President?" Clay asked.

"Here's a rough text, you can toy with it all you want as long as the central clause is clear," Hamilton said. He handed Clay a folded sheet of paper, and the Speaker read it out loud.

"Neither slavery nor involuntary servitude shall be introduced or allowed in any territory that the United States may take into its possession as a result of the current war with Spain," Clay intoned solemnly. "I can almost guarantee that this will bring about some fanfare, Mister President! Georgia and South Carolina are both eager to expand plantation agriculture into Florida."

"They have the rest of the Southwest Territory to expand their horrid system of bondage into," Hamilton said. "But that is where I have drawn the line. I want no new slave territories or slave states beyond that! If they push the issue, I will simply return the territory to Spain."

Clay whistled. "You are truly committed to the principles of liberty," he said. "I must admit, I was skeptical when we first spoke. But I decided to try your free labor system on my own lands and have been impressed with the result. Men do work harder when they are rewarded for their labor with a fair wage. I am now encouraging the leading citizens of Kentucky to follow suit, and I think that, before you leave office, my state may abolish slavery and go to a wage labor system. So, I am your man on this bill, Mister President. I'll pass it through the House or die trying!"

"Spoken like a true American!" Hamilton said, clapping the lanky Kentuckian on the arm. "I look forward to working with you, Speaker Clay."

Hamilton's proposed amendment to the Military Appropriations Bill of 1811 was sponsored by Josiah Quincy of

Massachusetts, his longtime congressional ally. It was immediately pounced upon by John C. Calhoun of South Carolina, who saw it as further proof of Hamilton's perfidy and hatred of the South.

"How do you ensnare a powerful beast, when you have not the courage or firepower to face it head on?" he thundered from the floor of the House as the appropriations debate for the war began the following week. "You encircle it, casting your net on all sides, surrounding, immobilizing, and trapping it to be slaughtered at your leisure! Even so, King Alexander Africanus now seeks to bring about the destruction of the South by encircling it with the noose of emancipation. Slavery has been practiced by the Spanish in Florida for two centuries now; what reason is there to rip it up from the fertile soil where it has flourished? There can be only one: to destroy the South's domestic institutions and way of life, by denying them the room for expansion—ensuring the permanent ascendancy of the Yankee states and the permanent debasement of the South! Already the vast territories west of the Mississippi are closed to the enterprising Southern planter; now the President seeks to block us in the only path of expansion that remains to us. I tell you, Mister Speaker, that South Carolina will go down fighting, as will all of the South, before we stick our head into such a noose!"

"Mister Calhoun, you make a fundamental mistake in your philippic screed against our President," James Breckenridge interjected. "You equate the end of slavery with the death of the South. The two are not one and the same. Virginia has now outlawed the peculiar institution you seem to think is so indispensable, and we are doing quite well for ourselves. Profits on my own plantation have risen considerably since I started paying my Negroes for their labor, and I no longer have to worry about runaways and slave revolts! If you would simply try the system devised by our President, you might be surprised at the result. Instead you spout nonsense—'Spain has practiced slavery in Florida for two centuries' indeed! They've also practiced the Inquisition and the burning of heretics; would you like to import those practices into South Carolina as well?"

The debate grew so furious that Speaker Clay had to gavel down the two combatants, but when the vote was held the following day the appropriations bill, with the Quincy Proviso attached, passed the House by a margin of ninety-one to fifty-two. The Senate passed it the following day by a six-vote margin. Slavery would be banned in Florida—if the Army could conquer Florida. The next few months would tell that tale.

Colonel Winfield Scott, now armed with a promotion and the support of the President, worked like a man possessed to build up America's invasion force for the drive into Florida. Outrage over the ambuscade and death of General Jackson had swept up and down the frontier, and thousands of angry Southerners, many of whom might have otherwise refused to fight for the New York President, flocked to the colors to avenge their hero. By the time General Brown arrived in New Orleans to relieve Wilkinson, Scott already had some seven thousand volunteers under arms. They were rough and rowdy men, ill disposed toward military discipline, but the towering young colonel brooked no insubordination and quickly began whipping them into shape.

He had transferred his forces from Ft. Hamilton, in the far southwest corner of Georgia, to the coastal town of Savannah over the spring, a long and arduous march across the swamps and forests of South Georgia. The thriving port would serve as his principal supply base, and he ordered his men to begin constructing a military outpost halfway between Savannah and the Florida border that would serve as the jumping-off point of the invasion. He named the outpost Fort Jackson in honor of his murdered commander.

Further west, Brown arrived in New Orleans on the first of May and reported to the Governor's house, where the commanding general resided. Wilkinson griped and blustered about being relieved, but Brown had brought a sealed letter from the Secretary of War to be given to the general if he proved recalcitrant. After arguing with the rotund Wilkinson for fifteen minutes, Brown reached into his kit and pulled the letter out, handing it to the southern commander. Wilkinson read it quickly, and his flushed face paled.

"This is outrageous!" he replied. "I should demand a court martial to clear these baseless slanders against my character!"

"The Army is sick of you, old man," said Brown. "We are going to war with the king and country that you have sold yourself to. If you demand a court martial, I will provide one. Just remember, since we are at war, if you should lose this time, you won't just be broken in rank. You will be found guilty of high treason, and I would have no problem with hanging you for it! The choice seems simple enough to me, General. Go north, keep your rank and titles, and retire with a nice pension in a few years. Or fight me on this, and you will lose even if you win. You will wind up making war on one of your masters at the behest of another, and frankly, your talent has always lain with scheming rather than fighting. If you stay here, this war will not end well for you, mark my words!"

Wilkinson slumped at that news, for he knew the truth of it. Defeated, he boarded the USS *Liberty* that afternoon, and she weighed anchor and set sail for New York the next day. General Wilkinson never took command of the Northern Department, however. During the voyage he contracted a malarial fever and died at sea. He was buried in Wilmington, North Carolina, with military honors, one of the last veterans of the Revolution still on active duty.

Once he had seen his predecessor safely underway, General Brown sprang into action. Thousands of Americans were coming southward, anxious to get involved in the fight against Spain. He wanted to be with the main body of the Army in its drive on Florida; however, he could not leave the vital port city of New Orleans unprotected with Spanish forces just a few days' ride away in East Texas. Should he go east, and take the field with Scott's forces, or should he stay in New Orleans and prepare to fend off a potential invasion from Texas? He questioned one of the local officers, Lieutenant Augustus Magee, as to the likelihood of a Spanish attack.

"Well, sir, I have been in communications with a Mexican revolutionary by the name of Bernardo Gutierrez for about a month now," Magee stated. "He was a follower of the independence leader down in Mexico, that Padre Hidalgo who stirred up so much trouble for the Spanish last year. He's been trying to get me to leave the Army and join him in organizing an invasion of Texas, to free it from Spanish rule."

"Deserting your country in time of war is not a good choice for any American officer," Brown said sharply.

"I know that, sir, and I would not dream of doing so," Magee said. "Had we not gone to war, I might have considered it, though. What the Spanish did to Hidalgo and his revolutionaries was downright cruel and excessive—gunning down troops after they had surrendered and burning their homes down, killing women and children. They went far beyond the military needs of the situation. The Spanish military governor, Joaquin Arredondo, is a brutal man—and also a formidable soldier. If he is ordered to attack New Orleans, he will do so. I know Winfield Scott—he and I served together during the Creek uprising. He's a meticulous planner, cool and methodical, and brave under fire. If San Augustine can be taken, he will take it! But General Arredondo— well, sir, if I were in command, I would not turn my back on him."

"Thank you for that advice," said Brown. "I think that you are right, Lieutenant. We will move our forces west to Natchitoches and stand ready to repel Spanish forces from Texas, and let Scott take command of the invasion of Florida. There are no settlements of any size south of St. Augustine for a hundred miles or more, so if Scott can take the city, East Florida will effectively be ours. I do share your confidence in his abilities; Jackson also trusted him. Now, what I want you to do, Lieutenant, is take charge of this flood of volunteers we're getting! I want you to institute a strict training regimen; they may know how to shoot a musket, but so far I haven't seen a one of them that knows the most basic rudiments of military discipline!"

Within a month of taking command, Brown marched to Natchitoches at the head of a mixed force of a thousand regular troops and nearly four thousand militia. They were a motley crew, surly and grumbling under the demands of military life, but eager to strike a blow at the hated Spanish. Before leaving New Orleans, he dispatched a swift ship for Savannah with orders for Winfield Scott to proceed with his march on East Florida's capitol with all dispatch.

There was an old French fort at Natchitoches, largely abandoned in favor of the town that had sprung up around it. Brown and his men quickly occupied it and rebuilt the rotten log walls, expanding its perimeter and beefing up its defenses. By midsummer, the men were about as disciplined as they were going to become, and the fortress was ready to fend off a major assault. Every day, Brown sent cavalry patrols as far west as the Sabine, and his men carefully interrogated travelers coming from Texas to see if there were any rumors of a Spanish advance.

While Brown waited to see if the Spanish were going to attack from Texas, a thousand miles away in Georgia, Winfield Scott was preparing for his own thrust into Florida. His force had swelled to nearly ten thousand strong; Massachusetts Yankees whose fathers had fought at Bunker Hill rubbed elbows with buckskin-clad Tennesseans, and staunch Hamilton abolitionists shared tents with Calhoun-supporting slave owners. The political quarrels of 1810 were forgotten in the shared outrage and hatred for the perfidious Spanish in the summer of 1811.

On the first of June, Scott gave orders for his men to march south. It was less than fifty miles to the Spanish border, and another eighty from there to St. Augustine, their objective. Enrique White, the Spanish governor of East Florida, was in a difficult spot and he knew it. He had four thousand second-rate troops under his command—most of Spain's best regiments were fighting in their homeland, either for the Bonapartistes or for the Junta—and he had scraped together another thousand or so auxiliaries, Seminole Indians, runaway slaves, and freebooters that he did not trust but needed, if he were to stand a chance against the advancing American horde.

White was seventy years old and his health was failing rapidly when word of the American declaration of war reached his ears. He had not ordered the raid on American territory, and did not know who had. Initially, he halfway believed that the Americans may have staged the whole thing themselves as an excuse to take Florida from Spanish control. But the death of General Jackson made him question that assessment. White was Irish born, but he had been a Spanish citizen for over fifty years. He knew little of the Americans, only that they were mostly descended from Englishmen, and he hated the English with all the passion of both his nationalities' accumulated grudges. But even he doubted they would murder one of their own generals in cold blood to start a war of conquest.

White was also a military veteran of Spain's wars, and knew a thing or two about defending territory against superior numbers, having fought in the Seven Years' War and as an ally of France in the wars of the American Revolution. From his sickbed, he sketched out the design of a broad, arcing set of fortifications designed to protect St. Augustine from the American barbarians. His lieutenant governor, Juan Jose de Estrada, another old soldier, supervised the building of the ramparts and positioning of the cannons, commandeering slave laborers, and taxing the local plantations heavily to buy arms and gunpowder from merchants in Cuba.

Estrada sent spies to the American border to watch for the invading force and received word late in the night the day after Scott's army began to move. He hurried to share the news with the governor, only to find that White's illness had run its course and that the old governor had died in his sleep. Estrada summoned a priest to administer last rites and arranged the governor's funeral even as his soldiers were scrambling to fend off a massive American invasion.

The Battle of St. Augustine opened on June 21, 1811 and lasted for three days. The Spanish were well dug in and managed to repel two American bayonet charges on the first day of fighting, leaving over two hundred Americans dead or dying on the field before the hastily constructed ramparts. Scott had allowed the initial assault because so many of the volunteers were eager for it; he did not think they would be able to breach the Spanish fortifications, but the rowdy frontiersmen were convinced the Spanish would break and run. After the second assault was thrown back, the men decided that maybe the young commander knew what he was talking about and agreed to wait for the artillery to arrive.

The next day Scott's cannons arrived. Consisting of five twelve-pounders and a dozen six-pounders, the artillery train had been slow and difficult to pull through the sandy coastal marshes. The Colonel personally supervised the positioning of the guns as the nervous Spaniards watched and occasionally fired their own artillery to disrupt the American's dispositions. Scott ignored the cannonballs—the Spanish aim was execrable, and Tennessee sharpshooters kept up a steady covering fire that dropped two dozen Spanish gunners. Eventually the Spanish abandoned their artillery barrage, deciding to wait for the main Yankee assault before expending more lives to keep the cannons manned. By three in the afternoon, the American artillery was in position, and Scott ordered them to open fire on the Spanish batteries.

The sturdy cannons belched fire and shot on the Spaniards' guns until the sun set, shattering their caissons, killing more gunners, and wrecking the morale of the defenders as they saw their artillery silenced. One lucky American shot caught a wagonload of black powder, destroying it in a spectacular explosion that caused part of the rampart to collapse.

There was a full moon that night, so Scott ordered his gunners back into action after they had eaten a hasty supper. Using solid shot, they concentrated their fire on the weakest points of the fortifications, shattering log walls and bringing down two sentry towers. At midnight, he had them switch to heated shot, which set the splintered wood of the Spanish fort on fire. The Spaniards gallantly battled the flames, and their silhouetted forms against the ghastly glare of the burning fort gave the American riflemen another chance to demonstrate their marksmanship.

By dawn, Fort St. Augustine was a smoking ruin, and the Spanish were in full retreat towards the city itself. Scott had a difficult time restraining his men long enough for them to form into companies and brigades; by eight in the morning, they were charging through the smoking rubble of the Spanish presidio and storming the gates of the city. St. Augustine had been built to withstand an assault from sea, not land, and soon the fighting was raging in the streets of the city. Although Scott had sternly warned the men against attacks on civilians, some women and children were killed in the deadly crossfire of house to house fighting.

By noon, Estrada bowed to the inevitable and raised a white flag from the roof of the governor's palace. It took the American colonel nearly an hour to get all his men to cease firing at the enemy, but the battle of St. Augustine was over, and East Florida was in American hands. When Estrada handed over his sword, Scott treated the Spaniard with great courtesy and offered the assistance of American surgeons to help tend the Spanish wounded. All told, over four hundred Americans had fallen seizing St. Augustine, and three hundred were wounded. There were over a thousand Spanish dead, as well as seven hundred wounded. By the end of the day most of the casualties had been treated, bodies were being gathered for burial, and the Stars and Stripes flew over the governor's palace.

In Natchitoches, General Brown eagerly awaited word on the success of Scott's expedition while keeping his eyes peeled toward the west. Bernardo Gutierrez, the Mexican revolutionary, had joined himself to the Americans and sent runners west into Texas, as far south as San Antonio, to see if the Spanish were coming. After a couple of weeks, two exhausted *vacqueros* rode into the American camp, bringing word that they were.

Spanish General Joaquin Arredondo was in San Antonio, they said, commanding a column of three thousand Spanish *soldados* and conscripting local *Tejanos* as auxiliaries. He was under orders from the Viceroy, Antonio Mendoza, to cross the border into the Louisiana Territory and attack any American forces he encountered.

"This is the same son of a bitch who burned my village and killed my wife and daughters in Mexico last year," Gutierrez snarled to Brown. "He's a vile Spanish dog that needs to be put down, Señor General!"

Brown was consistently surprised by the hostility to Spanish rule that was expressed by virtually every *Tejano* he met. He wondered at the cruelty and incompetence of a colonial administration that could engender so much hostility in the hearts of its own people. In the Revolution, he had heard, over a third of the colonial population were Tories. But to hear Gutierrez tell it, perhaps one *Tejano* in ten supported the Spanish government.

But ruminations on the loyalty of the Mexican population to Spain took a second place to military preparations. There was only one road that led from Nacogdoches, the northernmost Spanish town in Texas, eastward to Natchitoches. It crossed the Sabine river about seventy miles east of the American position, and Brown decided to give Arredondo an early—and hot—reception when he entered the Louisiana territory!

Gutierrez's spies kept up a constant flow of intelligence to the Americans as Brown moved his army eastward, quickly closing the gap between himself and the advancing Spanish army. The pine forests provided excellent cover as he marched his men eastward, wading through swamps and bayous and dragging half a dozen cannons behind them. Fortunately for the Americans, it had been a dry summer thus far, or the bulky guns might not have made the trip. The *Camino Real* was less rutted and muddy than it had been in the spring. Brown waited till the Spanish were only two days' march east of him and split his army in two, posting two thousand men on each side of the road where it passed between two low ridges. He sent his cavalry out to screen his position, and that night they returned with a prisoner—an angry young Spanish lieutenant who was the only survivor of a six-man patrol they had caught spying out the American force.

Gutierrez acted as an interpreter for Brown, whose Spanish was virtually non-existent.

"What's your name, son?" he asked the Spaniard, hoping to put the prisoner at ease.

"I am Antonio Lopez de Santa Anna," snapped the Spanish officer, "and I am not the son of you or any foul *gringo!*"

"Well, Lieutenant," said Brown, "you may not see it this way now, but being captured is probably the best thing that could have happened to you right now. Your General Arredondo is about to put his fist into a hornet's nest!"

"Our glorious army will make short work of your band of pirates and mercenaries!" Santa Anna said angrily. "No force on earth can stand before the fury of our lances!"

"I don't doubt that your men could give a good account of themselves in an open field battle," Brown said. "That's why we're attacking them here in the forest. Ambuscades may not be glorious, but they are effective, as poor old Jackson found out last fall—and as your General Arredondo will find out tomorrow morning. Señor Gutierrez, see to it that our guest is kept comfortable. I may need him to take my demand for surrender to the Spanish tomorrow."

The next morning, the Spanish force rode right into the trap Brown had set for them. Banners flapping and lances gleaming in the morning sun, they strutted through the hollow below the two wings of the American army. A few cavalrymen rode out to either side, heading to the crests that overlooked the old road, not suspecting that four thousand Americans were lying in wait. Brown had his best sharpshooters near the front ranks, and on his signal, they opened up, dropping the Spanish scouts off their horses. At the sound, the entire American force surged up the low rise and took aim at the Spanish column. A storm of gunfire raked the surprised lancers, who fell from their saddles as the musket balls found their mark. Brown reared his horse and waved a blue flag to the Americans on the opposite ridge. On that signal, the gunners wheeled their cannons up to the crest and aimed at the mass of confused, swirling horsemen and infantry trying to form up below.

Brown only had six cannons, but each one had been double charged with grapeshot, and they all opened up at the same time. Men and horses screeched as the leaden messengers of death sped through their ranks, killing and maiming as they went. Once the guns had spoken, the Americans charged down the ridge, bayonets at the ready, tearing into the Spanish ranks even as the furious Arredondo tried to restore order.

It was over in less than an hour; nine hundred Spanish soldiers lay dead on the field and about half that many were wounded. Arredondo survived the fight, but one of his arms was shattered by a musket ball and had to be amputated. A surly Lieutenant Santa Anna conveyed Brown's surrender terms to his commander, and Arredondo grudgingly accepted. Brown ordered the Spanish General placed under guard and conferred with his officers that night as to the next step.

"I beg you, sir, march onward to San Antonio!" said Gutierrez. "The people will welcome you as liberators, and you will bring great glory to the United States as the man who added Texas to the Union!"

"And what happens when the Spanish send another army into Texas to retake their territory?" said Brown.

"Arredondo was the best they had, and you beat him like a child," said the revolutionary. "I don't think they have another general anywhere near his caliber, nor a vast reserve of experienced troops to draw on. The people of Mexico are smoldering, and the news of this defeat may well cause our revolutionaries to come out of the shadows and storm the Viceroy's palace! America's support could help create a free and democratic Mexican republic, forever indebted to the American people for their help in our time of need."

Brown considered for a moment, and then turned to Magee and Shasteen, the Major who commanded his cavalry wing .

"See to it that the wounded are taken back to Natchitoches," he said. "The Spanish are to be held for six weeks and then paroled. Shasteen, I am leaving you in command of the American position in Louisiana. Magee, you tell the men to gather their gear, eat their fill, and be ready to march tomorrow. We're taking San Antonio."

"Yes, sir!" the two officers saluted, and Gutierrez beamed at the American general.

It was July 4, 1811. Andrew Jackson had been fully avenged.

CHAPTER TWENTY-SEVEN

FOR PRESIDENT Hamilton and his war cabinet, the spring and summer of 1811 formed one long, anxious season as they waited to see what the results of their strategy would be. Other than military appropriations and diplomatic initiatives, the machinery of government stood still, and Washington City became a ghost town. Six Senators and twelve Representatives had abandoned their seats in Congress to go and fight in the war; the spring session of the Congress disbanded early so the legislators could go home to their districts and drum up support for the conflict.

Anxious to follow the progress of America's armies, Hamilton opted not to return to New York and instead journeyed southward after Congress adjourned. He paid a courtesy call on President Jefferson at Monticello, and there he found the retired Virginian as friendly and courteous as ever.

"Life is a fickle thing," Jefferson told him as they sipped coffee on the veranda on a fine spring morning. "If anyone had told me five years ago that I would be happily hosting President Hamilton in my home during a war between America and Spain, I would have questioned their sanity!"

"You and I had our share of battles, didn't we?" Hamilton said with a chuckle. "But in the end, I am glad that our love of liberty was strong enough to overpower our hostility to each other."

"I must confess, Mister President," said Jefferson, "I fancied myself a true champion of liberty, until you revealed the hypocrisy of my public persona contrasted with my domestic self. You forced me to a moral reckoning that was long overdue. Now I am as happy as I have been in many years."

"Speaking of domestic bliss, how is Mrs. Jefferson?" Hamilton asked.

The former President smiled, and the expression made him look ten years younger.

"She is shy, owing to her former station in life, and often retires upstairs when I have guests," he said. "Would you like to meet her?"

"I should be delighted," said Hamilton.

Jefferson stood and walked inside, and a few moments later he returned to the sunlit veranda with a lovely mulatto woman on his arm. Sally Jefferson was younger than her husband by many years, but she held his arm tightly and it was obvious from her expression that she was deeply fond of him.

"President Hamilton," she said with a deep curtsy as Alex stood to greet her. "It is a pleasure to meet you, sir."

"The pleasure is all mine, madam," Hamilton replied, kissing her hand. "I hope the morning finds you well."

"It does, sir," she said. "If I may be so bold, Mister President, I should like to thank you for all that you have done for my people."

"The love of liberty knows no skin color," Hamilton said. "In giving freedom to the slave, I hope we can ensure freedom to the free. The freer all its people are, the freer our nation will be, and our children shall thrive and prosper. I only hope Virginia's neighbors to the South will come around to our way of thinking before I leave office."

"I have been quietly exercising some influence among those in North Carolina who are my friends," said Jefferson. "I think that the next session of the legislature may be more favorably disposed towards emancipation than the last was."

"After I visit Secretary Madison at Montpelier, I am journeying south to Raleigh to visit Governor Smith," Hamilton said. "My main concern right now is our war effort, but I may take advantage of the situation to try and sway opinion our way."

Arriving a few days later at Madison's house, Hamilton found letters from Winfield Scott waiting for him. Preparations for the Florida offensive were well underway, it seemed, and Scott was hopeful that St. Augustine would be in his hands by midsummer. Hamilton had no desire to interfere with his generals—he remembered all too well how frustrated Washington had been with congressional second-guessing of his strategies during the Revolution. He dashed back a quick letter to let Scott know of his travel itinerary and wishing him the best of luck in the upcoming campaign.

Hamilton was traveling light, having sent Eliza and the younger children back home to New York for the summer; he had a small escort including the indefatigable Cartwright and four young military officers. It was a beautiful spring, and as they cantered across the countryside from one plantation house to another, Hamilton felt young again. The camaraderie of the group brought back some of the happier memories of the Revolution, when he, Lafayette, and Laurens had juggled the responsibilities of helping Washington run a war with the amusements of drinking, playing cards, and romancing young women.

At Montpelier, Hamilton enjoyed the hospitality of James and Dolley Madison for two days, and during the cordial visit, Secretary Madison asked if he could accompany the President on the rest of his journey southward. Alex, who had come to enjoy the brilliant Madison's company, cheerfully assented. Both men were anxious to find out how the war was progressing, and the closer they were to the southern border, the quicker news would reach them. Hamilton had sent a travel itinerary to both commanders by ship, several weeks before leaving Washington City, and thus far he had managed to stick to his timetable.

The night before they headed south to Raleigh, North Carolina, Hamilton spread out a map of America's southern border and studied the two potential points of conflict.

"The drive to attack St. Augustine should be short and simple," he told Madison. "The distance to be covered is negligible, and the Spanish defenses are simply not equal to the force Scott will be bringing to bear. I don't doubt that they will put up a fight, but when you consider that Scott will have a fleet in readiness to support him, I don't see how we could fail, unless a huge Spanish army shows up out of nowhere."

He pointed westward, to New Orleans, and the Sabine River to the west. "This is the front that concerns me," he said. "I know little about the province of Texas except that the Spanish had done virtually nothing there until a hundred years ago, when the

French tried to stake a claim to it. The Viceroy sent about a thousand soldiers, priests, and settlers into this area, here around the Sabine, to show that the territory belonged to Spain alone. They built some missions and towns, and then as French interest in the area waned, Spain abandoned most of them. It is my understanding that there are only three remaining Spanish settlements of any size—San Antonio de Bexar, hundreds of miles south and west of Louisiana, a small town called Goliad, between there and the coast, and this settlement, far closer to our border, which is called"—the President hesitated a moment over the odd mouthful of consonants—"Nah-cog-doches. I have heard that a number of American families have settled in that region too, quietly and unobtrusively, coming over from Louisiana."

"Why does this front concern you?" Madison asked.

"There have been troubles," the President said. "American adventurers wandering down into Texas, some looking to detach it from Spanish rule; Mexican revolutionaries fleeing north from the ruin of Hidalgo's uprising, and Spanish armies determined to kill every last revolutionary they can get their hands on—all of them converging on this area. The Spanish solution to uprisings is brutal and bloody, and if they decide that America has been encouraging the rebels, I would not put it past them to march across the border and try to seize New Orleans in retaliation. That's one reason I sent Brown there; it would be a shame to seize Florida only to have New Orleans then snatched from under our noses! But with the flood of volunteers coming into our armies, I think the Spanish will have their hands full."

Madison studied the map, and then looked at Hamilton with admiration.

"I am glad, sir, that you are at the helm of the government now, and not me," he said. "You seem to have an intuitive grasp of where to dispose forces and how to anticipate the enemy's next move. I have read military history, but my practical experience is virtually non-existent. My health prevented me from serving in the Revolution, so I never had the chance to see a real battle unfold. I fear I should be a terrible wartime President."

Hamilton clapped him on the shoulder.

"You are one of the most brilliant men I have ever known, James," he said. "I am sure that you would be a quick study should the occasion ever arise. Although, while I would not be troubled at the thought of you succeeding me in office, I pray that if you do, your term would find the nation at peace with itself and with all our neighbors!"

Madison smiled, still bemused at times to find this man he had once detested as a reactionary radical had become both his political chief and his close friend.

"During the war I wondered," he said, "why Washington always chose you to be at the head of his military family. There were so many other fine young officers around him, but you were the one that he entrusted with the greatest responsibilities, both as a soldier and later as a cabinet minister. I must confess that the longer I work with you the more clearly I see his reasons."

"I hope that trust was not ill-placed," Alex said with a smile. "What I wanted most was to please him and to be of good service."

"I think His Excellency was well-served indeed!" Madison replied.

"Well, I want to ride out early in the morning," Hamilton said. "A hundred and seventy miles lie between us and Raleigh and I should like to cover it in six or seven days if we can."

"There is much fine, open country to our south," said Madison, "and we will make our best time in the first half of the journey. After that, the country gets rougher. But I still think we can do it, as long as there are fresh horses along the way. Fortunately, these old bones of mine are still pretty comfortable in the saddle."

Despite Madison's confident prediction, it took them eight days. The first half of the journey was both pleasant and quick; they covered over twenty miles a day and enjoyed the hospitality of a number of Madison's friends, spending the night in large, comfortable tidewater plantation houses. But the day that they crossed over the boundary line into North Carolina, heavy clouds gathered overhead and the sky opened up, unleashing torrential rain that followed them all day, soaking their clothes, their horses, their luggage, and turning the hardened dirt track roads into slippery red mud that left their horses sodden and stumbling. After ten dreary miles, Madison leaned over and shouted through the storm.

"My cousin Thomas Madison has a plantation about a mile from here," he said. "I know you wanted to make further progress, but we would be better off staying there for the night and waiting for the weather to improve!"

Hamilton sighed and nodded, sending droplets of rain cascading from the brim of his hat.

"I'm forced to agree," he said. "No sense making a few extra miles if we catch our deaths in this miserable storm! Lead the way, sir."

An hour later, the two men were clad in clean, dry clothes, courtesy of their host, and the horses were contentedly champing on oats as Madison's grooms brushed the mud from their coats. The military escort was comfortably quartered in a large outbuilding, and the smell of supper was wafting from the kitchen. Even though it was June, their host had kindled a small fire in the parlor, and their sodden clothes were strung before the fireplace, slowly steaming dry.

They enjoyed a fine meal and an early night, but then woke to another day of torrential rain. Madison and his cousin pored over a map together that morning, trying to figure out if it was worth it for the presidential party to set out in such forbidding conditions. It was nearly twenty-five miles to the next plantation house that Hamilton had planned on visiting, a long ride under optimum conditions and an impossible one during the current deluge. So, they spent the day playing cards and discussing politics both past and present with their host and each other. Thomas Madison was a stout, friendly, engaging man with a ready grin and an enormous supply of funny stories, and Hamilton laughed more than he had in a long time listening to him. Finally, around three in the afternoon, the rain let up and the clouds began to break. The sun emerged for an hour or two before sinking into the west, and the puddles began slowly soaking back into the earth.

The next morning the presidential party set forth again, and the blazing summer sun quickly turned the puddles to steam. The heat and humidity were almost unbearable, and by midday both Hamilton and Madison had removed their coats and loosened their collars. The roads, still slick at first, grew harder and firmer throughout the day, and their time gradually improved, although they did not reach their destination until six o'clock that evening, by which time everyone was soaked in sweat and the horses were nearly blown.

Roger Effingham, a South Carolina state senator, was their host for the evening, and he was standing on the steps when they arrived.

"President Hamilton!" he exclaimed. "And Secretary Madison! I was originally expecting you yesterday, but then that storm rolled in and I figured it would slow you down. I am delighted to see you have made it safely."

"Many thanks for your kind welcome and gracious hospitality, sir!" Alex said, extending his hand. "I don't know that I've had a more miserably hot day on horseback since the battle of Monmouth!"

"Well, sir, I took the liberty of having my servants draw a tepid bath for each of you. Cletus, my butler, will take you to your rooms. As for your escorts, I have arranged for them to be housed and fed at a tavern which is a half mile further down the road. Supper will be ready once you have refreshed yourselves. It is a great honor to have you both under my roof," the young planter said, almost gushing.

"You do us too much honor," Hamilton said with a smile. "We shall be glad of a soft bed and a good meal. Only forty miles yet lie between us and Raleigh, and I am anxious to get there. Have you heard any news of the war?"

"Colonel Scott's force was supposed to march on Florida this month, the last I heard," said Effingham. "And I have no news from further west; although rumor has it that General Brown has arrived in New Orleans."

"That's as much as I know, either," Alex said. "I am hoping that dispatches will be awaiting me at Raleigh."

After a few more pleasantries, Alex made his way upstairs. With a groan of pure pleasure, he stripped out of his sweat-stained riding gear and slid into a tub full of tepid, soapy water. He could feel the day's fatigue leaching out of his bones as he soaked. Cletus, the butler, tapped on the door discreetly.

"May I take your clothes to wash, Mistuh President?" he asked.

"By all means, sir," said Hamilton. "They are unfit to be worn again otherwise! But I plan to head out early in the morning; will you have time to wash and dry them?"

"Hannah, our laundress, done said she have those clothes clean as a whistle and ready to wear by tomorrah, suh," Cletus told him. "All of us honored to have you as our guest, seein' all that you done for our people."

"Are you a free man, Cletus?" Hamilton said.

"Not yet, suh, but Massuh Roger, he say he gone free us all at the end of the year and start payin' us wages to work for him," the old Negro said. "My daughter, she got sold upstate to Virginny when she only twelve years old. She a free woman now and she's learned to read and write! She send me letters all the time, talking 'bout how you gone free all of us."

Hamilton got out of the tub and wrapped a towel around his middle, then took a second one and dried his thinning hair. Then he sat on the bed and looked at Cletus, who had Alex's travel-stained clothes draped over his arm.

"I want you to know something, my friend," he said. "While I would love nothing better than to end slavery throughout America and see you and all your people living as free men and women, I too have a master. It's a document called the Constitution, and it places limits on the powers of the government, even the President himself. I can persuade, I can suggest, and I can encourage, but I cannot force any man to free his slaves against his will. So, as much as I desire for you all to be free, that does not mean I can make it so for all of you."

"But you tries, suh," said Cletus. "How many white mens does dat? We slave folk cain't do nuffin for the likes of you, and yet you sticks yo neck out fo' us. We never be forgettin' it, suh."

Hamilton looked at the butler, who was sixty if he was a day, and found himself deeply moved by the man's expression of gratitude.

"I will tell you what I told my own people," he said. "I cannot force my will on anyone, but I will do as much as I can for as long as I can with all the strength that I have to free as many slaves as I can."

Cletus bowed deeply.

"Cain't no one ask fo' more than that," he said. "Supper be ready downstairs, suh. I'll have your clothes ready for you fust thing in the morning. Agin, I thanks you from the bottom o' my heart for all you done for my people."

With that, the Negro butler left, and Alex dressed in a clean set of clothes and headed downstairs. The meal was most excellent, and Roger Effingham was clearly overjoyed to have the President of the United States dining at his table. The meal was excellent—chicken soup and fried pork chops, with a nice red wine to wash them down. After it was done, Alex turned to his young host with a smile.

"Tell me, Senator Effingham, where do you stand on emancipation?" he asked.

"I'm a reluctant convert, Mister President," he said. "I was skeptical at first, but all my friends in Virginia have reported good results from freed labor, and just last week I announced to my Negroes that I will be freeing them all at the first of the year and converting them to paid employees."

"Splendid!" said Hamilton. "Secretary Madison here was one of the first to institute the new system of labor, and he has enjoyed excellent harvests and good relations with his workers. I am sure that he can give you much useful advice."

"I would be grateful for it," Effingham said.

"Since you have opted to free your slaves, Senator, can I count on your support when the Emancipation Bill is brought up before the state legislature next time?" Hamilton asked.

Effingham hesitated for a moment.

"I must admit, sir, there is a great deal of pressure on me from both sides of the issue," he said. "On the one hand, I like the idea of freeing this captive people and raising their station in life; on the other, I am loath to strip someone of their property against their will. Many of my neighbors are adamant about keeping their Negroes; who am I to deprive them of their property?"

"Well, sir, you have already led by example, showing them that there is another way," Hamilton said. "I would urge you to further give voice to your convictions about liberty by voting for what your heart has already told you to be the cause of justice. There comes a time in each man's life where we must choose the ground on which we will stand, and if need be, die, for what is right and true. I have chosen my place to stand, Senator Effingham. Now you must choose yours."

"That is most eloquently put, Mister President. I shall carefully consider the issue," Effingham said.

"I cannot ask you for more than that," said Hamilton. "I am hoping for a better result than last year's deadlock in the next session. Now, sir, it has been a long ride and I am most weary. I bid you a good night."

Hamilton rose with the sun the next morning, feeling refreshed and relaxed after the previous day's exertions. A brisk south breeze had kicked up in the night; breaking up the oppressive humidity and helping him sleep soundly despite the heat. His clothes from the previous day were hanging in the window, clean and dry, just as Cletus had promised. He dressed quickly and headed downstairs, to find James Madison had beaten him to the breakfast table.

"A fine day for a ride, Mister President!" the Secretary said, rising as Hamilton entered the room.

"Hopefully less miserable than yesterday," Hamilton rejoined. "I begin to see why you Southerners are so hot-blooded and passionate! I must confess I will be glad to return to New York when our journey is completed. We are two days from Raleigh, James. I cannot wait to hear what news awaits us there!"

After a quick meal, the two men left the Effingham plantation house. Their horses were saddled and waiting outside, and as they checked their mounts, the military escort came trotting up, ready to resume the journey south. The old butler Cletus was holding Hamilton's reins, and the President tipped him a ten-dollar gold coin.

"My best wishes for you and all your companions as you embark on your new life of freedom, my friend," he said.

"Thank you kindly, suh," Cletus said, pocketing the coin with a grateful smile. "All we has ever wanted is a chance to live free, to come and go as we please, and to take care of our own. Thanks to you, Mistuh Pres'dent, we gonna have dat."

"You are too kind, Cletus. All I can do is lead, and pray that others follow. Your master has made the right choice; I pray that others in the South will do the same."

With that, Hamilton swung into the saddle and turned to the cavalry squad that was waiting.

"Lieutenant Murphy, I trust you and your men were well accommodated?" he asked.

"Better a lumpy bed in a tavern with a good mug of beer than the rocky ground of the Piedmont crawling with rattlesnakes," the lieutenant said with a smile. "The folks there were actually quite hospitable, so much so that I fear a few of my men may be a bit hung over this morning."

Hamilton looked at the young soldiers and saw that one or two of them were looking a little green around the gills.

"Come, lads!" he said. "One thing I learned in the Revolution is that the best cure for a night of excessive celebrating is to drink a lot of water and then ride it off! Let's set forth."

One of the soldiers nodded, then suddenly lurched forward in the saddle and heaved, emptying his stomach's contents onto the ground at the horse's feet. The startled animal reared and the queasy cavalryman was nearly toppled from the saddle.

"Well, I suppose that works, too!" the President said; the men laughed, and then they spurred their mounts and set forth.

They made twenty-two miles that day, arriving around four thirty in the afternoon at the plantation house of David Stone, the former governor. Stone had been a supporter of the Constitution during the battle for ratification, and a staunch supporter of President Jefferson. Hamilton had met him when they served together in the Senate and had been impressed with the man's intellect and his passion for education.

Stone rode out to meet the President and his party at the small town of Wadsworth, a mile from his home. Hamilton raised his hat in greeting when he recognized him.

"Well, Governor, it was kind of you meet us on the way!" he said.

"My pleasure, Mister President!" he said. "I would rather have greeted you in the capital, but the voters of my state chose otherwise. I trust the journey was not too unpleasant?"

"The heat was brutal yesterday," Hamilton said. "Today the breeze made riding much more bearable. But the trip has taken longer than I had wished, and I am anxious to get to Raleigh and see what dispatches are waiting for me. I'm especially eager to find out about the progress of our arms."

"The whole nation awaits news from the Southern border," Stone said. "I have my own sources—a number of North Carolina men have volunteered to fight under Scott, including my son. My last letter from him came this morning, dated two weeks ago, and he said they were preparing to march for the Florida border the next morning. For all we know, St. Augustine may have already fallen—and I have no idea if my son is still alive or not!"

"Scott is an excellent young commander, and I am sure your son will conduct himself heroically," Hamilton said. "Along with you, I pray for his safe return. I tell you, Governor; the worst part about being President is ordering men into harm's way and not being able to accompany them! In the War of Independence I took pride in not ordering my men to face any danger or perform any task that I was not going to face alongside them. My greatest frustration serving on Washington's staff was not always being able to ride into battle with the troops. I understand the reason why I cannot do that now, but that does not mean I like the situation!"

"At least, sir, you have faced enemy fire and know what it is you are sending our lads to face," Stone told him. "Too often, politicians start wars and send young men to die in them without having any idea of what it is like to fight themselves!"

"I was just telling the President last night," Madison interjected, "that I am glad Providence placed him at the head of our country at this time. His military gifts are considerable, and he seems to intuitively know what to do in situations that would leave me worrying and second-guessing myself!"

"Talking about the war will not do anything to help our soldiers right now," Hamilton said. "But I would like to confer with you, Governor Stone, about the subject of compensated emancipation. Where do you stand on the issue that so engrosses the nation?"

The two men talked far into the evening, even as, a few hundred miles to the south, American guns opened up on the Spanish fortifications around St. Augustine.

The next day, President Hamilton and Secretary Madison rode into the state capitol of Raleigh, where Governor Benjamin Smith awaited them. He had ordered the state militia into service for the duration of the conflict, and while most of them were down on the border with Scott, about a thousand of them remained in the city, drilling and training. The President was invited to attend a military review, and the sight of the earnest young men marching by, arms shouldered, to the tune of drum and bugle brought back many heady memories.

As the review ended, a courier came riding up with dispatches for the President. Hamilton retired to the guest quarters in the governor's house to read them away from public scrutiny, although he made a point of inviting Madison and Governor Smith to accompany him. Scott's note was short and direct.

2 June 1811
U.S. Expeditionary Force
Northern Florida

Mister President,

We have crossed the border into Spanish territory and are a few days' march from St. Augustine. So far, we have encountered little opposition, although we have noted a few enemy scouts flanking us in the distance. My men are eager to fight, and although most of them are inexperienced, I do not doubt that they will acquit themselves well in the coming battle. Intelligence reports indicate that the Spanish are concentrating their forces inside fortifications around St. Augustine, hoping to exact such a high price in blood that we will abandon our attack. You know, sir, that I have no intention of doing so! God willing, my next report will bring you the news of an American victory. I shall send my next set of dispatches to Charlestown, and if you have not arrived there yet, then I shall see them forwarded to Wilmington. God keep you safe, Your Excellency, and may God bless the holy cause of liberty in which we are engaged!

Your obd't servant,

Colonel Winfield Scott, Commander

The next letter's return address caught the President's eye right away, and he tore the envelope open curiously. As Madison and Smith pored over Scott's message, Hamilton read the letter from John C. Calhoun.

June 1, 1811

Mister President,

The news has come to my ear that you are planning to visit Charleston in the next few weeks, and I would like to offer you the hospitality of my home there during the time of your visit. While I know that we have clashed sharply on matters of domestic policy, you are still the President of the United States, and our country is at war. Therefore my home and myself are at your service, and I must confess I would also like to discuss at length with you the issue that divides us, in hope of finding some common ground. I shall be in Charlestown for the entire month of July in expectation of your visit, and can tarry longer if I receive word that you have been delayed. May God bless the progress of our arms! I have the honor to remain

Your obedient servant,

Representative John C. Calhoun

United States House of Representatives

"What's that letter, Mister President?" Madison asked him, having finished Scott's dispatch while Hamilton was reading the invitation.

"The Lion of the South invites us to visit his den," the President said, showing Madison the letter.

CHAPTER TWENTY-EIGHT

HAMILTON STAYED in Raleigh until the Fourth of July, at Governor Smith's request. An endless series of balls and parties were given in his honor, and when he was not being serenaded by bands and politely declining requests to dance, the President took the time to meet with as many members of the North Carolina legislature as possible. He sounded them out individually on the topic of emancipation and found that many were still considering their positions. Always charming, ready with a smile and a quip, a legal precedent, or a passionate argument—depending on his audience—Hamilton exercised his years of political savvy and considerable powers of persuasion to move them in his direction, as once, long ago, he had pleaded, cajoled, and bargained New York's reluctant legislature to ratify the U.S. Constitution.

He had agreed to stay in town long enough to speak on the Fourth of July, and then was heading south to the Cape Fear river, whence he would catch a ride on a special barge the governor had commissioned for him down to Wilmington, and from there he would take ship to Charleston, South Carolina. He was anxious to get closer to the border where word of military developments could reach him sooner, but he also wanted to take full advantage of the opportunity to speak to the citizens and lawmakers of North Carolina on the emancipation issue.

By the time the Fourth rolled around, word of his presence had spread throughout the state, and a crowd of nearly ten thousand gathered on the capitol grounds to hear him address the assembled dignitaries there—governors past and present, most of the state's congressional delegation, and the entire state legislature were seated before the special platform that had been erected on the capitol building's front steps. The state militia passed in a military review, and Hamilton returned the crisp salutes of the soldiers with great affection. A select group of Revolutionary War veterans, mostly now in their fifties and sixties, marched by under the banners they had carried during the war. Hamilton saw a few familiar faces in that crowd; he did his best to make eye contact and give an individual wave or shouted greeting to each man he knew. It was a hot day, but there was a pleasant breeze and the humidity had dropped enough that the heat was much more bearable than the previous week.

Governor Smith spoke first, and he paid a moving tribute to the spirit of American independence, and then he saluted the veterans of the Revolution who were in attendance. Finally, he spoke glowingly of Hamilton:

"For the second time in our state's history, it is our honor to welcome a President of our United States to our capital! On the thirty-fifth anniversary of our nation's independence, we salute this unparalleled patriot, a courageous warrior for liberty in both peace and war, the architect of America's prosperity, President Alexander Hamilton!"

Alex stood and bowed as the applause of the crowd washed over him. For a moment, his mind flashed back to his childhood; he recalled his hardscrabble upbringing on the streets of Nevis, his relief when his mother had relocated them to a much better home on St. Croix, and the devastation that had overwhelmed him when she fell ill and died. He remembered the terrifying hurricane that swept the island when he was a teen, the horizontal rain lashing his skin and the roof of their house being ripped off by the storm's raw power. The essay he had written about the storm for the *Royal Danish American Gazette* had first brought him to public notice and had generated a wave of public sympathy that had eventually sent the penniless orphan Hamilton to New York to get an education. That was where his odyssey began. Now it had brought him here, as President of the United States, about to address a vast crowd of people on the anniversary of the independence that he had helped win for his adopted country. It was all so overwhelming that Alex simply stood there for a moment, blinking as the applause continued. He looked down at the carefully prepared speech he had labored on for a month, and then folded it and put it in his pocket.

"My friends," he began, "fellow citizens, patriots, noble veterans of the Revolution, volunteers of the North Carolina militia, and Americans all—I cannot express to you the honor I feel just having the opportunity to stand before you today. I have always prided myself in my ability to craft appropriate words for any occasion, and I had labored long and hard on a speech to share with you. But I have decided, instead of reading prepared remarks, to simply address you from my heart. Thirty-five years ago on this day, the immortal words of Thomas Jefferson were adopted by the Continental Congress, informing the world that a new nation had been born, conceived in liberty, dedicated to the noble idea that all men are created equal, and that our rights and liberties are not a gift of government, but rather our divine inheritance from the God who made us."

The crowd rose to its feet, applauding again as he paused for a moment. When they resumed their seats, he continued.

"I was a lad of twenty years when I heard those words for the first time," he said. "I had already decided to take up arms to defend the rights of a nation where I had barely resided for a year, but had come to love. Even as we struggled and fought and killed for this notion of a nation that we had only begun to build, I knew that America, as deeply as I loved her, did not fully live up to the noble creed which we had declared to be our founding principle. I have come to realize that perhaps this was what Thomas Jefferson intended all along—that the words of the Declaration were not a statement of a goal realized, or a mission accomplished, but rather a quest, an ongoing experiment to refine and build upon the foundation of liberty that was laid on the Fourth of July in that glorious year of 1776!"

The crowd applauded again, and the assembled veterans joined in with loud huzzahs. Hamilton nodded in appreciation, and then continued.

"We live in an age of marvels, an age where reason has put superstition to flight, an age where men can still acknowledge the sovereignty of the Almighty and yet recognize that He has gifted us with an extraordinary measure of free will, the power to shape and alter this world we live in—the right to change our course and more fully realize the spark of divinity God placed within each of us! We can now embrace our God-given intellect and appreciate our God-given freedom more fully than any generation in the history of mankind. We have harnessed the power of steam to drive boats against the wind and current, Doctor Franklin showed us how to capture the essence of lightning, and who knows what marvels await as we continue to explore the full extent of our divine gifts? The children of the nineteenth century will see change on a scale that our fathers could only dream of!

"Yet, despite our remarkable achievements in the arts, in science, in technology and invention, we are still a primitive people in one aspect—we deny liberty to our fellow men in the name of profit! How can we truly call ourselves free when we buy and sell men, women, and children at the auction block? How can we hold ourselves worthy of God's love when we violate the very Golden Rule taught by our Savior Himself? I would never want to be a slave, so I have committed to never owning a slave. What I would ask on the Fourth of July is for the people of North Carolina to embrace this idea of liberty as well—that we are only deserving of freedom when we grant it to those we hold in our power."

There was some scattered applause, and a few jeers, but most of the crowd kept their silence, Hamilton pressed his point, hoping that the silence meant that some, at least, were considering his appeal.

"I have heard the arguments in favor of slavery passionately made by men who sincerely believe them to be true," he said. "I have heard how slavery benefits the benighted sons of Africa by exposing them to the twin lights of Christianity and civilization; how the sick and elderly among slaves are lovingly cared for by their kind masters; how labor gives purpose and dignity to a life that would otherwise be spent in squalor and pagan misery. I have heard that the slave in the South is better off than the mill worker in the North, who has no guarantee of care or compassion in the event of sickness. I do not doubt the integrity or sincerity of the men who make these arguments, but I would pose a question to them, a simple inquiry that cuts to the heart of the inherent flaw in their position: Have any of them ever been a slave?

"If slavery is as benevolent and beneficial as its defenders make it out to be, why do not poor Southerners, suffering in economic distress during hard times, simply volunteer to become slaves? And why do those who are held in bondage constantly seek to regain their liberty, knowing the penalties that await them if they are recaptured? If freedom is as dangerous and fraught with peril as the slaveholders claim it to be, why do slaves constantly risk all to gain it? If slaves are happy and content in their state of bondage, then why has every plantation in Virginia which has adopted my plan of emancipation seen its productivity increase, and its rate of desertion drop from what it was in the days of the lash and the bloodhound? And let me ask the single most important question of all—would any of you, my friends and fellow citizens, volunteer to become a slave? Is there any inducement that could compel you to place yourself on the auction block to become another man's property? Of course not! Then why, if none of us would ever choose to be a slave, should we choose to inflict that condition on others?

"North Carolina stands on the brink, my friends, of a momentous decision. While I know some here in the South have accused me of tyranny, of coveting other men's property, and even of outright theft, the fact is that they are wrong. As I recently told an elderly black man who stands on the brink of emancipation, I too have a master whose will binds me. That master is an idea, a concept, a set of principles and rules embodied in the United States Constitution. Although it is the fondest wish of my heart that every man in America be free, I will not force a single person to give up his slaves against his will. It is rather up to you, the people of North Carolina, and the legislators that you have elected, to make the momentous decision. Will you rise up, and help America live out the meaning of its creed? Will you take a stand for liberty and justice? Will you see your children and children's children guaranteed to enjoy the blessings of liberty, granted to us by Almighty God? Or will you bequeath to them the whip and chain and the auction block as their inheritance? The choice is yours, but I would ask you today, as we celebrate the liberty we won at our blood's expense, at the loss of so many good men, from our own British masters, to strike a blow for liberty! Help America rise up and truly embrace the creed that we fought a Revolution to establish. Rise up, as free men, and share the gift of freedom with those who labor among us. Sow the seeds of hope and future prosperity for ourselves and our children, and they will rise up and call you blessed."

The crowd surged to its feet, and cheers enveloped the President. He looked at the sea of joyous faces and realized that he had won. Oh, there were still a few scowls scattered among the crowd, but the vast majority were applauding his sentiments, and the legislators behind him were taking note. God willing, another Southern state would emancipate its slaves by the end of the year.

He knew that South Carolina would be a much harder sale to make—its slaves were more numerous, its planters more conservative and aristocratic, and its people more dependent on slave labor. He doubted that the state would ever voluntarily free its Negroes, but perhaps he could win a few souls over during his visit. If even a small handful of planters would embark on the experiment of paid labor, perhaps the example of prosperity they set would encourage others. Eliminating slavery in the Deep South would be a generational project, and Alex prayed that future Presidents would continue to work at it as hard as he had.

The applause began to die down, and Alex stared out at the crowd, smiling at their enthusiasm.

"My friends, you have filled my heart with gladness today. State legislators, I pray that you will take note of the enthusiasm for liberty that has been expressed here this morning when you take up the Emancipation Bill in your next session. To all who have listened to me today, and to all who are not here, but will read what I have said in the newspapers, I ask you to calmly and rationally consider the proposal before you. In giving freedom to the slave, you will ensure freedom to your posterity. Now, as we celebrate the independence of our great nation on this Fourth of July, let us lift our hearts in appreciation of the gift of God that is freedom! I thank you for the privilege of standing before you today, for the enormous honor that has been granted me, to lead this great nation of ours. May God bless you all and may His face shine with favor on the United States of America!"

The crowd roared its approval once more, and Alexander Hamilton returned to his seat as the local Episcopal bishop prepared to offer his benediction.

The next day the presidential party rode southward, escorted by a small party of North Carolina militia in addition to the President's cavalry escort. Madison rode next to Hamilton, looking thoughtfully at Alex.

"You know, Mister President, when I worked for your predecessor, he often expressed a fear of your skill with a pen," he finally said. "He commented that as long as you held ink and quill, you were 'a host unto yourself.' Having watched you for the last three years and read your work, I am inclined to agree. But I think Thomas sold your oratory short. That was one of the most impressive public addresses I have ever listened to! You won that crowd over by simple power of persuasion. I am glad that you have chosen to use your skills for the greater good of our Republic, because you would have made a formidable demagogue had you chosen a different course!"

"Well, I thank you for that, James," said Alex. "When I was given a second chance at life, I purposed myself that I would do something to be worthy of the Almighty's mercy. Preventing a civil war that could consume an entire generation of Americans seemed to fit the bill perfectly."

"A civil war, Mister President?" asked young Cartwright, who had ridden up quietly behind them. Madison looked at him sharply, but Alex smiled and nodded.

"It's not something I know for sure to be coming, my young friend," he said. "But it seemed to me that if it were to happen, slavery would be the root cause of it. So, I decided to do what I could to remove the cause of the conflict before the conflict itself could break out. If my premonition was wrong, then I have still at least managed to free tens of thousands of people from bondage. If it was correct, then I have liberated tens of thousands of people and may have saved hundreds of thousands of lives as well!"

"That must have been quite the premonition, Mister President!" the young secretary said with a smile. "Such things are beyond my ken. All I know is, I will be glad when we get back to Washington City! This trip is a bit much for me."

"Surely a young man such as yourself is not oppressed by this miserable climate," Madison said.

"Climate has nothing to do with it, Mister Secretary, it's the bloody temptation that is proving difficult to handle!" Cartwright said. "I have pledged to be a true and faithful man to my Lily-Beth for the rest of my life, and these Southern belles are doing all they can to make me forget that pledge!"

The two older men laughed, and Cartwright blushed a bit.

"Well, sirs, it's the truth," he said. "I think that this climate must keep their animal passions in a constant state of upheaval!"

Alex reached out and patted his young aide on the shoulder.

"The path of marital fidelity is not always easy," he said. "But it is worth staying on, as the straight and narrow way usually is."

Madison looked at the two men and cracked a smile. As usual, the expression of mirth looked a bit out of place in his normally stern, schoolmaster-like visage.

"Why, I have no idea what you two are talking about!" he said. "I've never once been tempted to be unfaithful to my dear Dolley. She is the finest woman any man could ever wish for!" Then he leaned closer and lowered his voice. "Besides which, she's bigger than me!"

Hamilton looked at his Secretary of State and gave him a wink.

"That's not saying much, James," he said. "Pretty much everyone is bigger than you!"

Madison shot the President a fake glare, then threw his head back and laughed out loud. Cartwright looked back and forth at the two most powerful men in America lost in mirth before deciding that maybe it was safe to join in, and then he laughed too.

It took them four days of hard riding south to reach the Cape Fear River, where a nicely appointed barge was waiting to bear them downstream to Wilmington. The flatboat had a draft of only three feet, but it was sixty feet long and thirty feet wide, and with a crew of expert river men to pole it along, they made excellent time. There were four cabins; one for Hamilton, one shared by Madison and Cartwright, and two larger ones that were used by the crew and by Hamilton's cavalry escort.

The river was deep and swift for most of the way, and they made excellent time as they floated downstream. Alex spent most of the time on the deck, enjoying the breeze and seeing the river communities on either side of the stream. Often the entire town's population would be gathered on the banks to cheer him as he passed by, and he always tried to acknowledge their greetings with a friendly wave and a shouted greeting.

But he also told the boat's master to make no unnecessary stops, as curiosity about the war's progress was consuming him. When he arrived in Wilmington after four days aboard the flatboat, a group of prominent local citizens were waiting for him on the dock. After thanking them for their hospitality, his first inquiry was as to whether any dispatches awaited him. The town's mayor, Thomas Chadsworth, presented the President with a bundle of letters.

"Two of these arrived yesterday," he said. "The others came last week on a ship from New York."

Ignoring the crowd, Hamilton eagerly untied the ribbon and looked at the envelopes. Sure enough, one of them was from Winfield Scott. He tore into it before all the rest, even the one from Eliza. He scanned its contents eagerly:

22 June 1811
St. Augustine, Florida
The Governor's Palace

Dear Mister President, it began.

It is my great pleasure to inform you that Florida is ours. St. Augustine was captured after a brisk three-day fight which saw our forces contend with great valor against a strongly entrenched opponent. Our losses were higher than I would have wished, but the bravery and determination of our men was wonderful to behold. On the third day I accepted the surrender of Florida from the Spanish governor, Jose Estrada, who had stepped up to the office when the old governor, Enrique White, died just before the battle began. He has sent word to the scattered Spanish forces to the south of us to surrender their posts and recognize the de facto authority of the United States over Florida until such time as a final peace treaty shall be signed.

Full details of the battle are included below in a formal dispatch addressed to yourself, the Congress, and Secretary of War Tallmadge, but I simply wanted to let you know at the outset the most important result of our campaign: the battle for

Florida is over and the United States has won! With the deepest of respect, I have the honor to remain,

Your obedient servant,

Winfield Scott, Col., United States Army

Hamilton gave a shout of glee and grabbed a startled James Madison by the arms and began to dance a merry jig as the welcoming committee looked on in astonishment.

"He's done it, James! Scott has prevailed!" Hamilton finally shouted. "St. Augustine has fallen, and Florida is ours!"

The local dignitaries began cheering, and word spread like wildfire throughout the crowd. Soon people were running from all directions, congregating near the waterfront, and Hamilton and his party had to board a large merchant ship to avoid being crushed in the press. He stood in the stern and watched as all the docks filled with cheering, eager faces. Within a half hour, most of Wilmington's population had gathered on the waterfront.

Alex had excused himself belowdecks for a moment to read the lengthier dispatches from Colonel Scott, and now he looked out on a sea of happy faces. Many were waving American flags left over from the celebration of the Fourth a couple of weeks before, and when they spied the President standing on the stern of the ship, the cheers and shouts grew even louder.

"For heaven's sake, Mister President," said Madison, who had nearly been knocked off his feet in the press, "go ahead and address them! Maybe if you share the news with them, they will all go home, and we can find our lodgings for the night!"

"I don't know if hearing from me will get them to go home or not," said Hamilton, "but I will certainly be glad to share the news with them. Why don't you go below and read Scott's dispatches before I forward them to Washington City?"

Madison gratefully accepted the letters, and President Hamilton turned to the ship's master.

"Could I trouble you for a bullhorn?" he asked.

"Of course, Mister President," the captain said, and handed him a well-worn speaking tube. Alex, still lithe and quick despite his fifty-plus years, climbed into the rigging until he could see above the heads of the crowd.

"Good citizens, listen to me!" he shouted into the bullhorn, and the crowd began to calm down, although it took a few minutes for them to grow silent enough for him to be heard.

"It is wonderful to be greeted with such enthusiasm, and while I don't know how much you may have heard, please allow me to share with you the news I have just received by urgent dispatch from Florida," he began.

Complete silence fell over the crowd as the President's words echoed up and down the waterfront. Hamilton smiled and spoke as loudly and distinctly as he could.

"There has been a great battle before the ramparts of Saint Augustine," he said. "There were heavy losses on both sides, but the American forces, led by Colonel Winfield Scott, have prevailed. The governor of Florida is in American custody, and Florida is ours!"

Loud cheers and huzzahs erupted from the crowd, and it took several minutes for Alex to get their attention again.

"I will see to it that full details of the battle are submitted to the newspapers tomorrow, and I will make a public address to you all before I embark for Charleston tomorrow morning," he said. "But let us thank God for His singular blessings, and for the victory that we now savor. Now I would ask as a favor that you clear a path for my companions and I to the mayor's home, for we have been long on our journey and are ready for a good night's rest. I promise that I will address you all in the morning!"

The crowd cheered, and someone began setting off fireworks over the harbor. Church bells tolled in honor of the victory, and it took over an hour for the local militia to clear the roadway enough for Hamilton and his companions to mount up and ride the short distance to the mayor's house.

"I am deeply sorry for the delay, Your Excellency," Mayor Chadsworth said as they finally arrived before his handsome red brick home as the shadows were lengthening and the heat of the day faded. "The people were just so excited to hear the news!"

Hamilton laughed.

"I have been delayed by many things on this journey," he said. "Endless receptions, tedious balls, swollen rivers, torrential rains, and worn-out horses, to name a few. But no delay has been more welcome than this one!"

"My servants will have baths drawn for you and your party within the hour," Chadsworth said. "There will be a late supper at nine, and then you may retire whenever you like. A very special conveyance is arriving in the morning to take you from here to Charleston, Mister President."

"A special conveyance?" Hamilton asked, raising an eyebrow. "I wonder what that could be?"

Chadsworth shrugged.

"I don't know, sir, but Secretary Tallmadge sent a letter bidding me to be ready for its arrival on the morning of the thirteenth of July, and that's tomorrow. Your arrival could not be more timely," the portly Southerner said.

"Excellent," said Hamilton. "I look forward to a swift journey southward. I may even pay a call to Florida before this trip is done!"

CHAPTER TWENTY-NINE

THE NEXT MORNING Alex rose early and spent an hour and a half answering all his correspondence. He spent the most time on a lengthy letter to Eliza and the children, filling them in on all the details of the trip and of Scott's capture of St. Augustine, and finally he added a personal postscript to Eliza, expressing his loneliness without her and how much he longed to see her again. He also wrote an official letter to his Vice President, John Quincy Adams, and enclosed a copy of Colonel Scott's dispatch along with it.

After a splendid breakfast of slow-cooked ham, eggs, and freshly squeezed orange juice, Alex met briefly with a group of newspaper editors. He had asked Cartwright to make several copies of Scott's dispatch, and gave a couple of them out to the most widely circulated newspapers, along with a short cover letter he had composed for the American people. Within a few weeks, he figured, the story of the battle of St. Augustine would be known from one end of the states to another. If only there were a more rapid means of transmitting the written word from one place to another than couriers on horseback carrying letters and papers, he thought, the business of informing the public would be much easier.

At nine-thirty, President Hamilton stood on the steps of the Wilmington courthouse and delivered the address he had promised the day before to the townspeople. He gave them more details about the struggle for St. Augustine, giving full credit to the heroic fighting skills of the southern sharpshooters who had kept the Spanish from effectively using their artillery. The public mood was still jubilant, but less hysterical than the night before, and the crowd gladly gave way for Hamilton's party to leave when his address was done. By half past ten, Alex and the rest of his party were on their way to the waterfront. The President was startled to see the craft tied up at the docks waiting for them.

The ship was over a hundred feet long, with a massive, twenty-foot wheel at its stern, studded with wooden paddles all the way around. A tubular chimney or smokestack projected from pilot house amidships, and white puffs of steam were rising from it; there was also a large mast rising from the forecastle. A tall man with curly hair and sharp features came down the gangplank to meet the President.

"Welcome aboard the USS *Washington*, Mister President!" he said. "This is the world's first steam-powered, seagoing vessel."

"Mister Fulton, I presume?" Hamilton said. "I have seen your steamboat the *Clermont* moving up the Hudson River, but I did not know you were working on a seagoing vessel!"

"I've kept the project largely secret," Fulton said. "But we embarked from Newport, Virginia, just three days ago and have averaged five miles an hour the whole way, despite a mild headwind. Secretary Tallmadge thought that you might enjoy a faster means of conveyance for the last leg of your journey."

"Well, bless his soul," said Hamilton. "We do indeed live in an age of wonders! How long will this contraption take to reach Charleston?"

"We just loaded up our bins with coal, and I think, with any luck, we can be there in two days' time," Fulton said.

"Marvelous!" Alex exclaimed. "Well, let's be aboard then!"

However, as he prepared to board the ship, he heard the clatter of hooves approaching from behind. He turned to see a young soldier, mounted on a horse that had obviously been ridden long and hard, making his way through the crowd of well-wishers that had gathered to see the President off.

"President Hamilton!" the young man said. "Urgent dispatch for your eyes only, from Colonel Scott!"

Hamilton pressed forward and took the envelope from the young man's hand.

"Do you know what is in here, Corporal?" he asked. "Has there been some military setback?"

"I don't know what the Colonel wrote you, sir, but all was calm in St. Augustine when I left there nigh on two weeks ago," he said. "The Spanish have been docile enough since we whipped them back in June."

"Very well," he said. "I am about to take ship for Charleston, South Carolina. Why don't you board with us, soldier, and you can convey my reply to Colonel Scott when we make landfall?"

"On board that thing?" the young man said, staring curiously at the paddle-wheeler. "Well, I suppose if it's safe enough for the President, I can't refuse! It will be good to be out of the saddle."

"What's your name, lad?" Hamilton asked him.

"Roger Whitaker, sir, from the Fifth New York Volunteers!" the soldier said cheerfully.

"A fellow New Yorker!" Alex smiled. "A long way from home, aren't we, Corporal Whitaker?"

"Aye, sir, and I am ready to return there, now that the fighting is done," Whitaker said. "I have a girl waiting for me, up in Albany."

"Did you take part in the battle for St. Augustine?" Hamilton asked.

"Yes sir, and a hot bit of work that was, too!" exclaimed the corporal.

"Once we are underway, I'd love to hear all about it," the President said as they boarded the steamboat.

After they left the harbor, Hamilton went below decks and opened the seal on the envelope. A small table was bolted to the wall directly beneath a skylight, and he quickly perused the letter's contents.

28 June 1811
St. Augustine, Florida

Dear Mister President, it began.

I believe that I may have discovered the answer to a question that has troubled our nation since this unfortunate conflict began. You may remember how General Jackson wrote to you that the attack on American territory was carried out under forged orders carried by an officer named Raul Vega, who was killed in our initial skirmish with the Spanish. At the time we had no idea of his significance and his body was buried in a mass grave with the rest of the enemy dead. But after taking possession of St. Augustine, I made careful inquiries about him, both publicly and privately.

Governor Estrada remembered him as arriving by ship late last fall, directly from Spain, but Vega refused to divulge his purpose in coming to Estrada at the time, and if he revealed it to old Governor White, the latter never spoke of it. But one of my sergeants, a Spanish-speaking Creole, began to investigate Vega's arrival and see if he had any known associates, and after a few days, he informed me that there was another Spaniard, named Dante Gomez, who had arrived with Vega and was said by many to be in cahoots with him.

Apparently this Gomez, an ill-favored and rather fat fellow, lingered about St. Augustine until the conflict began and then tried to take ship back for Spain as soon as word of the fall of Fort Pensacola reached here. However, his ship was forced to return to port by our naval blockade, and he dropped out of sight after that. My creole sergeant, Gaston Thibodaux, located him holed up in the back room of a seedy dive near the waterfront with a jug of wine and a mulatto whore, and we took him into custody.

Gomez was reluctant to talk at first, but then I arranged for him to be present when some of my Tennessean soldiers administered rough justice to a Spanish soldier whom they had caught raping a twelve-year-old girl. I don't know (nor do I care to find out) what they did to the ravisher, but when Gomez was ushered into my presence he was splattered with blood and hysterically eager to tell me the full story.

He and Vega were appointed by Joseph Bonaparte to come to America and stir up a border incident with the U.S.A. to provoke us into declaring war. Bonaparte knew that the governors of both Floridas were loyal to the Junta, and he believed that he would be able to strike a favorable deal with the United States if we blamed them and their masters in Cadiz for the attack on our territory. It seems Bonaparte fears that the war in Spain is tipping against him, and that an all-out attack on Spain's North American territories by the United States might weaken the Junta's standing and turn public opinion in Spain towards his own government.

It's a fantastic tale, sir, but Gomez produced a well-worn and much stained letter of instructions from Joseph Bonaparte to Captain Vega, bearing what he claims is King Joseph's signature. I have enclosed it with this report. The diplomatic implications of all this are far over my head, Mister President, but it seems to me as a simple soldier that rewarding those who attacked our soil without provocation would be a bad idea. I will bring Gomez north with me as a prisoner whenever you order me to return to the States.

Moving on to other matters, the occupation of St. Augustine has continued without incident. The locals do not seem to *resent our troops much, and I have ordered the men to be on their best behavior. I confiscated several chests of gold and silver bullion from the Spanish governor's palace and have used them to pay the militia and regulars for their service, and they have been free with their spending in the local grog shops and houses of ill repute—which may account for the lack of resentment by the locals!*

Governor Estrada is under house arrest awaiting whatever fate you assign to him and has been cooperative in making sure the remaining Spanish soldiers do not give us any trouble. Overall, the invasion of Florida has been as successful a military operation as we could have asked for under the circumstances, and I hope that my actions meet with your approval.

I have the honor to remain,

Your obedient servant,

Colonel Winfield Scott,

Commandant of St. Augustine

As Hamilton read and reread Scott's report, the beginnings of a plan began to form in his mind. However, he kept it to himself for the time being, determined to attend to domestic affairs in Charleston before making his next move regarding Spain.

The *Washington* made excellent time, and Alex watched with fascination as the huge paddlewheel turned at a constant rate, driven by the power of steam. He had always been interested by new gadgets and inventions, and he asked Fulton to provide him with a full diagram of the ship's propulsion system, so he could understand how it worked. He even went below and braved the intense heat radiating from the boilers to watch as the crew kept the fires stoked with bucketloads of coal.

After two grueling months in the saddle, and then being poled down river in the sultry Southern heat, the President was exhilarated to be on the open waters of the Atlantic, even if they never got completely out of sight of land. The bracing salt air and constant breeze cooled his body and lifted his spirits, and the soldiers who formed his escort were also cheerful and appreciative of the easy travel. Only Madison was ill at ease—he did not have strong sea legs, and although he never got all the way seasick, he also never got particularly comfortable.

It took them just under three days to complete the journey, and the *Washington* arrived in Charleston late in the evening on the twenty-eighth of July. Rather than go ashore and try to find lodging so late, the President sent his military escort ashore to announce his arrival to his hosts, while he and the others enjoyed another night in their small but comfortable cabins. The steamboat was anchored a half mile out from land so that the crew would have the advantage of daylight for mooring the vessel the next morning.

By nine o'clock the next morning, as they steamed up to the pier, a full welcoming committee was waiting to greet them, including a militia regiment under South Carolina's proud flag, and an impressively uniformed musical band.

"Looks like nearly all the powers that be in South Carolina are here," said Madison, surveying the welcoming party.

"Indeed, I see both Pinckneys, our friend Congressman Calhoun, and Governor Middleton, Senator Gaillard, and his counterpart, Senator John Taylor," Hamilton said. "Well, two friendly faces are better than none, I suppose."

"A Federalist background does not guarantee support for emancipation, Mister President," Madison said, lowering his voice as they walked down the gangplank.

"True enough," Hamilton whispered. "But I've been writing Cotesworth Pinckney for some time now. He is at least open to conversation on the subject. Nonetheless, the task before us here is great, and I have little confidence of victory. So for now, we shall be gracious guests, and enjoy the legendary hospitality of Charleston." By now they were approaching the platform where the assembled dignitaries awaited them, and Hamilton gave a gracious bow as the band struck up a patriotic tune.

"Mister President, welcome to Charleston," said Governor Henry Middleton. "It is our honor to welcome you as we celebrate our nation's victory over the perfidious forces of Spain, which attacked us unprovoked!"

Hamilton gave the obligatory speech before the gathered crowd and dignitaries, tailoring his remarks to his audience. He focused more on the glorious victory over Spain and less on his emancipation project, although he did insert a few pointed references to liberty to remind the people of his principles. Afterward, he reviewed the local militia and enjoyed a magnificent feast at the Representative Calhoun's palatial home. It was a very full day, and at its end, Hamilton and Madison found themselves seated around a dining table with Calhoun, the two Senators, Taylor and Gaillard, the formidable Federalist brothers,

Thomas and Charles Cotesworth Pinckney, and Governor Henry Middleton.

As the dishes were cleared away and coffee was poured for the guests, Calhoun rose and bowed to the assembly, and then began to speak.

"Mister President, I have invited you here to my home in Charleston because the policies of your administration are deeply troubling to the people of South Carolina. I have also invited these men, the leaders of our state past and present, because I wanted them to have a chance to hear how you respond to the questions I wish to ask today."

Hamilton rose and bowed to his host.

"I am honored to be your guest, Representative Calhoun, and I wish to assure you and all the men at this table that I bear no animus against the state of South Carolina or its people," he said. "My policies are driven by my love of country first and my love of liberty second, but I have purposed in my heart to bear malice to none and charity to all."

"Noble sentiments to be sure, Mister President," said Calhoun. "But the fact remains that your crusade against slavery is inimical to our entire way of life. Our economy is so strongly interwoven with slave labor that to destroy it, sir, is to destroy us, and that seems to be your purpose. Why would you attack the domestic institution that is the cornerstone of our culture, our way of life, and our commerce if you bear us no ill will? It is difficult, sir, for us to interpret your actions in any other light. You may claim to bear malice to none, but the effects of your emancipation policies are most malicious to us."

Charles Pinckney nodded at this and then also rose to speak.

"Alex, if I may be so bold, you and I are old friends. We fought together, we served President Washington together, and we have both been leaders of the Federalist Party. You supported me for President, and I in turn supported you. I flatter myself to think I know your heart as well as any man, and I believe your claim that you do not act out of intentional malice," he said. "I share your love of liberty, Mister President, but to abolish slavery is to drive a dagger through the heart of our state's economy. I have supported and defended you, but your policies have made it difficult for me to do so. Nonetheless, I have urged my friends at this table to attend this dinner and to listen to you make your case. But I would urge you, as an old friend, to think carefully on the course you have set for our nation. We in South Carolina feel surrounded and isolated by this dangerous impulse that you have encouraged, one which may turn our own workers against us and see us all murdered in our beds! Servile insurrection—that is the fear that every slaveholder goes to bed with at night, Alex. Your actions are making this apprehension more palpable every day for us. Why must you continue to press for emancipation?"

There were mutters of agreement around the table, and Alex shot Madison a quick smile before he rose and began to speak. He remembered the words of Martin Luther, when the great reformer had been invited to defend his works at Augsburg—*"The Devil invites us to preach in hell!"* With that idea forefront in his mind, the President began to speak.

"Gentlemen," he said, "first I want to thank you for the opportunity you have given me to defend my policies. Sirs, I am as aware of the economic power of slavery as any man at this table. I grew up in a place where slavery was even more firmly entrenched than it is here in the Carolinas, where its morality was never questioned, and where its baleful influence was felt from the lowest grog-shops and brothels to the homes of the richest planters and grandees. My first job was to keep the books of a company that traded as freely in slaves as it did in molasses, rum, and tobacco. I know that your economy depends on the safe and reliable harvest of your crops, and I also know that you believe slave labor is the only way to secure that harvest year after year. I would not seek to remove the main pillar of commerce without offering up a reasonable replacement for it."

He paused and looked around the table at the skeptical faces gathered there, and then continued.

"Had I died in that fateful duel seven years ago today," he said, realizing for the first time that it was indeed the anniversary of his "interview" with Burr, "I imagine slavery would have continued to spread unchecked across the southern half of our Union. Virginia would not have abandoned it, the territories beyond the Mississippi would have embraced it, and if the warm plains of Texas and Florida should have been added to our nation, then they, too, would have fallen under the plow and the lash. In time you would have had two distinct economies, one Southern and one Northern, one dependent on slave labor and the other becoming more resentful of it every year. As men's dollars go, so follow their hearts. The North would become a booming wellspring of shipping and manufactures, the South a vast plantation with millions toiling under the lash. Two separate cultures would have grown from one nation, and eventually some spark—perhaps a Southern attempt to expand slavery into the furthest reaches of the West, or perhaps a Northern bill to limit that expansion—would provide a spark to ignite a firestorm. I believe, if slavery is allowed to grow and expand unchecked, that a great civil war will visit America in the future, one that will consume an entire generation and sow seeds of bitterness for centuries to come."

"Preposterous," snorted Calhoun. "It sounds like a fevered dream from a Chinese opium den!"

Hamilton winced a bit inside, for he had come as close as he dared to telling these men about the vision he had seen while hovering at death's door seven years before.

"Perhaps, but I have been right in many predictions I have made before," said Hamilton. "I believe this one might have also come true. But whether I was kissed by the muse of prophesy or simply had a moment of moral clarity, I have made emancipation the central goal of my life for over six years now. Think on this, gentlemen—if I am right, then in delivering our nation from the scourge of slavery, I am sparing our children and grandchildren a horrible ordeal, a trial by fire that would consume them by the tens of thousands! But if I am wrong, what is the worst that has happened? We have lived up to our founding principles and given the gift of liberty to an oppressed people!"

"If slavery is such a godawful scourge, Mister President, why doesn't the Bible ever condemn it? Why did our Savior not speak against it?" demanded Senator Gaillard.

"Christ came to save our souls, not to reform our governments," said Hamilton steadily. "But did He not say: 'Do unto others as you would have them do unto you'? Gentlemen, does buying and selling human beings at the auction block in any way fulfill that commandment? Does forcing women into concubinage and then selling the children sired on them through rape honor God in any way? Does flogging men for seeking the same liberty that you fought the British to gain honor the commandment, 'You shall love your neighbor as yourself'? Christ may not have spoken against slavery directly, but living by the principles he taught should restrain us from ever holding another human soul as our property!"

Governor Middleton leaped to his feet, his face florid with anger.

"Concubinage?" he roared. "Do you dare suggest that any Southern gentleman at this table would sully himself by bedding some black wench from the cotton fields?"

"Oh, stow your false outrage, Henry!" James Madison said wearily. "You may not be bedding the black wenches that labor in your fields, but I'll wager some white man on your plantation is, be it your son, your nephew, or your overseer! That's who was raping all black women on my plantation, every time I left Montpelier in his hands, and I was utterly blind to it until one former slave had the courage to tell me. You know as well as I do that thousands of mulatto children are born to slave women in the South every year. Are you going to tell me they are all immaculately conceived?"

The governor stared at the Secretary of State, astonished, and then slowly sank back into his seat. Hamilton shot Madison a quick wink, and the Secretary sat down, abashed by his own outburst.

"Our own Declaration of Independence holds that all men are granted the right to liberty by our own creator," Hamilton continued. "I fought for that Declaration, and for the government we created. But I often ask myself if we are truly deserving of liberty when we so ruthlessly deny it to others!"

"Mister President," Calhoun interjected, "I'm going to come out and say what every one of us is thinking. They . . .are . . . NEGROES!" He enunciated each word in his rich baritone voice, pouring scorn on the final epithet. "They are barbaric savages at worst and simple-minded children at best, altogether incapable of understanding the concept of liberty or appreciating it in practice. If we freed them now, they would be at our throats in a year's time. The only way for blacks and whites to live together is for one race to hold the other in bondage, and I refuse to wear a chain!"

Hamilton looked sadly at the young man and then shook his head.

"I do not doubt that you believe what you said, Mister Calhoun," he said, "but that does not make it true. During the war, I saw free black soldiers fighting for both sides, and they fought as bravely and skillfully as any white soldier. I remember once—and I think you may have been there, too, Charles—just before Yorktown, we intercepted a patrol of British soldiers foraging beyond the fortifications for food. It was a company was made up of Negroes, former slaves who had been promised their freedom if they fought for the crown. We outnumbered them and had our guns on them, and I ordered them to surrender. One of them looked at the others and said: 'If we going to die, boys, let's die as free men!' And they charged our muskets and bayonets with pistols and sabers. We killed every one of them—they left us no choice—but that was the only time during the whole war when I wondered if perhaps I was fighting on the wrong side. They understood what it was to be free, Congressman, and they were willing to die for their newfound liberty. Would not any of us have done the same!"

"I do remember that," the elder Pinckney said. "You were quite grave when you came back into our camp that night."

"I have traveled throughout this land," the President said. "I have seen free blacks hard at work, trying to better their fortunes. I've seen black men plying honorable trades and living in peace with their white neighbors. Secretary Madison's plantation is very ably managed by a black overseer now—and has been for two years. One free black man told me that his people will become what we make them to be. If you want them to be savages, Mister Calhoun, continue to treat them as such and that is what they will be—and then may God help you if the chain you hold them with ever breaks! But if we want these people to be our peaceable neighbors, then we must follow God's command to love our neighbors as ourselves."

Hamilton paused, and looked around the table at the state leaders assembled there.

"Change is hard," he said. "Especially when it is a change as deep and fundamental as this. It will not come easily, nor quickly, to a place as steeped in the traditions of bondage as South Carolina has become. But may I issue a challenge tonight. Would just one of you men be willing to undertake an experiment in wage labor, as Secretary Madison has? Try it and see if it will not work just as well here as it has in Virginia! Let one brave man lead by example, and see if others will not, in time, by the grace of God, be willing to follow?"

"Never," said Calhoun. "You seek to uproot the very natural order of our world!" Several others loudly echoed his sentiments, but then the room grew silent as Charles Cotesworth Pinckney, former Governor, Ambassador, and Federalist presidential candidate, rose to his feet.

"I'll do it," he said. "I'll give your program a try. Secretary Madison, would you be good enough to lend me a few hours of your time, to show me how you did it?"

"Well, I can't let my brother stick his neck out alone!" Thomas Pinckney exclaimed, rising to stand beside his sibling. "I'll give it a go, too."

The respect these two Revolutionary heroes commanded was so great that even Calhoun fell silent. Hamilton nodded to himself in satisfaction. It was a start, he thought.

CHAPTER THIRTY

AFTER THE LONG dinner was over, most of the guests departed, and Calhoun invited Alex and James Madison to join him for an after-dinner brandy. The South Carolinian was quiet after the lengthy dinner conversation, although unfailingly courteous. The windows were open to admit a breeze from the harbor, and the distant sounds of the waterfront came wafting in with it. Calhoun's butler poured each man a glass and then left the snifter on the table, bowing to his master as he left the room. He was like a black phantom in evening dress, Hamilton thought, hovering over the entire evening, never saying a word beyond "Yes, suh" or "Thank you, suh." His presence was ubiquitous but unremarked upon; a metaphor for Southern slavery if ever there was one.

After the butler left the room, Calhoun turned his piercing gaze upon the President, studying him intently.

"First of all, Mister President, I want to thank you for being my guest tonight. I hope you will forgive my passionate outburst during our conversation," he said. "I imagine you think me something of a fanatic."

"Mister Calhoun, it is the very nature of mankind to hold on to the familiar, and to regard change with fear and suspicion," said Hamilton. "You are no different than most men in that regard. No doubt you probably find me fanatical as well. In the end, sir, we must all stand before the throne of the Almighty and give account for our lives. I will be unashamed to say that I took a stand for liberty; I believe that justice and right are on the side of emancipation, and I believe future generations will agree."

Calhoun sighed deeply, and then looked at Hamilton with more sadness than anger.

"Mister President," he said. "You speak of slavery as if it were just an economic institution and nothing more. But to us in the South, it means so much more than that! It is not just a system of labor that can be plucked up and replaced, sir—it is the basis of our social order! Slavery is the natural and normal condition of the colored race, just as mastery is that of the white. That is the reason why the poorest dirt-grubbing farmer of the Piedmont may look the wealthiest planter in the state eye to eye as an equal—because both of them are members of a race that is divinely ordained to mastery of the world."

Hamilton raised an eyebrow at this exposition.

"Sir, I don't recall reading in Scripture anywhere that God ordained white men to rule over all other races," he said.

"What about the curse of Ham?" asked Calhoun. "Was he not condemned, and all his progeny, to be a hewer of wood and a drawer of water for the descendants of his wiser brothers?"

"As I recall, sir, Ham was the forefather of the Canaanites, not the Africans," Alex replied. "In fact, the only two places I recall in the Old Testament where dark skin color was mentioned specifically, one Negress was the wife of Moses, and the other the true love of King Solomon!"

"Be that as it may, sir," said Calhoun with a sigh, "have you considered the long-term consequences of liberty for the dusky sons of Africa, if you free them and leave them here, to live amongst us? If they are to be free workers, paid for their labor and treated as equals in the eyes of the law, how long will it be before they demand the privileges of citizenship? How long before they demand the right to vote, the right to run for office, or the right to intermarry with white women? Do you really think that the gentlemen of the South will stand still for such abominations?"

"It seems to me that many men of the South have no problem taking black women as their concubines," said Hamilton. "And President Jefferson has done the honorable thing by marrying the woman that he had treated as a wife for many years. I often wonder how much of the outrage felt by Southern men at the idea of any black man ever touching a white woman is rooted in the suppressed guilt for their own behavior towards their helpless female property? Not that I am accusing you, Mister Calhoun, but surely you recognize that such actions do occur."

Calhoun's face was frozen in a mask of anger, but he managed to rasp his reply through clinched lips.

"No offense taken, Mister President, but Southern gentlemen cannot always answer for the actions of the lower classes among us!" he said.

"Let us leave that issue aside, then, for the moment," the President said, not liking the glint in Calhoun's eyes. "Liberty, sir, is a birthright of all humanity. That is our founding principle as a nation, and it is a good one. Citizenship is a privilege to be earned. I am willing to leave the issue of Negro citizenship, and all the responsibilities that go with it, for future generations to determine. My goal is to leave America a greater, freer nation than

I found it when I took office, and to remove the yoke from as many shoulders as the powers of my office allow me to. I have no desire to see the country torn apart by civil war over slavery, or any other cause, for that matter. Americans should not ever be driven to soak this land in fraternal blood over a difference of political opinion."

"You may very well create the thing you hope to avoid, if you push too hard, Mister President," said Calhoun. "South Carolina will never consent to 'voluntary' emancipation, even if some misguided individuals among us attempt it. You are my guest, and as such you are entitled to every courtesy while under my roof. But mark my words, sir, I will oppose you on this; I will oppose you so long as there is breath in my body! For, no matter your protestations of good will, what I see you attempting is nothing less than the death of the South as I know it and love it. I will fight you at the ballot box, on the floor of the House, and in the pages of our newspapers. I do not doubt your sincerity, sir, but it is possible to be both absolutely sincere and absolutely wrong."

"Indeed, it is," said Alex, "and I think that description may definitely fit one of us! History will disclose which one it is. But in the meantime, Representative Calhoun, I thank you for your hospitality and your candor. Sometimes I believe that clarity is more important than agreement, and I think we now understand each other, at the very least."

Calhoun offered his hand.

"That we do, Mister President," he said. "You know, sir, it is a damned shame you are such an agreeable gentleman! If you were a boor, I should challenge you to settle this difference of opinion on the field of honor."

Hamilton smiled and bowed to his host.

"My days of dueling ended on the day I took poor Burr's life," he said. "I swore a sacred oath that day that I would never again take up my pistols, no matter what the provocation. Not to mention, our difference is not a matter of personal enmity, but rather one of political philosophy. To resort to violence would cheapen the views we both hold so dear!"

"You are right, of course," said the Congressman. "And on that note, I bid you a good evening. Julius will show you to your quarters—I have placed you and Secretary Madison across the hall from each other. My library is also located along that hallway; you two may wish to relax and confer for a while before retiring for the evening."

"Indeed, sir, Secretary Madison and I do have some matters of state before us that we have lacked the opportunity to discuss," said Hamilton. "You are a most gracious host."

With a final bow, Calhoun exited the room, and moments later the Negro butler came to escort the two men to their bedrooms. He showed them each room, and then pointed out the library, which was next door to Hamilton's room and across the hall from Madison's.

"Thank you, Julius," said the President. "That is your name, if I am not mistaken?"

"Yes, suh," said the butler. "If you or Mistuh Madison need anything during the night, you just pull the bell rope by your bed and I shall be right up!"

"If you would be so kind as to bring us a small pot of coffee, I doubt we will trouble you the rest of the evening," said the President.

"My pleasure, suh," said Julius. "I be right back with it."

Hamilton sank into a comfortable chair next to a small end table and gave a deep sigh. Madison sat across from him and gave him a sympathetic glance.

"I did not envy you one bit this evening, Mister President," he said. "Not during the dinner and not during Calhoun's interrogation that followed!"

"It was a lively exchange, was it not?" Hamilton said with a smile. "Well, I think at the very least each of us understand the other a bit better now. Calhoun is locked into a vision that is almost medieval in its understanding of human nature. It's a shame, really, that he was too young to serve in the Revolution. Had he seen black soldiers fighting as hard for their liberty as I did, it might have shaken his convictions a bit."

"Perhaps, perhaps not," Madison said. "Most Southerners did not change their opinions of Negroes as a result of the war."

"I think that events like the skirmish I described probably planted the seeds of doubt in a few minds, at least," Hamilton said.

Julius, the butler, returned with a pot of coffee and two fine porcelain cups on a silver tray, and placed them on the center table. Hamilton thanked him, and then asked him to tarry a moment.

"Julius, if you will pardon my asking, what kind of master is Mister Calhoun?" he said. "I promise your answer will never leave this room."

The old Negro looked at the President and smiled.

"Mistuh Calhoun is as kind a master as any white man can be," he said. "I tell all the new slaves that they be lucky he bought them! He don't let his overseer whip us, and he makes sure we has good clothes and plenty to eat."

"I suspected as much," Alex said. "So, if you were given the chance, Julius, to remain here and be a slave to Mister Calhoun, or to be set free up North without a penny in your pocket or any assurance of employment, which would you choose?"

The butler thought for a few moments, cast a furtive glance at the door, and then spoke in a whisper.

"I'm an old man, Mistuh President," he said. "I was born a slave and so was my pappy before me. Servitude is all I have ever known, and this life here—it ain't so bad compared to what many of my people suffer. But—iffen I could be my own man, beholden to no one, free to come and go as I please! Suh, in that case, I'd rather starve to death a free man than die in my bed with a full belly as a slave!"

"Thank you for your candor, Julius," said Hamilton, tipping the slave a silver dollar. "I hope someday you get to taste the freedom you crave."

The butler pocketed the coin and bowed himself out of the room. Once he was gone, Alex turned to Madison and smiled.

"I know that slaves are conditioned by years of servitude to say what they think white men want to hear," he said. "But I do believe that old fellow was sincere. Liberty, my friend, is the urge of every human heart!"

"I always believed that, even before I met you," Madison said. "But you have shown me just how true it is. Now, my friend, I must admit I am bone-weary from our day's exertions. What is it you have to discuss with me?"

"I have kept this to myself until now," said Hamilton, producing the letter from Colonel Scott. "Take a moment to read it, and then tell me what you think."

Madison pulled a pair of spectacles out of his pocket, donned, them, and carefully pored over the letter, his eyebrows arching in surprise as he digested its contents.

"So it was Bonaparte!" he said. "Apparently scoundreldom is a family trait of those accursed Corsicans!"

"It seems he was attempting to set up the Junta to be blamed for the incursion, in hopes that we would line his pockets the way my predecessor lined his brother's," Hamilton said. "But I have another idea in mind, and that's what I wanted to discuss with you."

Madison's eyes gleamed brightly, his fatigue forgotten.

"Tell me what you have in mind," he said.

"Do you know where Minister Oniz went after he left the country at the beginning of this conflict?" the President said. "Did he return to Spain or not?"

"He informed me that he was going to report to the Viceroy in Havana, Cuba," Madison said. "From private conversation, I gather his family estate is in Bonapartiste-controlled territory, and he has no desire to return there until the civil war in Spain has ended."

"Excellent," said Hamilton. "How would you feel about a journey to the warm Caribbean before returning to Washington?"

Madison shrugged.

"Do I have a choice in the matter?" he asked.

"I will not order you," Hamilton said. "Nor would I send you alone. But I was thinking that, if we proceed carefully, we could. . ."

He leaned forward and outlined his ideas to the Secretary of State, and as Madison listened, the gleam in his eyes grew even brighter.

"I don't know if it can be done, sir," Madison said, "but if I can achieve this, I will! You have my word on that!"

The next day, the President rode down to the docks to confer with Robert Fulton. The inventor was standing on the decks of his steamboat, supervising the deck hands as they unloaded a wagon full of coal into the ship's scuttle.

"Mister Fulton," he said after the man was done instructing his crew, "a moment of your time, if I may?"

"Of course, Mister President!" said Fulton. "What can I do for you?"

"Is the *Washington* seaworthy enough to conduct Secretary Madison and myself to Saint Augustine?" Hamilton asked.

"I'm afraid not, sir," said Fulton. "The ship requires large quantities of coal to run, and there's no place in Florida or Georgia to pick up any. I had planned on coming this far south and arranged to have several wagonloads sent to Charleston in advance, but even with this lot, I only have enough to get me back up to Virginia. Not to mention, storm season is looming nigh, and this vessel isn't as strong as a sailing ship. I would not risk the hazard to you, sir, even if I had the fuel."

Hamilton nodded, frowning slightly. He wanted to meet with Scott personally, but overland travel all the way through Georgia in late summer was not one bit appealing.

"However, sir, a fishing boat captain told me that the USS *Plymouth* is sailing north from blockading the Florida coast, and should be in port in the next day or so," Fulton said. "That's a right seaworthy craft there, and I bet Captain Hopkins would be willing to take you south!"

Hamilton broke into a broad grin at that, and firmly shook the inventor's hand.

"That is good news, sir," he said. "Better than I could have hoped! A safe journey home to you. When do you set sail—or whatever it is you call moving this behemoth out of port?"

"Tomorrow morning," Fulton said with a laugh.

"I will send a packet of letters north with you," Alex said. "I'll have my man Cartwright drop them off later this evening."

With that he left the ship, mounted his horse, and rode back to Calhoun's stately mansion. He made his apologies to his host and retreated to the upstairs library with a stack of foolscap, several quills, and two full inkwells.

Eliza had always teased him about his incredibly swift writing style, but Hamilton had discovered long ago that if his thoughts were organized and carefully channeled, he had no need of repeated drafts. Concentrating intently, he first penned a long letter to Vice President Adams explaining what he had learned and what he planned to do. Hamilton was no fool; he knew that sea travel, even in the best of seasons, was hazardous, and should some incident befall him, he wanted to make sure that his successor would be armed with all the knowledge that he himself possessed. He also attached a copy of Scott's most recent letter, so that Adams could read for himself what had transpired in Florida.

Next, he wrote a letter to Secretary of War Tallmadge, discussing the latest developments in the military situation, and outlining his ideas for further campaigns in the event the Spanish refused to make peace. He fervently hoped they would; wars were ruinously expensive and had a way of drawing in other nations if they were not concluded quickly.

His third letter was to the Speaker of the House, Henry Clay, an ally whom Hamilton had come to value greatly. In this letter, he outlined some legislative ideas, as well as a broad strategy for the upcoming election—just a little over a year away now, Alex thought. He had every intention of seeking a second term, since there was so much work yet to be done. Clay had become a strong supporter of the President, and Alex knew that he could play a vital role in securing the electoral votes of the Western states for the administration. Of course, Clay, a horse trader by nature, would expect something in return, but Hamilton was willing to make a bargain if it did not compromise his principles.

Finally, he wrote a long letter to Eliza, explaining why his absence might be extended by a month or two. He hesitated and thought heavily over each paragraph that he wrote; unlike his political writings, words from the heart did not always come to him quickly. But as he continued writing, his pen flowed across the paper more quickly.

> *Heart of my heart,* he concluded, *how melancholy is the call of duty that keeps me from your arms! I had no idea that this journey would achieve the magnitude it already has, and it galls me that now I see it being extended yet again. However, I have a chance to bring this destructive conflict to an honorable end that shall bring credit to our country and do justice to those who have been wronged. Therefore, I shall endure the agony of separation a while longer, although I would a thousand times rather be enfolded in the domestic bliss you have always provided for me! But know this, my dearest Eliza, best of wives and best of women — never again shall I undertake such a journey without the bride of my heart by my side! Our children are now old enough that they can be left on their own, or in the charge of your dear sister. Honestly, I do not foresee another such sojourn in my future, whether I serve another term as President or not.*

> *All I ask is that you wait for me, and give our children a hundred kisses each, and reserve a thousand for yourself, until I return! And should ill fortune overtake me, so that I am unable to fly to your arms, know that my spirit will forever hover round you until we meet again in that place where death shall ne'er hold sway. Being loved by you, sweet Eliza, has been the greatest honor and privilege of my long life. Guard my heart well, for it is in your keeping until I return.*

When he was done, he pressed his lips to the letter, and then sealed it in an envelope and rang for Cartwright.

"Yes, Mister President?" the young secretary asked as he responded to the bell.

"Take these letters to Mister Fulton, on board the *Washington*," Alex told him. "He sets sail in the morning."

"I don't suppose you'd like me to deliver them in person?" Cartwright asked hopefully.

Alex stood and cheerfully clapped the young man on the arm.

"Come now, Elijah!" he said. "Where is your sense of adventure? We are bound for Florida! Don't you want to see an alligator?"

"I'd rather see my sweet Lily-Beth than all the alligators in the world!" groaned the young man.

"We'll be back home by autumn," said Alex, "and I promise to give you a few months off when we get there! But this one last port call beckons, and it is an important one. So now, run these letters on down to Fulton, and ask the harbor master if he knows when the *Plymouth* will be docking."

"Yes, Mister President," said Cartwright. "And thank you, sir, for that time off you mentioned. I am hoping to be wed before next spring!"

As it turned out, the *Plymouth* had just cleared the bar and was sailing into Charleston Bay as Cartwright arrived. Alex was overjoyed to hear the news, and borrowing a horse, he rode down to the docks to greet Captain Hopkins.

The ship had obviously seen some action—the rails along one side of the ship were splintered. one of the masts was missing a spar, and two dozen wounded men were offloaded when she moored. Hamilton waited until the casualties had been sent ashore, and then hailed the captain.

"Ahoy there, permission to come aboard!" he cried out.

"Mister President, is that you?" the captain said. "Of course, sire, come on up, welcome to the *Plymouth*! This is a rare privilege!"

"It is my privilege to see you again, Captain!" the President said jovially. "It looks like you have been victorious once more!"

"Those Spanish ships are decided inferior to the *Plymouth*, sir," said Hopkins. "They are heavily armed enough, but ponderously slow, and their gunners couldn't hit the broad side of a barn! Three of them came, too late for the battle, to bring reinforcements to Saint Augustine. We sent one to the bottom and the other two scampering back to Havana with their tails between their legs. I left the *Constitution* and the *Independence* on station and sailed north to bring our wounded here for treatment, and to deliver dispatches, but I intend to sail back to Florida in two days' time."

"Excellent," said Hamilton. "With your permission, Secretary Madison and myself shall come with you."

The normally unflappable Hopkins swallowed hard and looked at the President to see if he were joking. Hamilton's mouth was set in a smile, but his eyes showed he was in dead earnest.

"Well, of course, sir, if that's your wish!" Hopkins finally said.

"It is exactly that," said Alex. "We shall board day after tomorrow, for there is no time to waste!"

CHAPTER THIRTY-ONE

TWO DAYS LATER, President Hamilton, James Madison, and Thomas Pinckney boarded the *Plymouth* together and set sail southward. The weather was beautiful, and the bracing sea breeze moderated the July heat, but the prevailing winds from the southeast made the voyage difficult—Hopkins had to swing wide out to sea and tack repeatedly, multiple times a day, to make any progress.

"Well, the silver lining to the cloud is this, Mister President," the captain said. "As long as you don't tarry overlong in Saint Augustine, we should fairly fly on the return voyage! Wind tends to hold like this through mid-September, and we'll also have the ocean current with us on the way back."

Hamilton smiled and nodded, watching a school of dolphins sporting in the ship's wake.

"Aye," he said, "I remember my first sea voyage to New York, many years ago, from the Caribbean. We had following winds for most of the way, and the ocean was fair white in our wake!"

"Mister President," the captain said. "I was a wee lad when the Revolution ended. My da, he was at Bunker Hill and Concord, and he told me about those battles, but he never left Massachusetts after that. I know that you served under

Washington himself through most of the war. If I may be so bold, sir, what was that like? Helping a new nation win its liberties, knowing the price of failure was likely to be your life? I've always wondered what it would have been like to serve under His Excellency, and I know you were by his side in the thick of it."

Hamilton smiled as the memories rose up in his mind, and he sat on one of the capstans and pulled a pipe out of his pocket. He rarely smoked at home, since Eliza detested the smell of tobacco, but on such a fine day, a full pipe seemed a good accompaniment for an afternoon of war stories. He lit the tobacco on the bowl, drew a deep puff, and blew the smoke into the morning breeze.

"I was elected captain of a New York artillery company right after the war began," he said, "and I first saw George Washington in the summer of 1776, when he came south from Boston to defend New York City from General Howe. . ."

He spoke until the sun began to slant westward, and Hopkins had to take the helm to tack into the wind once more. Over the next few weeks, Hamilton often sat on that same capstan, watching the waves roll by and chatting with Captain Hopkins, or with Madison and Pinckney. Scott's courier, Corporal Whitaker, had taken ship with the President as the shortest route back to his command, and often sat, entranced, as he listened to the President and Thomas Pinckney swap war stories. Madison, while lacking in military experience, had plenty of political anecdotes from his years in government service, some of them quite amusing. The way he told them, with his dour parson's demeanor, made them all the funnier, and when he laughed, his face was transformed. Hamilton often thought these days that he was even happier to have Madison as a friend than he was to have his invaluable services as Secretary of State.

The voyage took nearly a month, and by the time they arrived in Saint Augustine, July had given way to mid-August. The heat was brutal, and as they drew near to shore, the humidity soared and the breeze died down, making conditions even worse.

"Please tell me that your business here will not take too long!" Madison said. "This is intolerable, even for one used to Virginia summers!"

"I hope to be back aboard ship headed north within a week," Hamilton said, "although I am sad to say that your mission will take you to Havana before you can return north. But, on the bright side, it will be nearly winter when you do arrive home."

"I swear I will roll in the first snowbank I see after this!" the Secretary of State exclaimed.

"You Yankees!" Pinckney exclaimed. "This is a fine balmy afternoon, nothing more!"

"I'm a Virginian, not a Yankee!" Madison said in mock outrage.

"Then quit complaining like one!" the South Carolinian shot back.

"Now boys!" Hamilton said, laughing out loud. "We are the first American political leaders to set foot on the newly conquered Florida territory, let's act like statesmen, shall we?"

The port was all abuzz as the frigate neared the docks—a watchman had spotted the presidential flag flying from the

Plymouth's yardarm, and a military band was scrambling to take their place on the shore as the lines were tied up. Colonel Scott, towering a head higher than anyone else in the city, was barking orders as his staff lined up to greet their Commander in Chief. As Hamilton prepared to walk down the gangplank, the band struck up "Hail Columbia" to welcome him ashore.

Scott snapped to attention and rendered a sharp salute, which Alex returned warmly, and then he shook hands with the huge American commander. Hamilton had seen Scott once, long ago, from a distance, but up close the man's height was even more impressive—at six foot six, he stood head and shoulders above the President and the Secretary of State. Even Thomas Pinckney, who was a respectable six feet tall, was dwarfed by the Army commander.

"Welcome to Saint Augustine, Mister President!" Scott said. "It is an honor to have you here, sir!"

"A privilege indeed to be here, sir!" Hamilton said. "It is an honor to visit the newest piece of American territory, won by your martial skill and the valor of your troops. In fact, sir, I wanted to be the first to let you know that I will be applying to Congress to promote you to Major General when I get back to Washington. Your meritorious service has more than earned it!"

Scott blinked in surprise, and then smiled broadly.

"Thank you, sir, that is more than I ever expected!" he said. "I'd like you to review my soldiers, and then I have news from Texas that I think you shall be most interested to hear."

Hamilton's eyes lit up. He had wondered often during the sea voyage how Brown's Louisiana corps had been doing, and if they had seen any action against the enemy.

"Well, let me review the soldiers then," he said excitedly, "and then I am most anxious to hear what General Brown has to say! Is Governor Estrada still in your custody here?"

"Why yes, Mister President, and he has been most cooperative," Scott said. "He insists that he never wanted a conflict with the United States, and he has instructed his citizens to treat our soldiers as guests. There are some hard feelings, of course—we killed a lot of Spaniards in the assault on the city—but I have ordered the Spanish wounded to be treated with the same level of consideration as our own, and our surgeons saved many of them. That has gone a long way towards healing the ill will between our peoples."

"Well done, then, sir," Hamilton said. "It sounds to me as if you have the skills of a diplomat as well as a soldier."

"I don't know about all that, sir," said Scott. "I prefer the battlefield to the honeyed words and black hearts that seem to be the opponents of the diplomat!"

With that, they reached the makeshift reviewing stand, and Hamilton stood at attention in the sweltering heat as the soldiers marched by, arms shouldered, saluting their leader. A large crowd of curious locals gathered, and Hamilton gave a short address after the soldiers had passed by—one of Scott's soldiers who was fluent in the language acted as his translator, since Hamilton's own Spanish was rusty from long disuse.

"It was never my intention to be a wartime President," he said, "for the goal of my administration was to extend liberty within our own nation, not to conquer the territory of our neighbors. But the United States became the victims of an unprovoked and perfidious attack, the challenge to our national sovereignty had to be answered, and you became the victims of war as much as our own frontiersmen whose homes were destroyed by Spanish soldiers under a renegade commander! As our forces have prevailed on the field of battle, it is now my intention to pursue a treaty of peace with the government of King Ferdinand under such terms that Florida will become a permanent possession of the United States. If such a treaty is ratified, each of you will have the opportunity to become American citizens, with all the rights and liberties of any native born American. Or, if you prefer, you may retain your Spanish citizenship and continue to reside here as legal aliens under the full protection of the laws of the United States. That will be your choice in the future; however, for the time being, I will promise that your lives, liberty, and property will be protected by the American soldiers who are stationed here. Those who have suffered property damage will be allowed to seek restitution under U.S. law. The wounds of war are slow to heal, but in time it is my fond hope that we will all live together as citizens of a great and free country, where all will be treated as equals. In the meantime, we ask your patience as we strive to establish peace between our two great countries, and to restore life in Florida to a state of peace and tranquility."

There was a smattering of polite applause as the translation was finished; a few scowls and a good bit of conversation as the crowd broke up. Hamilton turned to Winfield Scott and smiled.

"Now, sir, I believe that you have some correspondence for me to read," he said.

"Indeed, I so, sir," Scott said. "My carriage will convey us to the governor's palace, where you may read it in private, and out of this infernal sun."

It was a short ride up the hard-packed dirt street to a large stucco residence with a wide porch; "palace" was a bit of an overstatement, Alex thought. It was far less ornate than some of the southern plantations he had already visited, but it was large and had wide windows, most of them open to catch the breeze. Colorful paintings hung in the spacious foyer, and the stone floors were polished till they shone.

"The best rooms are on the third floor," said Scott, "above the dust of the streets and catching breeze from every direction. I'll be giving you my rooms; Governor Estrada is one floor below you, and there's a large bedroom across the hall where Secretary Madison and Governor Pinckney will be quite comfortable. Corporal Whitaker—thank you for allowing him to travel back with you, sir—can bring your bags up. Here are the letters from General Brown; one is to myself, and the other was to be forwarded to you. They just arrived yesterday, or I should have already sent it on a horse to Charleston, hoping to catch you there!"

"I'll let you keep his missive to you, General," said the President, mounting the stairs at a trot. "Unless you feel there is something in it that demands my attention. I'm sure he has made a full report to me in his dispatch."

"Well, I haven't read both," said Scott, "but you may read mine anytime you like. It contains many interesting details about—well, about the events that have transpired since the Fourth of July!"

With that the President could stand it no more. He dismissed Scott with a polite bow, then sat down on the edge of his bed and broke the seal on the letter.

20 July 1811
San Antonio de Bexar, Texas
Major General Jacob Brown, Commanding

Dear Mister President,

Much has transpired since you sent me southward with instructions to defend New Orleans against a possible Spanish attack. A large Spanish force under General Joaquin Arredondo attempted to invade Louisiana from the West; informed in advance by Mexican rebels who hate the Spanish for their barbarity, I marched my forces to the border between our countries and set up an ambush near the town of Natchitoches, just west of the Arroyo Hondo. The Spanish marched right into our trap, and in a sharp engagement, I was able to destroy or capture their entire force, including General Arredondo, who lost an arm but survived—he has been a most surly and resentful captive ever since!

Many of the Mexicans who live in the province of Texas are active revolutionaries, and they have long resented the brutal tactics and high-handedness of the Spanish viceroys. One of them, Bernardo Gutierrez, has joined himself to our forces, along with about a hundred "Tejano" volunteers. Apparently, before this conflict broke out, they were planning to break Texas away from Spanish rule and declare their independence.

After conferring with Gutierrez and my fellow officers, we decided that a forceful response to Arredondo's violation of our borders was in order, and we set out southward, along the old Spanish road known as the Camino Real, towards the largest settlement in Texas, San Antonio de Bexar. As soon as we crossed the Sabine, Tejanos came flocking to our banner, eager to strike a blow against the hated Spanish. By the time we were within a day's ride of San Antonio, nearly a thousand of them had joined us.

I conferred with their leaders extensively, and I have found that there is a strong popular sentiment for annexation to the United States. They fear the armies of the Viceroy and the long arm of the Spanish King would eventually reach out to reclaim Texas if they proclaimed it an independent Republic, and express great admiration for America's constitution and democratic institutions. So they say, at least.

The governor of Texas, an old Castilian gentleman named Antonio Martinez, sent a force of several hundred lancers to bar our entrance to the city, but by this time our force numbered into the thousands, and I had made a point of bringing along six artillery pieces. Between several rounds of grapeshot and the fearsome accuracy of my Tennessee riflemen, nearly two hundred lancers fell from the saddle, and the rest fled back to San Antonio faster than they had come! Our losses were about two dozen men totaled, and one officer—a Tennessee captain of volunteers named Sam Houston—was *grievously wounded but is now recovering and should regain his mobility.*

I was afraid of the heavy casualties that might result from street to street fighting in San Antonio, but the Spanish forces decided to spare the residents of the city such horrors and retreated to an old mission that had been converted into a fortress on the edge of town. Originally known as Mission San Valero, it had been renamed "Los Alamo" when it was secularized and converted into a barracks. It wasn't designed to withstand attack; the adobe walls were crumbling and one area next to the chapel had no wall at all. Still, I decided that it would be preferable to take the province without another bloody battle if I could help it.

I sent riders forward under a flag of truce to see if the Governor was willing to negotiate, and it turned out he was. He had some five hundred men inside the fortress; we outnumbered him more than ten to one and he did not have enough food to last more than a couple of weeks. After some heated discussion, Mendoza agreed to take his soldiers and retreat southward, ceding the province of Texas north of the Nueces River, some eighty miles south of San Antonio, to American military control.

And with that, the battle for Texas was won. I sent a thousand-man force to escort Martinez and his men to the border, and several hundred more to secure the only other fortification of any size, the town of Goliad, about sixty miles to our east. Gutierrez and his Tejanos have proven invaluable allies, rallying the people of San Antonio and Goliad to our cause. For the moment, Texas and its people are ours for the taking. I hope I have not exceeded your wishes in this, Mister President, but the Spanish did invade our territory (Gov. Martinez told me that Arredondo may have been acting without orders; he's apparently known as an arrogant hothead throughout Texas and Mexico). I have not had word from Florida, but I trust that Col. Scott has conducted the campaign there with his usual competence and skill. I plan to remain here in occupation of San Antonio until I receive orders to withdraw, or until the war is concluded with a treaty of peace. I was given to understand that you were coming south to monitor the progress of the Florida campaign, so I am forwarding this to Col. Scott, who may have a better idea of your current whereabouts than I do. May it find you quickly, and in good health.

I have the honor to remain your obedient servant,

Jacob E. Brown,

Major General, United States Army

"Secretary Madison, Governor Pinckney!" Hamilton called after he had read the letter through twice. "I want you to read this, and then we need to have a talk."

The two men crossed the hall, and Alex spread the letter out on a writing table and stood back so they could read it at the same time. Madison gave a low whistle when he was done.

"Our forces have acquitted themselves well on every front!" he said.

"General Brown has done a fine job," Pinckney said. "The American flag waving over northern Mexico! That is quite an accomplishment."

"It certainly strengthens our hand for negotiating," said the President. "Now, Pinckney, you have dealt with the Spanish before, and James, you are our nation's chief diplomat. I would like to bring Governor Jose Estrada into the room and lay out for him the same proposal for a treaty of peace that I discussed with the two of you, just to see what kind of response we get from a Spanish official."

"I understand he knows the Viceroy well," Madison said. "His response may help us predict how the Spanish government will react."

Hamilton rang for his trusty secretary Cartwright, who had been given a small room on the first floor, and told him to ask Scott to prepare a room where he could confer with the Spanish prisoner. Within a half hour, the three Americans were sitting at the head of a polished wooden table with a map of the Spanish-American border region spread out before them. Jose Estrada was escorted in by two American officers, with a young Spanish captain by his side. General Scott brought up the rear, towering over the Spanish soldiers.

"President Hamilton, it is an honor to make your acquaintance," Estrada said in passable English, bowing deeply. "Although I must confess that this is not the manner of meeting I would have chosen!"

"It seems to me, sir, that neither of us chose to be at war with the other," Alex said after returning the Spaniard's bow. "That decision was made for us, without our knowledge, by King Joseph Bonaparte."

"I will not grant the usurper a royal title," Estrada said, "but such news does not surprise me in the least. The Bonapartes, all of them, are intriguing scoundrels! Do you know for certain that he was behind the attack on America?"

"Thanks to the investigative skills of General Scott, I am quite certain," the President said, "although I will admit I have suspected he was behind things from the beginning of this unfortunate business. Now, I have an offer to make to the Junta that supports King Ferdinand. Secretary Madison and Governor Pinckney are going to convey it to your Viceroy in Havana, and I would like you to accompany them, so that you may give the Viceroy your version of the events that transpired here."

"I will not betray my country!" said Estrada.

"Nor would I ask you to," said Hamilton. "The offer we make is advantageous to both our countries, and I think when you see what I am proposing, you will agree."

"I would like to know what terms you are offering before I would agree to be a party to any negotiations," Estrada said.

"Of course," said Alex smoothly. He leaned over the map.

"At the moment, American forces occupy every major Spanish post in Florida and in Texas, and Spain's armies in both those colonies have been captured, killed, or driven out. Spain is currently torn in a civil war between the Junta and the Bonapartistes. American has maintained neutrality in that war, refusing to recognize either government as legitimate until we see the outcome of the struggle. Simply put, it is not our fight and we have abstained from taking sides. But, since Joseph Bonaparte is behind the attacks on American soil, we are now prepared to offer full diplomatic recognition to the government of King Ferdinand—and to pay Spain ten million dollars in exchange for that which we have already won on the battlefield, the ownership of Florida and Texas."

"The Viceroy will never agree to such conditions!" said Estrada.

"Come now, let us be reasonable," Hamilton said. "Spain was already struggling to hold onto these colonies. Texas was pitifully manned by less than two thousand soldiers, and barely that number of permanent residents. Florida has long been a point of contention between us. Even when the long civil war in Spain is over, do you think King Ferdinand will have the treasure or strength to send a large enough force over here to retake both territories? Especially when American settlers will have poured in and our armies have had time to fortify? Indeed, we could simply take both territories as an indemnity for the loss of lives and treasure we incurred as a result of the raids on American soil. Instead, we offer an honorable settlement as well as diplomatic recognition to a struggling government, in exchange for two territories Spain is bound to lose eventually regardless!"

Estrada paused for a moment, lost in thought, and then turned and conferred in Spanish with the young officer who had accompanied him. Finally, he faced Hamilton again.

"I see the strength of America's position, and given the circumstances Spain is currently faced with, there are advantages for us in your offer. I do not know that the new Viceroy, Francisco Vinegas, will agree to the terms, however. He is a proud, grasping man, fresh from crushing the Mexican revolt this spring. He only came to Havana when he heard of the probability of war with the USA."

"That is why I want you to accompany Secretary Madison," Hamilton said. "You have seen America's soldiers fight, do you really think that Spain, beset and divided as she is, can muster enough force to drive us from Florida and Texas? You need to help the Viceroy understand where King Ferdinand's true interests lie, and that is not further war with America. I will send three frigates to Havana, under a flag of truce, and you shall go ashore and ensure that they are granted safe conduct and an audience. Beyond that, the conclusion of the matter shall lie with the diplomatic skills of these two gentlemen, and your Viceroy's ability to see reason."

"I make no promises, other than to do my best to ensure that the Secretary and the Governor are treated with respect," Estrada said.

"That is all I can ask," Hamilton said, extending his hand. "You serve your country well, sir."

The President stayed in Florida for another week, writing orders for General Brown in Texas and discussing the governance of Spain—and its defense, should it prove necessary—with General Scott. True to his word, Alex also made sure that he and young Cartwright got to see a real Spanish alligator, up close.

By this time there were four American warships moored in Saint Augustine's harbor, and the President met with the captains to explain his orders for their deployment. Finally, on the twenty-eighth day of August in the year 1811, Secretary James Madison and former South Carolina Governor Thomas Pinckney boarded the flagship *Plymouth* to set sail for Havana. President Alexander Hamilton boarded the newly commissioned USS *Constitution* for the long sailing trip back to New York City and his beloved Eliza. As he saw the white sands and palm trees of Saint Augustine fading in the distance, Alex prayed that the Spanish-American War was truly over.

CHAPTER THIRTY-TWO

IT WAS OCTOBER by the time Alex finally made it all the way back to Washington, DC, despite favorable currents and winds. By that time, news of the American victories in Florida and Texas had spread throughout the entire nation, and the President was greeted with banquets, torchlight parades, and cheering crowds wherever he stopped. Domestic disputes over slavery, tariffs, and other matters were put aside as the young nation basked in the glow of victory in its first foreign war.

Alex's only disappointment was that his family was not waiting at the White House for him. He had originally hoped to return to their home in New York, but due to the delay of the Florida excursion, Congress was now in session and there were bills waiting for his signature. The southern jaunt had lasted longer than he originally planned by nearly six weeks; the nation needed its President to return to his duties. However, he did find a letter from Eliza waiting for him when he arrived in the capital; it informed him that she and the children were en route and planned to be there by mid-month. Cheered by the thought of seeing his sons and daughters again, as well as his darling bride, Hamilton threw himself into his work with a vengeance.

The war had been expensive but not ruinous to the young nation so far. Still, until a peace treaty was signed, Alex was not willing to draw down the forces on the frontier, so funds would continue to be allocated for the soldiers' pay for at least another quarter. The nation's debt had been reduced substantially under Hamilton's fiscal leadership, but it appeared that some significant borrowing would be required to finance the costs of occupation, not to mention the expense of the territorial settlement, if Spain agreed to his terms. At the same time, Alex thought, if a just and lasting peace could be achieved, with significant new territory added to the Union in the process, it would be money well spent.

For the moment, it seemed to Alex that he could have almost anything he asked from the Congress. The frenzied adulation that had accompanied his journey from Virginia to Washington City was mirrored, in a more subdued fashion, by the Congressmen and Senators who flocked to the White House to congratulate the President on the successful prosecution of the war. Many were anxious for details about the Florida campaign; others wanted the President's help with some pet legislative project, and many were simply trying to acquire some of Hamilton's newfound popularity by association.

The day after he got back to Washington, Alex received a letter from Thomas Jefferson, written only a few days before. Hamilton had come to value Jefferson's correspondence; the man was an eloquent writer who rarely touched on politics, but he was also one of only two men in the country who had served as its President. This gave him unique insights, as well as a strong sense of empathy for his successor. Alex broke the seal and unfolded the rich sheets of vellum.

Dear Mr. President, Jefferson began,

Allow me to congratulate you on the signal success of American arms in the recent conflict with Spain. War is the most regrettable form of diplomacy; yet at the same time there are times when the honor of a nation requires her sons to take up arms. In the event of that sad necessity, it is far better for a nation to achieve its aims through victory than to have terms of surrender dictated after defeat.

I spent much of my public career believing that you, sir, were altogether too fond of centralized power to be entrusted with the affairs of our nation. Indeed, at one point I was quite certain that you were intent upon destroying our Constitution and substituting a monarchy or something close thereto, in its place. That is why I opposed you so vigorously for so long, often with means that were, I realize now, less than honorable.

You can imagine my relief, then, as I have watched for the last three years, and seen you wield the power of the Executive Branch moderately, reasonably, and with great restraint, while moving towards the admirable goal of human liberty. Few discoveries of my later years have brought me as much pleasure as the realization that I was wrong about you.

But now you stand in a precarious position, my friend. Victory in warfare has set you upon a pedestal no President has yet occupied; public adulation echoes from all quarters as the gratitude and relief of the American people centers upon the Commander in Chief who delivered that victory. For a brief season—for the people, as much as I love them, are as fickle as any teenage girl in their affections—you can have almost anything you wish from the American people and their legislators. That is a power that could easily become intoxicating, Alex.

So as one of the few men who has sat in the chair you now occupy, and as one who, after many years, is now pleased to call himself your friend, I humbly ask one favor. Do not be corrupted by the opportunity this power presents! Use it for the good of the nation, use it for the cause of liberty, but do not be seduced by the siren song of tyranny. It took a great deal for me to reach the point where I now stand; that of trusting you with the Chief Magistracy of our nation. I wish to see that trust continue to be vindicated, as it has been thus far. Therefore, after much hesitation, I felt impelled to stir from my pleasant retirement to sound this warning. I hope you will not take affront at my doing so, because I offer it with nothing but the best wishes for you, and for our young nation. Tread firmly, Mister President, but tread wisely, on the ground that lies before you. I have no doubt that you will seek another term of office to complete the work that you have thus far so nobly advanced, and I wish to be able to support you in it. May the faith that I, and so many other Americans, have placed in you continue to be vindicated!

Yours very sincerely and respectfully,

Th. Jefferson

Alex smiled fondly as he read the letter. He was as astonished as Jefferson had been to find that his rival, the same man he had once damned as an American Jacobin, a threat to the very fabric of Christian civilization, had become not just a supporter but a friend. Jefferson had always feared that a government whose powers were too great could become a threat to the liberties of the people; Hamilton, on the other hand, had feared that a government whose powers were too weak and poorly defined would be unable to defend the liberties of the people. It was only in the last few years that he had been able to see that, while they approached the issue from different sides, their goals were the same—to see the Union strong and the rights of the people protected.

Hamilton made a point to sit down and write a reply later that evening; in it he thanked Jefferson for his concern and for his warning, and then promised that he would reflect carefully on the policies he undertook during this window of opportunity that the war had presented him. Even as he penned the letter, though, he was weighing his course forward and thinking of ways to cement his legacy.

Two days later Eliza arrived in Washington with the children, and Hamilton enjoyed a blissful reunion with his bride, who was still quite fetching as she neared her fifties, and with his sons and daughters. Angelica, he was thrilled to see, had continued to emerge from the shell of trauma that Philip's death had imprisoned her in some ten years before. She spoke more often and more freely and laughed more than he had seen her do since she was a little girl. She still had long spells during which she would fall silent, and occasional fits of melancholy, but she no longer withdrew into the childlike state where she had hidden her hurts for so long.

Alex's eldest child was disappointed that Cartwright was not there—the President had given his secretary a month's leave on their return to spend with his adored Lily-Beth—but she was happy when Alex assured her that Elijah had behaved himself properly during their long sojourn away from his beloved.

"That gladdens my heart, Father!" she said. "I know that he wanted very much to prove himself a true and faithful lover to his intended, but he had formed some very bad habits during his days as a bachelor. I am glad they are together now, but I do miss him. His stories always made me laugh!"

Alex was seated on a divan, with "Little Phil"—now a strapping boy of ten—on his right, Angelica on his left, and the other children seated in chairs or on the floor before him. Eliza stood behind her husband, hands on his shoulders.

"Mister Cartwright has had his share of amorous adventures," Hamilton said, "but he assured me several times on our journey that he intends to walk the straight and narrow path from this day forward—and he proved that on our journey, for he did not lack for opportunities to stray!"

"Even the wildest of tomcats can be tamed eventually," Eliza said, kissing the growing bald spot on the top of Hamilton's head.

"What does 'amorous' mean, Papa?" Phil asked, and the whole family shook with laughter as the President of the United States blushed.

Hamilton canceled his appointments for the next two days, spending the time reading and playing games with his younger children, and having long talks with his older boys about the directions they wanted their careers to take. He also strolled around the White House grounds with Eliza, cherishing her company and the warm feel of her hand in his once more. Unfortunately, nearly every time they set foot outside, a crowd of excited citizens would form around them, and they got little of the privacy they desired. Finally, Alex took his bride back into the White House and the couple barricaded themselves in the Executive bedroom for the evening, where Hamilton showed his wife that he still knew the meaning of the word "amorous."

As October gave way to November, the business of Congress wound down, and Alex's day-to-day duties became less onerous. His adult sons returned to their jobs or schools, and the younger children resumed their own studies under the watchful eye of a private tutor, Elias Wimberley, whom the First Lady had hired before leaving New York.

Alex had wanted to spend some time back in his home state, but he also wanted to be in Washington when Madison returned from abroad, hopefully bearing a treaty that Alex could present to the Senate. Finally, in the first week of December, the President received a letter from the Secretary of State, postmarked from Havana, Cuba, and dated the first of October.

Dear Mister President, it began;

Our journey to Havana was completed without incident, and the firepower of our fleet was impressive enough that the two rickety Spanish naval vessels in the harbor chose not to challenge our presence. Governor Estrada and I went ashore under a flag of truce, and the Viceroy's emissary agreed to conduct us to the Governor's palace where that august official was presiding.

His Excellency, Viceroy to King Ferdinand, Francisco Vinegas, was none too pleased to see his governor escorted in by two American diplomats and a squad of U.S. marines, although his anger was a bit mollified when he found out that I was the U.S. Secretary of State and not some lesser functionary. However, once we presented your proposed terms of Spain's surrender, his wrath returned tenfold. He blustered and sputtered and threatened, and it was all Estrada could do to keep him from seizing us as hostages on the spot! Governor Estrada, I might add, has been a model of diplomacy and tact throughout this whole affair and was instrumental in the negotiations that followed. I think, with some encouragement to King Ferdinand's government from the Executive, he might be most effective as Spain's ambassador to the United States once the peace between our countries is ratified.

At any rate, a week of intense negotiations, with many incriminations and protests from the Viceroy, followed our arrival. Vinegas is indeed a proud and vindictive man, but the arrival of a report on the battles in Texas from General Arredondo which arrived a few days after we did sobered him somewhat—I think he believed we were exaggerating the degree of our victory there. Finally, on the fifth day, he conceded that our terms were not unreasonable, given the military and political circumstances under which they were offered.

"However," he said, "although my mandate from King Ferdinand is quite broad, negotiating the surrender of so much of Spain's sovereign territory is beyond my purview. I cannot conclude this treaty under the authority that I possess, and if I did His Majesty would reject it out of hand—and most likely

hang me as a traitor! If you truly wish peace and diplomatic ties with our King, Secretary Madison, you must travel to Cadiz and negotiate it with him in person. What I can do for you, however, is send you to him with my official blessing, as well as my recommendation to His Majesty's government that the terms of your treaty, while they might seem odious upon first glance, are in fact the best bargain that our government can hope for at present."

After Pinckney and I conferred, we both agreed that the Viceroy was correct, and so we began preparing to take ship for Spain. Estrada has been assigned by the Viceroy to accompany us as his personal emissary to King Ferdinand VII. The King recently escaped from French custody—he had been imprisoned by Napoleon at one of Talleyrand's estates, the Chateau de Valencay—and found refuge with the Junta in Cadiz. The military situation in Spain is still precarious, although the Junta's forces, working with the British, are beginning to gain the upper hand. By all accounts King Ferdinand is a grasping, vindictive, and selfish ruler, but our offer contains enough advantages for him that I believe he can be persuaded to accept it.

Therefore, I am writing you as we prepare to board ship for Europe. I will travel aboard the USS Plymouth *again; the* Liberty *and the* Independence *will accompany us to Cadiz, while Commodore Hopkins is dispatching the brigantine USS* Jamestown, *the smallest vessel in our escort fleet, to convey this letter to you in Washington, where I hope it will find you before too many weeks have passed.*

Our party is in good health and spirits, although this infernal tropical heat is most oppressive, and I ran a slight fever last night—which I am sure is nothing serious. Hopefully, the next time you hear from me will be in person, with a treaty of peace in hand to be ratified by the Senate. I want to conduct these negotiations as quickly as I can and return home to my beloved wife, and in the future I will hope to serve my country from within its borders! Governor Pinckney sends his greetings as well; now I must make haste to sign and seal this before our ship sails. Adieu!

Your obedient servant,

James Madison,

Secretary of State

Hamilton studied the letter carefully; it had taken four weeks for it to travel from Havana to Washington City, so with fair winds and following seas Madison might well be in Cadiz by now. That afternoon he called a cabinet meeting and read the letter to his principal advisors, inviting their comments.

Benjamin Tallmadge looked over his spectacles and spoke first.

"I think that the Spanish government, if they are wise, will accept your terms, Mister President," he said. "We've had no further hostilities in Florida, and only a couple of minor skirmishes in Texas with hostile Indians and a body of Spanish cavalry who were unaware of the surrender of San Antonio. I've set our troops improving and enlarging the fortifications along the frontier, and Spain will have a hard time ousting us from the territories we've taken."

"Secretary Wolcott," said Hamilton, "how stand the nation's finances after our campaigns?"

"We have incurred about two million in debt since the war began," said Wolcott, "but the vast majority of the debt is in bonds purchased by citizens at a modest rate of return. If hostilities cease in the next six months, the financial cost of the war will be negligible. Now, the cost of purchasing Florida and Texas from Spain, as you propose, will require either another massive bond sale or some new form of taxation. That being said, I think that if you exercise the persuasive powers of the presidency, you can convince the people to meet the financial obligations of the war cheerfully enough. Right now, Mister President, the nation is flush with the joy of victory and ready to listen to its architect. Use that influence wisely while it lasts, would be my advice!"

"That is my intent; I only hope that Secretary Madison returns with a treaty in hand while public sentiment is still running so strongly in our favor," said Hamilton. "Mister Jay, do you have anything to add?"

The Attorney General shook his head.

"Of course, there is no actual treaty for me to review yet," he said. "But the terms you have outlined seem fair and just from a legal standpoint—indeed, you were more generous with the Spanish than I would have been! When Madison brings us a treaty, I will of course be happy to provide you with a legal analysis of the obligations it places on us."

"Do you think the Southern states will support annexing new territory that is closed to their peculiar institution?" Vice President Adams asked.

"We made it clear from the outset that any territory gained as a result of this war would be closed to slavery," Hamilton said. "I think we would have enough votes in the Senate to conclude the treaty without the support of South Carolina and Georgia, as long as we can get at least three Senate votes from the other slave states."

"That reminds me," said Jay. "The settlers in the Alabama and Mississippi territories plan to file for statehood next year."

"Well, under the terms of the Louisiana Purchase Act, they should be the last two slave states to join the Union," Hamilton said. "I wish I could have kept slavery out of them, as well, but it was already too well established when I took office."

"If Kentucky and North Carolina emancipate their slaves, that would nullify the advantage to the South of those two states being added," Adams said.

"I'm fairly sanguine about North Carolina in that department," Alex replied. "I am not so certain of Kentucky. Well, gentlemen, if no one has anything else, I suggest we adjourn."

The meeting broke up, but Vice President Adams hung back, obviously wanting to speak to Hamilton about something.

"What is it, Quincy?" Hamilton asked his friend after the others had left his office.

"Mister President, please understand that I am honored that you have asked me to serve as your Vice President," Adams said, "and that my support for you continues undiminished. It is your intention, is it not, to seek a second term of office?"

"I have little choice," said Hamilton. "I have too much field remaining before me to take my hand from the plow, so to speak. Why do you ask?"

"Sir, the vice presidency is the most miserable office ever conceived by the mind of man!" Adams said. "I understand now why it turned my father's nature so melancholy. I have no official duties other than to preside over the Senate, and on occasion, cast a tie-breaking vote. I'm not even allowed to speak out during the debates over legislation! I will happily continue to the end of your first term, but I beg you to consider another candidate for my office next fall. I am perfectly willing to serve in any other capacity, if you should wish it, but if I have to sit in that miserable chair for another four years and listen as Senators drone on and on about every point and detail of every bill put before them, I shall go mad!"

Alex laughed and clapped his friend on the shoulder.

"A mad John Quincy Adams is indeed a frightening prospect!" he said. "Do me a favor, sir, and tell no one of this conversation till after Christmas. Then we shall see about finding you another task within the administration after next fall's electoral contest."

Christmas came and went in Washington City, and Hamilton remained at the White House with his family. The older boys stayed in New York for the holiday, caught up in their studies and courting their sweethearts, but Alex, Eliza, and Angelica, as well as the three younger children, enjoyed a merry celebration at the White House. Eliza's beloved elder sister Angelica and her husband, John Church, joined the Hamiltons in Washington, the first time that the two couples had been able to be in the same place at the same time since Alex had won the presidency.

It was a joyful time for Alex; he and Angelica had always enjoyed a close and intimate friendship—so much so that tongues had once wagged about the possibility that the two sisters shared his love between them. The truth was that, while he had initially been drawn to Angelica's sharp wit and vivacious beauty, the thing that truly brought them together was their deep love for her sister, Alex's wife, as well as a common interest in politics and philosophy. On more than one occasion Alex had thought that Angelica might have been a formidable political leader had she only been born a man. Still, Hamilton would have been lying to himself if he did not acknowledge that he often envied her husband.

John Church, Angelica's husband, was a jolly soul who seemed to fit equally well into American and English society, having lived on both sides of the Atlantic and having served as a member of the House of Commons for several years. He was an effective touchstone for English public opinion, and Alex often relied more on his letters for insights into British politics than on the boring, stodgy reports sent home by the American ambassador, James Monroe.

The two couples and their children had a joyous Christmas celebration together, but as December ended, the Church family returned to New York, and Alex's older children to their schools and careers. This was the first winter since his election as President that Hamilton had not returned to New York, and while he missed his adopted hometown, he also discovered that the nation's capital was not without its own charms, especially when snow came drifting down and blanketed the young, bustling city in white.

Not long after Christmas, a beaming Elijah Cartwright showed up at the White House, excitedly sharing with Hamilton the news that his wedding was scheduled to take place in April. Alex warmly congratulated his secretary, and after conferring with Eliza, he informed Cartwright that his wedding gift to the young couple would be a small house in Washington City, not far from the White House. Hamilton acknowledged to himself there was a small bit of self-interest in the gift; he did not want to lose the services of his talented young secretary.

Early in January a warm spell came, and much of the snow that had covered the ground melted away, exposing the muddy roads and dead grass of a dreary winter. Alex found himself wishing for another blizzard to mask the deadness of the winter foliage, but he also took advantage of the better travel conditions to draft up a flurry of letters to friends and political allies regarding his reelection campaign.

On January 15, Alex was drafting up some proposals for Congress when he heard horses clopping up the White House drive, and the tramp of boots advancing up the corridor. He poked his head into the hall to see who was being brought in, and was astonished to see Thomas Pinckney, his boots and coat spattered with the mud of long travel.

"Governor Pinckney!" he exclaimed, taking his old friend by the hand. "I am glad to see you safely back in our country. Where is Secretary Madison?"

"He is coming along behind me in a carriage," the South Carolinian said. "He is not well, sir, not well at all. But he insisted on coming to the White House himself to present the peace treaty to you."

"I am sorry to hear that," Alex said, "although I am glad to hear that we secured a treaty with Spain."

"Secretary Madison would not leave without one," Pinckney said. "He may be small in stature, but he is the most dogged negotiator I have ever seen. King Ferdinand is a surly and childish man, and stubborn as a mule, but Madison figured him out pretty quick."

"His diplomatic skills were a big part of the reason that I retained his services," the President said. "I believe I heard the carriage outside; let us go out and meet him."

"Alex!" said Pinckney sharply, causing the President to turn and face him. "Try not to betray shock when you see him! He is not the man he was."

Hamilton's eyebrows shot up and he nodded curtly, taking his old friend by the hand for a moment. Then he turned and opened the door, heading down the front steps of the White House. A carriage was pulled up there, and the driver was carefully opening the door and lowering the wooden step-down. A black cane poked out from the shadowy interior, held by a trembling hand, and then James Madison stepped down very slowly, holding on to the door of the carriage for support.

Despite Pinckney's warning, Hamilton could not help but gasp at the sight of his friend. Madison had never been a big man—he was barely five foot four and weighed perhaps a hundred pounds after a good meal—but the figure that came slowly tottering up the White House steps was nearly skeletal, his skin yellow with jaundice, and his frail form racked by a deep cough. The Secretary of State paused to swipe his brow with a handkerchief, and Hamilton saw that there was a pale sweat exuding from his pores. He rushed forward to take his friend by the hand.

"My dear James, whatever has happened to you?" he said, trying not to let his voice register his deep alarm.

"Malaria," came the reply. "I must have been infected before I left Cuba, but the disease did not hit with full force until I arrived in Spain. I was flat on my back in bed for two weeks, but a Spanish priest gave me a tea concocted from the bark of a South American tree that is quite efficacious against the disease. I was able to get up and meet with King Ferdinand and the Junta—I tell you, Mister President, they are quite a formidable crew, the most grasping, venal monarch in Europe surrounded with a band of passionate idealists who are anxious to make their country a constitutional monarchy! Each side despising the other, yet making common cause against a common enemy. At any rate, sir, we have our treaty. There are a few minor alterations in the language and terms, but we have permanent possession of Florida and Texas, Mister President!"

With that, Madison handed a leather portfolio to Alex, who took it gratefully and clasped Madison's hand in his own.

"Well done, Mister Secretary!" he said.

Madison began coughing—deep, racking coughs that shook his tiny frame. He started to lose his balance and tip over, but Hamilton steadied him, and Pinckney came to his other side.

"Damned fever came back on the homeward voyage," said the Secretary. "I was feeling much better and putting weight back on, and then woke up covered with sweat and cold chills. I don't remember much of the last two weeks, except that I wanted to get back here. I wanted to make sure you knew that we had done it . . ."

With that, his knees crumpled under him, and Alex had to catch his friend to keep him from falling headlong.

"Help me carry him into the White House," he told Pinckney. "And you, coachman, please go fetch a doctor—quickly!"

As they carried the unconscious Secretary of State up the stairs and into the guest bedroom of the President's home, Hamilton prayed that God would spare his friend Madison.

CHAPTER THIRTY-THREE

JAMES MADISON hovered between life and death for a week, his frail body racked with fevers and intense sweats. Notified by presidential courier, Dolley Madison hastened to Washington and tended her husband constantly. She fed him warm broth when he was awake, talking softly to him, and cradling his bald head to her ample bosom when he shook with chills. Alex and Eliza relieved her periodically, when she was too exhausted to keep watch, and the President spent much of the time kneeling beside Madison's bed, praying for his friend's recovery. For the first few days he feared that his prayers were in vain, but on the sixth day Madison's fever broke and his senses returned, and for the first time Alex thought perhaps the crisis had passed.

Leaving Mrs. Madison talking softly with her husband, Alex slipped downstairs to meet with his cabinet after he convinced himself Madison was not going to suddenly relapse. He had asked Thomas Pinckney to fill in for the Secretary of State, since he had been present during the negotiations with Spain and was familiar with the treaty. Since the others had not heard much about the mission to Cadiz, the President asked Pinckney to relate the entire story to them.

"When we arrived, Secretary Madison was already in the early stages of his illness, but he insisted on being introduced to

King Ferdinand anyway, and handed over his initial proposal. Ferdinand is a dreadful character, the walking embodiment of everything Americans find loathsome about monarchy—proud, cruel, stubborn, profoundly self-centered, venal, and rather stupid. His initial response to the treaty proposal was a sneering and insolent refusal, so venomous that I was half prepared to walk out of the audience room. But Madison, fevered though he was, looked the King in the eye and spoke directly to him thus: 'Your Most Catholic Majesty would do well to carefully read the report of your own Viceroy regarding conditions in Mexico and the rest of New Spain. You should also listen closely to the account of Governor Estrada, who faced the fury of American firepower in person. It is no longer a question, Your Highness, of whether or not you are going to lose Texas and Florida, for they are already beyond your means to recover. The only question remaining is whether you will be compensated for their loss or not.' And with that he bowed, turned on his heel, and walked out. By God, gentleman, Madison may be a small man, but he has more sangfroid than any American I've ever met! By the time we got to our quarters, his strength gave out, and he collapsed from fever and hovered between life and death for days on end."

"Allow me to interrupt for a moment," Alex said. "Secretary Madison, as you know, is upstairs in the living quarters, recovering from a relapse of his illness. I grew up in a place where malaria is quite common, and my own mother died of the disease. I do believe he has now passed the crisis. If he avoids reinfection, each return bout of the illness will be less intense, and he should, in time, make a full recovery. But it will be a long recovery, if my memory serves me correctly, and he may not be able to return to his duties anytime soon. I want to discuss his future in my administration with him first, of course, but I fear that he will not be able to continue as Secretary of State."

"That would be a shame," said Pinckney, "because you'll find none better. At any rate, I think King Ferdinand, for all his bluster, did not want America's senior cabinet officer expiring in his palace, for he sent his personal physician to attend Madison and inquired daily as to the Secretary's health. In the meantime, I conferred deeply with Governor Estrada and the leading members of the Junta—the military and civilian coalition that supports the King. They cared little about Texas or Florida, to be honest, for their struggle is for Spain itself. What they were very interested in, however, was our offer of ten million dollars for those two territories. That much money could pay for a great many muskets, bayonets, cannon, and tons of powder and shot, which Spain desperately needs. I could tell every day that they were working on King Ferdinand, playing on his greed and self-interest as well as appealing to his patriotism and loyalty. By the time Secretary Madison had recovered enough to return to the audience room, the King was in a different frame of mind. He inquired most solicitously after Madison's health and held forth for some time on the dangers of malaria—something the Spanish have had three centuries to get acquainted with! Then, flanked by his advisors, he informed us that he was willing to discuss the terms of the treaty. Madison and I were invited to a large, spacious library where we went over the proposed terms point by point with the King and a group of advisors from the Junta. You could tell that they had pushed Ferdinand hard to accept the terms of the treaty, but he also had a nasty glint in his eyes as he looked at these idealistic liberals who were doing their best to return him to his throne. I'll warrant, Mister President, that when they finally succeed in restoring him to power—and I do believe that they will, the tide seems to be turning against Bonaparte in Europe— that he's going to prove an unpleasant surprise. But, to get back to the story, after Madison had gone over the entire treaty, the King asked everyone else to leave the room—myself included. Secretary Madison told me what transpired then, after the rest of us had left. That royal bandit wanted to adjust the terms so that two million of our ten-million-dollar purchase price for the territory be paid to him directly, not to the Junta or any other arm of the Spanish government!"

Hamilton threw his head back and laughed.

"Oh, avarice," he said, "you are the one great constant of human nature! Well, ten million is ten million, let the Spanish divide and spend it how they will. What about the rest of the treaty? Did we get the boundaries we asked for?"

"The entire province of Texas, from the Nueces River northward," said Pinckney. "I suspect the rest of Mexico will break away from Spain in the near future, and if we are generous and wise in our governance of Texas, some of the northern provinces may well petition to join the union when they win their independence. There is much opportunity for our country there in the future, I think. We also have possession of both East and West Florida, including the small chain of islands known as the Keys. In short, Mister President, Spain gave us everything we asked for."

"I concur," said John Jay. "The King's request about the payment for the territory is irregular, but nothing that would render the treaty invalid. I suspect the Senate will ratify it with little or no debate. It is, in the end, an offer too good to refuse."

"Thank you, gentlemen," Hamilton said. "Secretary Wolcott, we need to draw up a plan of taxation and bond sales to help cover the cost of the Florida and Texas purchase. See what you can come up with and bring it by my office in the day or two. Now, gentlemen, I have asked Speaker Clay to join us for the discussion of the next issue, and I believe I hear his step in the hallway. Secretary Tallmadge, would you be so good as to show him in?"

The tall young Kentuckian was ushered into the room moments later, bowing to the cabinet and to the President. Clay had grown into the job of Speaker, presiding over the House with dignity and competence, and he had become one of Hamilton's most valuable allies in Congress. After greeting him warmly, Alex returned to the head of the table and began to speak again.

"Gentlemen, I sought the office of Chief Magistrate because I felt compelled to do something to stop the spread of slavery in America, and to begin the process of its eventual abolition. I have worked within the Constitution, persuading rather than coercing, and have met with some limited success. But much work still must be done if our land is to ever be truly free—more work than can be done in the scope of a single four-year term. Therefore, I wish you all to be the first to know that I shall be seeking another term as President in November."

"Let me offer my congratulations, sir," said Clay, "and my promise that I will do all in my power to secure you Kentucky's electoral votes!"

"I will be delighted to support you, Mister President," said Wolcott, "but I would ask that, after the election, perhaps you find someone else to fill in at Treasury. It is grueling work, and I am ready to retire to my home and family."

"You have my support, likewise," said Tallmadge, "but I will stay on at the War Department if you so wish. I have found the work there challenging and invigorating!"

"I will be delighted to help you carry Massachusetts," said Vice President Adams, "and while I would like to continue to serve in your administration, as we discussed earlier, I should prefer it be in another capacity."

Hamilton smiled broadly as his cabinet members voiced their support. He felt truly blessed to have been served so effectively by such a talented and diverse group of men. He thanked them for their endorsements, and then continued.

"Much of what I have done regarding slavery has been in the form of legislation—the Louisiana Purchase Act, and the Quincy Amendment, and so on. However, the distressing thing about laws passed by Congress is that they can be nullified by later laws, or simply repealed if the mood of the nation changes. There is only one way to make a policy change permanent under our government, and that is to pass a constitutional amendment. Therefore, the goal of my second administration will be to amend the Constitution to state that no new slave states will be admitted to the Union from the date of its passage forward. We have seen how quickly the South has pushed forward statehood for Mississippi and Alabama after the territories west of the Mississippi were closed to them, and how hard they fought against Josiah Quincy's amendment banning slavery from all territory acquired from Spain. At some point, a candidate from the Deep South will win the presidency, and I will not see my life's work undone by Executive Order, or by a Congress cowed by slaveholders. An amendment is the only solution!"

There were general expressions of agreement around the table, but then Henry Clay spoke up again.

"I think you are right, Mister President," he said. "The only permanent solution is to amend the Constitution, but Kentucky and several states have not yet decided whether or not to emancipate the slaves within their own borders. Frankly, I would hold onto that amendment until after you have secured your reelection. Right now, the victory over Spain has made you all but invincible. But if you couple your candidacy with the success of this proposed amendment, you make the task of your reelection needlessly difficult."

"I would second that advice," said Adams.

Hamilton nodded in appreciation of their support.

"That was my own inclination as well," he said. "In two weeks, I will submit my annual report to Congress, and in the course of it I will let the nation know that I will be willing to serve again if the electors should choose me. In addition, I will announce my plan to request a moderate increase in the tariff. This will help pay for the new national territories and promote useful industries in the South, as well as improving travel between the two sections of the country through internal improvements, as recommended recently by Speaker Clay. I will also use the opportunity to continue to propound the doctrines of liberty to the nation; to challenge more states to dispense with slavery, and to urge peaceful relations with the belligerent nations of Europe. Then I will announce the Madison-Pinckney Treaty with Spain!"

"Sir, if you will, just call it Secretary Madison's Treaty," Pinckney interjected. "I was little more than a spectator to those negotiations."

"I think you were a bit more than that," Alex said with a smile, "but I also think that your version is a wonderful tribute to our Secretary of State."

"You will have the attention of the nation focused on you in a way none of your predecessors have," observed Clay. "You are our first warrior President, and you have led the country to victory. I think our Congress will be inclined to give you whatever you ask!"

"Then I must ask wisely," said Hamilton. "Now, gentlemen, I thank you for your time and your service to the country. All of us have much to do over the next two weeks, so I suggest that we get to work."

With that the meeting broke up, and Alex retired to his study to begin drawing up the speech he would give before Congress. He chose his words carefully, for while he was aware of the strength of his administration's accomplishments, he also knew that no one liked a braggart. The memory of how arrogant he had been on occasion as a younger man shamed him now; how much more he could have accomplished if he had been more generous in sharing credit with others! At the same time, he realized that it was that passionate ambition to rise up and excel in his adopted country that had driven him to reach the heights he did. Now as a mature man and seasoned political leader, Hamilton felt he'd finally found the balance he had spent much of his life searching for.

Later that evening, before going upstairs to see his family, he paused at Madison's room to check on his recovering Secretary of State. He found his friend sitting up, propped with pillows, and sipping some hot tea; obviously weak but just as obviously improving. As Hamilton stood in the doorway peering in, Madison looked up and saw him and smiled.

"Mister President!" he said. "Please, come sit with me for a while."

"It is good to see you looking so well," Alex said. "For a while I was afraid that you were not going to survive."

"For a while I wasn't too certain myself," the Secretary said. "I've never been so ill in my life! But now I do feel my strength beginning to return, although I fear it will be a long recovery."

"It will be," Alex said, "if I know anything at all about malaria. You will have occasional relapses, but they will grow weaker over time, and your strength will gradually increase to where it was before."

"That is one thing I wished to speak to you about," Madison told him. "Sir, the office of Secretary of State is a demanding one, and in my current debilitated condition I cannot serve you or the country as well as I should like. I fear I must tender my resignation, although I want you to know that I will still support you. It may be, as my strength returns, that I can serve in some less strenuous capacity in your second term. You are seeking a second term, aren't you?"

"Indeed, I am," said Alex. "I just informed the rest of the Cabinet this afternoon. You know, James, I have an idea I want to discuss with you. I was expecting that you might need to step down as Secretary of State in order to focus on your recovery and have been considering who I might appoint to serve in your place. I mentioned the possibility to Thomas Pinckney, but he is anxious to return to South Carolina as soon as possible, and has no interest in further public service."

"That is unfortunate," said Madison, "for he was an excellent diplomat and a dogged negotiator during our recent excursion to Spain."

"Well, Vice President Adams has recently expressed to me his dissatisfaction with the office he holds," said Hamilton. "He finds it tedious, boring, and not demanding enough to engage his energies. What would you think about him resigning as Vice President in order to take over the State Department?"

"An excellent choice," Madison said. "He's traveled extensively abroad, is fluent in several languages, and is an excellent negotiator. I cannot think of a more qualified choice, to be honest. The only drawback I can think of is that would leave your cabinet without a single Southerner, and given how your policies directly affect the South's way of life, the choice of Mister Adams would leave you open to criticism from that quarter."

"I thought the same thing," said Alex, "but I have a solution in mind. Assuming your recovery continues, I would like for you to be my Vice President during the next administration."

Madison's eyebrows shot up, and his pale, drawn face broke into a smile.

"Well, that is certainly not a very demanding job," he said. "I remember sympathizing with John Quincy's father when he was Vice President. A man who cherished argument as most cherish food or women, so frustrated that he could not join into the Senate's debates! Of course, Thomas enjoyed himself a good deal more when he held the office—he would preside over the opening of the Senate and then retire to Monticello for the rest of the session. You know, assuming my strength continues to return, sir, I think I could serve you and my country in that capacity. As Jefferson said, the duties of the second office in the land are easy and light, while those of the first are but a splendid misery."

"Some days more splendor, some days more misery," Hamilton said. "I am glad that you are so agreeable to this. I fear that your service to your country has cost you heavily, my friend, and I would not wish to add to your suffering."

Madison reached out, his small hands pale but no longer trembling.

"There was a time, Mister President, when I had come to regard you not only as a political rival but as malicious and dangerous man," he said. "I am proud to say that I was wrong. You, my dear sir, have built most nobly on the edifice whose foundations Washington laid."

"My life changed that day in Weehawken, my friend," said Hamilton. "I was never the nemesis that you and Jefferson made me out to be, but I did have a marked talent for making enemies. Since I was given a second chance at life and public service, I have tried to make friends of as many of them as I could. But you were the first; and have become the dearest of them all to me. I am glad to see you on the road to recovery. My only regret is that I was the one who placed you in such danger."

James Madison looked up from his sickbed, his eyes gleaming with tears.

"I serve our country foremost, sir, as do you," he said. "But I took the assignment I was given willingly, because it was the right thing to do—and because my friend asked me to."

The President of the United States embraced the Secretary of State, and then bowed out quickly, lest his own tears become evident.

THE NEXT morning Alex summoned Vice President Adams to his office after breakfast. The sturdy New Englander came quickly, his sharp features ablaze with curiosity.

"What can I do for you, Mister President?" he asked.

"I've been thinking about our last conversation," Alex said. "I assume that you still find the vice presidency to be an onerous duty?"

"Tedious would be a better description," said Adams. "There is simply nothing for me to do most of the time except sit and listen to other men argue and debate for hours on end. I enjoy a vigorous give and take as much as anyone, mind you, but politics is better enjoyed as a participant than as a spectator!"

"Secretary Madison is recovering from his illness," Hamilton said, "but he fears that he may not be equal to the demands of his position for some time to come, and so he has offered his resignation as Secretary of State. Would you be willing to resign the vice presidency to take on that position in my cabinet, and serve through my next term, assuming I am elected?"

"Secretary of State?" Adams asked, suddenly beaming. "That is a position that I have often thought I could fill quite ably. Why, yes, Mister President, I should be honored!"

"Your education and years of experience abroad certainly make you as well qualified as any man living," Hamilton said. "I will announce your nomination during my annual speech to Congress, and I'm sure the Senate will confirm you quickly and unanimously."

"But who will serve as Vice President?" Adams asked. "Will you leave the office vacant until the election?"

"There is no precedent for the second office in the land being vacated," said Alex. "I have asked Secretary Madison to announce his availability for the office in my second term. The election is nine months away; I may poll the cabinet as to whether I should appoint an interim Vice President until then."

"I think it would be wise to do so, even if there is no constitutional precedent," said Adams. "The point of there being a Vice President is so that, if the worst were to happen, there is someone ready, qualified, and able to step into the Chief Magistracy without triggering a battle for the succession."

"You're a wise man, Mister Vice President," said Hamilton, "a worthy son of a brilliant father. How is President Adams these days?"

"Spry and happy," said the younger Adams. "It is almost as if losing his bitter hostility towards you has lanced and drained some malignant boil on his soul. He writes letters to Thomas Jefferson, takes my mother for daily walks in the garden, and admonishes all of my siblings and our children on how to live virtuous lives. Young politicians come flocking to his dinner table to listen to his stories and ask his counsel. He enjoys his role as family patriarch and elder statesman greatly."

"May he enjoy it for many years to come!" Alex said with a smile. "I was never so happy as when I cracked through that shell of anger that he had built against me, and was able to reach the wounded man beneath, and try to heal or at least atone for the wounds I inflicted on him."

"What happened to you, Mister President?" Quincy Adams asked, curiously. "You were always brilliant, but you were also erratic and often vindictive. But ever since the duel, you have become a different man. Something changed you, made you wiser, happier, and more tolerant of others. I've seen you subjected to the most monstrous calumnies, and you absorb them with equanimity and good cheer, where once you would have lashed back at them with vindictive glee!"

Hamilton smiled softly, as he remembered his vision from all those years before. Was it ever real, he wondered, or had his brain conjured it to help him exorcise his personal demons? It mattered little in the end, he thought. Slavery was evil as few things in history were, and liberty was a cause worth fighting for.

"When a man sees his end before him," he said, "he takes stock of his life and his accomplishments. I was half-dead, racked with fever and chills alternately, and I saw a vision of an America torn by a civil war over slavery. I was told—by voices that I recognized and remembered well—that only I could prevent such a conflict. Whether those voices in fact belonged to the men my dream attributed them to, I do not know. But I remain convinced that they were correct. I have done all I can to block the spread of slavery, and to encourage its abolition in the North and South alike. The question that haunts me, is a simple one—will it be enough? I am not sure. That is why I feel I must seek another term."

"If any man can accomplish this, sir, it is you," Adams said. "And even if your vision was merely a fevered dream, you have served the cause of human liberty. There are far worse things to be remembered for."

"Thank you, my friend," said Hamilton, extending his hand. "Let us fight for freedom together, you and I, for the rest of this year, and for four more years beyond!"

"I will drink to that, by God!" said Adams. "A brandy, Mister President?"

"By all means," said Hamilton. "Raise a glass to freedom!"

CHAPTER THIRTY-FOUR

TWO WEEKS LATER, Alex appeared before a joint session of the United States Congress to give his annual report on the state of the union. Reviving the tradition of the President directly addressing Congress had been controversial at first, since Jefferson had abandoned it for eight years. But this would be the third time that Hamilton had reported to Congress in person, so the legislators had now grown accustomed to hearing the President speak. Speaker Clay gaveled the House and Senate to order, and then introduced the President proudly.

"Distinguished gentlemen of the House, Senators, and honored guests, it is my privilege to present to you our nation's Chief Magistrate, His Excellency the President of the United States, Alexander Hamilton!" his deep, resonant voice boomed throughout the well of the House. The galleries were packed with curious onlookers, foreign dignitaries, several elected officials from nearby states, and even a few Indian leaders from the Shawnee and Cherokee nations, who had been in Washington City to negotiate treaties with the administration. Hamilton had, with difficulty, persuaded Governor Harrison to renegotiate the Treaty of Fort Wayne from the previous year, which had seized vast tracts of land from the Shawnee, in favor of a more equitable agreement that left the tribe most of its hunting grounds.

Alex stood and courteously bowed to the applause of the Congress, waiting for the applause to die down before addressing them.

"My fellow citizens," he began, "the Constitution requires that the President shall, from time to time, report to Congress concerning that State of the Union. I have submitted my full written report to the Clerk of the House this morning, but I wanted to come and speak to you—and through you, to our great nation which you represent—about the events of the last year. A little over a year ago, the territory of the United States was violated. Spanish forces crossed our border with fire and sword, burning our towns, plundering our farms, and murdering our citizens. It is a terrible thing to lead a mighty nation into war, but it is a far worse thing to basely endure such outrages. Thus, in my role as Commander in Chief, I requested a declaration of war from you, and then ordered our soldiers and sailors into action. The loss of lives in our frontier settlements, and the death of the illustrious General Jackson, so beloved of his kinsmen in Tennessee, have now been fully avenged, and the American flag flies over the Spanish ramparts of Saint Augustine and Fort Pensacola, and the far-off cathedral of San Antonio de Valero in Texas. In short, my dear countrymen, if I had to sum up the state of our Union in a single word on this auspicious day, I would tell you that our Union is VICTORIOUS!"

The Congress erupted in applause, and Hamilton smiled and bowed. The young nation had answered the call to the colors with enthusiasm and valor, and even though Spain was not the strongest of opponents, the victory had been hardly and fairly won. The United States, in a single decade, had now expanded its borders from the Mississippi River in the west and Georgia in the south to the Rockies, the Nueces River, and the Florida Keys. In the process, lives had been lost and battles won, but America had stood tall. Hamilton recognized that the frenzied applause was not so much for him as for the nation he embodied, the young soldiers who had done the fighting, and the officers who had commanded them. He waited for the applause to die down, and then continued.

"I am also happy to report that the territories of Louisiana, Mississippi, Alabama, Illinois, and Indiana have completed or else are in the process of completing the requirements for admission to the Union, and all five should become full members of the United States of America by the end of this year. Our people are an industrious and prolific people, conquering the wilderness, building towns, clearing and plowing new farmland, and creating new families at a pace that sees our population doubling every twenty years. We welcome these new states, and to the territorial representatives in my audience I say that I look forward to greeting you this time next year as full members of our illustrious Congress! Therefore, if I may be so bold as to reduce the state of our Union into another single word on this proud day, I would say that our Union is GROWING!"

Once more the combined Congress rose in loud cheers and huzzahs for Hamilton's words, and once more he bowed deeply to his audience. When they resumed their seats, he continued.

"Three years ago, this great country, through its electors, bestowed on me its highest honor and elected me to the office of President. Since then, I have gone to work each day deeply grateful for the opportunity to lead our government, and humbly aware of the greatness of those who have led it before me—and those who may well lead it afterward. Isaac Newton once said: 'If I have seen further than other men, it is because I stood on the shoulders of giants.' I lay no claim to any superior will or intelligence over those who came before me, but if I have dared to reach higher, it is only because they have already borne our nation to the lofty promontory it now bestrides. I set out upon this journey with a destination in mind, with a cause that I was willing to fight for, and that cause was the advancement of human liberty. I have long believed that slavery was a cancer that could consume our Republic, were it not carefully contained and eventually excised. Mindful of the limits our Constitution places on the powers of the Executive, I have worked within those limits to oppose the spread of slavery and to begin the process of rolling it back from those regions where it holds sway. Through the grace of God, through the generous support of men like Secretary Madison and Presidents Adams and Jefferson, and most of all through the will of the American people, whose love of liberty has sustained me on this journey like a mighty ocean current, we have seen slavery abolished in Virginia, Maryland and Delaware; we see the legislatures of states like North Carolina, Tennessee, and Kentucky debating emancipation and the adoption of paid labor in place of slave labor. We see slavery abolished throughout the Louisiana Purchase, and from any and all territories that America might gain from our war with Spain. America is now a freer and prouder nation for those great strides, and I offer my thanks to Secretary Madison, Speaker Clay, Governor Tyler, and all the others who have helped make these steps possible."

The Congress applauded once more, not as loudly or for as long as it had before, and many of the representatives of the Deep South simply sat and glared.

"But there is much work to be done!" Hamilton continued. "Simply put, the cause of liberty is too great, and the obstacles ahead too formidable, to be overcome in the few months remaining in my term of office. Therefore, on this day, I will simply state that should the electors choose to return me to this noble seat that I have occupied for these last three years, I shall be willing to serve. If, in my first administration, it could be said that the forces of human bondage have met an implacable foe, let it be said of my next administration that they have met their master! For I will not stop fighting to roll back the tide of servitude, and to preach the gospel of liberty, and to break the chains of the bondsman, for as long as my heart still beats and there is breath in my body! And if any nation should threaten the liberties of the American people, or wish to test the mettle of our steel in defense of those liberties, they shall be met with as swift and forceful a response as those brigands were, who violated our borders and slew our citizens!"

Once more, the audience rose to their feet in thunderous applause. Hamilton beamed—even his most diehard critics from the South were on their feet, for they dared not be seen refusing to applaud America's successful defense of its southern frontier.

"Finally, my fellow countrymen, I wish to return to the issue of our recent conflict with Spain. After our forces conquered Pensacola and Saint Augustine, their commander, the illustrious General Scott, discovered that neither the Spanish governor of West Florida, nor his counterpart in the East, were aware of any orders from Madrid to carry out offensive operations against the United States. Whence then came the attack, and who ordered it? It was only after careful investigation that the General was able to determine the source of those orders, which sent bloody-handed soldiers across the border on their mission of rapine and murder—orders which originated with none other than King Joseph Bonaparte, brother of the mad French butcher Napoleon!"

This was the first time most of the men in the room, much less the nation at large, had been officially informed who was to blame for the Spanish invasion and the murder of General Jackson.

Hisses and jeers echoed around the room as the impact of Hamilton's statement was felt.

"The Bonapartes have portrayed themselves as champions of liberty, equality, and fraternity—the noble principles which the French Revolution once claimed to represent but has long since abandoned. Under the bloody rule of Napoleon, France has invaded its neighbors, raped and pillaged its way across Europe, and left death, devastation, and starvation in their wake. Napoleon showed his true stripes when he proclaimed himself Emperor—for he is as ruthless and ambitious a despot as Nero! So is it any surprise that his brother Joseph, while painting himself as a progressive and enlightened monarch planning to elevate Spain to a new age of reason, should coldly plan to invade a neutral country, murder its citizens, and then seek to cast the blame to his rival, the Bourbon monarch King Ferdinand, whom he supplanted?"

"The United States have deliberately remained neutral in Spain's civil conflict, favoring neither Bonaparte nor Bourbon, observing the principles of fairness and impartiality that were the hallmark of the immortal Washington's European policies. Desiring only peace and fair commerce with the rest of the world, we were prepared to bide our time and eventually recognize whatever side emerged from the Spanish conflict as its permanent government. Even when Spanish forces raided our frontier, I refrained from naming either government in our declaration of war, since we did not know at the time which, if either, was responsible for the heinous attacks on our soil. But after our forces carried the day in Florida, I visited the scene of the conflict myself, and there it was determined by careful investigation that Bonaparte himself had ordered the invasion, hoping that America would blame King Ferdinand and thus be more favorably inclined towards his own regime. I resolved immediately that such a blackguard could not only never be rewarded for his perfidy, but also to make overtures to King Ferdinand to bring an end to the conflict and guarantee America's future security. To achieve this, I sent Secretary of State Madison to Cuba, to speak with the Viceroy of Spain's New World Empire. When Viceroy Vinegas informed Secretary Madison that he lacked the authority to conclude any peace treaty that involved a loss of Spanish territory, our brave Madison took it on himself to travel to Cadiz to negotiate with Spain, despite the dangers created by the hostilities in Europe, and at great cost to his personal health. There he negotiated a treaty with King Ferdinand, under the terms of which the Spanish territories of Florida and Texas have been transferred to the United States! This treaty will be submitted to the Senate for ratification tomorrow, but its terms are fair and generous to both parties and will see America at peace with Spain and all of Europe, and our national territory enlarged yet again!"

This was the bombshell that Hamilton had carefully kept under wraps ever since Madison's return, and he could tell that his cabinet and Speaker Clay had kept their oaths of silence, for the effect on the room was electric. Congressmen and Senators from both parties and all regions of the country surged to their feet and roared with cheers at the news of the peace treaty. Hamilton waited, smiling, until the chamber finally settled down.

"As our nation returns to peace, I will see to it that our brave militia are allowed to return to their homes, and, as further events warrant, that our military is cut back in size to reflect the reduced threat. There will be a need for some small increases in taxes to cover the costs of the conflict, and to pay for the transfer of Spanish territory to American ownership, but my administration will do its best to insure that the tax burden is minimal and equitably administered.

"Last of all, I should note that Secretary Madison returned from his diplomatic mission gravely ill—so much so that we despaired of his life for several days. Although he is recovering now, he has informed me that he feels he can no longer discharge the duties of a senior cabinet minister and has tendered his resignation as Secretary of State. I will be issuing a formal commendation for his meritorious service above and beyond the call of duty and pray that the Congress of the United States will likewise grant its heartiest approbation to this worthy servant of our great Republic!"

The Congress applauded once more, roaring their approval of Madison and the treaty he had negotiated.

"There is little left for me to say at this point," Hamilton replied. "However, I do wish to point out that the office of Secretary of State is a vital one, which I do not wish to remain vacant for an extended period. After careful consultation with Secretary Madison, I have chosen his successor, a man of considerable diplomatic skill and experience, who will doubtless serve our country as well as his illustrious predecessor has. I have already spoken to this candidate, who has agreed to serve if confirmed by the Senate, which I do not doubt that he will be. His name is already known to you all, for he is none other than my own Vice President, John Quincy Adams!"

There was a momentary pause as the Congress processed this unexpected announcement, and then the Senators and Representatives rose once more to show their approval of the President's choice.

"Of course, this creates a vacancy in the office of Vice President, an unprecedented occurrence in our young history as a Republic," Hamilton said. "Therefore, I will seek the advice and consent of the Senate as to whether the office of Vice President should be allowed to remain vacant until next fall's election, or if I should appoint an Acting Vice President in the interim. I am sure their advice will be timely and will abide by their will in this matter. It is with great confidence in our country's future and pride in its noble past that I draw these remarks to a close. As God has favored our land with His blessings from the days of our struggle for independence until this very day, I feel no hesitation on invoking His blessing and guidance for our future course. May the richest blessings of heaven rest upon our Republic, and upon each of you. God bless the United States of America!"

With that, the President bowed and returned to his seat, and Speaker Clay waited until the thunderous applause died down to gavel the joint session of Congress to a close. Across the nation, the speech was reprinted in newspapers and broadsides, and within a few weeks had been read in every state. Approval was universal and unconditional in most of the North; Southern states were more conditional in their approbation, hailing the victory over Spain while heaping scorn on Hamilton's "obsession" with emancipation.

From the *Boston Federalist:*

THE TRIUMPH OF OUR PRESIDENT

Many New Englanders were skeptical of Alexander Hamilton's ability to lead our country when he took office; while his financial skills were acknowledged throughout the country and his tenure as a Cabinet minister helped launch our Republic, his abrasive manners and flaming pen had earned him many enemies. Many noticed the change in his personality after his near-fatal encounter with Vice President Burr; the new Hamilton seemed more gracious and conciliatory, willing to reconcile past differences and cooperate with former foes for the good of the country. Still, despite his rapprochement with his former critic and rival, President John Adams, many wondered if this leopard could truly have changed his spots so completely. Was a man as mercurial as Alexander Hamilton fit to lead our Republic, or would the pressures of the presidency cause him to revert to his old nature, and bring his fiery temper and impulsive nature back to the fore?

The naysayers have received their answer in the President's performance of his duties, and most notably in his remarkable address to Congress last week. What was displayed to the nation was a Commander in Chief of unerring military skill, a diplomat with a rare gift for negotiating from a position of strength, a champion of liberty with remarkable powers of persuasion, and a Chief Executive whose performance in office has earned him the trust and approbation of every American who values liberty over bondage, victory over defeat, and heroism over histrionics. It is therefore the opinion of this editor that no American statesman is more fit to lead our country through the next four years, and therefore we offer ALEXANDER HAMILTON our strongest endorsement. . .

From the *Charleston Courier*:

MONOMANIA ON DISPLAY:

HAMILTON'S OBSESSION WITH SLAVERY TAINTS AMERICA'S VICTORY OVER SPAIN

Whilst no one can doubt Alexander Hamilton's military prowess, as evinced by his service in the Revolution and his skilled command of our military forces in the recent Conflict with Spain, his continued obsession with destroying the livelihood of the South and promoting a false doctrine of liberty that takes into account none of the laws of Nature or of Nature's God negates these virtues.

The victory of the U.S. Army and Navy over the forces of Spain is as complete and decisive as the most ardent patriot could possibly wish, and vast tracts of fertile land now should lie open to settlers from both North and South, land to be cleared and plowed and put into productive use after centuries of being owned and governed by a corrupt and despotic monarchy that has seen them lie fallow and useless. But even as the long arm of the Executive Branch has driven our Spanish foes from Florida and Texas and annexed these territories to the United States, at the same time it has flung down the gauntlet to the men of the South who were instrumental in winning those great victories. "You are welcome here," says our President, "but the source of your prosperity and wealth is not." The rights of personal property guaranteed under the Constitution shall be respected and protected for every citizen, except for the industrious planters of the South. The Yankee factory owner may abuse his workers as he sees fit, but the Southern gentleman who tenderly cares for his slaves when sickness, old age, and debility overtake them need not apply. In barring slavery from the Louisiana Purchase, and now from the territories of Florida and Texas, President Hamilton has declared war on the South's culture and economy. It is therefore the duty of every patriotic Southerner to oppose his continuance in office with all of our energies, and to ensure that the next President of the United States understands that the Fifth Amendment's protection of property rights includes ALL property, both inanimate and conscious, and that domestic slavery—the oldest, wisest, and most just way for a superior people to manage the savage races of the world—is

allowed to expand into all Federal territories; not just for the
good of the South, but for the good of the nation, and the
advancement of all mankind."

A week after Hamilton's message to Congress, John C. Calhoun rose and asked Speaker Clay for permission to address the House. Once recognized, he rose and began to speak.

"Gentlemen of the House, it is with a heavy heart that I stand before you this day to deliver a message that must mar our joy at the great victory that our brave soldiers and sailors have recently won. For three years we have seen our country led by a man who is implacably hostile to the domestic institutions that are not only the cornerstone of the South's prosperity, but also the foundation of all civilized societies in the history of the world. Let us remember that the political resurrection of the current President began with the cold-blooded murder of the noble Vice President that he slandered. Since that dreadful day at Weehawken, Alexander Hamilton's abundant energy and boundless ambition were driven by one objective: to become the President of the United States. But he did not share his true motivation for seeking that office until he had achieved it, by manipulating the emotions of the public with a sentimental appeal to the memory of the great commander he once served under. Once in office, President Hamilton's fanatical crusade for what he calls 'liberty' became nothing less than an all-out war on the South's way of life. Speaking as a Southerner, I can say that we have entreated, we have supplicated, we have engaged in lengthy civil discourse over this matter. I have welcomed President Hamilton into my own home in Charleston and spoken with him for hours, expressing with deep honesty and candor our concerns, and it is obvious that he has stopped his ears to the voices of reason and consanguinity. The ties of the Union that bind our great Republic together cannot withstand such an assault forever. Slavery has followed the flag from the beginning of our Republic; while the institution now peculiar to the South was never more than a luxury for our northern neighbors, whose economic activities are so different from ours, for us in the South it has been the direct source of our wealth and the foundation of our social order. Hamilton's war on slavery is a war on the South, no more and no less, and has been from the beginning. I have done my best to persuade the President to cease and desist from tearing down the foundations of our society, but he will not. In the end, it is Western Civilization itself that Alexander Hamilton seeks to destroy, for every great empire that preceded us was built on the idea, not that all men are created equal—for anyone who observes mankind knows that to be an untruth!—but rather on the concept that some men are born to rule others. Whether it be the classical culture of Athens under Pericles, or Rome in its early days as a Republic, or the British in their creation of the world's most dynamic commercial empire— all are built on the concept that the lesser are born to serve the greater. President Hamilton has taken a phrase coined for political purposes during a struggle for liberty against our former colonial masters and turned it into a creed that mankind was never meant to live by!"

Southern Congressmen rose and cheered as the tall South Carolinian's deep voice echoed in the well of the House, while many northern members sat with raised eyebrows and skeptical expressions.

"History, experience of centuries, even the Word of God Almighty all bow to the necessity and logic of slavery," Calhoun continued. "Now in a single generation, Hamilton and his northern allies have decided that four thousand years of human experience are wrong, and that they and they alone are the measure of justice and compassion. Are we in the South expected to lie supinely on our backs while they strip away from us the institution that builds our homes, feeds our families, and gives meaning and dignity to our lives? Never! Therefore, in the name of God, and of the United States of America, and of the very spirit of liberty that animated our founders when they established this Republic, I call on the people of America to reject Alexander Hamilton's bid for another term of office, and to undo the damage he has done by electing a successor who will recognize the distinct and peculiar institutions of the South as being just as worthy of protection and preservation as those of the North; a man who will seek to be the President of ALL Americans instead of serving one region or section above the others. In that tone, gentlemen, I wish to announce the candidacy of Henry Middleton, the governor of my native State of South Carolina, for presidency of the United States! Let us pull back from the precipice of disunion that King Alexander has pushed us towards and restore the right and proper relations of master and slave, north and south, east and west!"

And so the presidential election campaign of 1812 began.

CHAPTER THIRTY-FIVE

ALEXANDER HAMILTON entered the presidential race of 1812 in a remarkably favorable position, but he knew it was a long road to the election in November. The odds were in his favor in February, but would they remain so through the next fall? That was the question he contemplated in the weeks after his address to Congress.

The American political process was changing, rapidly transforming the original system that Madison and the other Framers had envisioned when they created the Electoral College. How naïve they had been, he thought, to believe that political parties would never take root in America! The very men who created a system that did not allow for such parties had gone on to create the first two factions themselves. First the Federalists and the Republicans, now the Federal Republicans and the Democratic Whigs; he wondered if the two current parties would endure, or would they also transform, change, and be replaced over time?

But of more immediate concern to Alex was the simple problem of securing enough electoral votes to win the second term that he craved. It would be so much simpler, he thought, if he could just go out and make his case to the people in person, explaining to the masses why they should support him, just as he had openly campaigned in New York twenty-four years earlier on behalf of the new Constitution. But if he were to do such a thing, he knew the result would be his almost certain defeat. "The office should seek the man, not the man the office," was a creed Americans still believed in. Alex had taken a big enough risk simply letting the people know he would serve if the electors chose him a second time; anything more would mark him with the stigma of "ambition" that was the kiss of death in American politics.

Hamilton shook his head as he undressed that night, reflecting on the hypocrisy that the system forced upon all men who strove to win the nation's highest office. Tradition required that he and Middleton maintain a public air of complete indifference, never commenting on the campaign being waged on their behalves, or even responding directly to the flood of invective that would be hurled at them. One reason that Aaron Burr had failed to secure the presidency in the forty-two ballots the House had taken after he and Jefferson had tied the electoral vote was the fact that he had openly gone out and canvassed for votes during the campaign. A man who so brazenly put himself forward was not to be trusted; such was the conventional wisdom of the day—and in Burr's case, Hamilton believed that the convention was right.

But was it right about him? Was he just another self-promoting politician, seeking the presidency from raw ambition? Alex had spent hours in prayer, seeking the guidance of the Almighty, and searching the depths of his soul. It was true, he acknowledged, that he enjoyed being the President of the young republic. All his life he had longed to rise up and make his mark on history, and to be remembered after his death as a man whose life, in the grand scheme of things, had mattered. But there was more to his quest than that; he still believed in the fundamental truth of his vision those many years ago. If anything, his conviction had been strengthened when he saw the fanaticism with which Calhoun and others responded to any perceived threat to slavery. Holding human beings in bondage, he had come to realize, was a potent opiate that poisoned the mind of man. The longer white Southerners held their bondsmen in chains, the more tightly those chains wound around their own necks as well. They were just as much slaves to slavery as were the wretched Negroes who toiled in their fields under the threat of the lash.

It was to break those chains that Hamilton sought to remain in power; to free men, both white and black, from a system that warped souls and ruined lives. He had no difficulty believing that in another generation or two, Southerners would willingly resort to fire and blood to maintain their system, blind to how venomous it was. Saving the nation from civil war was a noble goal, an unselfish one, but more than anything, he wanted to restore to America the spirit of liberty that it had kindled in 1776. To do that, he simply needed four more years in office.

The calculus of the Electoral College was simple enough. With Alabama and Illinois poised to enter the Union before the election that fall, there would be some two hundred and twenty-seven electoral votes available. Hamilton needed to secure a hundred and fourteen of those in order to win the election. But a razor-thin margin was not enough to claim a mandate from the people; Alex wanted a win big enough and convincing enough that Congress would be forced to take his wishes seriously, as a genuine tribune of the people. The larger his margin of victory, the more support he could gain for his Thirteenth Amendment when he announced it in his second inaugural address.

A week after Calhoun's fiery speech announcing the candidacy of Henry Middleton, Alex summoned five of his closest political allies to the Executive Mansion for dinner. Madison, his health returning more every day, attended, as did Speaker Henry Clay. The newly minted Secretary of State, John Quincy Adams, was also there, along with Governor Dewitt Clinton of New York. The son of Hamilton's longtime rival George Clinton, whose health was rapidly failing, the Governor had made his peace with the President after the 1808 election and had become a faithful ally over the years of Hamilton's first administration. In addition, Hamilton's old friend from the earliest days of the Revolution, Hercules Mulligan, attended the dinner. The six men enjoyed a repast of clam chowder, fried cod, and slow-roasted ham with potatoes and onions before beginning their strategy session.

"Gentlemen, I have asked you here because you have shown yourselves to be the friends and allies of this administration," Hamilton said. "I have the utmost confidence in your discretion and loyalty. As you know, the presidential electors will be making their choice this fall, and I have indicated my willingness to serve should that choice fall on me."

"Who else would they choose?" snorted Clinton derisively. "That South Carolina slave driver Middleton? You, sir, are the hero of the hour. Even my father, who was your obdurate foe for so many years, has come to recognize your political genius. New York's votes are yours; my state is proud to hail you as its adopted son!"

Hamilton bowed, moved deeply by the Governor's words.

"I do not doubt," he said, "that I shall be able to secure enough votes, with the help of you gentlemen and other allies not present, to win another term. But I want you all to understand, I do not seek this term for myself. My paramount object in my second administration, should Providence grant me one, is to place slavery in America on an irrevocable course to ultimate extinction. To achieve this goal, dearer to me than life itself, I need support from all sections of the country—east, west, north, and at least in part from the south as well. If I am to succeed in ending human bondage in the United States, I must bury Middleton in an avalanche of electoral and popular votes, so that none can doubt that I speak with the voice of the whole country!"

"So you seek not just victory, but a landslide!" Madison said. "That is a more difficult task, but I can think of no President who has been in a better position to achieve it. I have served by your side these four years now, and I have come to share your vision, Mister President. Although I am far from fully recovered, my strength returns to me a little bit each day. I think that I can deliver Virginia's electoral votes to you. The program of emancipation has been a notable success there, and many of my planter friends report crop yields have nearly doubled since they began paying their workers."

"Excellent!" said Hamilton. He unrolled a map of the United States on the table and called for a quill and pen. "Look here, gentlemen. There are going to be nineteen states by summer, providing a total of two hundred and twenty-seven electoral votes. New York has twenty-nine of those, Virginia and Pennsylvania twenty-five each. Massachusetts comes next with twenty-two, North Carolina fifteen, Kentucky twelve, Tennessee, South Carolina, and Maryland eleven each. Connecticut has nine, and New Jersey, New Hampshire, Vermont, Georgia, and Tennessee claim eight each. Louisiana currently has only three votes, and the new state of Alabama may have enough people to claim four. That leaves Ohio with seven, Delaware and Rhode Island with four each, and Illinois appears ready to lay claim to six."

"How many of those do you think you will need for this election to qualify as—what did you call it? A landslide?" Henry Clay asked.

"A good question," Hamilton said. "Let's start with the states where I don't have a chance and subtract them from the total. South Carolina, of course, will vote for Middleton, and I imagine Georgia will, too. The new state of Alabama has been rushed into statehood for the sole purpose of voting against me. Many Louisiana planters resented the Louisiana Purchase Act, and I imagine those three votes are lost as well. That gives us a total of twenty-six electors that will certainly go for Governor Middleton. How many of the remaining two hundred and one am I likely to secure, gentlemen? You represent nearly every section of the country, so please be candid. I summoned you here to have the benefit of your collective wisdom and experience."

"Massachusetts is solidly in your corner," said Secretary Adams. "My father's influence in the state is still considerable, and the fact that you took the time to come to him and seek his forgiveness and friendship made a deep impression on many. Not to mention he is now full of praises for your administration!"

"I am deeply grateful for his support," Alex said. "What about the rest of New England? Any dangers of defection?"

"None that I am aware of," said Adams. "Your administration has been good for trade, your shipbuilding program has enriched our seaports, and most New Englanders have become quite hostile to slavery—perhaps in a belated attempt to atone for our region's role in the slave trade? At any rate, I think all the New England states will be in your corner."

"That is fifty-one electoral votes," said Hamilton. "With New York and Virginia, that brings my count to one hundred and five. Secretary Clay, what of Kentucky? Do you think my prospects are good there?"

"Many Kentuckians are skeptical of your war on slavery, Mister President, but that doesn't alter the fact that they like you. The victory over Spain, in which our troops played a role, enhances your popularity. My own voice does carry some weight as well, and I think I can persuade our governor to take your side," Clay explained. "I do think Kentucky will be close, but in the end, I believe you will win there."

"Well, I hope you are right," Alex said. "That would put us at a hundred and seventeen."

"I have some good friends in New Jersey," said Hercules Mulligan. "I think you can chalk that state up in your column as well. Folks are mighty fond of you in those parts!"

"Eight more electors!" Hamilton said. "Excellent. Now, what about Pennsylvania? I have always felt that I should have included someone from Philadelphia in my cabinet, but it just did not work out for me to do so."

"Governor Snyder is a member of the Moravian Church," said Adams, "and an inveterate foe of slavery. Indeed, anti-slavery sentiment runs strong in the state, especially among the Quaker population."

"And among the non-Quakers, the war with Spain was quite popular," Clay interjected. "You have strong support on two different fronts in Pennsylvania, it seems. That should give you another twenty-five electors."

So they went down the list, assessing the administration's chances in each of the remaining states, while Alex carefully jotted down their results in three columns—the electors he felt he could count on, the ones he was uncertain of, and the ones that would definitely be supporting Middleton. He frankly didn't share the optimism of his advisors regarding some states, but still, his lead was impressive. Still, there were sixty electors that he was reasonably sure might go the other way—seventy, if Clay's prediction about Kentucky proved overly optimistic. That was certainly not enough to deny him the election, but enough to give solid voice to his opposition.

But if he could peel away two or three of those states, he would have a lead almost as commanding as Jefferson's impressive 1804 win over Charles Pinckney. While the Deep South was lost to him, he felt that Maryland, North Carolina, and Tennessee might be within reach.

One thing Alex had come to realize over the years was that American citizens loved the personal approach. He recalled a story from Washington's presidency, when a French visitor to New York had been astonished to see the President walking down the street without any kind of uniformed escort or retainers, only the burly form of Henry Knox, who was deep in conversation with him. The Frenchman had looked at the barber who was cutting his hair and said:

"Is that not your President?" The barber had replied in the affirmative, and the astonished foreigner asked: "Where are his bodyguards?"

The barber pointed at his own burly chest and said: "You're looking at one of them!"

American Presidents walked freely among their citizens, and Washington had made a point of visiting every one of the thirteen states during his first term. As loath as Hamilton was to embark on yet another marathon journey, he thought that a swing through the nation—especially through the upper South and those states that hung in the balance—might be an excellent way to garner support for the November elections.

He would not leave Eliza behind again, he decided, unless she demanded it. So the next evening, after supper, he broached the idea of a grand tour of the country to her.

"I am not averse to travel, Alexander, but what of the children? Phil is only ten, Lizzie thirteen, and Will is fifteen! The trip would take months, and I do not want to leave them for so long," his wife said.

"Then let's bring them!" he replied. "Let's show them this grand country of ours and give them an experience they will never forget! We can make much of the journey by sea, or else by traveling up the Hudson. I'll see if Mr. Fulton would be interested in letting us use his steamboat again—it's a remarkable vessel, my dear, utterly independent of wind and current!"

"Do you really think this will help you win reelection?" she asked.

"I think it will help me a great deal," he said. "I have so much work left to do, my dear, that I cannot complete in the time I have left. I know that this job has been hard on you and on the children, but I do not want to leave you for so long again, and would be most grateful for your comfort and company on such a long sojourn."

Eliza sighed and kissed her husband. "I always knew being married to you would fill my life with challenges," she said. "But it has also been a life of grand adventure! I would be lying if I said that I do not enjoy being the First Lady of the land, although I'd be just as happy to be the wife of a New York lawyer, as long as his name was Alexander Hamilton!"

"Shall we summon the children and tell them?" the President asked her.

"We can tell them tomorrow," she said. "Right now, I do not wish to be mother, or First Lady, or anything other than a much-loved wife!"

"And how much do you want to be loved?" Alex asked with a sly smile.

She smiled back, and in that smile the years fell away and Alex once more saw the young woman who had dazzled his heart at a winter ball so long ago, during the height of the Revolution.

"As much as you still can, at your age!" she shot back.

"My age, my dear, is always twenty-five when I am alone with you," he said—and for the rest of the evening, that was how old he felt.

THE HAMILTONS set out one month later, traveling down the Potomac and thence into the Chesapeake on board the USS *Washington*. The children were fascinated with the big paddlewheel that drove the vessel downstream, and the presidential party made good time to Baltimore, where the governor of Maryland, Levin Winder, had invited the President to speak to the state legislature.

Maryland had been the second slave state to adopt Hamilton's emancipation plan—their economy was similar to Virginia's, once based on tobacco but now primarily on other crops, as well as shipping and manufacturing. Winder, an old Federalist and veteran of the Revolution, was a great admirer of Hamilton, and an early convert to the program of emancipation. So many Marylanders crowded into the capital city to hear the President speak that Winder decided to move the entire event to the capitol building's south lawn, where Hamilton spoke from a raised dais to the State Assembly and several thousand spectators.

He discussed the importance of liberty as a defining element of America's character, and how he had always felt that the sentiments of the Declaration, so noble in expression, fell short in practice. He held forth on justice, but also praised the practical aspects of emancipation and the benefit of having workers who stood to gain something from their labor. By now he had polished and honed his anti-slavery speeches to glistening oratorical perfection, and the crowd loudly cheered when he was done. He never once mentioned the presidential election, or Governor Middleton, his opponent—but by painting such a clear picture of the greatest issue of his presidency, he also painted a clear picture of the choice the state's electors would be facing. After spending a single night as the guests of Governor Winder, Hamilton and his family returned to the *Washington* and headed northward to New Jersey, where Hamilton was scheduled to speak in Newark, and thence to his beloved New York, where the state's dignitaries were planning a thunderous welcome for the warrior-president's victory lap around America.

Governor Middleton, on the other hand, found excuses to visit several neighboring states, where he gave passionate speeches in defense of the South's culture and institutions, and attacking the President's emancipation policy as a threat to both. However, he was bound by the same traditions as Hamilton, and could not publicly pronounce himself as a candidate to replace the President, whose military accomplishments were still popular in the South, even if his anti-slavery stance was not.

John C. Calhoun, however, was not bound by that tradition, and the energetic South Carolinian embarked on a marathon journey of his own, traversing the entire South and many of the border states as well. He ventured as far north as Ohio and Illinois to carry his own message of bluster and warning that a second term for Hamilton was a grave threat to the Union.

"Our President," he declaimed in a speech in Cincinnati which was widely covered in northern newspapers, "belongs to a growing segment of the population in the North which regards the South as being morally as well as geographically beneath them. They refuse to understand that slavery is the cornerstone of our economy, the central pillar of Southern commerce, and a vital part of our social order. So thoroughly is slavery interwoven into the society of the South that to destroy it is to destroy us as Southerners! Already, our domestic institutions have been barred from vast new territories uniquely suited to them. A Southern gentleman who wishes to settle across the Mississippi cannot take his work force with him, nor can a planter from Georgia purchase farmland in Florida unless he is willing to abandon the key to prosperity there."

The fiery young Congressman, now seeking a seat in the Senate, fixed his audience with a piercing stare as he continued. His impressive mane of dark brown hair was swept back in a striking pompadour, his gestures were theatrical and yet seemed authentic, and his rich baritone carried a note of pleading undercut with a faint tone of warning.

"Gentlemen of the South stood side by side with our brothers from the North against the British thirty-five years ago," he said. "We proclaimed our independence together, and we won it together, against mighty odds, fighting the most powerful empire on earth. The heroes of Valley Forge, of Saratoga and Yorktown, of Trenton and Princeton, came from all over America to offer up—and sometimes shed—their life's blood in the name of our national freedom. But just as this nation rose up against the British when 'a long train of abuses and usurpations evinced a design to reduce us under absolute despotism,' so must I warn you that the people of the South will not suffer forever under the tyranny that the man we aptly name 'King Alexander' seeks to impose on us. The rights of property are sacred, protected by the very Constitution our President once forcefully argued for. Why now does he seek to supplant it? Why should his false concept of 'liberty and equality' be allowed to tear up the young and delicate plant of our Union whilst its roots are still tender and easily injured? I beseech you, men of the North, suffer us not to be betrayed with a Judas kiss by this false champion of liberty. He cannot, with the stroke of a pen, make equal what God Himself has made unequal. But what he can do is drive the people of the South one long step closer to fratricidal conflict.

"Therefore, I pray you men of Ohio will join me in rejecting President Hamilton's bid for a second term of office this fall, and elect a man who will undo the damage Hamilton has done to our Union, a man who will draw north, south, east, and west together in a sacred compact that respects the liberty of equals, but protects the property of all men, in all sections of the country. Vote for Henry Middleton, my friends, if you wish to preserve the domestic tranquility that this current administration has so gravely threatened!"

Such was the force of the South Carolinian's oratory that the audience applauded when he was done, even if few in the crowd agreed with him. A month later Hamilton himself visited the same city, and his speech in favor of emancipation pointed out the ridiculousness of Calhoun's main thesis, that the South could not survive and prosper without slavery by citing the increased profitability of virtually every plantation that had adopted his system of paid labor. By now Hamilton had fallen into a familiar routine of travel punctuated by a few consecutive days of rest after a week on the road, and his family had adjusted to the schedule quite well. His speeches were always well-received, but it was the President himself, and his lovely family, that the people flocked to see. Everywhere he went, parades were held, bands played, and noteworthy citizens lined up to shake his hand, share the platform with him, and most of all, they vied to host him and his family in their homes.

It took almost six months, but in the end Hamilton managed to visit every state except for South Carolina and Georgia, where he had already been last fall, and Louisiana, which was so far removed from the rest of the country that he hesitated to take his family on so long a trek. It was a bone-weary President who returned to New York in October, determined to enjoy a month in his hometown before the election finally took place.

Calhoun wound up visiting eleven states himself, but the further he got from the South, the less credence people gave to his speeches. In Philadelphia, he was jeered and heckled by the crowd when he denounced as "pernicious" the Declaration's statement that "all men are created equal." But the dogged spokesman for the slave states did not give up, and by the time he returned to South Carolina, a week after the Hamiltons arrived in New York, he was resigned to the outcome of the election.

But not even Calhoun could have predicted just how sweeping Hamilton's victory turned out to be. In the end, Middleton carried only South Carolina, Georgia, Alabama, and Louisiana outright—a total of twenty-six electoral votes. Tennessee and North Carolina were so close that the electors there split their votes, giving eleven to Middleton and twelve to Hamilton. The President was reelected by a margin of one hundred and ninety to thirty-seven—a remarkable achievement for a man whose political career had been considered dead beyond all hope of resurrection a decade before. James Madison was unanimously chosen to be Hamilton's Vice President for the next four years; no one else had even sought the office once his candidacy was announced.

Hamilton and his family spent the days after the election at home in New York, savoring the moments together as the votes from one state after another were reported. It took almost two weeks for the final tally to reach New York City, but when the result was announced, the whole city erupted in celebration of the victory. The orphan teenager from the Caribbean, once derided as a bastard and a monarchist, was now the most celebrated resident of the largest city in America, as well as a two-term President.

Alex spend the entire evening on the balcony with his family, waving to well-wishers as they crowded the streets in front of Hamilton's uptown home, and watching the spectacular fireworks show the city fathers had arranged in the President's honor. Finally, at midnight, Hamilton put his weary children to bed, kissed Eliza goodnight, and slipped downstairs to begin working on his second inaugural address.

CHAPTER THIRTY-SIX

IT WAS MARCH 4, 1813—Inauguration Day! Spring had come early to Washington, DC; a warm, gentle rain had washed the streets of the city, melting away the last ragged remnants of a late February snowstorm. Alexander Hamilton had risen early and spent almost a solid hour in prayer, his mood both hopeful and solemn. After being sworn in, he planned to announce the major initiative of his second term: a thirteenth amendment to the U.S. Constitution that would forbid the entry of any new slave states into the Union after the date of its ratification. He knew—or at least, hoped—that if he could succeed in persuading the states to ratify this amendment, his goal would be accomplished. Even if the remaining slave states attempted to launch a rebellion, they were now too few to unleash the kind of holocaust he had seen in his vision. Still, he prayed, asking God to give him words that would fire the conscience of the nation.

Alex had always believed in God, a faith he learned at his mother's knee from early childhood. The sanctimonious planters on Nevis had scorned Rachel Faucett as a scarlet woman for leaving her first husband, an abusive lout, and moving in with James Hamilton, Alex's father. She was never the whore that Hamilton's enemies claimed; it was not her fault that Johann Lavien, her former spouse, refused to grant her a divorce. Strong-willed, intelligent, and beautiful, she refused to live without love because Lavien was a selfish ass who would not release her from her vows. But despite the disdain of many congregants, she had raised her two boys in the church and prayed with them every night, encouraging them to read the Scriptures and seek God in their lives. Fortunately for Alex, the rector of the local church had been a kind and understanding man who refused to blame the boys for the circumstances of their birth. It was through the eyes of this reformed Dutch clergyman that Alex had first felt the love of God shine through.

Since those days, Hamilton's faith had never left him, although he knew he had not always lived up to what he believed. But ever since losing Philip on that fateful day twelve years before, he had spent more time in prayer, more time in the Word, and had felt God's hand moving more powerfully in his life than ever before. He had been spared at that dreadful moment in Weehawken when, by all rights, he should have died at Burr's hand. He had been granted a vision that filled him with purpose and conviction, and he had acted on it. Hamilton was convinced he had been carried to the place he currently occupied by the hand of the Almighty, and he was desperate to make the most of his high office; to prevent, if he could, the future bloodbath his vision had shown him.

He was full of hope, however, on this morning of his inauguration. One thing that buoyed his spirits was the news from North Carolina—the voters in that state had approved emancipation by a substantial margin. Kentucky and Tennessee were expected to vote on the issue in the next year or so; he prayed that they, too, would choose liberty over bondage. Across the nation, except for the Deep South, newspaper editorials had reacted favorably to his reelection and most applauded his stand against slavery, at least in principle.

The eyes of the nation would be focused on Washington City on this fine day, and Hamilton had labored long and hard on his address. It was short, heartfelt, and to the point. He planned to ask Congress to meet in a special session the week following his inauguration to debate the Thirteenth Amendment and vote on sending it out to the states for ratification. He knew some would criticize this haste, but Alex had learned long ago that there was a time to wait and a time to move. He felt that on this issue he had to strike while the iron was hot, while the nation was still united behind him.

He neatly tied his cravat and combed his thinning hair. Given that this was his second inaugural, there was not nearly as much pomp and celebration as had accompanied his surprising win over Madison four years before. He would go to breakfast with the members of the House and Senate and thence to the Capitol steps, where a special platform had been erected. Several thousand people were in attendance, many of them were already streaming towards the long green hillside below the Capitol so they could have a good view of the President being sworn in.

"You look dapper, my dear," Eliza's voice sounded from the bedroom door.

Alex turned and looked at his bride, who was wearing a lovely blue dress with silver trim and a dark green sash that stood out sharply without clashing. She was winter and spring, frost with the promise of warmth, reserve and passion, all woven into one striking combination. The small streaks of gray in her hair and the laugh lines around her eyes and mouth enhanced her beauty rather than detracting from it, adding wisdom and maturity to her natural allure.

"You are ravishing, my love," he said, and she was. In the joy of the moment, and in her fierce pride in her husband's accomplishments, the cares and worries of the years had fallen away, and Eliza Schuyler Hamilton was once again the girl who had won his heart so many years ago. He crossed the room and pressed his lips to hers.

"The greatest accomplishment of my life is being loved by you," he said, and meant every word.

"That is too much, Alex," she replied. "You have led a campaign that has liberated hundreds of thousands of people and woken the conscience of a nation. How can the affections of one woman compare to that?"

"Without you, my love, I would never have found the courage and will to do the things I did," he said. "You have believed in me and stood by me through good and ill, thick and thin, even when I did not deserve it."

"No man is perfect, Alex," she said. "But you are perfect for me. I never quit loving you, even at my angriest, and I am proud to be your wife."

Alex had finished his prayers, but even as he held Eliza in his arms, he closed his eyes and thanked God that this woman found him worth loving. Then he stepped back, smiled brightly, and offered her his arm. Together the President and First Lady left the White House and climbed into the carriage that would take them to the Capitol.

The United States Congress had grown by a few members since Alex took office four years ago, with the addition of Alabama and Illinois to the Union. Many new House members and a few new Senators had been elected that fall, most of them from Alex's Federal Republican party—with one noted exception. John C. Calhoun had been elected to the Senate by the South Carolina state legislature, no doubt as a reward for his quixotic crusade against Hamilton's reelection. As Alex and Eliza entered the grand dining room where the Congress was having breakfast, he saw the young Southerner sitting with several other Senators from the Deep South.

"Members of the United States Congress, please welcome the President and First Lady of the United States!" the House master-at-arms announced, and the assembled Congressmen stood and applauded. Many of them had their wives with them for this celebratory lunch, and after Alex had escorted Eliza to their seats at the head table, he moved around the room, greeting the new members by name and shaking hands with all.

"Senator Calhoun," he said when he got to the southerners' table, "congratulations on your election, sir. I am sure the people of South Carolina will be well served."

Calhoun rose, his penetrating gaze fixed on Hamilton's violet-blue eyes. His handshake was firm and manly, but Alex could feel a slight tremble, as if a powerful emotion was barely held in check by the young politician.

"Thank you, Mister President. I cannot pretend to be happy with the outcome of the election, but it is obvious that you are the choice of the people of the nation. We in the South will have to find a way to live with that—but I pray you, sir, do not make it too difficult for us!" he said.

"I regret, Senator, that we have been unable to find common ground," Alex replied, "But even as you must obey the mandate of your state, so am I bound by the will of the American people, and by the dictates of my conscience. What I do, I do because I must."

"Likewise, Mister President," said Calhoun. "As the great Martin Luther said, 'it is dangerous indeed to force a man to go against his conscience.' This is your day, Mister President, and I hope you enjoy it to the fullest."

Hamilton walked away, greeting other members of Congress as he passed from table to table, but Calhoun's words lingered in his mind as he returned to his table and rejoined Eliza and Vice President Madison. Before long, the meal was done, and Alex prepared to mount the Capitol steps to wait in the Senate Chamber until it was time for his inaugural ceremony to begin. Eliza went on out to the reviewing platform to take her seat.

At the stroke of noon, the doors to the Senate Building opened wide, and Alex followed Vice President-elect Madison to the platform. As tradition dictated, Madison was sworn in first, and then gave a short address, thanking the people of the nation for their trust in him, and offering his support to the President in his second administration. There was a surge of applause when he was done; Madison had become a hero to the people for his role in ending the Spanish war, and for his miraculous recovery from a near-fatal bout of malaria.

Alex rose next, and took his place before Chief Justice John Marshall, who was a picture of judicial rectitude in his flowing black robes. Hamilton placed his hand on the Bible—the same one Washington had been sworn in on—and said the words that formalized his acceptance of the electors' choice:

"I, Alexander Hamilton, do solemnly swear that I will faithfully execute the office of President of the United States, and will, to the best of my ability, preserve, protect, and defend the Constitution of the United States, so help me God."

Then he bent and pressed his lips to the well-worn leather cover of the Scriptures and rose to face the crowd. Senators, Congressmen, dignitaries, and spectators rose to their feet in a standing ovation to show their respect and approval of America's President. Hamilton bowed to the crowd, and they gradually cease applauding and resumed their seats. Alex removed the speech he had written and spread it before him but did not look down—he'd committed the words to memory as he crafted them.

"My fellow Americans, Senators, Congressmen, judges, and all of you who have gathered here today to witness me taking this oath, I would first offer my heartiest thanks to this divinely favored nation. You took an orphaned immigrant to your bosom and lifted him up, entrusted him to defend your rights and liberties, and have now, for the second time, conferred on him the highest office in the land. As I prepare once again to assume the duties of the presidency of the United States, I do so with the greatest of humility, recognizing the service of those who have gone before, and the hopes that will be pinned on those who follow after me. May I always prove worthy of this great trust, and may I redeem it with the purity of my intentions and the accomplishments of my administration."

He looked down at the front row, where Thomas Jefferson was sitting. John Adams had begged off, saying that the trip to Washington City was too long and arduous for one of his advanced years, but John Quincy Adams, Secretary of State, sat beside Jefferson in a show of support from the second President's family. Hamilton smiled at them and continued his speech.

"Over the last four years, the focus of my administration has been to fight for the liberty of the oppressed, and especially to encourage the emancipation of those held in unjust bondage. I have heard many arguments in favor of slavery from my Southern opponents, but none have been so effective as the single greatest argument against it: that all across the breadth of this great land, not one free man has ever volunteered to become a slave. All the endless statements about the benevolence of the South's domestic institution founder upon that rock. So now I say again, if I had said before—if no free man would voluntarily be a slave, then how can any free man justify owning slaves?"

Many in the crowd applauded this sentiment, even though Calhoun and the rest of the delegation from the cotton states simply sat and shook their heads.

"As I have preached the gospel of liberty from this magnificent pulpit to which the people have elected me, much of the nation has come into agreement with me. Virginia, Maryland, Delaware, and now North Carolina have voted to emancipate their slaves; Tennessee and Kentucky will soon be voting on the issue as well. I have also made it my policy to bar slavery from the Federal Territories—from all of the Louisiana Purchase, and most recently from Texas and Florida. I am proud to say that America is a freer nation now than it was when I took office four years ago, and my goal is to make it freer still, that we may truly rise up and live out the words of President Jefferson's immortal declaration, that ALL men are entitled by their Creator to life, LIBERTY, and the pursuit of happiness!"

Alex had to pause as the crowd rose to its feet again to applaud his words. He swallowed hard and mouthed a silent prayer; the easy words were done. Now it was time to lay out his bold proposal and pray that the people would approve it.

"But as I look back at the accomplishments of my first administration, and forward to what I hope to accomplish in the next, I am increasingly aware that no President serves forever. I will honor the example set by the great Washington and step down when this term is done, and another will follow me here. While I hope that my successors will continue and build on the work of emancipation that I have begun, I also recognize that not all Presidents are created equal; the mood of the country can change. My greatest fear is that, at some point in the future, I might be followed by one who does not share my convictions about human freedom, and that the liberties I have fought so hard to advance might be threatened."

He ran his eyes across the audience and saw that Calhoun had fixed him with a fiery gaze, as if anticipating what Alex was about to say.

"But there is one way, one legal and constitutional way, to make policy permanent in this country, and that is to add an amendment to the United States Constitution. That is what I am asking the people of America to do, right now, at the beginning of my second administration. We do not lightly tinker with our Constitution in America, recognizing it as a work of inspired genius that needs little improvement. But if we are to continue as a nation of free men and women, then let us commit to freedom in a way that leaves future generations no choice but to bow to the will of the people. The text of my proposed Thirteenth Amendment is short and simple: 'Neither slavery nor involuntary servitude, save as a penalty for felony crimes of which the accused shall have been duly convicted, shall be established or allowed in any territory or state admitted to the Union and its commonwealth after the ratification of this amendment.' No new slave territories, no new slave states! That has been the policy of my administration, and I would see it become the law of the land forevermore. I will keep my promise to the gentlemen of the South—no outside force shall interfere with slavery in the states where it is already established. But the days of extending the kingdom of bondage in America, so antithetical to the founding principles of our nation, will be done when this amendment is passed. I am summoning the Congress of the United States into a special session next week to take up this proposal, and should it meet the requisite support of a two thirds majority in each house, then it shall be sent to the states for ratification by this summer."

The impact of Hamilton's words rippled across the crowd like a wave. Men turned and began whispering to their neighbors; Calhoun rose to his feet and balled his fists in fury, fixing Alex with a glare of sheer hatred. But many legislators rose to their feet and cheered, and gradually the buzz of disbelief and shock transformed into another ovation, albeit not a universal one. It was nearly five minutes before the crowd fell silent again. Finally, Hamilton was able to make himself heard.

"This is a bold step, my fellow Americans. The eyes of future generations will look back at this moment as the time when Americans bravely confronted their future and made a choice between liberty and bondage, between democracy and despotism. My fellow countrymen, we cannot escape history. The choice we make here, in our nation's capital, over these next few weeks, will light our generation for good or ill in the eyes of the world, and in the minds of our children and their children's children. I urge you, my dear friends, to choose the more difficult path, the challenging, narrow way that leads our country into the sunlit uplands of liberty, and leaves behind us the dark valley of bondage, slavery, and wrong that have afflicted our land ever since the first slave ship offloaded its cargo of misery at Jamestown two hundred years ago. Let us leave to our posterity a legacy of liberty; so that they may rise up and call us blessed! Now, with confidence in the blessings of the Almighty, and faith in the wisdom of the American people, let us set forth to do their work!"

Hamilton bowed deeply, and the crowd rose to its feet and applauded him once more. He turned and took Eliza by the arm, and followed by the Madisons and Chief Justice Marshall, they walked back up the steps and into the Capitol.

ALEX HAD printed up dozens of copies of his speech and dispatched them from Washington via post riders that very afternoon. Within a week, newspapers all over the country had printed Hamilton's address, and editors had added their thoughts and opinions to the mix. The President hoped that the people would be with him, but he had already decided to capitalize on his impressive victory the previous fall by pushing Congress to act now, before the opposition could recover its wits and muster its forces.

Henry Clay had read an advanced copy of Hamilton's speech, and when the House was gaveled into session the following Wednesday, he immediately declared them dissolved into a Committee of the Whole to debate and vote on the proposed amendment. A fiery young South Carolina planter named Roger Brooks had been elected to fill Calhoun's vacated seat, and he took the lead in opposing the amendment, while another congressional freshman, Daniel Webster of New Hampshire, emerged as one of its strongest supporters.

"King Alexander is not content to reduce the South under absolute despotism during his own benighted term of office," declaimed Brooks in his opening remarks. "He now seeks to make sure that his tyranny will continue long after his term is ended, and he returns to whatever New York den of iniquity that spawned him! He would see the pillar of the South's prosperity so weakened that it topples from lack of support, to see Southern planters impoverished and destitute any time they attempt to leave their native states and seek prosperity elsewhere. Make no mistake, my friends, this amendment is nothing less than a death-blow, not just to the fortunes of the South, but to the future of our Union itself!"

Webster, a powerfully built young man of some thirty years, demanded the floor to respond to Brooks's screed.

"How is it," he demanded, "that you South Carolinians have come to define human liberty as holding the other half of humanity in chains? Why must you deny freedom to others in order to be sure of your own? And how is it that your pronunciations of doom to the people of the South are not being played out in the Southern states that have renounced slavery already? Are Virginians no longer Southerners, just because they have ceased to sell men and women at the auction block? Have not crop yields in Virginia increased? Has not the flood of Negroes fleeing northward from there to escape from the horrors of bondage almost ceased? South Carolina, Georgia, and Alabama need not fear abject poverty if slavery is abolished; the only thing they will lose is their ability to impose absolute despotism on the lives of their unfortunate human property! The gentleman from South Carolina is not in danger of losing earthly goods, only of losing his right to be a tyrant, lord, and master over those poor benighted souls who toil in his fields, cook his meals, and tend to his every need. There, my distinguished colleagues, you see the true evil of slavery exposed in all its selfish wickedness—it takes decent men and turns them into malevolent despots, and then convinces them that despotism is nothing less than the essence of liberty!"

In the Senate, Calhoun personally took charge of the opposition to the amendment. His opening remarks were less strident but no less eloquent than those of Congressman Brooks.

"Gentlemen of the Senate, I would rather be addressing you on almost any other topic this day," he began. "For I love this country no less than any man here, and my fondest wish is for the future prosperity and cohesion of our national Union. But our President, the all-seeing, all-knowing epitome of morality and justice, Alexander Hamilton, has decided to begin his second term by cutting away at that Union with a two-edged sword! My friends, I have conversed deeply with President Hamilton. I will confess, I do not believe him to be an evil man at heart. But he is a fanatic, and fanaticism will perform any evil in the name of what it perceives to be good. Our President's myopia on the subject of slavery will destroy this country if this pernicious amendment is adopted! The states which make up our Republic did not sign away all their rights when they ratified the Constitution; why should future states not have the same free choice we did? Is Hamilton so uncertain about the prospects of his radical ideas of emancipation and equality that he must force them on future generations, without giving them a chance to decide for themselves? Should not popular sovereignty be allowed on the issue of slavery, as it is on so many other issues? I was the one who coined the phrase 'King Alexander' to describe our President, and sadly, the label fits better than I realized at the time. Hamilton is so convinced of his own righteousness that he feels he must bend the whole world to his will. We of the South say, enough! We will not bend the knee to a despot. Even if you do not share our views on domestic slavery, will you not stand with us on the sacred issue of states' rights? Will you not join us in reining in this runaway abuse of executive power?"

Samuel Dana of Connecticut rose to rebut Calhoun's remarks.

"I will admit, I had never given much thought about the Southern institution of slavery until President Hamilton was elected," he said. "But since then I have educated myself on the topic. I have traveled to Virginia, to witness the effects of emancipation there; I have spoken to free Negroes who live in my native state and heard their vivid descriptions of life in bondage. I have even undertaken a journey to Charleston to see what slavery is like in the Senator's own state. I feel that I have gained an understanding of both sides of this debate, but after much reflection, I must support our President on this issue."

He paused and raised one hand to the heavens, as if in silent appeal to divine justice, and then continued.

"Slavery is a vile institution," he said. "It not only binds the helpless toiler in complete obeisance to his master's will, but it gives every slaveowner a taste of the most complete tyranny imaginable. It is entirely up to the master whether the slave is fed or starved, clothed or naked, housed or compelled to sleep on the ground amid the elements. The slave's life, his children, even his bride is not his own. At any time the master may sell husband away from wife, children away from parents, siblings away from each other. He may even—and I know this is not a popular topic for discussion—tear a bride from her husband's bed to satisfy his own carnal lust, and then cast her back into the fields when he is done!"

Several angry Southern Senators began to jeer and interrupt, but Vice President Madison gaveled them down and fixed them with an angry stare.

"You, of all people, should not interrupt such a declaration," he said, breaking precedent for a moment. "We all know this happens, even if we choose not to speak of it. My own overseer was guilty of it, right under my nose, and I was too blind to see it! Now, Senator Dana, please continue."

"My fellow Senators, whether we like President Hamilton or not, he has taken a stand on the right side of history," Dana said. "Slavery is a cancer on the body politic, and it would have poisoned our whole country if allowed to spread. Perhaps we cannot excise this tumor yet, but we can contain it. We have been given this opportunity, right now, to take a stand for liberty and freedom and to quarantine this vicious malady that threatens the peace and order of our country. We are not trying to steal your slaves, Senator Calhoun. Nor will we prevent you from emigrating to one of the new territories for the betterment of your family's fortunes, if you so wish. You may even try and talk your laborers into accompanying you and working for wages. But what we will do, in supporting this amendment, is to make sure that you cannot sell them once you get them there!"

The debate raged on for two weeks in both houses, as newspaper editorials from around the country weighed in on the pros and cons of the new amendment. The anti-amendment forces became more and more strident as it became evident that a strong majority of the country agreed with President Hamilton's free-soil views. Calhoun attempted a filibuster when the proposed amendment came up for a vote; he and two other Senators spoke for three days straight, but it became apparent that the rest of the Senate was willing to wait as long as it took to bring the amendment forward.

Hamilton stayed out of the discussion as much as possible, although he did write a lengthy article explaining the necessity of the Thirteenth Amendment, which he forwarded to several newspapers that were friendly to the administration. He made no attempt to hide his authorship; he felt he owed it to the people to explain his views as fully and plainly as possible when asking for their support.

It was the thirtieth of March when the amendment came up for a vote in the Senate. Alex stood at the window of the White

House, looking out at the Capitol, waiting to see what the results would be. Madison's office there had a window that faced the Executive Mansion, and the Vice President had told Alex he would unfurl a blue banner from his window if the measure passed, or a red one if it failed, so that the President could know right away.

Alex paced impatiently all morning, knowing that the Senators would be giving their final remarks before the vote was taken. The House was set to vote the next day, but the President's Federal Republicans had such a large majority there that victory was near certain. Everything hinged on the Senate, and Hamilton was nearly beside himself as he walked from his desk to the window and back again, hoping to see some sign that the votes had been cast.

"You're going to worry yourself sick, Papa," came a voice from the door, and Alex turned to see his daughter Angelica standing there. Amongst the political victories of his first term in office, Hamilton had also seen a remarkable personal triumph: Angelica's mind had fully returned, and she was a normal young woman again. Indeed, several suitors had begun calling over the last few months, which filled Alex with a different kind of trepidation.

"The night we crossed the Delaware at Christmas of 1776," he told her, "I did not yet work on Washington's staff—I was just another junior officer in the Continentals. But I remember him and Knox standing and watching as our men climbed into those bulky Durham boats, operated by Glover's Marblehead fishermen. I'd never seen him look so frustrated or powerless as he watched that agonizingly slow process of loading men and horses from the docks into the boats, slowly being rowed across the river, and then doing it again. He paced and fumed and swore and finally crossed the river himself because he couldn't stand to wait any more. But today I think I know exactly how he felt."

He strode to the window and looked at Madison's office window again, and his heart caught in his throat was he saw the shutter slowly open. Angelica laid her hand on his shoulder as he stiffened in anticipation—and then a long strip of cloth rolled down from the window, catching the breeze and flapping gently as it unfurled. It was pure azure, as blue as the Caribbean on a sunny day, and the President of the United States froze as he watched it, tears welling up in his eyes.

"We've done it," he said. "America will be a free nation forever!"

"Oh, Papa, I'm so proud!" Angelica said, and Alex's tears were replaced with laughter. He spun his daughter around the room in an impromptu waltz, kissing her forehead, and then ran up the stairs to the White House living quarters, calling out "Eliza!" as church bells across Washington City began to toll in celebration of the vote.

The final vote in the Senate was twenty-nine for, and nine against—closer than Alex would have liked, but enough to send the amendment to the states for ratification. The House of Representatives voted the following day, and the Administration scored another victory—out of one hundred and eighty-nine representatives, a hundred and forty supported the Thirteenth Amendment. That was the level of support Alex had hoped for; the House was a better barometer for the feelings of the nation than the Senate. Three quarters of the states—fifteen of nineteen—

would have to vote in favor for the Amendment to be ratified, but the President felt a strange sense of peace as he studied the results. It would happen, he felt sure—the amendment would pass, and no new slave states would enter the Union thereafter. Was it enough? Had he done what Laurens and Washington had tasked him to do in that vision so long ago? He prayed it would be.

A few days later, Hamilton walked over to the Capitol Building to have lunch with Madison and a few members of the Senate. It was the most relaxed meal that Hamilton could recall in a long time; they laughed and told war stories and drank coffee for nearly two hours after the dishes were cleared.

"How is Calhoun taking all this?" Alex asked as the cheerful gathering broke up. "I haven't seen or heard from him since the vote in the Senate."

"Someone told me that he's been up at the Presbyterian Church, kneeling at the altar, for the last three afternoons," Senator Dana said. "I did not know that he was such a religious man!"

"Perhaps he is wrestling with his conscience," said Madison. "I have never seen a man more devastated when a vote went against him."

"It's a lovely day, Mister Vice President," said Alex. "Why don't you walk back to the White House with me? I have a cabinet meeting in an hour, I would appreciate your input."

"I'd be delighted," said Madison, retrieving his walking stick. "I am almost back to my full strength now. Would you like to invite Speaker Clay, also?"

"By all means," said Alex. "His aid will be indispensable in getting the Thirteenth Amendment ratified in Kentucky and hopefully Tennessee as well!"

Madison dispatched his secretary to go fetch the Speaker, and in a few moments the three men were walking along a newly constructed gravel walkway that connected the Capitol Building to the Executive Mansion. As they made their way down the hill, Alex was pleased to see the cherry trees that he had donated to the city beginning to bloom. Winter was receding, and life was emerging from its slumber wherever he looked.

"Well, speak of the devil," Madison said. "Here comes Senator Calhoun now!"

Alex looked up and saw the South Carolinian striding up the hill, his dark eyes twinkling with intense emotion. Calhoun fixed his gaze on the President, and Hamilton was surprised to see that his face was drawn with grief, and his cheeks streaked with dried tears.

"Good afternoon, Senator," he said. "I trust you are well?"

"Well enough, Mister President," Calhoun said in a surly voice. "Good day!"

Alex and the others let him pass and resumed their stroll, but before anyone could remark on the curt greeting, the Senator spoke again.

"Hamilton!" he exclaimed, and Alex turned to face him.

The mask of grief was gone, and fanatical hatred was suddenly blazing in Calhoun's eyes as he leveled a dueling pistol at the President of the United States.

Time stood still for a second; Alex opened his mouth to cry out, while Madison turned and saw the gun and raised his cane. Clay began to lunge forward, but it was too late.

"*Sic semper tyrannis!*" Calhoun shouted, and pulled the trigger.

Alex felt a sharp blow to his midriff, as if he had been kicked by a horse, and then looked down to see blood pouring from his stomach, just below his rib cage. He opened his mouth, but no sound came out. Instead, he slowly settled to the ground, managing to sit rather than to fall, as he saw Clay tackle the South Carolinian. Madison's pale face was crimson with anger, and as Calhoun wrestled with Clay the Vice President struck the Senator with his walking stick again and again till the younger man finally was knocked out. People who had heard the shot came running from all directions, and Alex was gently lifted in their arms and carried down the hill to the White House as word spread like wildfire through Washington City: "The President has been shot!"

Eliza Hamilton let out a piercing wail as her husband was carried into the living quarters, his clothes soaked with blood, but after that she gave no further vent to her grief. She called for physicians, hot water, and towels, and aided by her daughter Angelica, she removed the President's shirt and cleaned his wound. Hamilton tried to comfort her, but his voice was weak and rasping.

The injury was mortal, everyone realized as they saw the extent of the damage. The bullet had torn through the President's abdomen and exited from the small of his back, a wound no surgeon could repair. But Alex was awake and alert, and despite his great pain he only cried out when someone touched the area around the injury. Once he was settled into the bed and cleaned up, he took his wife by the hand.

"Eliza, don't grieve," he gasped. "I was given my life back, and I did my best to redeem the second chance I'd been given. I go to my grave with a clean conscience. I did all I could to make men free."

"Don't say that," she said, and suddenly her tears came like a flood. "Please, Alex, don't leave me. I can't bear to lose you."

"It's only for a little while," he said. "I'll be waiting for you. Take all the time you need, my love. Take care of our children. Tell the world that I did all I could. I only pray it was enough."

His eyes began to lose their focus, and Eliza Hamilton leaned forward and kissed him on the forehead.

"My heart," she said. "Oh my heart, come back to me!"

He opened his eyes wide, but he was no longer looking at her. He saw a radiant form materialize at the foot of the bed, and then the brightness began to fade, and a familiar smile greeted him.

"Laurens?" he said in a soft tone of uncertainty. "Was it enough?"

As Alexander Hamilton's eyes closed for the last time, his lips softly echoed the reply that only he could hear.

"Well done."

EPILOGUE

THE MURDER OF President Hamilton sent a shock wave across America like nothing else in the history of the young republic. There was a spontaneous outpouring of grief for the nation's great loss, and rage at Senator Calhoun specifically and Southerners in general. James Madison was sorrowfully sworn in as the nation's fifth President an hour after Hamilton breathed his last. The Virginian moved swiftly to make sure that the nation paid an appropriate tribute to its slain President. Eliza Hamilton was shattered by grief, but her daughter Angelica and the new First Lady, Dolley Madison, consoled her together and helped her plan Hamilton's funeral. It was President Madison who brought up the idea of laying Alex to rest in a monumental tomb not far from the Capitol Building and the White House; Eliza resisted at first, but ultimately agreed that President Hamilton belonged not just to New York, but to all of America.

The state funeral was the largest in American history, with the entire United States Congress in attendance and over twenty-five thousand mourners from nearly all the states. Eulogies were given by Thomas Jefferson, James Madison, and John Quincy Adams, as well as by Hamilton's former pastor from New York, Benjamin Moore. The polished wooden casket was laid in a temporary crypt while Henri de Plame, an expatriate architect from France, designed and built a magnificent marble edifice to house

Hamilton's mortal remains forever. It took a little over a year to finish, and when it was done, the remains of Hamilton's slain son, Philip, were exhumed and brought from New York to lie alongside those of his father; there was a space left in the crypt so that Eliza could also be laid to rest next to her husband someday.

President Madison spoke at the re-interment of Hamilton's coffin there with these words:

"Alexander Hamilton was a courageous soldier, a brilliant statesman, a cabinet minister without peer, a Senator of great accomplishments, and a President whose name will be spoken of with affection and reverence for as long as our Republic endures. He was my partner in the struggle to ratify the Constitution, my opponent during the debates that shaped our nation while Washington was President, and my chief rival during the presidential election of 1808. He was as magnanimous in victory as he was painstakingly honest in the discharge of his office. He rose above partisan rancor and asked me to remain in his administration as Secretary of State, despite our political rivalry. He was a Commander in Chief of remarkable skill and foresight, and an American patriot who loved this country as his chosen, adopted homeland. But above and beyond all of those, he was my friend, he was my President, my chief, and my superior. I only hope that when the time of my own service to our country is done, that I will not have disappointed the memory of this great man who honored me with his trust and his friendship. Let us honor his memory by completing the great work that he began."

JOHN C. CALHOUN was hanged for murder three months after shooting President Hamilton. He never denied the act and did nothing to avoid the penalty for his heinous crime. He simply claimed that, like Brutus of old, he had acted to save the Republic from a demagogue and tyrant. As the executioner fitted the noose around his neck, the former Senator cried out with deep emotion: "The South! The South! What is to become of her?" Those were his last words.

THE POLITICAL consequences of Hamilton's murder were far-reaching and immediate. The state legislatures of Kentucky and Tennessee immediately took up bills of emancipation, and both voted to free their slaves by the end of the year. South Carolina became a pariah state; even a heartfelt renunciation of Calhoun and an official declaration of mourning for the President from Governor Middleton did nothing to overcome the wave of revulsion for the slaveholding states that swept the North and West.

The Thirteenth Amendment was ratified in record time; being sent out to the states that spring, it was approved by fifteen of the nineteen states. Only South Carolina, Louisiana, Georgia, and Alabama rejected it. The Mississippi Territory was unable to meet the conditions for statehood before the amendment was ratified, and thus entered the Union the following year as a free state.

James Madison served out the remainder of Alex's term as President, three years and eleven months, and then stepped down as his health was becoming frailer; the occasional recurring fevers from malaria haunted him until his death in 1830. But his administration was remembered fondly as a time of peace, tranquility, and great national growth, with four new states joining the Union during his term of office. He was succeeded by John Quincy Adams, whose two terms saw the Union become even larger, stronger, and freer. One by one, many of the free states approved voting rights for the former slaves, and many industrialists began to move their operations from New England into Virginia and North Carolina, where the labor pool was large, and the shorter winters made for increased productivity.

In 1831, during the presidency of Henry Clay, South Carolina, Georgia, and Alabama, the last three slave states, attempted to secede from the Union and form their own slaveholding Republic. Clay, using the threat of military force combined with all his powers of persuasion, managed to avoid an all-out civil war. But even as he negotiated with Roger Brooks, the governor of South Carolina, something remarkable happened. All over the state, the slaves themselves rose up, seizing weapons and imprisoning their former masters. There was surprisingly little bloodshed; the mastermind of the revolt, a runaway slave named Horace Davidson, insisted that the bondsmen simply wanted freedom and justice, not revenge. Only a few of the most brutal slaveowners were killed; most were simply locked inside the cabins where their human property had been forced to reside until they agreed to emancipate their slaves. With Federal troops on his border and half the interior of his state now controlled by the slave insurrectionists, Brooks folded, and South Carolina repealed its ordinance of secession, and then proceeded to vote for a system of compensated emancipation. Georgia and Alabama took a bit longer to come around, but by 1840 there were no slave states remaining in the Union.

Eliza Hamilton lived to be ninety-five years old and kept her husband's memory alive for decades after his death. When Hamilton's birthday was declared a national holiday in 1834, she spoke to a joint session of Congress about her husband's life and legacy with such deep and heartfelt emotion that everyone in the chamber wept, and representatives from all twenty-eight states, as well as foreign dignitaries from England, France, and Spain attended her funeral in 1852.

In 1860, Senator Abraham Lincoln of Illinois sponsored the Fourteenth Amendment to the Constitution, which granted citizenship to all who were born in America, regardless of their color or previous condition of servitude; and also guaranteed basic civil rights to all Americans. During the debate over the Amendment, he looked back at the man who had led the crusade for emancipation, and shared his personal memory of Hamilton with these words:

"My father was a rough-hewn man with no education or ambition other than to make a living as a farmer. He had a simple sense of justice which he imparted to me from a young age; and he loathed slavery his whole life, moving to Illinois after I was born to escape its baleful influence in Kentucky. When I was a very small lad, he came in from town one afternoon and sat down at our simple kitchen table, put his face in his hands, and began to weep. I had never seen Pa cry before, and I asked him what was wrong. He took me in his lap and said: 'Abraham, our President, Mister Hamilton, has been cruelly murdered by a Southern slaveholder. He was a great and good man, and our country is a poorer place without him.' I was barely four years old, but I have never forgotten the tears flowing down my father's face that day. When I decided to pursue a career in politics, I swore that I would dedicate myself to finishing the work that President Hamilton began over fifty years ago, and make sure that all the rights and liberties guaranteed in our Constitution would apply equally to all Americans everywhere, north as well as south, black as well as white."

It took four years to push the Fourteenth Amendment through Congress and for it to be debated and voted on in every state, but in 1864 it was ratified, and equal citizenship for all races became the law of the land in America. Two years later, the first Negro was elected to the United States Congress—Frederick Douglass, who had been born in slavery, emancipated during the South Carolina revolt, and educated at Yale. He would have a long and distinguished career in Congress, ending up as Senate Majority Leader, and living long enough to see America's first black President elected in 1892.

Today, a marble statue of Hamilton stands across a giant reflecting pool from the Washington Monument, a memorial to the martyr of liberty, the man who lived when he should have died and died when he should have lived. The great civil war that he so feared never came to pass, thanks to his tireless efforts to change the heart of the nation and turn it to the cause of human freedom. Not far from the feet of the colossal likeness, Hamilton's tomb is constantly protected by an honor guard of American soldiers, sailors and marines, and is illuminated by an eternal flame kindled on the hundredth anniversary of his death in 1913. The simple words of his epitaph read:

HERE LIE THE MORTAL REMAINS
OF
ALEXANDER HAMILTON
GENERAL OF THE AMERICAN ARMY
SECRETARY OF THE TREASURY
SENATOR FROM NEW YORK
PRESIDENT OF THE UNITED STATES
HUSBAND OF ELIZABETH SCHUYLER
HAMILTON
FREEDOM HAD NO TRUER CHAMPION,
NOR TYRANNY A MORE BITTER FOE.

CONNECT WITH
LEWIS BEN SMITH

OFFICIAL WEBSITE
www.lewisbensmith.com

FACEBOOK PAGE
https://www.facebook.com/authorindianasmith

TWITTER
https://twitter.com/AuthorIndySmith

INSTAGRAM
https://www.instagram.com/authorindysmith/

BLOG
https://lewisliterarylair.blogspot.com/